To my best friend and wonderful wife, Barbara, who has put up with all of my antics over the past forty years.

THE HAT TRICK MURDERS

– 1 –

Jack closed the door of his dingy basement flat and heard the distant sounds of sirens as they came up College Avenue. The warm sun permeated the early summer morning air. It was Friday, June 11th, 1965. The first one hundred feet was a steep incline on Catharine Street, and Jack took it slowly due to a congenital heart defect. He wore brown loafers, gray flannel pants, and a white Hathaway button-down shirt with a knitted Karen Bulow tie. His Harris Tweed jacket was slung over his left shoulder, and he carried his three-ring binder, filled with "crib" notes and a clutch of pens in his right hand.

He turned left onto College Avenue and proceeded slowly through Collegetown toward his final exam at Cornell, passing the Collegetown Motel on his way. Every business immediately south of the Cornell gates in Ithaca was called "Collegetown" something: Collegetown Florists, Collegetown Cleaners, Collegetown Photos, and on and on. The motel's parking lot was packed, and Jack thought that they must have close to one hundred percent occupancy; perhaps proud parents arriving to bring home their graduating child, and after the obligatory congratulatory hugs they would begin persuading their progeny to continue on to graduate school. The motel's car lot was filled with huge Lincolns, with their very straight lines and gigantic trunks, and a few Chrysler Imperials. Over in one corner Jack caught a glimpse of one of his favorite cars, a 1957 Chevy. It was a light turquoise with a white roof, wrap-around windshield, a beautiful chrome grill and fashionable whitewall tires. Even though it was eight years old, it was obvious the owners took great pride in it. It was in mint condition.

Having spent four years at Cornell's famed School of Hotel and Restaurant Administration, Jack Souster thought only in terms of occupancy percentages and food costs when it came to the "Hospitality" industry. On the next corner he was almost overcome by the heavy odor of greasy fries. It smothered him like an oily blanket from the exhaust fan of the Collegetown Diner. He wondered if they'd changed the oil in their deep fat fryer this week, and he thought briefly back to his quantity cooking class, along with organic chemistry class. He could almost taste the fries after they'd been dropped into the two-week-old rancid cauldron, as the chemical formulas of the simmering sludge taxed his brain. The only time he went to the diner was on Friday nights, when they featured a bowl of chilli on "special" for ninety-nine cents, complete with toasted garlic bread. That was just to coat his stomach, so he thought, before he headed up the street to Johnny's Big Red, the local bar.

Johnny's was steeped as much in tradition as it was

atmosphere. There was a layer of hazy blue smoke that permeated every corner, Marlboro being the brand of choice. The room off to the left of the bar was filled with heavy, thick dark tables with endless initials carved in them. Some had a heart linking or encompassing the odd monograms as if to formalize some wish for betrothment. The silken patina on the tables was a result of years, perhaps decades, of oil from hands pawing the tables as points were being made and polished by the constant rubbing of the forearms of woollen sweaters.

The bar, to the right, was almost as long as the building. The mirrored wall behind the stepped shelves contained every liquor known to man but was lit only by neon signs of Budweiser, Miller High Life, Michelob and Schlitz. There was always a waiting line for an empty stool. Pictures of legendary Cornell crew, football and hockey teams were hanging everywhere. It was a Friday night ritual, as Jack met many of his friends at the bar to discuss the latest or an upcoming game. They rehashed them again and again as another pitcher of Schlitz was slammed down on the table, almost tipping over the basket of free, salted, unshelled peanuts. The shells, after being shucked by the voracious patrons, were simply brushed onto the floor and would crunch under the busy traffic to and from the bar or the washroom.

Just ahead of him, Jack could see a few people gathered on the stone bridge that marked the official southern entrance to the campus. They appeared quite animated, pointing over the bridge down to the gorge below. Cornell was framed by a couple of deep gorges carved out of the limestone by centuries of cascading waters as they headed downhill towards beautiful Lake Cayuga, one of upper New

York State's five Finger Lakes. As he approached the growing crowd at the College Avenue Bridge he could see the flashing lights of the police cars, an ambulance, and a fire department rescue vehicle.

Jack got there just as a couple of campus security guards began asking people to leave. He took a quick look over the bridge and caught a glimpse of a young woman splayed out on her back on the rocks below. Blood from her nose, ears and neck had matted her beautiful, honey-blonde hair and covered the upper part of her top, as she stared, wide-eyed, lifelessly; yet somehow pleadingly back at the onlookers on the bridge. She was wearing a white, blood-stained blouse, a light gray, pleated skirt that was up just above her twisted knees, and her limp ankles led to her feet, which were splayed in distorted directions and were capped by white socks and penny loafers.

Jack felt his legs go limp and was suddenly faint. A terrible nausea rose in the pit of his stomach. He was able to grab on to the side of the bridge but dropped his binder and his pens, which he scurried to pick up. He had to squat down until the light-headedness left him. It wasn't long until he recovered, and as he stood up, a security guard told him it was time to move on. He crossed the bridge and veered off to his right as the path led up a gentle grassy slope, past Carpenter Hall, the Engineering School, and then across the street and to Statler Hall, the home of the Hotel School, where Jack spent almost every waking hour. It seemed if when he was not in class, he was working in the kitchens or serving at a banquet in the attached Statler Inn. Off to the side he noticed Sky Muncey, quarterback of the Cornell "Big Red" football team, leaning up against a tree, quietly watching the activity on the bridge. Jack, having met Sky a few times in the past, was not a big fan of the self-professed "Big Man on Campus," or at least of his huge ego. He made eye contact with Muncey and acknowledged him with a slight nod. The quarterback quickly turned away, as if he didn't want to be recognized, which Jack put down to his incredible arrogance.

"Someone 'gorge out'?" a passing engineering student asked. Jack hated the term. It was so descriptive with its connotations of despair, hopelessness and finality, as does every suicide. Jack could almost feel the pain and anguish they felt as they took their final leap from life.

"Yeah, I guess so. A co-ed," he replied.

"Probably couldn't handle the pressure of finals or missed her period. That's usually the case," replied the engineer as he sped past.

Jack felt that his right hand was tacky. He looked at it and saw that his fingers and palm were coated in blood. He quickly went over to the freshly mowed lawn and wiped his hand on the cool, morning dewy grass. *It must be from the pens. I must have dropped them into a congealed pool of blood,* he thought.

Jack was a slow walker, especially when it came to inclines, regardless of how steep, due to his heart condition. At six foot one and one hundred and sixty-five pounds, he was the picture of good health, and nobody would suspect that he had a problem. Walking fast, and on an incline like this, he would turn a little cyanotic. He always left his apartment much earlier than anyone else would, just because he knew how much longer it would take him to walk to school. This morning his final exam was at eight. In his freshman year, when he was rooming in Boldt Hall at the bottom of "Libe

Slope," it had been almost impossible for him to walk up the steep incline of the hill without stopping to catch his breath three or four times. Even though he'd had a corrective surgery in the 1940s called a Blalock-Taussig shunt, he still had a hole between his ventricles about the size of a quarter. Eventually he'd gone to the Cornell Medical Clinic to get a permit to drive his car on campus and park in handicap parking. This cramped his style, because he would never have considered himself as "handicapped."

This morning was different. The southern entrance to the campus and Collegetown were only a gentle slope away from Statler, and Jack wanted to enjoy his last day. He could have driven but chose not to, and now as a result was faced with being late for his final exam because of the time he had spent on the bridge gathering his composure. He hurried, got to Statler and then had to climb three flights of stairs to get to room 311, where the final was being written. Jack arrived completely out of breath as Professor Elston was about to close the doors. That would have been disastrous. All latecomers would receive a zero, which surely would have caused him to lose his year. Jack did not have to look at the tips of his fingers to know that cyanosis was evident, and the bluish tinge in his lips and fingers would be recognizable to anyone who saw him. He dropped his binder on the floor, since no books or papers were permitted in the exam room. He took his seat and soon roll call began.

"Souster," Professor Elston eventually called out.

"Present," said Jack as he was still catching his breath.

Taking attendance at the university level really bothered Jack, as it always reminded him of his dreaded first grade teacher, Miss Brown. She was constantly taking roll call, and to make matters worse, she'd insisted that the first graders drink their milk after recess, even though it had curdled having sat in the sun on the classroom radiator all morning. The Hotel School had a reputation for discipline, and as was explained to the students when they got out into the industry, that's what would be expected of them. Human Resources was one of Jack's favorite subjects. In fact, Professor Elston had hired him to be a student instructor to the freshman HR seminars, and it was only two days ago that Jack had proctored the freshman final HR exam.

As the exams were being passed out, Jack looked at the collection of pens and pencils he had dumped on the desk when he sat down. They were covered in blood. There was one ballpoint that he didn't recognize, but it had the logo of The Bastion Bank of America. This was a continuous line of b's spiralling in ever decreasing concentric circles, not unlike the funnel cloud of a tornado. Jack, who had cynical views of banks, thought that this logo was most appropriate, since he shared the common belief that banks were well known for sucking the money out of all their clients.

The Bastion Bank of America was the second largest bank in the U.S. and traded well on Wall Street. The name "Bastion" was supposed to denote fortress-like strength, but it was often referred to as the "Bastards" Bank of America. The pen was not one of those pens that companies hand out to everyone as a cheap promotional item, but instead, with its gold cap, it looked as it belonged to an executive set, complete with matching fountain pen and pencil. Jack briefly explained to Professor Elston, in hushed tones, what he had witnessed on the way to class and why his pens were coated in blood. The professor gave Jack a tissue to help clean the pens off, but it was of little help. Jack wrote the exam with a gluey and gummy pen and hand. Going to the washroom to wash his hands was not an option, since once the exam room doors were closed, no one was permitted to leave until finished.

The exam covered a lot of the basics of human resources, questions on HR guru Peter Drucker's theories and a few "what if" scenarios. Jack thought that if he aced this exam, he had a pretty good chance of making the Dean's list. That would shock Dean Myers, who had little use for Jack and the antics he and his fellow classmate Jim Webster contrived. Jim had transferred from Dartmouth and was roughly Jack's age. The Dean would often tell them that they were the most immature mature students he had ever seen. Jack was now twenty-five years old and had come to Cornell after working for Canadian Pacific Hotels for a number of years.

The exam was a breeze, and Jack was finished a good half hour before the allotted two-hour time limit. As he walked up to the front of the classroom to hand in his paper, Professor Elston went to shake his hand, and Jack awkwardly pumped his fist, not wanting to get blood all over the Professor's hands. The instructor quietly wished him good luck. Jack smiled and mouthed the words, "Thank you." However, his mind was on the scene he had witnessed on the way to school. He just wanted to be alone and gather his thoughts. He went to the men's room to wash off his pens. He washed his hands so thoroughly; they turned very pink and tender.

Today was his last day of a four-year love affair with an incredible institution, one which he would always remember. He recalled the day when he got a letter from the registrar. It was three months after he had driven down to Ithaca from Toronto to have an interview and write his SATs. "I am pleased to advise you that you have been accepted..." it stated. The rest was a blur as he threw his arms up in the air and yelled "Yes!" He quickly ran out and bought current copies of Playboy and GQ magazines that featured "Girls of the Ivy League" and "Fashions of the Ivy League." He also went to the library to read all about the Ivy League.

He discovered that it was founded in 1876 when members of Harvard, Princeton, Yale and Columbia got together to set out to define certain rules of their athletic competitions. The term "Ivy" comes from the roman numerals for the number four, IV, as there were four schools represented at the meeting. The "IV League" was eventually expanded to include eight schools, the original four plus Dartmouth, Brown, Cornell and the University of Pennsylvania. He was so proud of himself for having been accepted at such a great institution.

Jack didn't want his four years to end, but especially not on a downer such as the scene he'd witnessed this morning. He couldn't get the image of the lifeless co-ed out of his mind. He unbuttoned his top shirt button and took off his tie, almost as a small gesture of defiance, but more so an act of freedom. "Hotelies" were the only students on the entire campus who were required to wear a jacket and tie. Dean Myers would often say, "If you want to hang out with 'the great unwashed' on the steps of 'The Straight,' then apply to some other school," and then he would add, "Like Fine Arts, God forbid."

*   *   *

"The Straight" the Dean referred to was Willard Straight Hall, the Student Union building. It was a large, imposing granite building with leaded windows and marble and parquet floors, depending on the room. It sat impressively on the crest of a hill overlooking Ithaca and Lake Cayuga. It was fairly close to Statler, as one would just walk across the street, pass Sage Hall, the Graduate Center and then the Cornell bookstore, which was Ezra Cornell's original home, then across one more street, and there was The Straight on the lip of "Libe Slope." The Straight was full of activities and rooms for Bridge Clubs, the Glee Club and every other social activity one could imagine, as well as a huge cafeteria that served typical student food such as burgers and fries, as well as hundreds of other items, none of which you would find at Statler. Jack would go there in his torn jeans and sneakers on a Saturday morning or afternoon just to hang out around the steps and listening to Bob Dylan, Tim Hardin or Joan Baez wannabes. There were always one or two purists who only would sing the songs of Woody Guthrie or Pete Seeger and the Weavers. One young co-ed, Amy Schechter, had the voice of an angel, not unlike Nana Mouskouri's. Jack would often ask her to do a Baez or a Judy Collins song. She was very prominent in the Cornell Folk Club. However, he was most appreciative, being Canadian, if someone played a Gordon Lightfoot song, or his all time favorite, "Four Strong Winds" by Ian and Sylvia. Amy did an amazing rendition, so wonderfully wistful. He could not help but feel a little bit homesick for those evenings he'd spent at The Riverboat Coffee House in the Yorkville district of Toronto, where he would spend countless hours listening to Lightfoot, Richie Havens, Joni Mitchell and others while drinking hot lemonade and honey. Jack had complimented Amy a number of times, and through their conversations he found out that she was from Calgary. Her father was a wealthy oilman, and because of his strong financial support for the sitting Liberal Party, he was appointed to the Canadian Senate and was the chair of the Senate Banking Committee. Alberta was Conservative territory, so any time the Liberals found a supporter in that province, he or she was treated like royalty. Unlike the United States, Canadian senators were appointed to the Senate, for life, by the sitting prime minister.

The noise in the cafeteria, as he recalled from the first time he had entered The Straight, was deafening. Everyone was talking over each other about their courses, their profs, their schedules, upcoming events and everything else a couple of hundred students could talk about. Jack could easily tell the seniors from the freshmen just by their swagger and their "done that" tone in their voices, while the freshmen were just filled with excitement and anticipation. Jack paid for his burger and fries and Coke and started wandering around looking for an empty seat. He finally found one opposite two co-eds and asked if the seat was taken.

"No, go for it," one replied.

The tables were actually picnic tables. Jack put down his tray, climbed over the bench, and sat down. "Thanks very much. Jack Souster."

"No problem," they replied in unison, then laughed.

"Ruth Golden," said one.

"Suzanne Kramer," said the other. Then immediately started talking to each other in French, as if they really didn't want to engage in any conversation with Jack. He knew a little French but was embarrassed. Being Canadian, he didn't know that much of his country's other official language. For some reason, he had come to university in the United States with a bias that Canadians were better than Americans, better educated, more tolerant, and nowhere near as pushy. He had heard his parents and many others talk about the "Ugly American," and yet here he was sitting across the table listening to two co-eds talking fluently in French, albeit with a very strange accent, a Long Island/Parisian mix.

Also, only a couple of nights ago, freshmen during Orientation had been treated to a musical show featuring everything from folk music and jazz to an incredible string quartet playing Franz Joseph Haydn's Serenade in "F" for a string quartet. This was a serious wake-up call for Jack. This was more than Peter, Paul and Mary singing "Lemon Tree" or "If I Had a Hammer."

"Ruth, Suzanne, where are you from?" he interrupted. His father always told him that people liked to be acknowledged by their name.

"Long Island," they again chorused.

"And you're fluent in French?" said Jack with a certain amount of incredulity.

"We try. Where are you from?" Ruth asked.

"Canada."

"And you don't speak French? I thought all Canadians spoke French."

"Only a 'petite peu,'" said Jack with an embarrassed smile.

Ruth had a dark page boy haircut and a swarthy complexion. She loved horses, and her family had a small hobby farm on Long Island. Her father tended his "boutique" vineyard when he wasn't working at his import and export business in Manhattan. She had a couple of horses which she and her brother rode at the farm. Her voice had a very charming throaty tone that Jack attributed to the numerous mentholated Newports she smoked, bucking the Marlboro trend. She was an "Aggie," having enrolled in the School of Agriculture, hoping to eventually become a veterinarian.

Suzanne, on the other hand, was a freckled redhead who was majoring in Fine Arts, with sculpture as her main focus of interest. They both took French as an elective and had met each other in class. A curl of smoke found its way into Jack's right eye, and he accidentally inhaled. He coughed and his eye watered as he moved the ashtray closer to Ruth. She apologized.

At this point the fellow and his girlfriend sitting next to Ruth got up and left and were replaced by another young couple. Jack acknowledged their presence with a nod. The young man put out his hand and introduced himself.

"Colin MacDonald."

"Hi, I'm Jack Souster."

"And this is my girlfriend, Yvette Bouchard." Colin motioned to the cute young blonde who accompanied him.

"With a name like, that you must be French."

"Oui, I mean yes," she replied.

"Well, Ruth and Suzanne here also speak French, and they're from Long Island."

"I know, we've talked before," Yvette said. The three of them started to converse in French. Jack could tell that Yvette was from rural Quebec, because his ear was good enough to pick up her rhythmic and lyrical Quebecois patois. She was blonde, with very short hair, blue eyes and a little turned up nose. She couldn't be more than five feet tall, and Jack thought that if they ever needed someone to play Peter Pan in a theatre production, Yvette would win hands down.

Ruth and Suzanne had to ask Yvette to slow down from time to time.

"L'entment, s'il vous plait," they asked.

"Where are you from, Colin?" asked Jack.

"Glace Bay, Nova Scotia."

"That's a coal mining town, near Sydney on Cape Breton, isn't it?"

"Right on, boy. My dad's manager of the Dominion Mines. They're not doing too well…a lot of layoffs."

Jack took an immediate liking to Colin. He loved the Nova Scotian accent and the way they called everyone "boy," but it was pronounced "by." Colin was also impressed that someone knew where Glace Bay was and what it was famous for.

"Yourself?"

"Toronto, I'm just starting in the hotel school."

"I'm in ILR," said Colin, referring to the School of Industrial and Labour Relations in Ives Hall, almost next door to the Statler Inn. "My dad's always having trouble with the union, so I thought ILR'd be a good place to go.

"Are you trying out for the hockey team?" Colin asked.

"No, I can't; congenital heart problem."

"Oh, sorry 'bout that. Congenital? That's since birth, right?"

"Right, and you?" asked Jack.

"Left wing," Colin said proudly.

"Hockey scholarship?"

"No, the Ivy League doesn't have sports scholarships

like the other U.S. college programs, but they do subsidize certain things like room and board. But I get by. My folks have scraped together every nickel they have to get me here, and the miner's union put on a fundraiser for me. Got two brothers in the mines, and I figure hockey's my ticket out."

Yvette, who had one ear on the conversation, piped in, "And he's a damn good hockey player. The NHL are keeping their eyes on him," she said in her delightful French accent.

"Well, I can hardly wait to see you play, 'cause I love hockey."

Jack had only been at school for a week, and had already met four friends at his new school. He couldn't be happier, and he knew that he would make many more friends, especially hotelies, but Ruth, Suzanne, Yvette and Colin he would never forget, since they were his first friends. He revelled in the memories of his first days at Cornell.

− 2 −

Jack shook his head and brought himself back to the present as he took stock of everything he had to do before leaving for Toronto the next day. He had returned all of his kitchen whites to the linen room the day before, as well as his waiter's outfit. He would go to the locker room, double check that it was empty, and remove the combination padlock, which was his. He also had to go to Day Hall, the administration office, to clear up his account. If there were any unpaid fines, parking, speeding, etc., or if his rent wasn't paid up in full, he would not be able to graduate. The landlords in Collegetown and the rest of Ithaca had absolutely no worries about a student damaging their property or skipping out on their rent, because if anything untoward happened, all they had to do was notify the university, and the student wouldn't graduate until everything was rectified. This was a good deal for them, but in return they had to meet certain Cornell standards in order to be accredited by the university as an approved student residence. Jack would go there tomorrow morning after he packed the little red Austin Mini Minor Cooper and said his final farewell to his landlady, Mrs. Smithyes. Jack was very proud of the Cooper designation to his car, since it meant that it had a more powerful engine than other Minis.

Still not being able to erase this morning's event from his mind, he played the image over and over again in his head. Finally it came to him: she hadn't gorged out. It looked, from the amount of blood around her neck, that her throat had been slashed. She was murdered: plain and simple. It gave Jack goosebumps, and he decided he needed to talk to someone.

His friends Ruth Golden, Suzanne Kramer and Yvette Bouchard had promised to meet him in The Straight right after their morning finals. Yvette's boyfriend, Colin MacDonald, had also hoped to make it, although he had some sort of meeting and might be a little late.

Jack got his padlock from the locker and went out to the main hall of the school towards the Dean's office to say goodbye to Mary Caldwell, secretary to the Dean. Mary had been there for over twenty-five years, and as deans and assistant deans came and went, Mary was the one constant. She had the unique ability to remember every student's name. Graduates would come by after being away for well over a decade, and she would always remember them and certain facts or situations pertaining to each individual. Jack would never forget the day in his sophomore year when he saw Mary cradling one of his classmates, Anne Metzger, while she was lying on the floor having an epileptic seizure. Mary had called an ambulance, and when it arrived she accompanied Anne to the hospital. She personally called Anne's parents in Barbados, where they owned a very exclusive resort, and were obviously grooming Anne to take over the family business. Mary cared.

Jack looked in, and Mary was on the phone. He waved and he mouthed the word "Goodbye." She put up a hand to tell him to stop. She quickly ended her call, got up, came around the desk, and gave Jack a big hug. "All finished?" she said.

"Yep, this is it."

"I hear that you're going to be working out in Lake Louise. Is that right?"

"Yeah, I'll be out in God's country in a week or so."

"I've seen many pictures of it, and it's the one place on Earth that I've always wanted to go."

"Well, now you have a reason. I'll get you a room whenever you want," Jack promised.

"You look after yourself and promise to drop in the next time you're in Ithaca." She gave his hand a little squeeze.

"I promise," he said, winking. Tears welled up in her eyes, and a great feeling of sadness came over him as he opened the main door and stepped out into the summer sun. And yet it was bittersweet, because he knew that he had accomplished something that no one could take away from him: a degree from Cornell University. He'd been much older than most freshmen, since he had worked four years with Canadian Pacific Hotels after he left high school. He worked on the front desk during the summers, at the Banff Springs Hotel and Chateau Lake Louise, in Banff, and at the Royal York Hotel in Toronto in the winter. So he was considered a "mature" student, since his work in the hospitality industry had weighed as much, if not more, than his high school grades in getting him accepted at Cornell.

Jack walked down to The Straight and found his friends. The conversation of the group quickly turned to the co-ed who'd allegedly jumped over the Cascadilla gorge bridge that morning.

"It was Nicole Watson," Yvette said, "head cheerleader for the football team, and goalie for the women's hockey team. She was pinned to Jimmy Cartwright, one of Colin's fraternity brothers. He's taking it very hard. The police have taken him in for questioning, although we all know that he was back in Lincoln attending his uncle's funeral...heart attack." She continued, "For the love of Jesus, I don't know what would possess her to do that. The two of them had everything going for them."

"I think every time I see a pink ribbon from now on, I'll think of Nicole," added Ruth. "Here she is skating with all those heavy goalie pads, shoulder pads, gigantic gloves with a blocker and a huge goalie stick, and she has this little piece of tattered pink ribbon tied to a buckle on her goalie mask. It must have been her little touch of femininity in such a tough sport."

The five of them dropped the subject and continued to enjoy each other's conversation much longer than expected, although Nicole's death sobered a lot of it. They talked so long, in fact, that they were almost alone in the cafeteria.

*   *   *

Jimmy Cartwright was the center for the Cornell football team. He weighed in at over 325 pounds and was six foot two. There wasn't a pound of fat on him. He was quarterback Sky Muncey's best friend, simply because, as the center, Jimmy gave him the best protection any quarterback could ever ask. He came by his nickname "Hoss" honestly, after the well-known TV character Hoss Cartwright on *Bonanza*. Jimmy came from just outside the small town of Fullerton, Nebraska, which had a population of barely 800. His family owned ten sections of land that had been in the Cartwright family for over three generations. A section was roughly one mile square or 640 acres, and multiplied by ten, they controlled a huge tract of land. Wheat, corn and soybean were their main crops, although they had just added soybeans within the last few years as it became a more popular choice. The corn was contracted exclusively to Purina Foods for the production of dry dog food. Jimmy's father also had a substantial feed lot, where he fattened steers on his own corn before sending them off to market.

Jimmy chose Cornell over the Big Ten because of its excellent agricultural school, which hopefully would lead him into the veterinary college.

* * *

Ever since she was a toddler, Nicole Watson was always doing summersaults, and eventually cartwheels and back flips. While all of her little friends were enrolled in ballet and tap dance classes, she was happily entered into the "Bethlehem Tumbleweeds," a young gymnastics group that gained considerable notoriety as it performed in many competitions, state fairs and high school football halftime shows. She had always wanted to attend Cornell, as it had an excellent women's physical education program. In her freshman year, she had made the varsity women's gymnastics team and also became a popular member of Cornell's cheerleading squad. Her back flip, after back flip, after back flip, followed by numerous cartwheels to do a final back flip and end up standing on one of her male counterpart's shoulders, wowed the thousands of fans. She was also known for scampering to the top of her teammates' human pyramid then doing a triple somersault as she jumped down to the ground with a giant smile and arms outstretched. Her athletic prowess and agility also won her the starting position on the Cornell women's hockey team. Although she had been raised in Bethlehem, Pennsylvania, where her father was Chief Financial Officer for Bethlehem Steel, she had recently moved to McLean, Virginia, an enviable area just outside of the Washington Beltway. Her father had recently been appointed by President Kennedy to the onerous post of Chairman of the Federal Reserve Bank. He had not endeared himself to the banks on Wall Street, since he was proposing sweeping new regulations to restrict some of the dubious actions of the banking industry.

Nicole soon became the sweetheart of the campus, and although she had many suitors, Jimmy "Hoss" Cartwright was the only one for her. He approached her after a game, bloodied and sweaty, complimented her on her cheerleading, and thanked her for getting the fans excited. As he explained, "It just spurred the team on." Nicole was taken by Jimmy's "aw shucks" responses when she congratulated him on the team's win. She was also taken by his midwestern drawl. They agreed to meet after he'd showered and cleaned up, and the pair became inseparable from there on in.

Even though Jimmy and Sky Muncey were fraternity brothers, there was a little bit of jealousy, since Sky considered himself the best catch on the campus, with his good looks, his athletic ability and plenty of money. For the life of him, he couldn't see what Nicole could see in an overweight, midwestern center lineman, but he needed Jimmy's protection on the line, so he wasn't about to create any waves.

*   *   *

"Why don't we all go for a swim at Buttermilk State Park this afternoon and then go out to a flick tonight?" asked Jack.

"Great idea, let's try and forget about all this stuff and enjoy our last day."

There were four movie theatres in Ithaca, and no one could remember which one was which, let alone name them all. The Bijoux, the Roxy, the Tripoli and the Seneca were just a bunch of meaningless names and were constantly confused with each other. They were all strung down West Seneca, the main street of Ithaca, like four sparkling diamonds with their flashing marquees lighting up the nightscape. So the theatres became known as the "Near Near," the "Near Far," the "Far Near" and the "Far Far." The Near Near was playing *The Sound of Music*, and just down the street the Far Near was showing *Dr. Zhivago*.

"Let's go and see Julie Andrews in *The Sound of Music*,"

chorused the girls.

"*Dr. Zhivago* was partly filmed in the Lake Louise area and in Field, British Columbia. Don't you want to see where I'm going to be working this summer?"

Field was just a few miles west of Lake Louise, and staff from the hotel would often drive across the Great Divide, which was the border between Alberta and B.C. From there they went down to the Monarch Hotel, which had a "Beverage Room," a euphemistic term for a fluorescent-lit beer hall filled with plastic chairs and Formica-topped tables. It had great burgers, and pickled eggs were only five cents each. One of Jack's favorite stories was about the times they were driving home to the Chateau, from the Monarch, and they would ritually stop at the Great Divide. The guys would urinate in either the western or the eastern part of the stream where it divided, joking that either the Pacific or Atlantic oceans were running low and needed to have their water levels raised.

*   *   *

Jack recalled that a month or so after he had arrived, Colin had asked him if he wanted to join his fraternity, Delta Chi Upsilon, because, if so, he would "rush" Jack and invite him to a number of "rushing" parties so that the brothers could get to know him and decide if they wanted to have him as a "brother." Jack was a little dubious, since he was a little older than other freshmen on campus and was not really interested in taking part in the silly initiation rituals new "brothers" were put through. However, at the urging of the little group, he finally agreed to go to a "rushing" party on the next Friday night.

"Great, I'll see you at the Delta Chi House on Friday at seven," said Colin.

It wasn't that far from Boldt Hall, his first year residence, so he could easily make the walk, since there were no hills to climb. Colin met him and began to introduce him to a number of "brothers" as well as many other "rushees," all of whom were trying to make a good impression. They talked about what other houses they had been "rushed" by and compared notes and experiences. Colin introduced Jack to Kevin Brandt, a senior, then excused himself, as he had to go and tend bar. Kevin took over and introduced Jack to a number of other "brothers."

"Sam," Kevin called out, "I'd like you to meet a friend of Colin's, Jack Souster...from Canada. Sam Wainright."

"Hi, Sam, nice to meet you," Jack said as he gave Sam a firm handshake.

"Sam plays wide receiver and is Sky's go-to guy," continued Kevin, referring to Sky Muncey, the star quarterback, and then added, "Jack's a friend of Colin MacDonald's."

"From Canada?" echoed Sam, at which point Sky Muncey joined the conversation.

"Play hockey?" Sky asked.

"No," said Jack.

"I thought they let Canadians into this place only if they were hockey players."

"Apparently not."

"Didn't MacDonald tell you that this was *the* Jock House on campus?"

"Yeah, and what about that president of yours selling wheat to the Russians. What are you, a bunch of Commies up there?" added Sam.

"Actually, we have a prime minister, not a president, and I don't really think that this is the best place to have a political debate," Jack said, then added, "Nice meeting you," and left to find Colin.

Skylar Muncey came from an incredibly wealthy family. It was "old money," some said, and others said that it was his mother's money but also that his stepfather was very well connected on Wall Street. Sky and his sister kept their mother's name, Muncey, since she was on her third marriage to Chadwick Richardson, financier. Chadwick was an old family name, and the shortened form "Chad" was never permitted. This marriage looked solid, and Chadwick spoiled the kids rotten, hoping that money and gifts would garner great favor.

The family had a large apartment overlooking the Hudson River as well as a large country estate and horse farm just outside of Essex, Connecticut, which had been in his mother's family for generations. Sylvia, Skylar's mother, and his sister Cicely showed their horses at the Essex Hunt Club, and for many years had the top jumpers in the State. Cicely was hoping to try out for the U.S. equestrian team, and "Daddy" was searching the world for her perfect mount. The family kept its forty-eight-foot Ketch at the Essex Yacht Club, and when they wanted to let their hair down, they would often go to the Griswold Inn and have a number of Beefeater and tonics with lime, then an incredible dinner which the chef prepared especially for them.

Skylar was always very athletic and was sent to the

prestigious Andover prep school, Phillips Academy. He excelled in most of the sporting activities but was head and shoulders above all the others when it came to playing football. When he graduated, he was given a brand new Corvette and when he was accepted at Cornell, a large trust fund, reportedly in the low seven figures, was set up for him, available to him on his graduation. He, however, had acquired a reputation throughout his years at Phillips, where he had been charged twice with arson and once for break and enter. He was also a well-known bully, always picking on the youngest and weakest of the new boys shortly after their enrolment. His parents had always been able to clear his name with numerous generous gifts to the school and the community.

Sam Wainwright, who also came from a wealthy family, was born and raised in New Hampshire and started his college career at Dartmouth. However, he decided to transfer to Cornell because of its excellent electrical engineering program. He was having difficulty keeping his grades up to a C or 72 average due to the fact that he had to work for every mark he got. This average must be maintained at the Ivy League Schools if the student were to remain, regardless of athletics. Sam's love of football and partying was getting in the way of his studies.

Jack found his way to the bar, realizing that he would clearly not be welcome, nor feel comfortable as a "brother" in Delta Chi Upsilon, so he thanked Colin for the invitation and let him know that he was heading out early to write a paper that was due on Monday.

"Jack," Colin said, "let me introduce you to Jimmy Cartwright." He motioned to a large group of people talking to the large football center.

"Not right now, thanks, this isn't the right time," said Jack, not wanting to meet another ignorant, wealthy, spoiled jock. He couldn't get to the door fast enough, hoping he would not bump into "Skylar" Muncey's ego or Sam Wainwright's ignorance on his way out.

"Listen, thanks for the invitation, but I really think that this isn't the place for me."

He remembered going to his first Cornell hockey game. They'd defeated Dartmouth ten to nothing. He recalled watching Colin the first time he stepped onto the ice. Colin was small but incredibly fast and quick enough to dodge the checks the larger opponents threw at him. He had a powerful slap shot yet had incredibly soft hands, as he deked with the puck around every defenseman, and his shots were almost always on target. This game alone he got a perfect hat trick by scoring three goals in succession. Jack, a huge fan of the Toronto Maple Leafs, could only compare Colin to Dave Keon.

It was 1965. Cornell had won the NCAA hockey championship by handily defeating the Michigan Wolverines. Colin was named MVP of the tournament, having scored a hat trick in each of the seven tournament games, a feat never before accomplished. Coach Weiss took Colin aside and introduced him to one of Canada's foremost hockey agents, Chuck Trimble. NHL teams were definitely looking at signing Colin.

*   *   *

Jack had walked up the steps to The Straight, passing someone who was practicing his juggling while another was singing Dylan's "Blowing in the Wind."

These guys have got too much time on their hands or else have finished their exams, Jack thought. He quickly went down the stairs and into the half-full cafeteria. Not sure what he wanted to eat, he grabbed a plate of fries and a Coke and soon found Suzanne, Ruth and Yvette engrossed in a very animated conversation in French.

"*Bonjour*, Jack," they chorused.

"*Bonjour*," he replied, "where's Colin?"

"He'll be along shortly," Yvette said.

Colin and Yvette had now been going out for four years, and Jack was expecting their engagement announcement very soon. They were obviously deeply in love, and Colin had given her his fraternity pin earlier in the year, which was a precursor to engagement. Colin eventually arrived and gave Yvette a quick peck on the cheek.

Yvette was from St. Foy, Quebec, just west of Quebec City. Her father, Pierre Bouchard, a well known accountant and community leader, had decided a number of years before to run for politics and was elected to the Legislative Assembly. He was a bright man and had a star quality about him. He was soon named Minister of Finance. In his first term he was able to bring down a surplus budget, which hadn't been seen in years. He continued on with his policy of strong fiscal management, and during his second term, he caught the eye of the prime minister, Pierre Cadeau, who enticed him to run in the next federal election. He easily won and was promptly named Canada's Minister of Finance.

They took up Jack's suggestion to go to Buttermilk Falls

State Park, just outside Ithaca, and later perhaps to an early show at the movies, then finishing the day at Johnny's Big Red.

Jack, being the only one with a car, said, "Do you want me to go home to get the car and pick you and Yvette up at the dorm, Ruth at your flat, and you Colin, at Delta Chi?"

Ruth said, "At the speed you walk, we could all be changed, go to your flat to get your car, and be waiting for you."

They all laughed, and Jack didn't mind the ribbing from his friends. In fact, many times he would refer in a self-deprecating manner to his lack of speed and stamina.

"Try me," he said, and they all agreed that he could pick them up. After they were all crammed into the Mini, they decided to go to Obie's Diner at the far end of town to pick up some subs and cold sodas for a picnic. Obie's was one of Jack's favorite eateries. It just had one long Formica counter with stools and five booths. Chrome, stainless steel and dark red plastic seats finished the Art Deco decor. Jack would often order two poached eggs on toast for no other reason than to hear Carla shout out to Obie, who was busily dicing some home fries and onions on the grill, or frying a couple of eggs.

"One Adam and Eve on a raft," she would bark, to which Jack would shake his head and laugh.

"One more time, just for me, Carla."

"What? You want two orders, hun?" she would laugh.

Carla was as much an institution as was Obie. She had a tough exterior, and although Jack had never seen her smoke, she had the telltale wrinkles and fine lines of a smoker, and a raspy voice. However, the twinkle in her eye and her wry little smile revealed a soul that was as warm and as soft as the poached eggs Jack had just ordered. She called everybody either "Sweetie" or "Hun," and Jack felt honored if he got called both during the same meal. When totalling up the cheque on her pad, ripping it off, and putting it down on the table, she always, without fail, gently touched the diner's arm and said, "You be good now, hun."

The picnic area in the state park was right beside the water and close to the falls. They had been to this spot many times before and enjoyed the shade, a great grassy area for sunbathing, a picnic table, as well as change rooms and nearby washroom facilities. The girls spread a couple of blankets on the grass and Jack put the subs and soda in a cooler.

They decided to go in for a swim, and Colin went off to the change room while all three girls and Jack simply peeled off their outer clothes, since they'd already changed into their bathing suits back at their rooms. The girls were wearing bikinis, Ruth with her olive complexion looked stunning in orange, while Suzanne, with her auburn hair and freckles, was wearing a green print bikini. But the stunner was the little pixie, Yvette, already working on a tan and in a beautiful deep yellow, very skimpy bikini. Colin and Jack were both in psychedelic, California-style surfer trunks. Jack had always been quite self-conscious of the large scar from his childhood surgery that went down from the top of his sternum then turned and crossed just under his left nipple and proceeded up and under his armpit. His friends had all seen it before, but he caught Ruth, Suzanne and Yvette all taking a furtive glance at it as he took his shirt off.

"It's OK," he joked, "it hasn't grown."

They all blushed with embarrassment and Ruth came over to give him a little kiss on the cheek.

"You're such a sweetheart."

Ruth and Jack had become very close friends over the years, like brother and sister. They confided their deepest feelings in each other, and Jack always wondered if it was because they had a common interest in horses, or if it was something stronger. He was reluctant to take the relationship to the next level. It was so perfect the way it was, and besides, he had an old flame, Consuela, back in Toronto. However, one night they couldn't resist. Jack had driven her back to her flat, and she invited him in for a late night drink. They found themselves giddy with excitement over something Jack couldn't even now remember, dancing to "Cara Mia" by Jay and the Americans. They started undressing in the middle of her living room and found their way into her bedroom, where it all happened to the tune of Petula Clark's "Downtown" followed by the Supremes singing "Stop in The Name of Love." They both agreed that it was good and it was fun, but neither wanted it to ruin the wonderful relationship they had built.

They splashed about in the pool of water that collected at the base of the falls and delighted in the cool mist that descended on their backs. The Frisbees soon came out, and all sorts of games: diving, skipping and lunging began as the plastic fluorescent saucers were whipped around the pond. Before long they all went to the blankets to catch some sun and have their lunch.

"OK," what's with you two?" Jack asked, noticing that Colin and Yvette had been particularly giddy ever since they left The Straight.

"OK, you tell them," Colin said to Yvette.

"We're engaged," she said.

"Wow," everyone exclaimed in unison, "congratulations!" As Ruth and Suzanne hugged and kissed Yvette, Jack shook Colin's hand and put his arm around his shoulder.

"And to top it all off, this morning I signed my first NHL contract with the Leafs!" Colin continued. "I'll be starting with their farm club in Rochester, but it's a firm two-year, entry level draft, and we couldn't be happier. I report to training camp on the first of August. That's why I was a little late this morning, and I had to phone my folks back home. The first thing I do will be to pay them back for everything they have given me. If that's at all possible."

Jack, being the sentimental suck that he was, stood there with a huge grin on his face. Yvette came up to him, and with both thumbs firmly placed on each of Jack's cheeks, wiped a small tear away and kissed him. "You are such a good, good friend. Thank you."

"We haven't set a date yet, but it'll be sometime next spring after the season is over," said Colin.

"That may be June, because with the playoffs, the season lasts forever, and with you on the team, you *will* make the playoffs," Jack emphasized. "The Leafs," he said admiringly. "Do you realize who you'll be playing with? Mahovlich, Davey Keon, Red Kelly, Eddie Shack, Conacher and number 7, Tim Horton, probably the best defenseman who's ever played the game, and with Bower and Sawchuck in net, you've got it made. I can see it now splashed all over the front page of the *Cornell Sun*: 'Toronto Maple Leafs celebrate Canada's centennial with Stanley Cup win,' and then underneath it will say, 'Topped off with an overtime goal in the final game by Cornell's very own Colin MacDonald.'"

"Dream on," said Colin, "I'm only going to be on the

farm team."

"Don't worry, as soon as they see what they've got, you'll be brought up in a flash."

The air was filled with excitement as they all basked in the success and future of Colin and Yvette. Then Colin became embarrassingly serious.

"Jack, will you be my best man?"

"You're kidding! God, I don't think I've ever been so honored. Yes, absolutely!" Jack was filled with all sorts of emotions, wondering how a person with a serious heart defect, having never played on any team in his entire life, could have a "jock" for a friend. He had always assumed that most athletes were shallow, like Sky Muncey, and it took a very special person, like Colin, to look past Jack's physical ailment and see his real character.

"Did you and Yvette kiss in the center of the suspension bridge?" Suzanne said, referring of the Cornell tradition, or superstition, that if a couple kissed on the suspension bridge that spanned Falls Creek Gorge, they were destined for marriage. Falls Creek Gorge was the second gorge that framed the Cornell campus, along with the Cascadilla Gorge on the south side. The suspension bridge was known to be the smallest of its kind in the world.

"Of course," said Yvette. "Many times."

"Speaking of the suspension bridge," said Colin, "did anyone read this morning's *SUN*?" He was referring to the Cornell student newspaper.

"No, why?" someone asked.

"The police found Amy Schechter murdered on the rocks, yesterday, directly below the bridge." He added, "Her throat had been slashed."

There was a collective gasp from all of them, then silence.

"Not Amy, the folk singer," said Jack. "You must be wrong! What's going on? First Nicole Watson, now Amy."

He was truly shaken. They all were suddenly still and quiet. Ruth and Suzanne grabbed each others hands and bowed their heads. Yvette reached out for Colin.

"Well, that means there have been two murders in as many days, because there's no mistaking what, where and when I saw Nicole this morning," said Jack.

He had been a big fan of Amy's and would always stop on the steps to listen to her. If he heard that she would be singing at one of the many hootenannies the folk club put on, he would always be there. Amy got to recognize him as a "regular," and they often chatted. Jack would never forget how she sang Ian and Sylvia's "Four Strong Winds." "....*Think I'll go out to Alberta, weather's good there in the fall...*" The rich, soothing tones projected by Amy's silken voice were swirling in his head. He sat down on the blanket and put his head between his knees. A few minutes later, he looked up, and everyone else had red eyes and was sniffling.

"I'm scared," said Yvette. "I keep getting a spooky feeling that someone is following me."

Colin immediately jumped in. "Why didn't you tell me? From now on, you don't leave your dorm unless you're with me or friends you know you can trust. Do you understand that?"

"Don't get mad at me."

"I'm not getting mad at you, I love you," Colin said. "I want you for the rest of my life, and now you're making me scared."

Suddenly the quiet was broken as two cars came speeding into the park. One was a yellow Corvette convertible and the other a black two-door Mustang. The drivers were whooping it up and screaming as they tried to outdo each other's wheelies. They continued making donuts round and round on the grass and chewing huge ruts into the nearby baseball diamond.

"Those are your buddies, Sky Muncey and his go-to guy, Sam Wainwright," Jack said to Colin in a very derogatory tone.

"They must be celebrating the end of exams," said Colin, as if he was apologizing for them.

"Say no more," replied Jack, trying to reduce Colin's embarrassment.

"How the hell do they afford cars like that?"

"Probably their daddies," said Suzanne.

"Yep," replied Colin, "someone told me that their fathers made more money in their annual bonuses than it'd take to run Cornell."

"Go on," said Jack in disbelief, "that's obscene."

"That's the truth, boy," Colin said, but I'll tell you what, if they want to throw one of those new Mustangs my way, I'll take it. I think Ford's come out with a winner with that one."

They all mused about the rumors that Sky Muncey had been caught shoplifting at the Cornell Bookstore. It was also said that he was in the clothing section and picked up his own football shirt with his number on it. They all laughed at his immense ego. He had denied stealing the jersey and blamed the cashier for slipping it into his bag. It was reported that all charges were dropped after his father made a large financial contribution to the university.

Colin mentioned that Sky was also very tough on his teammates. Every time a play did not work out, he found someone to blame, and it did not endear him to the rest of the team. On top of it all, he would constantly brag about his sexual conquests, which prompted Yvette to label him as "Le Cochon," the Pig.

The events of the day still had Jack emotionally drained. "Guys, I'm really not in a partying mood right now, would you mind if we went home? Anyway, I have to do some packing if I hope to get out of here in the morning."

"What about tonight?" asked Colin as they started folding up and packing the blankets. "This will be our last Friday night together."

"Yeah, for sure," said Jack, "but I don't think we'll be in much of a party mood. It's such a downer, when we should be celebrating your engagement and your contract."

In spite of the tragedies of the last two days, they all agreed to pass on the movie and meet at Johnny's Big Red one last time.

After dropping everyone off at their various residences, Jack went home. His basement flat was in a house on a steep hill on the northwest corner of Catharine Street and College Avenue. It had its own private entrance. He unlocked the basement door to a room that contained his metal shower stall, an open toilet and Mrs. Smythyes' washer and dryer. There was a door to the left of the shower stall that led to the stairs up to the kitchen and the rest of the house. Jack's study was on the corner and had windows on two sides and lots of light. There was one old refrigerator, but cooking appliances were "not permitted." However, Jack had smuggled in a little heating coil apparatus, which he would put into a cup of water to bring it to a boil for tea or instant coffee. It wasn't long before he was able to master Minute Rice, or a poached egg, and with a little extra effort a larger cup made Lipton's Chicken Noodle Soup easily. Producing Kraft Dinner with a little coil was a feat of magic. The fridge was always stocked with Molson's Export when he returned from vacation in Toronto, and Budweiser the rest of the time.

The apartment was furnished in what Jack affectionately described as "Early Train Station," heavy oak desk, a very squeaky, oak chair with arms, a large oak lounge chair with wide arms and a very comfortable seat, the back covered in genuine leather. The bed was an old double spool bed that reminded Jack of his grandmother's. There was no closet, but instead a very functional stand made out of plumbing pipes on wheels, not unlike any coat rack found in some sleazy banquet hall, or bingo parlour.

Mrs. Smythyes was seldom seen, although Jack always worried that the stairway door would open as he was sitting on the toilet or having a shower. This never happened. Mrs. Smythyes had only three rules: no cooking, quiet conversation with any visitors and members of the "opposite gender" were not permitted. There was no parking on the street, so Jack had to park his car in the lot of the small plaza across College Avenue. Generally, this was only at night when the businesses were closed, since he parked on campus during most days.

Jack went into the furnace room, where he was allowed to store his two suitcases. He opened them up on his bed, opened the window to get rid of the musty smell, and emptied his chipboard drawers to pack as tightly as possible. His mother had always told him to roll his clothes up in very tight balls. He was so efficient at it that there was plenty of room to lay his sports jackets, pants and ties across the top. He folded his sheets and blankets and figured that they would lie on top of everything. The pillow could also go on the floor somewhere. He unrolled his down-filled sleeping bag for the night.

The local grocery store had given him a couple of boxes for his books. He then began to clean out the drawers of the desk, where he found a two-year collection of paperclips, erasers, rubber bands, staples and pens. His prized set of Henkel knives, in their own carrying case, was carefully packed along the side of one box. Every time Jack looked at his knife set he felt sick, for in his junior year he had worked for a catering company and his favorite boning knife had gone missing. He was sure it was stolen at one of the fraternity "Homecoming" parties he had helped cater. But he had no proof. He had hoped these knives would last him a lifetime and had his initials, "JAS," for Jack Andrew Souster, stamped into the handles just in case they were lost. Sitting on top of his large blotter were the pens he'd used at this morning's exam. For some reason the Bastion Bank of America's pen stood out. The blotter would be placed on top of everything in his car, so that it would lie flat.

It was seven thirty and just about time to go to Johnny's Big Red. He was going to forget about his weekly stop for chilli at the Collegetown Diner and head straight for Johnny's to treat himself to their fabulous burgers and fries. The burgers were fat and juicy, and it was the only place around that would cook them rare, just as he liked.

He got a table large enough for all of them as well as a couple more people, and ordered his burger and a pitcher of Schlitz. The place was filling up fairly quickly, although everyone seemed quite quiet. There wasn't the usual Friday night banter and bursts of laughter. Ruth and Suzanne showed up first and found Jack, then Colin and Yvette a couple of minutes later. It was obvious from her bloodshot eyes that Yvette had been crying.

"What's up with you two?" Jack asked.

"I want to invite the entire team to the wedding, and she doesn't want Barry Warren to be invited. He's such an asshole, and every time he sees her teases her because of her French accent. I say that we can't just leave one guy off from the team," complained Colin.

"Sorry, buddy, I'm sort of with her. Warren might get the message," Jack replied.

Colin dove into the basket of unsalted peanuts and put a pile of them in front of him. The beer and glasses arrived. Jack played bartender and poured everyone a glass. Soon his meal arrived and the others gave Shirley, the waitress, their orders.

Every now and then, someone would drop by the table to congratulate Colin on his signing, and girls would come over to give Yvette a kiss and congratulate her on her engagement, giggling with excitement.

Out the corner of his eye, Jack saw Sky Muncey and Sam Wainright come through the door. Sky came right over to the table and congratulated Colin, saying, "I hear you signed with the Leafs," and continuing, "there's no money in hockey. I'm heading for the NFL, either the Bears or the Jets."

Jack writhed inside, thinking that this guy couldn't play for the Big Ten, let alone for the NFL, unless his daddy bought him the team. He just couldn't believe the arrogance.

Sky then looked at Jack and said, "And what does a Canadian do who doesn't play hockey?"

"I'm headed out to the Rockies to be the assistant manager of a hotel out there."

"Big deal," Sky snapped, turned, and walked away, as if

to say the only things important in life were football and his conquests. Jack thought, *It'll be too soon if I never see him again.*

The conversation for the rest of the evening was on everyone's plans. Yvette and Colin were probably going to live in Rochester, where the Leafs' farm team was located. They were going to live together until they were married, and both sets of their parents were cool with that.

"I mean, this is the sixties, with free love and all. What else would they expect," Yvette said. "Although my dad is having a bit of a problem with it." The Righteous Brothers singing "Unchained Melody" came on the jukebox.

Beth and Jim Newton, married graduate students and Friday night fixtures at the bar, came and joined the group. The conversation immediately turned to the two campus murders.

Beth said, "I understand that the police are asking for everyone's help to assist them in trying to solve these."

Jim added, "Rumor has it that they're looking for a serial killer. The school has made it known that there are psychologists available at the campus clinic in case anyone wants to talk about the murders and has suggested that all co-eds use the 'buddy' system especially when walking after dark. When I was in Day Hall, I overheard that they're also bringing in some FBI agents because they think it's some kind of psychopath or a guy who's pissed off with the women and all that shit, or maybe he's even gay."

"Gay? What's that got to do with it?" asked Jack.

"Well, gays are known to hate women."

"That's a pile of crap! I know a gay guy, back home, and he's the life of the party when he's with a bunch of women," said Jack.

Suzanne and Ruth held hands and Jack said, "I don't care how close your dorm is, Suzanne, or your flat is, Ruth, *I'm* driving you both home."

There was no complaint about this. With that settled, Jack's mind turned to the odd ballpoint pen that had shown up with his others at the beginning of Professor Elston's final. A chill went over him as he suddenly remembered dropping his binder and pens on the bridge, when he felt light-headed after seeing the co-ed lying in the Cascadilla Gorge. He wondered if the pen happened to be lying on the ground when he went to pick up his own, and he'd picked it up as well, without noticing. He thought that he would take it to Campus Security in the morning when he turned in his handicapped parking licence.

They continued talking about their summer plans. Ruth and Suzanne were both staying on to take a few extra electives over summer school. Colin and Yvette, still giddy from their engagement and Colin's signing with the Leafs, were free until August 1st, when Colin would start training camp. They were tossing around the idea of actually coming out to Lake Louise to visit Jack and tour the Canadian Rockies. Neither of them had been west of Toronto.

"Yeah, come on out. I'll get you a room. I won't have too much time to spend with you, but I'll certainly show you a good time when I'm off duty. Fly out and you can use my car for day trips while I'm working."

Jack announced that he had a five-hour drive back home in the morning, and he still had to pack the car, say goodbye to Mrs. Smythyes, and return his handicapped pass. There were hugs and kisses all around, with everyone promising to stay in touch. They left feeling a bit better, but the murders of the last two days were not far from their minds. Jack drove Ruth and Suzanne home, as promised, and waited until they entered the building and the door had closed behind them. He went home and crawled into his sleeping bag.

The next morning, he busied himself packing the car with great care. It was small, and he had to use every inch of empty space. He still had seven bottles of Budweiser left, which he had planned to give to Colin. The last thing to be put in the car was the blotter, which would lie on top of everything. He went to pick it up, and the pen that he had found yesterday seemed to jump out at him. He knew that he had to deal with it, shortly. He grabbed it and shoved it into his pocket.

In two years, Jack had never used the back stairs to see Mrs. Smythyes. Somehow the door gave him the "willies," since the stairs headed up into an unknown part of the house. He went out the back door, climbed up the hill, and rang the doorbell at the front. Mrs. Smythyes answered, and they said their goodbyes. Jack had never been invited in.

"Are you on your way, Jack?"

"Yes, I'm afraid so. It's been wonderful, and I want to thank you so much. I've really enjoyed staying here, and I hope that I was a good tenant," Jack replied.

"Jack, you were wonderful, there was only that one time, but you corrected that as soon as you learned the rules," she said, referring to the one time well over a year ago that she had to come down the stairs and ask him to turn down the radio.

"Here's the key, and I'm sure that you'll find everything in order. I actually scrubbed the shower stall, the toilet and the fridge. And oh," he added, "you'll find a half carton of orange juice in the fridge, which you're welcome to use. It's still good, since I bought it on Tuesday." He handed her the key and they said goodbye.

The next stop was the Campus Security office to hand in his parking hanger. The room was painted a hospital green. The desk was gray metal with matching chair. There was an old, dented, brushed aluminum cigarette ashtray, overflowing with butts sitting next to a rustic Underwood typewriter. Just off to the side of the typewriter was a police car radio receiver with a microphone and switch on the end of a gooseneck stand with a blinking red light. There was a name plate beside the ashtray that read: "Gloria Stokes, Sect'y."

"Hi, I've come to return my handicapped parking hanger," he said to the aging, bespectacled secretary. "Do I give it to you?"

"No, I'll get you Sergeant Smith. He'll have to sign for it and give you a receipt," she said as she added another half-smoked cigarette to her nest of butts.

Jack always found it humorous that Campus Security had titles like Constable, Sergeant and Chief. He used to call them "rent-a-cops" and was amazed at how much authority they felt they had hiding behind a badge.

"Can I help you?" said the portly sergeant as he approached the desk.

"Yes, I would like to turn in my parking permit."

"What's your licence number?" Jack gave him his licence number followed by the name of his issuing province.

"Oh yeah, you're that *Canadian*. Let me see if there are any infractions. Nope, you're clean." Jack wasn't sure what he meant by "*That Canadian,*" but decided to let it slip by.

Jack pulled out the Bastion Bank of America pen. "They say that you're asking for peoples' help in solving the recent murders. I found this pen on the ground, I think, yesterday morning on the Stone Bridge close to where they found the co-ed in the Cascadilla Gorge."

"'You think,' but you're not sure where you found it. Listen, go back to Canada and leave the policing to the pros," the sergeant sneered then added, "Don't worry, we'll catch the perv. We don't need the help of any stoned students." He was referring to the rampant use of marijuana around the campus and the hippie revolution with free love and everything associated with the movement.

Jack nodded, thinking *What an asshole*, and thanked Miss Stokes. At that moment the static of the patrol car radio on Miss Stokes's desk crackled and broke the silence.

"Come in," Miss Stokes said into the old microphone to the right of her typewriter, pressing the red "Speak" button.

"Gloria, we've found Jake Snelling peeping in the windows of Dickson Hall," the officer crackled. "We're going to take him downtown and have him booked. We'll let you know what happens, over and out."

Jack's mother's name was Dickson. What really amazed him, however, was the fact that Dickson Hall was named after a Clara Dickson, the same name as Jack's grandmother. He wondered how many Clara Dicksons there could be.

Jake Snelling was a "Townie" and well known in Ithaca, and particularly on the Cornell Campus, as a Peeping Tom, a drug pusher and part of a gang known as "The Crew," named after the famed Cornell rowing team. He and other members of "The Crew" were constantly being ushered off the campus by security, and were often charged for being drunk, disorderly, and for the odd burglary.

As he left, Jack put the pen back in his pocket. The next stop was signing out at Day Hall, and he was pleased that there were no outstanding fines or work orders against him. He was reminded that, being Canadian, he must relinquish his student visa at the border, as it was no longer valid forty-eight hours after his final exam. The United States government did not want foreign students staying in the country and taking jobs away from Americans, which Jack thought was completely understandable.

Delivering the beer to Colin at the Delta Chi house was next on the agenda. He found Colin studying in his room. The house was huge, built in the style of a southern mansion, such as one might see in *Gone With The Wind*. It housed sixty-eight students, and with over sixty fraternities and sororities, all of the same magnitude, on campus, the university relied heavily on them to house many of the students.

Jack knocked and walked in. "Hi guy, here's some remnants from my fridge," he said, handing Colin the seven bottles of Bud.

"Thanks. So, this is it, you're off?"

They talked for a few minutes then Jack reminded Colin that he wanted a couple of tickets to his first Leafs game. They gave each other the traditional one-armed hug, shook hands, and Jack started for the door.

"You have no idea what your asking me to be your best man means to me. Remember, I'll be there. Just let me know where and when it's going to be. Guess I'll have to bone up on my French if it's going to be a bilingual crowd," he laughed. They shook hands again, and Jack was off. He couldn't help but feel lucky to have a friend like Colin.

The Mini headed down West Seneca, past the Tompkins County Savings and Loan, where he had closed out his account two days before. He found his way onto Route 96, and he looked out his right window for the last time to see a single scull gliding, like a ballet dancer, gracefully gliding across a watery stage along the Crew course. Route 96 took him up the west side of Lake Cayuga. It was a drive he'd always loved, not only because of its scenery but more because of the wonderful memories it held of his arrival at Cornell. Shortly after Geneva, he headed onto Interstate 90, the New York Thruway heading west to Buffalo.

There were three border crossings to enter Canada: Niagara Falls's Rainbow Bridge, Buffalo's Peace Bridge and the Queenston Bridge. Jack always preferred the latter because it felt like a shorter route, although he had never checked it out on his odometer.

After paying his toll, he pulled up to the office, knowing that there would be some paperwork as he surrendered his visa. He always got butterflies in his stomach, thinking that he was bound to get caught with something illegal, even though he knew that he never had anything to declare. This day was different, as he had all of his worldly possessions with him, including a stereo and his prized Martin guitar, both which he had purchased in Ithaca over the last four years.

"I'd like to surrender my student visa," Jack told the officer.

"All finished?"

"Yep, do I need a receipt?"

"Nope, as long as I've got it, you can't use it anymore," chuckled the guard.

Jack nervously said, "I've got nothing to declare."

"Well, you'll have to tell that to the Canadian guys when you cross the bridge, and if I were you, I wouldn't offer that information unless you are asked," advised the guard with a knowing smile.

Jack proceeded across the bridge with his mind racing, thinking that the U.S. border guard would phone his Canadian counterpart and tell him to pull over the guy in the red Mini.

He always played a silly little game of putting his hand up against the windshield as he crossed the bridge where the Canadian and U.S. flags flew side by side, just to see if his hand was in Canada before his foot pressed on the accelerator. For some reason, the hand always won. By the time he pulled up to the Canadian border guard booth, he was convinced that he had seen the end of his two most prized possessions.

"Anything to declare?'

"Not a thing."

"What's all that?" the guard said nodding to the pile of clothing, bedding and books in the back seat.

"I've been going to school at Cornell for the past four years, so that's pretty well everything I own."

"Hockey team?"

"No, I can only wish."

"Humph," replied the guard then added, "OK, go ahead, have a good day."

Jack gave a great sigh of relief and, although wanting to speed out onto the highway, purposely drove exactly at the posted speed limit for the next mile until he was out of sight. As much as he loved Cornell and Ithaca, it was always nice to come home, and a little shiver of happiness came over him.

− 4 −

Jack pulled into the paved double driveway at his parents' home at 12 Crestview Court in Scarborough, part of Metropolitan Toronto in the north east of the city and sometimes referred to by its detractors as "Scarberia." They were at the end of a cul de sac with only the driveway the frontage of the property. As the property lines went back in a deep pie shape, it created a huge backyard. Jack's father, Sam, being an accountant, and known to be very frugal with his money, particularly prided himself in his property. It was not because it was adorned with beautiful shrubs, flowerbeds and a tremendous stand of birch trees in the back, but because the taxes were the lowest in the neighbourhood, because the city only based their tax assessment on the frontage of the property.

As Jack put the parking brake on, his mother, Stephanie, came running out. They had a huge hug and it seemed that she didn't want to let go. They started unpacking the car.

They went into the house, and Jack's favorite dog of all time, Dylan, the Siberian Husky, came out to greet him. He started his familiar howl to show his great pleasure at seeing Jack again. Jack had named him Dylan because he never barked, and Jack would, jokingly, tell people that he sang like Bob Dylan.

Inside the house, his mom said, "I've cooked your favorite dinner tonight, you know, that chicken casserole with the onion soup mix in it, the one you've always liked."

"Oh, I was hoping to go over to Consuela's tonight."

"Well, invite her over here for dinner with us, and then the two of you can go out to a movie after."

Jack had something a little more exciting on his mind than a movie, and he chuckled to himself. Since it was his first night home, he thought it best to stay home and visit then drive Consuela home after dinner, and what happened after that would unfold, hopefully the way he wanted.

"Jack, Heather Stuart of Mr. Lawton's office called a couple of days ago and asked that you give Mr. Lawton a call when you got in."

Gordon Lawton was the Chief Executive Officer of all of the Canadian Pacific Hotels. Under his leadership, they were now thinking of expanding into other countries. Heather Stuart was Mr. Lawton's personal assistant, who Jack liked very much, but purely platonically. Their offices were on part of a floor in the Royal York, and Heather and Jack often had coffee together in the hotel coffee shop. Being front desk staff and part of management, they were permitted in the public areas with the guests and was not relegated to "The Beanery," the staff cafeteria.

Heather often told Jack what was going on, knowing that

he would keep it to himself. He enjoyed this, as it could help his long-term plans. As long as the chain expanded, he saw a good future for himself.

He called her. "Hi, Heather, it's Jack. You told my mom that Mr. Lawton wanted to see me?"

"Hi, yes. Welcome home, how about tomorrow morning at ten?'

"Perfect. Coffee after?"

"Wouldn't miss it, Thanks, see you then."

Next was a call to Consuela.

"Hi, I'm home. How'd you like me to pick you up, and you could have dinner here with my folks, and then we could do something after."

She agreed, and Jack said that he'd pick her up around seven o'clock. Consuela gave him her new address. She had just moved out of her parents' home and found a nice apartment on her own.

Consuela Gonzales was originally from Guatemala and had moved to Canada when she was thirteen. She had that lovely olive skin with jet black hair and still maintained her delightful, although weakened Spanish accent. She had started in the travel business as an agent for the Advantage Travel Agency in the concourse of the Royal York. Jack had noticed her a number of times on his way to the coffee shop, and eventually they struck up a fairly serious relationship. They seldom spoke at the hotel, to avoid tongues wagging, as they so often do in corporate environs.

Consuela was a hard worker, and by living at home was able to save just about every penny she had earned. This past year, while Jack was still at school, she'd purchased a Marlin

Travel franchise in the very upscale area of Toronto, on Bloor Street. Now that she was her own boss and having to hire her own people, cover the payroll, pay taxes, rent and those hated franchise fees, she was working harder than ever.

The dinner went well, with Jack doing most of the talking reliving his past year. Unfortunately, he had to tell them what had happened to the two co-eds. While it put a damper on the evening, they were so happy to have Jack home and to hear that he had done well in his exams that the rather remote lives of Amy Schechter and Nicole Watson really didn't mean as much to them. After dinner Jack and Consuela said their goodbyes and headed down the Don Valley Parkway, exiting at Bloor Street, and eventually to Consuela's new apartment, in Greek town along Danforth Avenue.

Jack was impressed at how tastefully she had furnished it. As soon as the door closed, they instantly found themselves in each other's arms. The embrace was long and passionate, as Consuela backed Jack up, leading him to the bedroom. By the time they had reached the bed, they were two bodies of writhing warm flesh, and Jack always relished that feeling of skin on skin. If it was at all possible, Consuela's lovemaking was more passionate than he had ever remembered it.

Afterwards, he stared up at the ceiling while Consuela was in the adjoining ensuite "freshening up," realizing what he had missed since spring break. She soon returned with a warm snifter of cognac. This led to another, but slower, lovemaking session.

It was now two thirty in the morning, and Jack realized that he had a ten o'clock meeting with Mr. Lawton. He hadn't even unpacked, so he had a quick shower and kissed Consuela goodbye. He rushed out the door to get home, grab some sleep, and find something suitable to wear to the meeting. He was quiet enough not to wake up his parents when he got home. Dylan opened one eye, slapped his tail twice on the floor, and went back to sleep.

The Parkway, which was finally being completed after being planned since 1954, was normally like a parking lot in the morning rush hour due to construction, was pleasantly fast-flowing this day, and Jack pulled into the east door entrance of the hotel to refresh his acquaintance with Tom Parker, the doorman who had been there for over fifteen years. Jack seldom took advantage of Tom's good nature, as the east wing entrance was strictly for the use of arriving guests and taxis, but asked him if he could leave the car for a few minutes while he went up to see Mr. Lawton. Tom said, "No problem."

The executive suite of offices for Canadian Pacific Hotels was opulent, to say the least. Thick, woven burgundy Indian carpets with the CP logo woven into them in gold were laid out as if to protect the highly polished mahogany floors. The ceilings were a good twelve feet high, yet seemed lower. Two matching crystal chandeliers mirrored each other. The sofas and chairs were in a deep mustard leather, accompanied by highly polished mahogany coffee and end tables with floral patterned china lamps crowned with shades of silk. The *Financial Post* and the *Globe and Mail,* Canada's National Daily Newspaper, were carefully set out on the tables flanked by *Business Week, Maclean's,* Canada's weekly news magazine, and *Guest*, the glossy international hospitality industry magazine. Gracing the front cover was a picture of Gord Lawton dressed in his blue suit looking at an architect's scale model of Canadian Pacific's latest venture, a beautiful new property in Dubai. Captioned in bold type under the picture was: "INTERNATIONAL HOTELIER OF THE YEAR."

Against the back wall was a beautifully carved desk, and sitting behind it was Heather Stuart, smiling as Jack walked in. She was always dressed very sharply, conservatively, one might say. Today she wore a pleated skirt, a white blouse with a brooch and a navy blue blazer with red piping around the collar, lapels and cuffs. Her hair was, as usual, perfect, precision cut, medium brown with a touch of frosted highlights.

"Hi, stranger," she said as she came out from behind her desk to give Jack a quick hug. "Mr. Lawton's ready to see you, so go right in," she added as she opened the door to the inner office.

"Jack," said Gord Lawton as he got up to shake hands. "Welcome back, and it's good to have you finally on board. Have a seat."

Jack pulled up an armchair. Gord Lawton was a large, imposing man, at least six foot three inches and two hundred and fifty pounds, but he carried his weight well. A large original oil painting of the Banff Springs Hotel, with the Vermillion Lakes in the foreground and Mount Rundle in the distance, hung on the panelled wall directly behind the desk. An oil of another CP hotel classic, the majestic Chateau Frontenac, perched high over the St. Lawrence River in old Quebec, hung on the wall to Jack's right. The sun poured in from the floor-to-ceiling windows on the left, framed by massive burgundy and velvet curtains and pinned back by golden tasselled ropes.

After a few minutes of casual banter about the school, Gord said, "There's been a change of plans. Alessandro

Carlucci's mother just passed away in Italy two days ago. He's allowed three bereavement days, but he's asked for a couple of weeks. Seeing as he has to fly to Italy, I've granted his request of a leave, without pay, and I'm going to get you to fill in for him. Harry Hickson of the Palliser will fill in for you at the Chateau until you get out there, which may possibly not be until the last week of July." The Palliser was the CP hotel in Calgary, so it made sense to send someone from there for the few short weeks, since it was only a hundred miles from Lake Louise.

Jack was very disappointed, since he'd been looking forward to getting out to Lake Louise as soon as possible, but he didn't let his dashed dreams show. It was only for three weeks, and he wanted to show he was a team player. He also figured he would enjoy a steady diet of Consuela while he was in Toronto.

"Not a problem. I can start tomorrow, or whenever." They parted with a warm handshake then Jack reminded Heather it was time for their coffee.

They made their way down to the coffee shop. Jack was delighted to see that Madge Williams was still there. Madge had waitressed in the coffee shop for over twenty five years. Her gray hair was covered in a hair net, topped by a little starched yellow and white cap, which matched her short-sleeved, freshly ironed yellow uniform and highly stiffened white French apron. She was getting on in age as she seemed to be shuffling in her white "sensible" shoes a little more than the last time Jack saw her. As Heather and Jack took their seat on the coffee shop stool, Madge came by with a hot piece of cherry pie, Jack's favorite, straight from the hotel bakery, and then she gave him a big welcoming wink and a smile.

"How's Tommy?" Jack asked Madge, knowing that she had been a single mother since Tommy was two, and the last he had heard Tommy was doing very well in law school, after receiving his B.A. from the University of Toronto.

"God, you don't forget a thing, do you?" Madge chuckled. "He just graduated, head of his class, and has just started articling for Ross, Hepson, Little and Burns."

Jack was impressed. Ross, Hepson, Little and Burns LLP was the top criminal defence firm in all of Canada. Most people referred to the firm as Ross and Associates. They took on the truly hopeless cases where the alleged perpetrator was already convicted in the press even before there was a trial. It was rumored that the legendary William Ross, who had since retired, never lost a case. His junior, Norman Caldwell, was now senior partner in the firm and had learned well from his mentor. Norm Caldwell hated to lose. He never left a stone unturned when he prepared for a case. He hated surprises when he went into court. He used Tommy a great deal to do some of his research, and he would question Tommy on every point and then double check all the pertinent case law. Only when he was completely satisfied would he let Tommy go or have him check out something else.

"Wow, you must be very proud of him," she said as Madge served them, then walked away to fill up someone else's coffee cup.

After they got their coffee, Heather said, "So, I've got some news. I've just handed in my notice and only have another week to go."

"What? You can't go, you practically run this organization."

"Thanks, but I got an offer that I just couldn't refuse... and I'm only moving one block away but fifty storeys up."

"Where? And what will you be doing?"

"I've accepted the position of executive assistant to Thomas Crowley, the president and CEO of the York National Bank. I'll be doing similar things to what I'm doing here, except dealing with bank branches instead of hotels. The money is twice as much as I'm making now, with a better health and dental plan, and a better pension plan. In fact, I only have to pay ten percent into it, whereas here it's fifty-fifty. On top of all that, I get stock options. It's a no brainer," she concluded. "You should know: the hotel business is not a big payer."

They knew that they would be having coffee a few times more before she left, and possibly a drink, but Jack was sorry to see her go, not only because he had lost his contact in head office, but he was going to miss her company and advice when he bounced ideas off her. He signed the check for their coffee, and as Heather went back up to her office, he proceeded to the main lobby.

The lobby was two stories high, with the mezzanine's wrought iron railings encircling the lower level. Massive creamy marble pillars every fifteen feet supported the overhang, and the floors were a highly polished, marble terrazzo in terra cotta. Mammoth red and gold area rugs, with the famous Royal York "RY" capped by a crown logo woven into them, were placed in perfect alignment over the terrazzo. There was a large circular staircase that snaked from the center of the lobby down to the Lower Concourse.

Alessandro Carlucci was at the assistant manager's desk, just a few feet away from the main registration desk. Jack said a few hellos to some of the cashiers and bellhops and then to Alessandro to express his sympathy.

"Hi, guy," Jack said. "I'm really sorry to hear about your mom. Listen, I'm here, so whenever Bill wants me to start, you're free to go." Bill Murphy was the front office manager and had been running the front office and reservations department since the hotel was built in 1929. He was meticulous, and there was seldom a problem.

"I appreciate that, Jack, and if you could suggest to Bill that you start in the morning, that would be great." So it was arranged, and Jack started back at his old job at seven the next morning.

It was good to be back, and Jack felt he knew the ropes well enough to avoid any surprises. Furthermore, he knew that this was only temporary, and it wouldn't be long until he got out to Lake Louise. He started the day by going over all of the reservations, showing a particular interest in what VIPs would be arriving and which ones required a personalized greeting. He would already have pre-registered before ushering them to their suite. He also checked which rooms required a complimentary basket of fruit or a vase of flowers, and went over all the arrangements with either room service, housekeeping or the hotel flower shop to make sure there were no slip-ups.

A few days after he had started back, he had his first dignitary to pre-register and greet: Harry Belafonte was performing at the O'Keefe Centre for the Performing Arts. It was just two blocks east along Front Street from the Royal York. Most of the performers stayed at the Royal York, partly because of its proximity and partly because of its prestige. Jack enjoyed meeting various personalities, sports figures, presidents, prime ministers, and of course, royalty. The hotel's main supper club, the Imperial Room, featured major

Las Vegas and Hollywood entertainers such as Peggy Lee, Tony Bennett, Mel Torme and many others.

Immediately after checking in Harry Belafonte, Jack was talking to Carole Crindle, the mail clerk on duty at the time, and he mentioned that she had missed seeing Mr. Belafonte.

"What," she exclaimed, "you checked in Harry Belafonte and didn't tell me? My god, Jack, I absolutely idolize him."

Jack just happened to look up at that moment and noticed Mr. Belafonte coming across the lobby.

"Shsh. Just be calm and treat him like any other guest."

"I'm expecting an envelope from the theatre, would you be kind enough to call my suite when it arrives?" Mr. Belafonte asked.

"Absolutely, sir, I will, I definitely will," Carole replied in a shaky voice.

Carole's total admiration was not lost on Mr. Belafonte, and he asked, "Would you care to come to the opening night?" He pulled two tickets out of his shirt pocket.

"Oh, sir," Carole said, "you're far too kind, I'd love to go…and sir," she stuttered, "I'd be just as happy to see you stand on stage for two hours. You wouldn't have to sing at all," she nervously blurted.

Belafonte laughed in his soft, smoky, sensual voice, turned to Jack and said, "Now you be nice to her, because she's holding the tickets, and it's up to her who she brings."

"I'll be extra nice, sir, thank you," Jack smiled.

Just at that moment a room clerk approached Jack and said, "There's an urgent call for you from Chateau Lake Louise."

Jack went to his desk and picked up the phone. It was

Harold McIntyre, the manager of the Chateau. They exchanged pleasantries and mentioned how eager they were to work together in just a few weeks.

"Listen," Harold said, "a Ruth Golden from Ithaca has been trying to get a hold of you. She said it's urgent, but I didn't want to give her your number in case...well, you know what I mean. Jack," he continued, "she seems almost frantic."

Jack knew company policy was that personal phone numbers were not to be given out, but he thought he could have given Ruth the Royal York's number. He asked the senior room clerk to keep an eye on his desk and to come and get him if there was any problem. He would be in the back office making an important phone call.

"Ruth, it's Jack, what's the problem?"

"Oh god, Jack, where have you been? Yvette's been murdered, and they've arrested Colin. In fact, they've also charged him with Amy's and Nicole's murders." She was rambling hysterically.

Jack immediately felt faint and nauseous. He reached for the waste paper container and threw up all the contents of his stomach. He felt lightheaded, and his right hand was starting to tingle so that he could barely hold the telephone to his ear.

"Jack, are you still there? Are you OK?"

"Yes, I'll call you right back." He wiped the vomit from his chin with the back of his hand and hung up. He went into the staff washroom to get a drink of water and clean off a spot of vomit on his tie. Looking in the mirror, he saw that his normally rosy cheeks had turned a pallid gray, and his eyes had slightly darkened. His hands felt clammy. He went back to the table in the staff room and sat there with his head between his trembling hands, trying to make sense out of what he had just heard.

Finally, he mustered up enough nerve to phone Ruth back. As he was dialling, his mind was filled with confusion, fear and apprehension. His very best friend having been charged with three murders, one being that of his fiancée, the adorable Yvette. Jack wondered how he could continue. It was like he was being smothered under a stone wall. His idyllic memories and his promising future seemed to be collapsing around him. How could he go on without the dearest friends in his life? He said to himself that he must be strong. Ruth answered.

"Tell me that what I just heard is not real. This is no joke?"

"No, Jack, I would not kid you about something like that."

"What happened?" He was terrified to hear the details.

"They found Yvette floating in Beebe Lake. She was naked and her throat had been slashed," Ruth sobbed.

Jack's stomach again started to heave at the images Ruth's words were putting into his head. There was nothing left in his stomach, so he simply gagged with each heave. Beebe Lake was in the center of the Cornell campus. Its waters flowed down Falls Creek, under the suspension bridge and down to Lake Cayuga.

"They're holding him in the Tompkins County Jail, and he doesn't have any faith in the lawyer the court appointed him. The only number he thought of was mine, because they wouldn't allow him to make a long distance call to his family in Cape Breton or to you in Lake Louise. Jack, he's innocent. You know that he loved Yvette like nobody has ever loved anybody. I'm scared. What can we do?"

"First of all, I'm in Toronto, and I get off duty at three o'clock, so I could conceivably be there by eight or nine tonight. If I can get someone to cover my shift tomorrow, I'll be there, but if not, I might have to phone in sick," he said. He hated that idea. He had prided himself on never having taken time off work due to illness one day in his life. He totally disagreed with faking illness as an excuse for a day off.

"We'll work something out. I'll see you at your place tonight, and tell Colin I'm on my way." He tried to make his voice sound consoling.

He finished the rest of his shift as if he were a zombie. He merely went through the motions of work until Chris Carter, his relief, came on duty. He quickly, but very briefly, explained the situation to Chris and asked him to work a couple of his shifts for him. He said he would work Chris's Christmas and New Year's Eve shifts. Chris and Jack had always gotten along well, and there was no question that Chris would help out, as long as Bill Murray, the front office manager, approved the schedule changes. In Bill's office, Jack explained what had happened in the hope that Bill would understand.

"Do you mean to tell me you know that guy?" Bill asked.

"What do you mean, 'that guy'?"

Bill Murray threw a *Toronto Star* newspaper on his desk, and the headline leapt out: *Leaf Hopeful, Charged in Multiple Murders!* There was a picture of Colin pulling his Toronto Maple Leafs jersey over his head right after the signing of his contract. The heading under the photograph: *Cornell Hockey Star Charged in Hat Trick Murders.* Bill also added that it was on CFRB, Toronto's most listened-to radio station, reporting that Colin was the serial killer for whom the police and FBI had been searching for in the past few weeks.

Jack's spirits nosedived.

On his way out, he stopped and made one last phone

call. "Ross, Hepson, Little and Burns," answered the efficient-sounding receptionist.

"May I speak with Tommy Williams, please?" asked Jack.

"One moment please," replied the receptionist. "I'm checking."

"Tom Williams speaking."

"Tom, it's Jack Souster from the Royal York...I know your mother, Madge," said Jack.

"Oh yeah, Mom's often talked about you. How can I help you?"

"I have a friend in upper New York State who really needs a top-notch criminal defence lawyer. Do you know of anybody?" Jack asked.

"Jeez, Jack, I've just started here, but I'll ask around." They left it that Tommy would call Jack at Ruth's number should he be able to find a criminal defence lawyer in New York State.

Jack quickly went over to speak with Carole at the mail desk, explaining that something had come up and he wouldn't be able to go to the Belafonte opening that night.

Jack raced north on the Don Valley Parkway at three thirty in the afternoon, darting and weaving in and out of traffic, to pick up a few personal items and head directly to Ithaca. He explained Colin's situation to his mother as she followed him up to his bedroom. After gathering up his toiletry kit, a couple of changes of underwear, socks and shirts, he quickly wrote down Ruth's telephone number. He gave his mother a peck on the cheek and tried to go down the stairs and out the door without wasting time, but he didn't neglect to give Dylan a quick pat goodbye.

Jack's route was Highway 401, across the north part of Toronto, south on Highway 27, onto the Queen Elizabeth Way, over the Garden City Skyway traversing the Welland Canal and then to the border crossing at Queenston.

"Purpose of your trip?" asked the female border guard.

Jack wished he hadn't surrendered his student visa, since it made life at the border so much easier and faster. He had always heard that the women guards were the strictest. "Taking over any gifts? How long are you going to be in the U.S.? What's your final destination? Any tobacco, alcohol, or firearms?" The questions came out in rapid-fire succession.

"Visiting a friend, no, a couple of days, Ithaca, New York, no, no, no." He answered the questions as fast as they were asked.

"Enjoy your stay."

By the time he got onto the Thruway and picked up his toll ticket, it seemed like he had been on the road for hours. He had traveled this stretch of road dozens of times over the last four years, but it seemed like forever before he reached Exit 41 and was onto Route 96 heading south to Ithaca. He turning on his radio and Roy Orbison came on singing "Pretty Woman" followed by the Beach Boys singing "Surfer Girl." These songs would normally get his mind thinking of his wonderful Consuela, but today he could only think of Colin and his situation. He had passed the Rochester exit and knew that it wouldn't be long before his exit and toll booth would be coming up.

Eventually he made it to his exit south. This route wound its way down the west side of Cayuga Lake and its numerous vineyards, but he soon realized that there were many speed zones that came up and slowed him down as he traveled through small villages, some with only four corners, three homes and a variety store. He eventually came to Trumansburg, and Ithaca was only fifteen minutes away. They were the longest fifteen minutes in his life, for it seemed like another hour as he worried what he was going to say to Ruth and eventually Colin.

– 6 –

Jack pulled up to Ruth's small apartment building, already out of breath at just thinking that he had to climb three flights of stairs to get to her flat. He was glad that it was summer at school and parking restrictions were somewhat relaxed. He knocked on her door, and she opened it and hugged him all in the same movement. She buried her head in his shoulder and started crying uncontrollably.

"Oh, Jack, what are we going to do? It's all so horrible," she sobbed. Jack took her hand, and they went and sat down at her table.

"Have you talked to Colin?" he asked, and she shuddered.

"Oh yes, but you can see him only between ten and eleven in the morning, and he's allowed just one visitor at a time, unless you're his lawyer, and he hates his lawyer. He's convinced that Colin is guilty and is telling him to plead guilty to second degree manslaughter to reduce his sentence."

"Where is Colin?"

"They've moved him to the Elmira Correctional Facility, and they have him in solitary confinement. Jack, it's just awful. They lead him into a little room with two chairs and a table, and he's in handcuffs and leg shackles. He looks just terrible. His eyes are all dark and his skin looks as gray as pewter," she said and started to sob again. "Oh, I forgot to mention, a Tommy Williams called for you."

"Great, maybe he's found us a decent lawyer. I'll call him in the morning. I'm famished," he said. "Let's go out and get a bite to eat."

They got in the car and drove down to Obie's Diner, where Jack ordered one of his favorite meals: sautéed liver, rare, heaped with fried onions and bacon, and instead of two scoops of mashed potatoes, he ordered his cherished hash browns. Ruth shuddered when the liver arrived at the same time as her toasted club house sandwich.

"How can you eat that, especially at a time like this?" she cried.

They talked for hours, ordering coffee after coffee. Ruth insisted that Jack stay with her rather than get a motel room; their relationship had always been strictly platonic—except for that one time—and sex was the last thing on their minds under these circumstances.

The next morning came soon enough, and Jack started breakfast. He always prided himself on cooking eggs well, and started what he considered his famous scrambled eggs with cheese. Ruth said that she'd start the bacon.

"What, you're doing bacon?" asked a surprised Jack. "I didn't think you people ate bacon."

"You people!" she said indignantly, "what do you mean

by 'You People'?"

Jack was embarrassed by his insensitivity and said, "God, I'm sorry, I meant to say that I didn't think that Jewish people were permitted to eat pork or any pork by-products like bacon."

"Well, Catholics aren't supposed to use birth control either."

"Touché."

It was now nine a.m., and they decided to call Tommy, as they had half an hour to drive to Elmira to visit Colin.

"Hi, Jack, I have a name for you. A couple of guys in the firm went to the National Association of Criminal Defence Lawyers, NACDL convention in Vegas last February. When they heard this young guy speak, they were just in awe." He gave Jack the name and number of Clayton McBride. Jack looked at the number and realized that it had the same area code as Ruth's. He couldn't be that far away.

Clayton McBride answered his own phone. Jack introduced himself and told Clayton how he'd come highly recommended by a friend at Ross and Associates in Toronto. Clayton said that he had heard about the three murders and had read some local newspaper reports.

"Where is he now?" he asked.

"He's being held in solitary confinement at the Elmira Correctional Facility."

"I know it well. I get a lot of my business out of there, mostly appeals."

"Where are you?"

"I'm just down the road in Binghamton."

After talking a bit about Colin and some of the circumstances, Clayton told Jack that he couldn't see him that day but could shuffle things around in his calendar and meet him at the correctional facility the next day at ten a.m. Jack had asked him about his fees and Clay said not to worry about that right now. Jack felt a little relieved that they had perhaps found a decent lawyer to represent Colin.

Ruth and Jack set out to visit the prisoner. When they got to Elmira and the Correctional Facility, Jack was shaken at its immense size, and the towering fences, capped by huge coils of razor wire like a giant, gleaming, outstretched Slinky. As they entered the massive front door, they were greeted by a guard with a revolver sticking out of an unfastened holster wrapped around his waist. Without saying a word, he motioned them over to a bulletproof glass window, where another armed guard sat. Jack spoke into a microphoned hole, implanted in the middle of the one-inch, green-tinted, bulletproof glass. He announced that he was there to visit Colin MacDonald. The guard looked at Ruth and said, "You know the rules, miss. Only one visitor at a time."

"I know, I'll just wait in the waiting room if that's OK."

The guard nodded and the second guard ushered them into another room. Jack could hear the lock click behind him. This room was totally devoid of anything except an overhead fluorescent light and an open counter on the right hand side. A third guard soon entered from a second door, complete with a metal detector wand, and then a fourth appeared behind the counter. Jack and Ruth were asked to remove their belts, shoelaces, watches and any jewelry as well as to empty their pockets. They created two piles of all of their possessions on the counter, and the guard put them in two large separate envelopes, labelling each one handing them each a receipt. Both Ruth and Jack were frisked. Ruth was taken to a small anteroom where a female officer patted her down.

Then they were ushered into a waiting room containing nothing but straight-backed chairs, and again a string of fluorescent lights. As the door slammed shut and locked behind them, Ruth took a seat and a guard opened another door to summon Jack to follow him into a hallway. He opened the second door on the left and entered the room with Jack. This room, again, was lit by the omnipresent fluorescent lighting, and the blank walls were painted the usual anaemic green, which, combined with the lighting, turned Jack's skin ashen, not unlike his mood. There was one metal table and two straight chairs opposite each other. In the center of the opposite wall was another door. The guard told Jack to sit down then backed into a corner and stood with his arms folded in front of him.

In a few minutes, which felt like an eternity to Jack, the other door opened and in walked Colin, hands cuffed in front of him, and his legs in shackles. Jack was a little relieved to see Colin was wearing a plain gray shirt and prison issue pants. Having watched too many movies, he was expecting to see his friend in a black-and-white striped chain gang outfit. Colin's incarceration number was stencilled above the shirt pocket: 572859632. At the sight of him, Jack jumped up and started around the table to give him a huge hug.

"Sit down," barked the guard. "There'll be no touching."

Jack and Colin sat down facing each other. Jack noticed how gaunt Colin looked. "How are you? Are you OK? This is crazy, man," Jack said. "What are they saying?"

"They say that I've killed Yvette, as well as Amy and Nicole. They say they have evidence that clearly links me to each of the murders, and they've assigned me a lawyer who's a total idiot and wants me to plead second degree manslaughter for each murder. They've put me in isolation 'for my own good.' They claim it's to protect me from the general population. This place is maximum security, and there are guys in here doing life. I know I won't ever find anyone again that I could love the way I loved Yvette. She was just everything to me, and they won't even let me attend her funeral. Her parents hate me, and I'm sure that everyone back home is having second thoughts about me. I'm just so alone and so devastated. Christ, I don't know what I'm going to do. Jack, you just have to believe me, please believe me. I didn't do it," he pleaded. "Man, I have to be at training camp by August 15th or I can kiss my hockey career goodbye. I've already had a call from my agent, Chuck Trimble, emphasizing that point. But at this point I don't even care about that anymore. As far as I'm concerned, the Leafs can fuck themselves." There was a pause, then he shuddered and broke down.

"Oh god, Yvette, who did this to you? If I ever find the bastard, I'll kill him with my own hands."

"Listen," Jack said. "Let's take this one step at a time. A friend of mine is an articling student at Ross and Associates, Canada's top criminal defence firm, and he's asked around the firm. They've recommended someone who actually works quite close to here in Binghamton and knows the jail quite well. Apparently he wins most of his cases. His name is Clayton McBride, and he's agreed to come and meet you tomorrow at ten. I'll be here to meet him as well."

Colin was concerned that he wouldn't be able to pay for a good lawyer and that the meeting would be fruitless, but Jack told him not to worry about that right now, and that they'd figure something out.

"Have you spoken to your parents yet?"

"Yeah, my dad called me yesterday after he got a call from the CBC news and another from the *Halifax Herald* within a minute of each other. He's pretty upset, and I told him that I didn't do it, but he says that the press has already convicted me. Mom's a total wreck. I told him that you were coming down to see if you could help, and he asked me to have you call him."

Jack asked Colin for his father's phone number, and since he didn't have a pen or a piece of paper, he asked Colin to repeat it four or five times. To lighten the mood, they talked about school, hockey, Ruth, Suzanne, but it eventually led them to Yvette, and Colin broke down again. Jack was convinced of Colin's innocence, but he had to figure out a way to prove it. The guard finally barked, "Time's up." Jack repeated Colin's parents' phone number as another guard appeared to lead Colin back to his cell.

"Hang tough, man, we're with you," Jack said.

"I know…thanks."

Jack met Ruth in the visitors' waiting room. Neither said a thing until they picked up and signed for their personal possessions. As soon as Jack opened the envelope, he grabbed a pen and wrote Colin's father's home phone number on a five-dollar bill, which was the only piece of paper he had. As the two left the prison, they were blinded by the blistering summer sun as the prison doors slammed behind them. They headed back to Ithaca and Ruth's room to read all of the press clippings that Ruth had saved.

Jack called Colin's dad, but his mother Moira answered. Jack introduced himself, and she started crying uncontrollably. Colin's father took the phone and said angrily, "Who is this?"

Jack again introduced himself as Colin's friend and told him that he fully believed in Colin's innocence. The news about the lawyer seemed to settle Colin's dad down. He was, however, very concerned about how they could afford a good lawyer, and he also wondered if the Canadian government could intervene and offer some assistance. They decided to sleep on those two questions then Jack promised Mr. MacDonald that he would call him the next day as soon as he had met with the lawyer.

Jack didn't feel like going back up to the campus. Instead, he took Ruth out for a quick lunch at Obie's. They carefully and thoroughly went over every detail they could think of that might give them a clue. Finally, Jack admitted he was exhausted, and they agreed to go to Ruth's for a nap.

The next day he drove to Elmira alone. Ruth had missed too many summer school classes already. He entered the prison door as he had done the day before and told the guard that he was waiting to meet Clayton McBride. This guard was a little more understanding and accommodating as he explained that Clayton was not on the record as Colin's lawyer, but he was sure that "Clay" would straighten that out when he got there.

"We know Clay, how did you ever snag him?" the guard asked.

"Through a friend."

"Good friend," replied the guard and told him to proceed. Jack went through to the next room and was again frisked and deposited everything on the counter. He waited patiently for Clayton McBride to walk through the door.

7

A fter about ten minutes a tall, thin black man walked into the waiting room.

"Clay McBride." He extended his hand.

"Jack Souster, nice to meet you."

They sat down for a couple of minutes.

"Listen, why don't you go outside, look around Elmira, or whatever, and I'll meet you after I talk to Colin. My guess is it'll be about an hour, and then we could go and grab some lunch," suggested Clay. Jack was very impressed with the richness of Clay's voice. He didn't know whether it was tenor or baritone, but it had the fullness of an echo in the mountains.

He went to the car and sat in the driver's seat, just a little surprised. He hadn't expected Clay to be black. He was shocked that he, himself, might be becoming judgemental based strictly on skin color. *Is this what four years in the*

United States has taught me? he asked himself. As a Canadian, he viewed the racial tensions in the U.S. from a distant perspective and thought it was one of the greatest problems the country ever had. Jack had taken an instant liking to Clay. He didn't know what to attribute this to, the incredibly resonant voice, the handshake, the look in his eyes or his wide smile, but Jack felt a little relieved and comforted.

*   *   *

Clayton Russell McBride was born September 30th 1942 in a small house off a dusty, dry dirt road just west of Pelham, Alabama, about fifteen miles south of Birmingham. His father, Bo McBride, was a carpenter by trade and a general handyman around Pelham. His excellent work could definitely qualify him as a cabinetmaker. His mother Lucy cleaned a number of homes and took in laundry and sewing to earn extra money for the family. She was known in Pelham for her ability as a seamstress and was often asked to make wedding dresses for the local brides. Clay had three sisters, Lucy-Sue, Mae and Eugenia. He was the youngest of the four children, and it was said that the girls spoiled him. The family attended the First Baptist Church in Pelham. The parents were in the choir, and they never missed a Sunday. Many times a week, after dinner, the family would gather in the parlour to sing old gospel songs, just for the pure enjoyment of the music and relishing the moments of being together as a family. The entire family loved music and all were gifted with great voices. Clay, especially, had an extremely rich baritone voice. His father had a very deep bass while his mother was an alto, and the girls were all beautiful sopranos. The six were often asked to sing at weddings and funerals and sang solos in the church. Eugenia's rendition of "Ave Maria" sent chills up everyone's spines, and when the six of them harmonized "Amazing Grace," people just listened, slack-jawed, with the hair on the back of their necks standing straight up and goosebumps on their arms.

Clay went to a segregated primary school and high school. He knew the feeling of having to drink out of water fountains designated for blacks, and having to sit at the back of the bus. Once he snuck into a "Whites Only" washroom just to see if there was a difference, and he was shocked to see how clean it was, with the crisp odors of disinfectant. He compared this to the filth of the washroom he and other black men had to use, with the pungent smells of urine and feces, and toilets that were plugged and had never been fixed. The flies were so thick, he had trouble keeping them off his face. He lived in continual fear of the Ku Klux Klan, having heard stories of his great Uncle James being dragged out of his bed and hanged from a tree in the middle of the night.

He would never forget the fear of the fangs and the heat of the breath of an attack-trained German Shepherd as it lunged at his face, straining at the end of a leash being held by a riot squad cop who, with dozens of fellow officers, tried to break up a civil rights march in Montgomery. All of the protestors were being rounded up and ushered into paddy wagons then taken off to be charged with disturbing the peace and unlawful assembly and thrown into holding tanks. Clay was able to sneak away when no one was watching, knowing that any charge against him would surely hamper his chances at getting accepted into university, and it would be a mark used against him for the rest of his life.

He was an exceptional student and was the valedictorian of his graduating class. His marks were high enough to win him an NAACP scholarship to Howard University in Washington, D.C., an "all black" university which had an outstanding reputation. Here he excelled not only in sports, basketball and track and field, but more prominently in academics. In his senior year he became the captain of the debating team and won numerous debates with rival white colleges. Over the four years at Howard, Clay decided that he wanted to go into law. His biggest problem was choosing what type of law to practice, civil rights law or criminal law. He knew he could do more for his race in America if he took up civil rights law but was touched by the number of wrongful convictions of blacks that seemingly took place on a daily basis. His good friend Bobby Kendall was arrested for burglary and held in jail for over thirty days without a trial, and Bobby wasn't even in Pelham the night the robbery took place. A few days after the incident, Bobby had just been walking towards the Hurry-Mart to pick up some cigarettes when the victim of the burglary told the police that she thought that he was the man who had robbed her home. He was black and the police wanted the case closed, simple as that. He was arrested and held without bail.

Hearing stories like that infuriated Clay. He applied to a number of law schools and was accepted at all of them. He had been elected to Phi Beta Kappa, the honorary society, and this did not go unnoticed by any of the institutions that were considering his application. He chose Yale for two reasons, the reputation of the Yale Law School and their offering him a very generous scholarship which, when combined with yet another NAACP grant, covered all his tuition and room and board. For spending money, he was sure that he could pick up some odd jobs in Hartford, even if it was washing dishes in some sleazy diner.

Continuing to excel in academics at Yale, he put sports aside as he was busy working for the City of Hartford doing everything from garbage collection to cutting grass in the parks. The city was very good to him, knowing he was a student. They found jobs for him that would fit his academic schedule. He became a member of the Yale debating team, giving him great confidence in his thinking and speaking on his feet, which stood him in good stead in future years when addressing a judge or a jury. In his senior year, for entertainment and social activity he joined the famed a cappella group called the Whiffenpoofs, a fourteen-member ensemble that was the oldest a cappella group in the U.S. with a tradition of singing down in Mory's Tavern. The richness of his voice and the fact that he had perfect pitch won him a spot on the famous ensemble when it came to the auditions. The Whiffenpoofs was a sought-after group for college concerts. This brought in a little extra money.

Clay had a number of offers from large legal firms but decided to go with Fuller, Cranston, Whelan and Smith LLP, with over 275 lawyers and offices in Manhattan, Chicago, Los Angeles, Dallas and Denver. After articling he was promised the position of junior to Bill Cranston, unarguably the best criminal lawyer in America. The year of articling went well as Clay learned the inner workings of the firm and the politics. This aspect of large law firms was something that bothered him. He also witnessed a few of the partners padding their bills from clients they knew could pay. It was often blatant, since many of them discussed the practice openly. Clay kept this information to himself and just went ahead with his job.

Bill Cranston often asked his opinion on various aspects of the law, and how it pertained to certain cases. Clay frequently snuck into the back of the courtroom during trials and was amazed at how many of his words and arguments were parroted by his senior. Eventually Bill Cranston asked him to accompany him at the defence table to look after files.

Clay was, without a doubt, the new and rising star in the firm. After his articling he was offered a position and given his own office, although it did not have a window. Window offices were reserved for the partners, and corner window offices were strictly for senior partners. He won a number of difficult cases that partners threw his way, since the defendant in their opinion didn't have a case, or as they would often say, "He's got only a whiff of a defence."

Clay received national recognition when he won a murder case involving a Tony Award-winning Broadway star who had allegedly bludgeoned to death his lover and partner, an acclaimed Broadway composer and orchestra leader. As it turned out, he'd been murdered by a fanatic homophobe.

It was his incredible diligence, to the point of fanaticism, and detailed research into every fact, that won his cases and the acknowledgement from his peers, not only from within his firm and its many offices but also from his colleagues throughout the NACDL.

Clay had found that one of the many private investigators he hired to do investigative work had the same work ethic. He followed every lead until the trail was totally exhausted. His name was Clive Scranton, and he did not fit the scruffy "Columbo" image that appeared first a few years earlier on

The Chevy Mystery series, but was extremely well kept. If anything, he might have worn a little too much Old Spice, and Clay sometimes felt a little underdressed next to him. Clive was always nattily attired, pale blue buttoned-down shirts, light tan chinos and penny loafers with matching brown belt. However, Clay's high opinion of Clive's work remained unchanged.

Often, when Clive was working on a case for Clay, he would take a totally different view and come up with ideas that had never occurred to Clay. They worked so closely on so many different cases that they were jokingly referred to in the office as "The Clay and Clive Show." There was a small room reserved just for Clive from which he could work with his own extension, right there in the firm, since he was there so often. Clive liked the "meat" of Clay's cases. He was tired of following around unfaithful spouses until he could get a compromising photo of them that would hold up in court.

The size of the firm, as well as the unethical billing practices, eventually got to Clay, and he never felt completely comfortable there. He attributed it in part to the color of his skin. He often wondered if it was just some sort of paranoia he had picked up as a youngster in Alabama. He could feel the uneasy eyes of new clients and their preformed opinions as they quickly looked away when he was introduced.

One day he received a hand-printed letter on lined paper written in pencil and using the most basic grammar. It was from a Billy Eckler, who was writing from the Elmira Correctional Facility, insisting that he had been wrongfully convicted of murder. He couldn't afford a good lawyer but was wondering if Clay could help him. Billy was a Tennessee mountain boy who had very little education and had had some minor brushes with the law such as possession of marijuana, bootlegging and petty theft. Instinctively, Clay felt that Billy was somehow innocent. He showed the letter to Clive and asked him if he'd consider doing a *pro bono* case with him. "Absolutely! Let's get the little guy the hell out of that hole," was the reply, and the next day they took off to the Elmira Correctional Facility.

After meeting with Billy, one at a time as the rules stated, they decided that there was some merit in his story. They had driven up in Clive's car, so he proceeded up to Syracuse, where the murder allegedly took place, while Clay caught a bus back to New York City. The next day Clay explained the situation to his senior, Bill Cranston. At the next partners' meeting, Bill took Clay's *pro bono* request before the partners. The verdict was that he could defend Billy Eckler as long as he kept track of his billable hours, paid the money to the firm at his going rate, and that he would be personally responsible for all expenses, including the salary of Clive Scranton.

Clay listened. He was quiet for a moment then asked, "So that's it?"

"I'm afraid so."

"I'll let you know what I'm going to do in a day or two. Thanks." He got up and quietly left the room.

When he got home, he called Clive, and they discussed it at length. They were both bachelors, and Clive had no problem moving to upstate New York. The decision was made: Clay would leave the firm and start his own practice in Binghamton. His girlfriend, Julia, he knew would understand. She still had a couple of years left at Columbia's famed med school, after which there would be two years of residency. They admired each other for their commitment to their professions, and Clay was sure the move to upstate New York would not jeopardize their relationship.

Clive, who had always liked the university scene, chose Ithaca. Apart from the many interesting co-eds, he found university life stimulating, from the amazing libraries that sated his voracious appetite for reading or a game of chess in some quiet corner. He was a big sports fan, and hockey was, without a doubt, his favorite. The bar scene he found fun; while others were quaffing down beers he would get into lengthy discussions with a bartender. He always hoped the barkeep wasn't a student just trying to make a few dollars to augment his weekly allowance, because the subject invariably was about the qualities of various single malt Scotch whiskies. Clive was convinced that he was the only person in Ithaca who knew anything about single malt Scotch.

With some very clever investigative work by Clive and his connections to the "darker side of the law," they got Billy Eckler out of prison within a month. He had broken in through the back door of St. Mary's Roman Catholic Church in Syracuse, not realizing that he could have walked right in through the unlocked front doors. He was hoping to find some cash from the previous Sunday's collection, but failing that he was certain that he would find some gold goblets, chalices and plates he could either pawn or fence. What he did find, however, was Father Martin O'Malley lying face down in a pool of blood with a small revolver in his hand. Billy picked up the revolver, believing it would be just the right size to carry on his person. But at that moment a parishioner walked through the front doors, expecting to go to confession, and instead found Billy standing over Father O'Malley's body holding a gun.

Billy didn't run, but instead tried to explain to the parishioner what he had found. The parishioner and Billy found the church office and called the police, who arrived and arrested Billy without incident on the sole basis that he was found holding the gun. It didn't take Clive long to get to the bottom of the situation once he started asking a few pertinent questions.

For years, it had been rumored all over Syracuse that Father O'Malley had been molesting young altarboys. It frustrated many parishioners, especially when the Bishop ignored their claims and continued to support Father O'Malley. A young boy named Alvaro Correa had immigrated to the United States with his family from El Salvador and was given refugee status due to persecution back home. The family worked hard in the vineyards of upper New York State and attended church faithfully every Sunday. At the age of ten, Alvaro became an altarboy then one of Father O'Malley's favorites to take on camping trips. It was during these trips that the molestations took place. Alvaro was too embarrassed to tell anybody and lived with the shame, until the day after his twenty-fifth birthday. He walked into the church and confronted the tormentor of his youth. "Never again!" he said as he held the gun to the aging priest's head and pulled the trigger with every ounce of hate in his body.

Billy confessed to break-and-enter and was released for time served.

8

Jack drove from the prison to downtown Elmira, where he parked and looked around at the various shops, eventually coming to a park, where he sat under the shade of a large maple. Although he did his best to divert his thoughts, he couldn't stop imagining the meeting. His fear was that Clay would come back to him and tell him that he thought that Colin was guilty, even though he knew a defence lawyer's job was to defend his client, guilty or not. Jack started to break into a cold sweat. Glancing at his watch brought that churning, gnawing feeling into the pit of his stomach once again. He realized that the hour and half was almost up, and it was time to get back to the prison to meet with Clay and hear the results of the meeting.

There were a few parking spaces just in front of the main gate. He impatiently pulled into one and waited. After a few people walked by, he guessed they were either lawyers or families of the inmates. Clay appeared in ten minutes. They decided to go to a nearby diner for a coffee.

"So, how did it go?" Jack asked tentatively. Clay said everything that Jack was hoping to hear. He believed that Colin was innocent and that he was being framed. He would start asking questions. He told Jack that Colin had asked him to represent him, but apart from his biggest fear of being found guilty, he had no idea how he could pay. Clay had told him that that matter could be discussed later.

"Jack, this is very serious. Serial killing is punishable by death. The electric chair was used in New York State only two years ago, in '63. I haven't mentioned this to Colin, and I tell you this, Jack, only because we have to start working on this immediately. Money is the least of our worries right now.

"I found out that Erik Wolfe, the local district attorney, is taking this case on personally. He's mean, he's aggressive, and he'll do anything for a conviction. On top of all this, one of the guards told me that Wolfe thinks this case is his ticket to being elected to the office of New York State Attorney General. He loves high profile cases, and this is the one he can hang his hat on. He'll do everything humanly possible to get a conviction." Jack was surprised that the guards would offer such opinions to a convict's lawyer.

"They are just guys doing their job, and it's not an easy job. My philosophy is if you give lots of thank-yous now, it makes future pleases a lot easier. Furthermore, they'll take it easy on Colin if they know that I'm on his side."

They discussed their plan of action over several cups of coffee. Clay was a smoker, and Jack was sorely tempted to ask Clay for a cigarette, although he knew it would be close to suicide with his heart condition. Clay would represent Colin and would notify the court that he was the defence lawyer of record. He would immediately request a bail hearing. He didn't give Jack much hope that this would be successful, since Colin was not an American citizen and was a definite flight risk. However, it was worth a try and it would at least let Erik Wolfe know that there was a strong defence team in place. He would have to divulge all of the evidence they had to hold Colin. He also told Jack about his private eye, Clive Scranton. He suggested that Jack tell all of Colin's friends to expect a call from Clive, and that they should cooperate fully. He would be asking all sorts of questions, whether they believed them to be relevant or not.

Jack agreed to discuss everything with both his and Colin's friends, and would call Colin's father about the possibility of raising some cash. They also agreed that Jack and Colin's father should write the minister of foreign affairs, the minister of justice and the prime minister to make this an international situation. "And get them to contact their local members of parliament. Down here in the States the local congressman would be flooded with mail if this had been the situation here," said Clay.

"The problem is, we are so much more passive by nature and just let the politicians do their own thing. If we do complain, they don't do anything anyways, so what's the use?"

"Jack, it's absolutely paramount that you get as many people involved as possible, and if possible make this a national issue, if Colin's going to have any chance at all."

Clay's main focus was to put enough pressure on the politicians to have Colin extradited back to Canada, incarcerated in a Canadian jail, and tried on Canadian soil.

Jack's feeling, also, was that treatment in a Canadian jail would be far more humane. There was precedent for this action, so they agreed that it might be worth a try.

"I'll give it my best shot. Heaven knows, hockey stars are treated like royalty back home, so if anybody has a shot at getting the public on his side, Colin certainly does."

Jack was up to the challenge. They finally got up and shook hands. He had to get back to work in Toronto, but he agreed to pay Colin one more visit before he left the following morning. He gave Clay the numbers for the Royal York and Chateau Lake Louise, and they would stay in touch on a regular basis.

Ruth had been waiting for Jack's return, and when he walked through her door, she jumped up, ran to him, grabbed his hands, and pleaded with him to tell her everything at once. They sat there for an hour rehashing everything. Jack told her that she should expect a call from Clive Scranton.

"What a time in my life," Ruth said, "first Kennedy was assassinated and now this. I hope I never see another five years like it." She started to sob and put her head into Jack's comforting shoulder. He didn't dare tell her about the possibility of a death penalty, or she would certainly become hysterical.

"Let's go for a walk and a swim in the park," he said as he offered her a Kleenex to blow her nose.

The late afternoon sun was still warm as they sat under an old apple tree. Jack said that he would visit Colin first thing in the morning and then continue back to Toronto directly from the prison.

"You can't leave now. Colin needs you now more than he ever has."

"Listen, Clay is the best thing that has ever happened to Colin, and there isn't anything more that I can do here. You know that I'll be calling both you and Colin regularly, and I'll come down whenever you think I'm needed. Colin knows that, and I just want you to have faith in Clay, because if you don't, then your fears will rub off on Colin. OK?"

"OK. I'll try."

Ruth promised she would visit Colin as much as possible. She would also keep in touch with Clay and Clive. For the rest of the evening, they talked of various happenings around campus, trying to avoid the topic of the murders and Colin's impossible situation, but they both knew that these conversations were just a shallow escape.

9

Jack left Ruth's apartment as early as possible to make the ten a.m. opening of daily visiting hours. He was used to the procedure by now, and it wasn't long before Colin was led into the room. Jack inquired about his state of mind, his treatment, listened to his opinion of Clay, and laid out the plan of action for Colin's approval. He thought that Colin should be kept abreast of each and every move. He thought it would be good for Colin's morale, and it would give him much needed intellectual stimulation. After a good hour, he was able to get a couple of chuckles from his friend, and eventually Jack said that he had to get back to Canada to work.

"Keep your chin up, we're going to win this thing," he promised. They broke all the rules and gave each other a hug. Jack, remembering Clay's philosophy, thanked the guard profusely. He acknowledged it with a nod and a rare smile.

"Jack," Colin said with a touch of embarrassment, "don't tell Dad he's black. He wouldn't be reassured or feel much confidence."

"I gotcha, not a problem."

It was noon when Jack got into his Mini. As he got onto the Thruway heading west to Niagara Falls, he thought that he'd better pull off at a service center and call the Royal York to let them know that he would be back tomorrow. This news was greeted with great relief and he continued on his way, using his time to compose, various ways to present Colin's situation to Prime Minister Pierre Cadeau.

"Cadeau" was most appropriate, as the English translation of Cadeau meant "gift," and Pierre Cadeau certainly considered himself as God's gift to mankind. His ego was enormous, and it matched his arrogance, but the Canadian public almost worshipped at his feet. Jack thought that his letter was going to have to, somehow, feed into his ego. This was going to be a gargantuan task because Jack, being a staunch Conservative, almost despised the prime minister because of his leftist policies, aided by arrogance and sense of personal omnipotence.

The mental composing of this letter, along with a few ideas of fundraising for Colin's defence, kept Jack's mind busy the entire drive home. He passed the various mundane milestones without any notice, although he had a bit of a start when he arrived at the border.

There was a long line of cars, and only two lanes were open instead of the usual five. There was a yellow Corvette about six or seven cars in front of him in the next lane. Jack immediately thought of Sky Muncey and Sam Wainwright and how they had bragged that they were going to spend the summer driving out west on U.S. Route 66. He naturally assumed that they would not be crossing into Canada if they were following their plans, so he quickly dismissed it as just being another yellow Corvette.

The trip went faster than expected. He phoned to check in with the hotel and found out he was due on the floor at seven the next morning. At the kitchen table he began the letter six times before he got the exact wording he wanted. He thought that he would add a personal touch by telling the prime minister that he had worked at Chateau Lake Louise with his daughter, April, the year before, but rejected the idea. Choking on his last sentences, he feigned support for the Liberal Party, hoping that might trick the prime minister into getting involved personally.

June 29th, 1965

My Dear Prime Minister,

I am a friend of Colin MacDonald, who is a Canadian citizen and a student at Cornell University in Ithaca, New York. Colin has just been charged as a serial killer in three separate murders including one of his fiancée, Yvette Bouchard, the daughter of your minister of finance. Colin was an outstanding student, most valuable player on the Cornell hockey team and has just recently signed a contract with the Toronto Maple Leafs. There is no doubt in my mind, and in the mind of many others, who know Colin, that he is not capable of committing such hideous crimes. It is the opinion of many that Colin is being framed for these murders.

I have always been a great admirer of yours and your lifelong pursuit of social justice. Colin has been incarcerated in the Elmira maximum security correctional facility and could possibly face the death penalty if convicted of being a serial killer. It is my understanding that the District Attorney representing upstate New York has taken this case on personally, since it is a high profile case that will advance his campaign for State Attorney General.

I beseech you, sir, to use your good offices to contact all relevant U.S. authorities and have Colin released on bail, and should that fail, ask that he be extradited to Canada where he would certainly receive a fairer trial and better jail conditions. I would hope that the Canadian government would assist its citizens in a foreign country. As a supporter of the Liberal Party of Canada and because I am aware of your personal commitment to personal justice for all mankind, I know that you can help Colin MacDonald in this matter.

I thank you for your consideration and I look forward to your reply.

Yours very truly,
Jack A. Souster

He showed his mother the letter and watched her holding back her laughter.

"Jack, you've got more nerve than a government mule!" she said. "What else can you say? You've said it all, but you'll go straight to hell for praising that twit." He signed the letter, addressed an envelope and sealed it, so it was ready for mailing when he got to work in the morning.

Getting back to the hotel helped him temporarily forget the last few days, until one of the bellmen began asking questions about Colin. He told Jack that members of the Toronto press were snooping around for information. They had heard of Jack's friendship with Colin, the "serial killer." Fortunately, it was early in the morning, and he had time to get his VIP reservations organized. At 9:15, Corrine Clancy, director of Public Relations for CP Hotels, suddenly appeared at Jack's desk. Everyone knew Corrine. She was always fluttering about whenever a dignitary was due to arrive, and her office, on the main mezzanine, was connected to a small press room, where she would hold court, coddling various members of the entertainment media. She handed out complimentary dinner invitations to the hotel's famed Imperial Room whenever a new show opened.

Corrine asked Jack if he could spare a couple of minutes to go to her office for a brief meeting.

"Jack, this is very serious," she started. "Rumor has it that you are involved with or assisting a serial killer. This is something that we cannot condone. The reputation of CP Hotels is far more important than your personal activities. A number of my friends in the press are calling me to ask some very pointed questions, so I am asking you to have nothing to do with this hoodlum."

Jack was shocked. "First of all, he's not a hoodlum, and he's not a serial killer. He is a very well-educated person and a terrific athlete as well as my very best friend. If you want to take this matter up with Mr. Lawton, then so be it, but I will not give up my friendship so that you can save face with your press buddies. In fact," he continued, "if the press ever got wind of what you're asking me to do, you would be toast. Now, what I will promise is if I'm ever approached by a member of the media asking specific questions about Colin MacDonald, I will answer: 'no comment.' If that is not good enough, then we'll have to continue this conversation in Mr. Lawton's office." He got up and sarcastically thanked her for her concern.

A number of staff members came up to him to find out what was happening. Many were just fishing for gossip. Those he trusted and liked he would fill in as best he could or tell them that he'd provide more details over a beer.

It seemed like forever that Alessandro was in Italy for his mother's funeral. Jack longed to get out to Lake Louise. Two days before he was ready to leave, Alessandro had phoned that he was back in town. Gord Lawton's new secretary called and told Jack that Mr. Lawton would like to speak to him. Jack was concerned that Corrine Clancy had complained. Instead, it was a very pleasant meeting as he received his ticket to go on the Canadian, Canadian Pacific's luxury transcontinental train.

"I was hoping to drive out."

"We need you there as fast as possible, and we don't pay mileage, gas, accommodation, food, or any other expenses when the train is available. If you require a car when you're out there, then you can rent one. I've reserved a compartment for you so you won't have to sit up in coach for the three days you're in transit. You'll leave tomorrow."

Jack was disappointed but knew that head office didn't spend money needlessly. Other assistant managers, who were married, always refused the summer postings in the mountains at the Banff Springs Hotel or the Chateau because they were charged full price for their spouses' rail passage, as well as their accommodation and food while they were with their husbands at the resort.

*   *   *

Alessandro dropped in a day early to get caught up on things and casually mentioned to Jack that he was lucky he had never had to fill out a form 15385B. If there were ever a suicide or murder in the hotel and a body was found in a room, the famous Form 15385B had to be filled out in quintuplicate. This required pressing firmly on the five onion-skin forms sandwiched among four sheets of fresh carbon paper. Jack always wondered what the "B" meant and why it wasn't Form 15385A or "Z." The original copy went to head office, the second to the hotel security, the third to the Metro Toronto Police, the fourth to the coroner's office, and the fifth was filed in a black folder, affectionately known in the accounting office as the "Death Book." This last one was used in case the deceased's estate had to be charged for any costs incurred in cleanup. Standard procedure was that if housekeeping had not been able to gain access to a room within a twenty-four hour period, it was reported to the assistant manager who went with his pass key to the room in question, accompanied by one of the house security guards. The job of the assistant manager was to enter the room first, something that Jack never relished. Much to his relief, it had always turned out that the occupants on his shifts had left their room through an adjoining room that may have been occupied by family members or friends.

It was Jack's last day before he boarded the Canadian at Toronto's Union Station, directly across Front Street from the Royal York, to head out to what he considered one of the most beautiful spots in the world: Lake Louise, Banff National Park, Alberta. He could hardly wait. His mother was busy getting all of his clothes cleaned. His tuxedo was being pressed. This he had to wear while on duty after six o'clock in the evening. His morning suit was compulsory attire during daytime shifts. *Thank God for Mom,* he thought. He'd never have been ready in time. She'd bought him a new set of cuff links to go with his dress shirts, as well as a new bow tie and a beautiful new cummerbund. It was one o'clock. He would soon be off duty and on his way home to meet Consuela. He was pleased that the train didn't depart until one thirty p.m. the next day, which meant he could spend one last lingering evening with his Guatemalan love. He fantasized about what her farewell gift would be for him.

The phone rang and jarred Jack back to reality.

"Mr. Souster?"

"Speaking."

"Miss Himmel, housekeeping."

"Yes, Greta, what can I do for you?"

"The girls haven't been able to get into rooms 13-185/87 for over a day now. We've tried calling, and the adjoining room doors are both locked."

Oh no, he thought as his heart sank and his stomach began to churn. *My first form 15385B. Why couldn't she wait until 3:05?* That was when he would be officially off duty. He placed a call to hotel security and got Ed McWharters, one of the senior Hotel Security guards.

"Ed? It's Jack Souster. Could you please meet me up at room 13-185. We have a room check to do."

They met in the corridor and knocked loudly. There was no answer, and a wary glance passed between them. Jack put his pass key into the keyhole and opened the door. According to procedure, he entered the room first. The stench was overbearing, and he thought that he was going to throw up. He quickly grabbed a linen handkerchief and covered his mouth as he unsteadily went over to the window. He opened the window, and the warm summer breeze helped dissipate the odor, but Jack wished it had been cooler. Ed opened the bathroom door. "Jack." There, lying in the blood-filled tub, was a slightly overweight man who looked to be about fifty. It seemed that he had taken his own life by slashing his wrists. They didn't see the large open gash on the right side of the man's neck

"Don't touch anything," warned the burly security guard. "I'll go down the hall and call 52 Division. I'll also call the coroner. You must stay in the room," he continued, "until they all get here and take a statement from each of us. You'll also have to take note of their names and badge numbers and the time of their arrival and departure. I'll have housekeeping bring you up a pad of paper. Remember, don't touch anything, and if you want to sit down, pull out the desk chair with your handkerchief. I'll be right back, don't let anybody else in."

Jack gently pulled out the desk chair, as instructed, and sat down. Unfortunately, it was positioned where he had a direct view of the corpse in the bathtub. The water was such a dark red, with a thickened emulsified opacity and a glistening creamy, textured scum, that the victim's entire body below the slimy surface was, thankfully, not visible. A number of flies were buzzing around his nostrils and walking on his open eyes, and a few were gathering around the area where the sludge met the unfortunate man's chest. Jack could hear the noise of the traffic. A horn sounded and he heard a distant siren, wondering if that were the cops heading to the hotel. However, he knew that the hotel had an unspoken agreement with the police that they would only come in unmarked cars if the problem was a private matter, and therefore of no concern to the public. Someone walked past the room and Jack could hear them gag. He kept his handkerchief over his mouth and nose.

It seemed like forever, but eventually four cops in full uniform appeared at the door. Ed was with them.

"I've filled them in," he informed Jack as introductions were made. They all peered into the bathroom. Sergeant Myers, the leader of the team, asked if they could get a bite to eat, and Jack glanced at Ed.

"Of course, what would you like?"

"A nice juicy sirloin, rare, with a baked potato and extra sour cream and chives."

"Sounds good to us," responded the other three, when all of a sudden the youngest one of them said, "Could I also have a side order of fresh asparagus with extra hollandaise?"

Myers looked at the young officer, who Jack thought must be a rookie, and said, "You learn fast, kid…oh…" and turning to Jack, he said, "Don't forget lots of coffee, we'll be here for a while."

"Jack, could you make that five, and that way I won't have to be subjected to that garbage they serve in the Beanery," said Ed.

Sergeant Myers asked, "Ed, have you called the coroner? If it's Doc Smithers, he'll take his sweet time…that's all we need."

Ed confirmed the coroner's office had been notified and Jack went out to the house phone to order the meals. He asked them to add two extra cups and an extra thermos of coffee for Ed and himself. He got a chair, sat out in the hall and waited for room service. He wanted to make sure that the waiter didn't enter the room with his wheeled table.

While waiting for room service, Jack couldn't help but recall Ruth's recollection of Colin's bail hearing. The courtroom was mahogany-panelled, with oak benches for the public. A mahogany bar separated the general population from both the prosecutor's and defence's tables, which faced the raised dais upon which the judge's bench sat. The American flag was hanging from a pole, topped with a brass bald eagle. On the wall was a large American seal. To Ruth's right were twelve seats for a jury. A jury was not required, since this was merely a bail hearing. The courtroom was packed, as it seemed everybody in Ithaca wanted to get a glimpse of the "serial killer."

Ruth arrived early and managed to get a seat directly behind the defendant's table. She wondered what motivated people. Was it simply a desire to witness the seamy side of life, not unlike the rubberneckers who slow down at a traffic accident looking for blood? Their morbid curiosity had always bothered her. She had met Clay only once as they passed each other coming and going at the Correctional Facility. She'd spoken briefly to him and wished him good luck at the bail hearing. Clive was also at the table and introduced himself.

"Do you recognize anyone here today?" he asked as his eyes scanned the courtroom.

"Not a soul," she replied, although she noticed a well-dressed woman with a notepad sitting behind the prosecutor's table. She was taking notes. Ruth thought that she must be a reporter and made a mental note to stay clear of her. Erik Wolfe had three members of his legal team accompanying him at the prosecutor's table. Ruth thought that this might be a bit of overkill for a bail hearing.

There was hushed silence in the courtroom as the door on the left opened and Colin was led in by two policemen, one on each side, holding his arms, which were handcuffed in front of him. He was wearing his standard gray prison uniform, and the shackles on his legs clashed and jangled as he shuffled towards Clay at the defence table. One cop removed the handcuffs, took one of the leg shackles off, and locked it to the leg of Colin's chair. Colin shook hands with Clay and gave a quick glance at the packed courtroom. He couldn't miss Ruth sitting directly behind him, and they exchanged smiles. He winked, even though he was noticeably shaking, and his lips quivered.

Colin was about to sit down when the court clerk shouted, "All rise." Another panelled door opened to the left of the raised judge's bench, and the judge walked in and sat down with a flurry of his robes. Ruth tried to size him up to get a feel as to whether he would be strict or lenient.

After everyone was seated, the court clerk read the charges. "Mr. Colin MacDonald, the defendant, is charged with three counts of murder and the possession of a deadly weapon."

The judge then directed a question to Colin: "Do you understand the charges against you, Mr. Macdonald?"

Colin nodded, to which the judge replied, "Nods are not accepted in this courtroom, it's 'yes' or 'no.'"

"Yes, sir," replied Colin, his voice cracking and his hands shaking.

Clay then rose, requesting bail be set at $25,000.00, having calculated the value of Jack's parents' home in Cape Breton, which could be put up for bail. He talked at length about Colin's background, his academic success, his athletic prowess and his contract with the Toronto Maple Leafs. He also talked of how Colin worked with underprivileged children in Tompkins County and how he coached the local junior hockey team.

Erik Wolfe promptly stood up and demanded that Colin be held in custody without bail, since he'd been charged with the most heinous of crimes, serial killing. Further, he was a Canadian citizen, and should he return to Canada, there was every possibility that he would never return to the U.S. to face the charges. He also requested that Colin's student visa be cancelled and that his Canadian passport be revoked. He also advised the court that he would be seeking the death penalty, and Canada over the past few years had commuted all death sentences to life imprisonment. As well, Canada had a history of refusing to deport criminals to countries that used the death penalty as punishment and a deterrent to murder.

Ruth looked at Colin, as did everyone in the courtroom, as soon as the words "death penalty" were spoken. There was an incredible quiet hanging over the assembly. Colin hung his head and stared at the table. Ruth glanced over at the female reporter, who had a curious small smirk on her face. Whoever she was, Ruth did not trust her.

The judge took no more than a minute to make his ruling. "Bail denied. The court is ordering Mr. MacDonald's student visa be revoked, and unfortunately, as much as I'd like to, Mr. Wolfe, this court has no jurisdiction over the passport of a citizen of another country. However, I will order that it be seized and held by the court." He continued. "I'll set a trial date for Tuesday, October 19th. Will that give you both enough time to prepare?" Clay and Erik Wolfe both agreed.

"The defendant is to be held over in custody at the Elmira Correctional Facility until such date. So ordered!" He cracked his gavel firmly.

"All rise," ordered the clerk, and Colin was again handcuffed, the leg irons reattached, and after a quick word with Clay, and a faint smile showing both fear and hope to Ruth, he was led out of court. There were hushed murmurs amongst the onlookers as they slowly made their way to the exit.

*   *   *

Jack snapped back to reality when he saw the room service waiter coming down the hall. There was not going to be enough room nor enough chairs in that room for all of them to sit down and eat, and then he remembered that it was part of a suite. He went into the room and mentioned this to Meyers. He asked the detective if he wanted to have 13-187, the adjoining living room, opened up. With the sergeant's approval, Jack unlocked the door. The room was neat and clean, although over on a corner table there were two empty martini glasses, one with a curled up, dried lemon twist in the bottom of one glass and the other host to four parched olive pits.

Jack was going to straighten a sofa cushion that appeared just a little askew when Myers shouted, "Don't touch a thing!" Jack stepped out into the hall as the officers started taking photos of both rooms. Dinner arrived. The waiter was looking for a tip, and Jack said that this was "on the hotel." The waiter rolled his eyes, tried to peek in the door and, seeing the police, quickly left. The table was rolled in, the folding leaves were lifted to expand it to fit at least six, and chairs were placed around so that all five men could enjoy their dinner. They unfolded and placed starched white napkins on their laps, and the banquet began in full view of a gray corpse, lying in a dark pink curdling tub of blood with a stench that would rival that of an abandoned abattoir. Jack's stomach began to turn, so he poured himself a coffee, adding two creams and two sugars, and went back out into the hall to escape this bizarre, grizzly scene. He found the scene of the police officers kibitzing and enjoying their steak dinners in the presence of a bloodied corpse most disturbing.

It was now four in the afternoon, and he should be home, packing and getting ready for his last dinner with his parents and his last evening with Consuela. He still had to fill out Form 15385B, which might take hours, to note all of the information he had already gathered. Doc Smithers, the coroner, eventually arrived and started his initial examination, looking at everything and listening to what Sergeant Myers had to say. The cops looked very sheepish as they tried to pretend that the feast in front of them was meant for someone else. Photos were taken by Doc Smither's assistant, a young, rather plain-looking woman named Janice. He then advised Sergeant Myers to call in the crime lab. Two men with a gurney and a folded body bag eventually arrived, and Jack, noticing some hotel guests coming down the corridor, ushered the morgue employees into the room as quickly as possible to avoid any suspicions or rumors. Nothing could be touched until the crime lab and homicide squad arrived. Jack asked the coroner if this was all necessary for a simple suicide. The coroner replied that he felt there was something suspicious about this death, and he wasn't ready to label it a suicide until a thorough investigation was completed. Jack thought of nothing but his ruined evening.

The crime lab and homicide squad finally arrived. More coffee was ordered all around. Jack wheeled the messy dinner table out of the adjoining room into the corridor so that room service could remove it and to make room for the additional investigators. Samples of the bloodied bath water were taken, put into two sealed jars and labelled. The martini glasses were dusted for fingerprints and bagged to be sent to the crime lab. The coroner ordered the bath drained while the man's corpse was still in it. Numerous photos were taken at various levels of the subsiding red sludge. Jack found this terribly troubling and again left the suite while the morgue attendants lifted the corpse into the body bag.

"Anyone see the razor blade?" asked Doc Smithers. "Nope" was the reply after they all did another thorough search of the bathroom.

"Gentlemen, at this point I'm treating this as a homicide. For reasons of my own, I don't believe that suicide note. Young man," he said to Jack, "I want everything you have on this gentleman, reservation phone numbers, credit cards, his registration card which he would have filled out when he checked in. Sergeant, you go with Jack and pick up all of this information, and I want you to wait until he has completed his report." He was referring to form 15385B. You will then keep a copy for your files and deliver a copy to my office in the morning. And," he continued, "I want these rooms sealed and put out of order until I release them. Nobody is to enter them without my authorization. Understand?"

"Yes, sir," replied Jack. Everyone left, and he locked the suite. The police taped a plastic yellow banner across the two doors: "POLICE LINE: DO NOT CROSS." Jack thought this a little excessive.

He had phoned his mother and told her that he would be late, as it was now 9:05 p.m. He had completed all of his paperwork, left letters for housekeeping, Bill Murphy, and the front desk, and made sure that all copies of form 15385B were placed in their proper envelopes and distributed.

He pulled into his driveway at 9:45 p.m. and walked into a house filled with a number of friends and neighbours. Consuela had conspired with Jack's mother and orchestrated a small surprise going away party. He was exhausted but tried to be as enthusiastic as possible, knowing that he still had to pack. After hearing about the events of the day, and what he still had to do, everyone, including Consuela, left by midnight. The two lovers said their quiet goodbye in a corner, where Consuela gave Jack a long, lingering kiss. It was obvious that he desperately wanted to go back to her apartment, and she knew it. The parting was tender, but they knew that they'd be together again in only a month or so.

10

Fortunately, the Canadian wasn't scheduled to pull out of Union Station until one thirty p.m., which gave Jack plenty of time to finish packing what his mother had already started for him. He put his Mini Minor in the garage, since his mom had arranged to drive him to the train in her station wagon. It would hold his large trunk, which he would ship in the baggage car, and he had a small overnight bag to take with him on the train.

They arrived at the station in plenty of time. The trunk was unloaded by a "red cap" and taken on a dolly to the baggage department, where it was tagged and labelled.

There was still half an hour before the train departed, so Jack's mom accompanied him up to the track. Walking through the large, vaulted, marble concourse of Union Station, they passed three newspaper boxes whose headlines instantly grabbed Jack's attention.

The *Toronto Telegram*, Toronto's conservative voice, headlined, **'DEPUTY FINANCE MINISTER DEAD IN DOWNTOWN HOTEL.'** The *Toronto Star*, the distinctly liberal-slanted paper of the city, shouted: **'FINANCE'S AARON HODGES DEAD...DEATH SUSPICIOUS, SAYS CORONER,'** and finally, The *Globe and Mail* trumpeted: **'TORONTO'S ROYAL YORK SCENE OF DEATH OF FINANCE OFFICIAL.'** The papers revealed the occupation of the victim. Until now, Jack had only known the name on the registration card. He grabbed a copy of each of the papers, folded them and put them under his arm.

They found his car, the Assiniboia. Each streamlined stainless steel coach, almost Art Deco in styling, had a distinctly Canadian name. The conductor welcomed Jack and his mother on board and ushered them to Jack's compartment. A porter came along and explained how the bed came down and how the toilet worked. He pointed out the various light switches, the closet, and of course, the button Jack should push if he ever needed service.

Jack thought that the compartment was better than sitting up in a coach for four days and three nights, but it was a little confining and allowed no human interaction. He dropped his overnight bag and the three newspapers, and they walked back to the acclaimed dome car. This led through the dining car, where waiters were setting up for dinner with fresh starched linen, Canadian Pacific silver plate flatware, and fresh flowers set out in matching silver plate bud vases. A few more coaches and they entered the Dome Car. The main level was the Club Car, where there was a full bar and chairs and tables arranged so that passengers could play cards or just enjoy conversations over a drink. Past the bar, at the back, was a spiral staircase leading up to the dome. The walls and ceiling were solid glass, providing a totally unobstructed view of the scenery as the train meandered through the vast Canadian landscape.

It was time for Jack's mother to say goodbye, and he walked her to the exit at the end of the platform.

"You look after yourself," she said as she gently stroked his cheeks with tears welling up in her eyes.

"Mom, this isn't the first time I've left home. I've worked out at the Banff Springs and the Chateau for five different summers, and I've been away at university for four years."

"I know, but I still worry, what with all you've been through lately."

"Don't worry," he reassured her, giving her a long hug and a peck on the cheek.

"BOARD!" shouted the conductor. Jack climbed on the nearest step and ascended to the platform. He decided to go back to the Dome Car and claim a seat before everyone else had the same idea. There was only one seat left. The girl sitting next to him was an attractive brunette, with honeyed highlights in her page-boy hair cut. She was wearing jeans, sneakers and a hand-knitted Irish knit sweater. She had a cute turned-up nose and a complexion that suggested that she may have been raised on a farm, with a steady diet of fresh air and milk. She wore barely any makeup or lipstick. She had a fresh soapy aroma. They struck up a conversation as the train started to creak and groan out of the station. They both waved to total strangers on the platform and giggled at their silliness. Jack noticed that her eyes squinted and had a little twinkle when she smiled. He found it endearing.

Her name was Mandy Jenkins, "short for Amanda," she

added. She had just completed her second year in library science at the University of Toronto and was heading out to Banff to see if she could get a job. She realized that she was late to apply but thought that if she went out in person, she might be able to find something. She was riding coach. Jack told her should she strike out in Banff to call him later and maybe there would be some work at the Chateau. Lake Louise was just over thirty miles west of Banff.

The train wended its way through the west end of Toronto, factories and older turn of the century townhouse complexes, and they waved to cars stopped at the railway crossings. As it headed onto the outskirts of the city and through large pastures, the train picked up considerable steam. Jack offered to go down to the bar in the club portion of the car and get a couple of sandwiches and drinks, maybe even two beers. She declined the food, since she had packed a sandwich of her own. "But a beer would go nicely," she added.

He asked her to save his seat. He quickly made his way up to the dining car and noticed that there were three sittings: five, seven and nine o'clock. Breakfast and lunch were open, and they were on a first come, first served basis. Jack made a reservation for two at seven p.m. then lurched back and forth through the swaying coaches as he went to tell his newfound friend that she had a date that night. She seemed pleased with the invitation. They talked for at least another hour as they nibbled at their respective lunches, and drank the two Molson's Export that Jack had picked up.

Eventually Jack decided to go back to his compartment to have a nap. Mandy said that she was ready to get into a good book. Her coach was called Portage La Prairie, and it was halfway between the dining car and Jack's car, the Assiniboia.

They agreed to meet in the club car for a drink before dinner around six.

*   *   *

As Jack entered his compartment, he noticed a well-dressed middle-aged woman stepping in to the adjoining room. He nodded a greeting smile, which she acknowledged with a grin and a nod. After entering, he promptly lay down on the sofa, which would later be folded out and made up into a double bed by the porter. He grabbed a pillow and a blanket and curled up, but his mind would not rest. Colin's very serious situation was foremost in his mind. He couldn't sleep, so he decided to look at the newspapers. He knew that PR Director Corrine Clancy would be furious the Royal York was mentioned in the *Globe and Mail* story. He began to wonder who had leaked the story to the press.

His speculations were put to rest as he realized a bulging body bag being loaded from the service elevator and into a waiting station wagon with privacy windows and the words "Coroner's Office" with the City of Toronto crest on the side, would certainly arouse no small amount of curiosity. On the thirteenth floor, the bright yellow tape would leave little doubt that something was amiss. Jack knew two things, though. Firstly, Corrine would put him on the top of the culprit list for leaking the story, and secondly there would be a phone message from her waiting for him when he arrived at the Chateau. He also believed that the two Toronto paper's editors probably left out the hotel's name because they wanted to protect the reputation of their famous hospitality gem. The *Globe and Mail,* on the other hand, taking the opportunity to boost national readership, would naturally blast the news to every corner of the land. Sure enough, Corrine was quoted in every paper: "No comment."

* * *

Jack's mind turned again to Colin and the Elmira Correctional Facility. Colin was only allowed one visitor or phone call a day. Clay and Clive were scheduled to have access to Colin all week, from Monday through Friday. Saturday would be reserved for Ruth and Jack, and Sundays for Colin's parents' calls. Jack was pleased that he had managed to reach Colin's dad before he left for the west. The conversation included Colin, his state of mind, Clay and Clive, and naturally led to the topic of financing the defence.

"Perhaps there could be a fundraising dinner or something," suggested Jack.

"Why don't we see if Liam would like to get involved," said Colin's dad, referring to Colin's cousin and best friend. "They've been inseparable since birth! Liam's the son of my brother, Archie."

Liam had the charisma and charm to make everyone in New Waterford, Glace Bay, North Sydney, and most of Sydney absolutely adore him. He had a great sense of humour and was a natural-born musician. He was accomplished on guitar, piano, bagpipes and especially, the fiddle, and was blessed with a fine tenor voice. He was in demand at every ceilidh on the island. He worked in the coal mines with his father and uncle, and he often sang with a number of the miners, not unlike the coal miners of Wales.

The conversation with Liam went very well. They hit it off over the phone and pledged that they would both do whatever possible to help free Colin. Liam suggested raising money by throwing a community lobster dinner. He knew he could get a number of "the boys" involved, who Jack presumed were some of the miners. Liam also proposed going to the various banks in Sydney in an effort to set up a "Colin MacDonald Defence Fund." Jack was really encouraged by Liam's enthusiasm and promised to call him again when he arrived at Lake Louise.

*   *   *

Jack woke up and looked at his watch: it was 6:35 p.m. The rocking of the train and the repetitive, muffled song of the steel wheels on the two ribbons of track had gently lulled him to sleep for much longer than expected. He quickly threw the blanket off, picked up and folded the papers, which had slid onto the floor. He got his toilet kit out and brushed his teeth, washed his face and combed his hair, getting ready for his dinner with Mandy. Having his own sink, mirror and toilet was particularly convenient. Final touch, a little deodorant, and he was off.

He saw Mandy as he entered the Portage la Prairie car. She was curled up on her seat with her shoes off and her heels tucked under her, reading an Agatha Christie mystery. "Good book?" She put the book down and made room for him then excused herself to go to the washroom. Soon they were off to the dining car. The lurch of the train pushed them into various seat backs as they headed down the aisle.

They entered the dining car and Jack slowed his pace past the galley kitchen, amazed at how much equipment was crammed into such a small space. Having designed a number of kitchens as projects at Cornell, he was aware of the efficient use of space, and a dining car's galley was the ultimate in economy. The tables were beside windows leaving the center aisle free for the waiters and other passengers. A menu was presented to both of them as they took their seats. Then the waiter asked if they would like anything from the bar. Mandy ordered a whiskey sour, and Jack said that he'd like a light Bacardi and Coke. He also asked to see the wine list.

Always the hotelier, he wondered if the menus and wine lists were printed in the Royal York Print Shop. The wine list was produced. They placed their orders and dug into the crusty rolls. Jack was amazed at how the waiter maintained his balance while the train rocked and lurched. He noticed that the waiter planted his long, aproned thigh against the table as the train careened around a long bend.

Jack had a wonderful feeling that this evening was going to be fun. The waiter enquired if he was with the other gentleman, pointing to the Cornell logo on Jack's shirt. Jack asked if there was someone else wearing a shirt with the same logo, and was told that it was someone a little younger than Jack who had been at the first sitting. Jack didn't give this much attention, because clothing with the Cornell logo could be purchased in many places and, besides, his mind was really on Mandy.

The meal was outstanding and conversation was kept to various happenings at school, friends and relatives. Jack was careful not to mention anything about Colin or the death at the hotel. He wanted to relax and enjoy the evening. Their hands touched as he passed her the butter and then again when he filled up and passed over her wine glass. The second time they let the skin of their fingers linger a little longer, smiling. Their feet had touched under the table and did not move.

"Do you play cribbage?" Jack asked. She told him that she had come in third in a crib tournament at school and loved the game. He suggested that they go back to his compartment for a game, and left with another bottle of wine but not before reserving the same sitting for tomorrow night with the maître d'. When they arrived back at his compartment, they found that the porter had already pulled down and made the bed. The sheets and blankets were turned down, ready to climb into. There was very little room left, so they decided to play cribbage sitting on the bed. Jack opened the bottle of wine and poured each of them a full glass. They spent a few minutes looking out the window as the train was passing northern Ontario lakes. It was nine thirty and the western sun was just beginning to set, giving off a warm glow and casting a golden sheen on all the waterways. The cribbage game and the conversation lasted for a couple of hours until the wine was finished.

Jack had to use the toilet. Mandy said that she had to go too and would use the public toilet just down the hall.

It was close to midnight when she returned and said, "I just saw that guy from Cornell...he had a bear sitting in the Cornell 'C.' Is that the Cornell logo?"

"Oh yeah," said Jack, "that's Big Red, our mascot. What did the guy look like?"

"Early twenties, maybe six feet, like any other jock...I

don't know. He seemed too preoccupied, looking for a certain compartment number. He must have found it, because he wasn't there when I came out." She emptied her last sip of wine then grabbed Jack's hand. They sat down and kissed. It didn't take too much convincing to get her to stay the night with him rather than go back to coach. They lay down on the bed and kicked off their shoes. The wine, the rocking of the train and the muffled noise of the wheels were perfect narcotics for a deep sleep, but they had something else in mind.

Mandy was a willing partner, as she countered each one of Jack's advances. Their lips were locked, and Jack wondered if they'd ever come up for air. Her firm breasts were highlighted by the bright moonlight coming through the window. He then slowly unbuttoned the top brass button of her Levis and slowly lowered the zipper as she fumbled with his belt.

Just as he was slipping his hand underneath the elastic waistband of her panties, they heard a loud THUD on the wall beside them, which was obviously not the thickest of partitions. They thought they heard a bit of a muffled scream, then all was quiet, until they heard steps running down the corridor. The coach door quickly opened to the coupling area of the cars: CLICKETY CLACK, CLICKETY CLACK, CLICKETY CLACK CLICKETY CLACK, CLICKETY CLACK. With a quiet but definitive click, the door closed, and all was silent except for the rocking, rolling and lurching. Soon Jack could tell that they were going over a large body of water by the low-pitched, reverberating resonance.

Jack quickly pulled on his pants and slipped into his sneakers, much to Mandy's disappointment. He knew that someone was in trouble but had no idea what he was about to witness. The door of the compartment next to his was quietly swinging. There were bloody shoeprints leading from the compartment leading down the corridor. He gently pushed the door open with two fingers and almost fainted at the sight.

"CALL THE POLICE, PORTER, PORTER, SOMBODY CALL THE PORTER, OH MY GOD!" he shouted at the top of his lungs. There before him lay the middle-aged lady he had nodded to earlier in the day. Her sheer nightgown was pulled up to her waist. She was lying stretched out on her back. Her head was hanging over the bed, attached only by her spinal cord, her throat slit from ear to ear, mouth wide open and blank eyes uselessly straining as if to cry out for help. Blood was splattered everywhere, and pools of it were starting to congeal. A few drops were still running down her cheeks, and into her eyes, as her almost decapitated head and blood-matted hair swung with the movement of the train. A large cluster of pink bubbles clung to the opening of her windpipe, where the knife had slashed it with great precision.

*   *   *

A memory of Jack's quantity cooking field trip to New York City instantly flooded his mind in great detail. It was their side trip to a kosher slaughterhouse, across the river in Elizabeth, New Jersey. A small rabbi, not more than five foot four, dressed in black, with a long black rubber apron and wearing a black yarmulke on his balding head, sharpened the largest knife Jack had ever seen. It was like a giant straight razor. The rabbi was continually, quietly saying prayers while a large, half-naked, sweaty worker led a beautiful Black Angus into a stall comprised of galvanized pipes. Once it was in place, the abattoir worker shackled the poor animal's back legs with some heavy chains that hung from an overhead pulley attached to a track. The rabbi finally stopped sharpening the gigantic straight razor and ran it across his thumbnail to check for any nicks. He nodded to the worker.

SLAM! A bar came up and pushed the animal's chin up as far as it could go. The poor beast's eyes were bulging and its tongue hanging out as it attempted to moo. The rabbi coolly slid the executioner's blade across its throat, just missing the spine. Furtive and hollow blasts were heard coming from its severed windpipe as its eyes continued to bulge out, as if to cling on to some last hope. Blood gushed out in pulsating quarts. The rabbi's apron was bright red and Jack and his class had to jump back to avoid being drenched. The chains tightened and the slaughtered beast was raised by its shackled hind legs to the track above, which ferried it away for "dressing." One final kick of its rear leg and a slight twitch of the right foreleg signalled the end to its life, as the rabbi ran the knife over his thumbnail again. A nick would have signalled that he had erroneously hit the spine and, if so, he would signal to the worker that it was to go to a "Gentile" area, as it was no longer kosher. Jack thought, *And this is supposed to be "humane."* The murmured prayers punctuated by the continual sharpening of the knife sliding along the cold steel set the stage for the next beast to be led into the killing cage. Jack could not believe that he would ever witness the murder of a human being done with the precision of the brutal slaughter of a steer.

*   *   *

People came out of their rooms in various states of undress. Jack told them all to stay in their rooms and wait for the porter. The porter finally arrived, and Jack pointed into the room he was guarding. The porter's dark skin almost turned gray when he looked in and took in the grisly scene.

"What do I do?" he asked.

"Well, if I were you I'd call the conductor, then get the engineer to contact the next station ahead and have him alert the police and wait for us until we arrive. Also, tell everyone to stay in their rooms."

The porter looked at his watch, and said, "We should be in Sudbury within the hour."

Soon, two conductors arrived and advised everyone on the car that they should stay in their rooms. There was an emergency on board, but they need not worry. They positioned themselves by the two doors at either end of the car to prevent other passengers from entering.

The train pulled into a siding at the Sudbury station. There were at least five police cars, two ambulances and two fire trucks. Each had circular flashing red and white lights that lit up the night sky and the surrounding buildings. Within a minute from when the train creaked to a jerky, squealing stop, the car was flooded with police, firemen and ambulance attendants. The sergeant in charge of the operation looked into the compartment and ordered all passengers in the Assiniboia to gather up their belongings and proceed to the dining car. This they did, some still dressed in their nightclothes, tiptoeing around the bloody footprints. Mandy stopped briefly at her seat to pick up her knapsack.

Fresh coffee was offered to everyone. The lead investigator asked Jack to go outside to answer some questions in the cruiser. Jack told them what he had seen as accurately as possible, and as he got out to go back on the train, he saw that Mandy was being questioned in another cruiser.

They compared questions and worried that they might be suspects. They both told exactly what had happened down to the details of their relationship, and knew they'd just have to wait and see what will come to pass. Soon, a yellow school bus pulled up and an announcement was made telling them all that they were going to be billeted at the Caswell Motor Inn. The train would continue on after their car was uncoupled and held for a homicide investigation. Their trip would be delayed one day, since Canadian Pacific couldn't get a spare coach to replace the Assiniboia any faster. They would be allowed one long distance phone call, and all meals and drinks other than alcoholic beverages would be covered, provided they were consumed in the coffee shop of the motel and charged to their rooms.

Jack and Mandy took one room at the motel and stayed up talking until 2:45 in the morning. Jack had gone to the pop machine down the hall and picked up a few Cokes and some ice. The two were both as wired as any two people could be. Then Jack broke down and started babbling everything that he had been through in the last few months: the three murders at Cornell; his best friend, Colin, being charged as a serial killer; the death at the Royal York, and now this. He told her about Consuela, and about his mixed emotions about what might have happened between him and Mandy on the train. In short, he was a basket case. She hugged him and told him not to worry; these things had a way of working themselves out. She told him about Trevor, who she had left behind, and promised him to tell him the whole story when the time was right. Their dialogue was cathartic for both of them. They took off their outer clothes and crawled into bed, and exhausted, fell into a deep sleep in each other's arms.

11

Jack and Mandy woke up around ten in the morning and went down to the coffee shop for a late breakfast. There was a notice that all passengers on last night's Canadian were requested to meet in the Algonquin Room at one p.m. Jack took a quick glance at the *Globe and Mail*. It was the morning newspaper, so it didn't have any news about the night before. He phoned the Chateau and spoke to Craig Simpson, the front office manager, to tell what had happened.

Jack had become good friends with Craig and his wife, Irene, who managed the Brewster Transportation desk, over the past couple of years. He always admired Craig's sense of humour in a difficult situation, but he always had the most practical solution to any problem. He also asked Craig to have the bellmen pick up his trunk and put it in his room, since the baggage car had gone on ahead of him. Next, at a pay phone, he called his mother to let her know what had happened. He warned her that she would probably read about it in the paper and that he would phone her when he arrived at Lake Louise.

Jack suggested to Mandy that they go for a walk in the warm sun and see what they could of "The Nickel Capital of Canada." They found it shocking and sad that the pollution from the smelters had killed off so much of the foliage, and all that was left on the distant hills were brown, naked trees. The meeting after lunch was merely to inform everyone that the bus would pick them up after dinner, and that they should have their tickets ready to present on boarding. Many questions were asked about what had happened, and the CP ticket agent told them that he was not permitted to discuss anything, since it was a police matter. They were also asked not to say anything to the press. Eventually all the details would come out.

"Will there be any police on the trip west to protect us?" asked one worried woman. "Yes, ma'am, there will be added security. Everyone's carryon luggage will be searched before they board the train. It will be an inconvenience, but we understand your concerns, so we have taken this measure just to ease your minds."

A number of the fellow passengers came over to Jack and Mandy after the meeting to ask them about what had happened. Jack, without going into any details, said that he'd found a dead woman in the compartment next to his, after a brief scuffle. The word spread amongst the other passengers, and some clutched their loved ones while others sat quietly with their heads in their hands.

The evening papers were out as they headed into dinner. The *Toronto Telegram*, being the more sensationalist of the three dailies, said: *'MURDER ON THE CANADIAN'* with the subheading: *'BANK OF CANADA EXEC. THROAT SLASHED'.*

The *Toronto Star: 'ALLISON SVENDSON, EXEC. ASST. TO THE GOVERNOR OF BANK OF CANADA, FOUND MURDERED ON TRAIN.'*

Jack reluctantly picked up the papers from the quickly dwindling stacks as they headed in to dinner. Everybody in the coffee shop was deeply immersed in the papers. The news articles were very general, but they did identify the victim as Miss Allison Svendson, a career bureaucrat who had been with the Bank of Canada for nineteen years, having attained her MBA at the University of Western Ontario in 1946. There were statements of grief, sorrow and feelings of great loss to Canada from the governor of the Bank of Canada, the prime minister, the presidents of banks who had worked with her, a number of her colleagues and even one from Carl Watson, chairman of the U.S. Federal Reserve Bank, with whom she had helped negotiate a number of transactions between the Canadian and American banking systems.

The bus picked up the passengers as scheduled and took them to the station, where they began boarding their new coach, the Prince George. The same Porter, Eli, and an RCMP officer were there to greet them. Their tickets were checked as they were helped up the steps onto the car. Mandy was stopped, since her ticket was good only for coach. Jack had to remind Eli, with a two-dollar bill, that Mandy had been his guest the night before last and that she could go back to a coach car, but she could simply walk up and meet Jack in his compartment.

Eli agreed. Jack asked the conductor how his day had been

so far. The man replied, "You wouldn't believe the paperwork I've had to fill out."

Jack said, "Form 15385B? Tell me about it."

The conductor looked at him as if he was some sort of ghost or a company spy, although all the legal forms for the corporation were the same.

The rest of the trip was uneventful. They spent most of their time reading, playing cribbage, and some spirited games of double solitaire. The quiet conversations were sometimes light and other times quite deep as they talked about life and their dreams. They tried not to talk too much of the murder. Their relationship remained platonic for the rest of the trip but their friendship deepened.

"I wonder what ever happened to that Cornell guy," mused Mandy. "He must have had a seat on another coach and continued on." They fell asleep in each other's arms for the next two nights, and both seemed comfortable and comforted by that.

Arriving in Calgary, they quickly went back to the dome car to get two seats, so they'd be sure to see the spectacular view of the Rocky Mountains. Banners were up all over the Calgary station announcing the opening of the Calgary Stampede the next week. Jack knew that there was no way he would be able to get time off to see his favorite fair. He loved his trail rides in the mountains, and he loved the Stampede's western spirit. Along the way, he had told Mandy about Ribbon, his favorite horse in the Brewster Stables.

*   *   *

The horse stables were just outside of the main entrance to the hotel and up a short treed laneway. They were situated beside the Brewster Barns, the name of the building where the sightseeing busses were serviced. One's senses would get an incredible workout. As you left the hotel you could smell the odors of wonderful cuisine being prepared by the army of Swiss chefs in the kitchens, and then the clear, fresh air would take over with the invigorating scent of pines and fir trees. Proceeding up the gravel roadway, the smothering blanket of diesel fuel would bring you back to the twentieth century, and as you rounded the corner to the corral, the pungent scent of horses, earth, leather and manure combined with the creak of the saddles and the jangle of the cowboys' spurs sung out the love of horses and mountain trails. Jokes and laughter were constantly heard coming from the hands, and there were always kind words and nudges directed at the animals as they were saddled up for yet another trail ride.

Jack often walked over, and if Ribbon hadn't been rented out to one of the tourists, he'd take her for the day on one of the many trails and enjoy the smell of the pines, the solitude and the purity of the clear mountain air. Ribbon loved it, too, because it was an easy ride and Jack would spoil her with an apple or some carrots, and always a sugar cube when they got home. Ribbon was a Cayuse, a Native/Canadian/American horse which was smaller than a quarter horse, with great speed for her size, but more importantly, she was incredibly sure-footed, making the breed perfect for the narrow mountain trails. She certainly wouldn't fit into the term "an old plug," so often used to describe horses used for dude ranches and greenhorn tourists. Ribbon was always bright and alert. Lifting her feet high, she was responsive to the slightest of Jack's commands, and many times would anticipate them well in advance. Her ears were always perked straight up, her eyes constantly searching the landscape, and her nostrils open wide, as if she were on constant vigil for a lurking grizzly. Jack hoped that she had wintered well on the Blackfoot Reservation, where Brewsters kept their herd of trail horses for the off season.

Mandy gathered her knapsack, and Jack got off the train at the Banff Station with her to say goodbye. She was heading to the hostel and then to the Banff Springs Hotel the following morning, and if there were no jobs available there, she would start hitting the restaurants along Banff Avenue. Her experience working in the pub at the U of T should help get her a job. Jack was sure that she would have no problem, as her bright appearance and twinkling eyes would persuade any person to hire her. To any business, this girl would be nothing but an asset. She agreed to call him as soon as she got settled, and Jack promised if she didn't have any luck, he would try to get her something at the Chateau.

He retrieved his seat in the dome car and settled in for the last hour of riding until the Lake Louise Station, where he expected to be met by a bus that would take him and the guests up the mountain on the switchback road, until it arrived at what was considered one of the world's greatest views, that of Lake Louise, beautifully colored in a soft milky turquoise by ice cold glacial streams sitting at the base of Mount Victoria and its magnificent glacier. Artists and photographers have tried, fruitlessly, to capture its beauty since the late 1800s, but neither palette nor lens has ever been able to seize the magnificence of the view. They passed Johnson's Canyon, where he again marvelled at the view of Castle Mountain, which had been renamed Mount Eisenhower in honor of former American president and general. Jack still preferred Castle Mountain, reminding him of Edinburgh Castle on Princes Street in Edinburgh. He felt as if he were coming home.

The train slowly crept into the station and Jack disembarked, thanking the porter and the conductor for their services. He was met by a smiling Gerry Graves, head bellman, dressed in his alpine uniform of black shoes, white knee-high socks, dark gray knickers shirt and tie and a dark green embroidered waist coat with knicker matching sleeves. They greeted each other with huge smiles and a hug.

"I've commandeered a car from Irene at Brewsters," Gerry chuckled.

"Nothing's changed," said Jack; Gerry could basically do anything he wanted at the hotel. He had put himself through law school and was now thinking of medicine. Gerry had started at the Chateau as a busboy, and he'd worked his way up over the years to the most lucrative position in the hotel. Many said that Gerry's tips far exceeded manager Harold McIntyre's salary. Gerry was from Digby, Nova Scotia, and had the gift of the gab. He also had his thumb on the pulse of the hotel. Whether it be management or staff, Gerry knew everything that was going on. "There's a party at Gables tonight," he said, referring to the building that housed the hotel's laundry on the ground floor and the bell staff's and doormen's residence on the top floor. A bellman's party was one not to be missed.

Craig Simpson greeted Jack with great enthusiasm, and they agreed that after Jack settled in his room, they'd meet for an early dinner in the Victoria dining room, the hotel's main dining room with a seating capacity of two hundred and windows three storeys high overlooking the breathtaking view of the lake and the mountains.

Jack got to his room, number 322. His trunk had been delivered earlier and was waiting for him to unpack. Rooms with even numbers overlooked the Pipestone Range, which was at the back of the hotel. They also overlooked the main entrance, the steward's/receiving dock, and one of the staff residences, Hillside. Room 322 was directly over the main entrance, and he had to make sure that his window was closed tightly to prevent the fumes from all the sightseeing buses from gassing him. He made short order of unpacking and arranged to have his morning suit and tux pressed by the laundry.

He then walked down the fire stairs, which were right next to his room, and popped his head into the Glacier Lounge, which was in the basement with a patio outside accommodating a great view for guests enjoying a drink. He was greeted with a big hug by Trudy Hellman, the lounge waitress. Trudy's last name had earned her the nickname of "Mayo" by a friend in grade one, and it followed her all of her life. Trudy had worked for the past four years for maitre'd Giorgio Bellanto as waitress in the Victoria Room, and since this was her last season before graduating from school, she had requested a transfer to the lounge where the tips would be larger. Giorgio had been with CP Hotels for seventeen years. He was a real professional in his trade and liked by guests and staff alike.

Next stop was the Poppy Room, the hotel coffee shop. Because most guests dined in the Victoria Room, the Poppy Room only served sandwiches, soup, which had been brought down from the main kitchen, milk shakes and soft drinks, and it also had a vanilla soft ice cream machine. April Cadeau, the prime minister's daughter and only child, basically ran the Poppy Room, reporting to the hotel's steward. She greeted Jack with a big smile and poured him a coffee. "Double double! There, and you thought that I'd forget."

– 12 –

April Cadeau was a small wiry young girl; one might call her "mousey." She had a pleasant, shy smile and drab, short hair. She wore the same yellow and white starched uniform that was standard attire in all CP hotels. She hated being the daughter and only child of Canada's Prime Minister. She hated the spotlight. She hated the press, and she hated any fuss being made over her. She was in her fourth year of veterinary college at the University of Guelph. If she wasn't working in the Poppy Room, she could always be found mucking out the stalls at the Brewster Stables, just opposite the parking lot and before Deer Lodge, a small but cozy hotel just outside the Chateau's main gates. Last summer, April and Jack had gone on a couple of trail rides together. Jack was sure that April would have taken care of Ribbon until he got out there. He hadn't had a chance to get over to the stables, but April assured him that his horse had wintered well and that she had taken Ribbon out a couple of times.

"Thanks," said Jack.

"And I gave her a good currying too," added April.

Jack went back to his room and started to make some phone calls. First to his parents, and then Colin's cousin Liam to see how plans for the lobster dinner were progressing.

"Great," said Liam, "people down here are some upset about what's happening to Colin. I think I've got every musician I know coming to play, as well as the Stephens Family and the Barker Brothers." These were two of Cape Breton's best-known Celtic singing groups.

In the tradition started by Welsh coal miners, the miners of Cape Breton also had wonderful choral groups.

"Some of the boys from the mine are also going to do a few numbers. We've sold so many tickets that we've had to change it from the hall to the arena, and just about every lobster fisherman is donating the lobsters. The lobster brokers are some pissed off!" he laughed. "Serves 'em right, the greedy bastards!"

"I wish I could help, is there anything I can do?" Jack asked.

"Nope, the York National has been really good and is looking after all the money in the Colin MacDonald Trust Fund. We're over twenty grand already."

Jack thought that moving the venue from the church hall to the arena was most fitting, since it was where Colin had spent most of his time when he was younger and honed his skills on the rink.

A call to Clay was next. "Clay? It's Jack Souster. I just wanted to let you know that the fundraising is going really well, and I'm ready to send you a cheque, except you've never given me an invoice."

"I've always told you not to worry about it, but I guess I'd better get some money to Clive in order to keep him in the lifestyle he's used to."

They laughed. Jack decided to get some fresh air and decided to walk up the west side of the lake. He would go until the trail started heading up to the Plain of the Six Glaciers, a little too steep for him, especially with the thin air being a mile above sea level. However, it was about two miles to the end of the lake and back, and by the time he got back and had a beer, it would be time for dinner with Craig and Irene Simpson.

Giorgio hardly ever gave a window table to a member of the staff, but tonight was different, since it was Jack's first night back. Harold, the hotel manager, and Mrs. MacIntyre were both ill in their suite.

"I think the flu," said Irene. They ordered their dinners then asked Jack what he'd been up to. He mentioned that school had been great then started describing the three murders and Colin being charged as a serial killer, then on to the death at the Royal York, describing everything in detail, including Form 15358B, and then to the murder of the executive assistant to the Governor of the Bank of Canada.

Craig laughed, grabbed Jack's arm, and said, "Well at least you have experience at filling out those forms...we have the same ones here. Listen, the good Lord doesn't give you anything you can't handle, and I thought that I had a problem being overbooked by ten rooms tomorrow."

They spent the rest of the meal getting caught up on the hotel, the town of Banff, where Craig and Irene wintered, and the politics of the CP Hotel chain.

"There'll be no charge for the car that Graves used today," Irene laughed, referring to Gerry Graves by his last name, as did everyone else.

Jack settled in easily into the daily routine and was thoroughly enjoying every minute of it until he thought of Colin. *Resorts are different,* he thought. All the guests were on vacation and wanted to enjoy themselves. There was no pressure, like there was in a large city hotel with businessmen dashing everywhere trying to get things accomplished and organized before they went on to their next meeting or catching a limo which would hopefully get them to the airport on time for their flight, fully aware that they had not left enough time.

Just like the Royal York had its celebrities, Chateau Lake Louise had its share, except the celebrities came to the resort to relax and didn't have to worry about putting on a performance every evening. Since there was no television in the mountains, the hotel provided evening entertainment. After dinner, guests, dressed in their finest, would proceed down to the lobby to listen to a one and a half hour concert, then proceed into the large ballroom, where they would sit at small cocktail tables in leather lounge chairs around a massive dance floor to dance the night away to the strains of the house twelve-piece orchestra. The concerts were put on by noted concert pianist Robert Rhind, who had been doing it for years. Every winter he taught at the famed Ontario Conservatory of Music in Toronto and worked as social host at the Chateau every summer while indulging his passion for mountain climbing. Each summer he hired a student in voice from the Conservatory to perform with him in the concerts.

This year he had hired the lovely soprano, Dorothy Rutherford, a tall, stunning brunette with a perfect hourglass figure. She, following concert traditions, always dressed in beautiful, flowing evening gowns and stood in the crux of the highly polished ebony Baldwin Concert Grand.

When Robert Rhind played a piano concerto, and he played them all, Tchaikovsky, Rachmaninoff, Chopin, Mozart, he would always have a designated bellman standing beside him ready to turn the page of music at his demanding nod. It was not unusual for a bit of "staff humour" to turn two or three pages at once, which would infuriate the absorbed maestro as he tried to fake the next few bars until his furtive, muted grunts would scold the offending bellman into getting him back on the correct page. The rest of the bell staff would be stifling their glee, folding over in their seats with their hands clasped over their mouths shaking. The odd guest might look over quizzically, trying to figure out what the bell staff found so amusing.

Dorothy Rutherford would sing at least one aria every evening, but Broadway show tunes, mostly Rodgers and Hammerstein, were favored. This year, "Climb Every Mountain" from *The Sound of Music* was ironically the show stopper, but Dorothy's powerful voice filled the lobby with hits from *Carousel* to *Oklahoma*, and now and again, for fun, she would throw in a current folk tune. Ian and Sylvia's "Four Strong Winds" would bring the house down, and even the bellmen, for that, would give her a standing ovation. There was no microphone, and the incredible acoustics in the lobby were nothing more than a happy architectural accident.

Jack had checked in noted Hollywood filmmaker Alfred Hitchcock and his wife. He personally took them up to their two-room suite, having advised Graves to be sure their luggage was in the suite before they arrived. Suite number 523/25 overlooked the lake and was one of the hotel's finest. He welcomed the Hitchcocks to the hotel and explained that a window table had been reserved for them.

"Please do not hesitate to call, at any time, in case there is anything I can do to make your stay more enjoyable." He also mentioned that they might enjoy the concert in the lobby that took place every evening.

This particular evening, Mr. and Mrs. Hitchcock had taken his advice and were sitting unobtrusively on a nearby sofa not far from Jack's office door, which faced the lobby. A few other guests recognized the master of suspense and whispered to each other. The lights in the lobby were dimmed, but not darkened, and the concert began. Robert and the singer were in the middle of "Some Enchanted Evening" when suddenly the entire hotel was thrown into blackness. The only light was the silver candelabra on top of the concert grand.

The artists didn't miss a beat, and the concert proceeded. Bellmen scurried to find more candles, and Jack went over to the Hitchcocks to apologize. Unfortunately, he knew the chief engineer had booked off for the evening and was dining with his latest "trophy," whom he had recently picked up in Banff.

"Is there anything I can get you or Mrs. Hitchcock, sir?" Jack enquired.

In his patented soft, heavy breathing English accent, Hitchcock said, "Yes….I'd like a glass of iced water…thank you."

Jack, with his flashlight, found his way to the bar in the lounge and retrieved a large glass of ice water. He brought a silver pitcher in case a refill was required.

"Thank you," said the master of mystery. "Please pull up a chair," he added.

Jack looked around and couldn't find a nearby seat, so he squatted down on his haunches. They were lit only by a nearby candle and his dimming flashlight.

"You've just given me a great idea for a script for a new movie."

"Sir?"

After a long pause, Hitchcock continued, "In a remote, wilderness resort, high in the Canadian Rocky Mountains, the power went out. When the lights came back on, the elevator operator was found murdered inside her elevator. Who did it? The maitre'd or the assistant manager?" During this exchange, Robert Rhind noticed who Jack was talking to and broke into Hitchcock's famous theme song, "The Funeral March Of A Marionette," much to the delight of everyone. Polite applause was heard from the assembled guests, to whom Mr. Hitchcock smiled and nodded .

Jack smiled and said, "The maitre'd, because the assistant manager was getting a glass of ice water for a guest, and there were lots of witnesses, since they were all wondering what was happening with this well known celebrity."

"Ah yes, but the assistant manager left the lobby to get the iced water, and there was a certain lack of alacrity in his step; it seemed that he took an exceedingly long period of time to perform such a simple task."

Mrs. Hitchcock said, " Oh Hitch, behave yourself." and turning to Jack said, "Never mind him. He never stops."

The movie mogul extended his hand and thanked Jack for everything. Jack smiled and thought, *I can't seem to get away from murder. Now I've got the 'master of murder' describing grisly scenes. When will this ever end?*

Fortunately, the head electrician and the assistant engineer went to the power plant, which was just down the road, past the main gate, across the road from Deer Lodge. The hotel generated its own power through runoff from the lake. The cascading waters turned the generators' turbines. The lights came back on to the applause of everyone in the lobby.

Jack went up to the Hitchcocks and told them, with a smile, that all elevator operators were accounted for. One had been stuck between floors but returned to ground level with great relief. Alfred Hitchcock replied with a wry smile: "I'm pleased, although I think I prefer my outcome." Again, he shook Jack's hand and thanked him.

The hotel was running smoothly, with only the expected little hiccups, dishwashers stealing steaks for their staff barbeque and bartenders slipping free drinks to waiters or bringing hotel liquor to their staff party, and switching rooms for guests who demanded that they get a Lakeview room, even though their travel agent had only reserved them a Pipestone room. General Manager Harold McIntyre had fully recovered, although Mrs. McIntyre was still "under the weather."

Jack had taken Ribbon out a number of times for a ride with April, knowing her love of horses. One time, Ribbon seemed a little skittish. Jack thought that he had heard something, and the last thing he wanted was to come in contact with a grizzly. April mentioned that she had been out the day before and felt uneasy, as if someone was following her. She had signed off on all security and said that she would be really mad if her father had ordered the RCMP to secretly follow her. All of a sudden they heard a small rock bounce down the hill, off pine trees as if they were pylons in a giant pinball machine. The rock came to rest on the path about twenty feet in front of Ribbon and Jack. Then they heard the neigh of a horse two or three switchbacks up the mountain. Jack looked back at April.

"See, I told you so, there's somebody up there."

Ribbon warily walked over the large rock, and they decided to go back to the stables. Jack was a little concerned and hung around the corral as they unsaddled Ribbon and April's mount. No one else showed up within the next hour, but Chet, the stable hand, said that a couple of young "university type" guys had left a few hours earlier, long before April and Jack had gone out.

The next day Jack received a phone call from head office advising him that he was to be in Toronto for a two-day motivational management seminar. His airline tickets on CP Air would be put in the courier bag from Calgary, and he would be staying at the Royal York. The answer was "No" when he asked if he could stay at home, because of the team-building nature of the event.

Harold McIntyre was not pleased, since Jack had only arrived a couple of weeks earlier, and now head office was taking him away for a few days.

When he arrived in Toronto, he immediately called Consuela. If he wasn't allowed to leave the hotel, at least he could find a way to enjoy himself. He also phoned his old friend, Heather Stuart, at the York National and invited her over for a drink after work. She was delighted to hear from him and accepted his invitation without hesitation.

"I hate it. I absolutely hate it. It's the worst move I've ever made in my life," she bemoaned as they sipped their cocktails in the Imperial Lounge.

"Why?"

"There's so much pressure, and everything is top secret, I can't talk to anybody about a thing. I'm thinking of leaving. Maybe Mr. Lawton will have me back," she said.

Jack told her what he had been through, some of which she was already aware from the press coverage, and as they had another drink, they began to open up. Heather explained that a major American bank had been trying to buy the York National, and that they were offering far more than the shares were worth. But they needed 51 percent for control.

"The Federal Government has gotten involved," she continued, "since they won't allow any foreign control of Canadian banks."

"What bank is it?"

"Jack, I told you, I can't say a thing. I would if I could, but I've been sworn to secrecy. This guy really scares me. He yells at everybody, even me, and I'm just sitting in on the meetings taking shorthand for the minutes. He stays in the Royal Suite in the Royal York and demands fresh caviar, Dom Perignon on ice, and a selection of the finest imported cheeses, at room temperature, awaiting his return to the suite, at any time. He's hired a chauffer with a Rolls Royce to take him over to our boardroom, and the chauffer must have the car waiting for him, running, on the street, at all times, until the end of the day, even though, as you know, our tower is connected to the hotel via a tunnel, and it's no more than a five-minute walk. He literally shouts at every meeting and demands to speak to the minister of finance or the governor of the Bank of Canada on the speaker phone when he's here."

She continued. "He's threatened almost everyone, and

he even suggested bribes if they all cooperated with him. He told me on his way out of the office one day that I should also watch my back, because he wasn't finished with this bank or me, yet. Not that I have any influence on anything. He's just mean and nasty, Jack. I just hate the whole thing. He thinks that I'm his little gopher...he sends me out for chocolates, cookies, olives...with pits in them, can you believe it? Yet the pay, benefits and bonuses are better than I'll ever find anywhere else."

Jack ordered another Heineken, grabbed a handful of salted peanuts, and pondered how he could help, but felt totally useless other than just being a listening post.

"Why don't you see if you can take some time off and come out west for a visit? I'll get you a room, and that way you'll at least get a break from this scene."

She said that she would consider it. They finished their drinks and Heather left. Jack had a "team" dinner he had to get ready for.

Before heading up to his room, he stopped by front desk to say hello to his former colleagues.

"Who's in the Royal Suite this week?" he casually asked.

"Some asshole from New York, Chadwick Richardson. You wouldn't believe this guy, he just has everyone jumping. In fact, people turn around and make themselves scarce when they see him coming."

The name didn't mean anything to Jack, and he didn't think of asking what company he worked for.

When he got up to his room to have a quick shower before the meeting, he noticed the message light was blinking, signalling that maitre'd Giorgio at Lake Louise wanted to talk to him. He asked the switchboard operator to patch him through the Green Line, which was a no-charge company long-distance line connecting all CP properties across Canada. Sissy Sanderson, who was operating the antiquated Chateau switchboard, answered in her husky voice: "Chateau Lake Louise, how may I help you?"

"Sissy, it's Jack in Toronto. Apparently Giorgio is looking for me, can you put me through the dining room please?"

"Certainly, Jack." He visualized her putting his line into the Victoria Room plug in the Lily Tomlin-styled switchboard.

"Dining room," answered Giorgio in his heavy Italian accent.

"Giorgio, it's Jack in Toronto, you wanted me?"

"Yes, sir." Jack wasn't used to being called sir by someone twice his age but accepted it, begrudgingly, since it went with the position of assistant manager.

"Do you know a Mandy Jenkins? I've had to fire the little 'poofer' in the Glacier lounge, and I need an experienced cocktail waitress. This Mandy appeared here this afternoon, and she gave me your name."

"Yes, I think that she'll do a great job for you. Get her a room in Fairview, and tell her I'll look forward to seeing her in a few days." Fairview was the girls' staff residence.

"I hope that she'll be a lot better than the last little poofer." Jack was wondering what "mayo" the former little "poofer" did, or didn't do, to raise the wrath of the excitable maitre'd. "Little Poofer" was Giorgio's term for any of his female staff: waitresses, hostesses, bus girls, etc., and the staff just knew by the tone of his voice whether it was a term of endearment, praise or severe scolding.

*   *   *

Jack proceeded to the British Columbia Room on the main mezzanine, where the "team dinner" was being held. Gordon Lawton was the host. He warmly welcomed Jack, and they had a brief chat about Heather. There were about twenty junior managers from hotels gathered there, and they all introduced themselves. Jack felt a little awkward. He was the only one with a degree in Hotel and Restaurant Management. All the others had worked their way up through the system. He already knew a number of them. There was an open bar, and hot hors d'ouevres and cold canapés were passed before they sat down to dinner. The menu consisted of smoked Atlantic salmon, chilled vichyssoise, a fresh Boston bib salad with a creamy cucumber dressing, and New York striploin steak, done rare, just as Jack had requested. He declined the cherries jubilee.

Gordon Lawton introduced the instructor, who would lead the sessions for the next two days. Everyone was asked to introduce themselves, state their present position within the corporation, and outline their aspirations for their future with CP Hotels, as well as their expectations of the "team building" sessions.

Jack hated these feel-good get-togethers and quietly looked at his watch, hoping that this would end quickly. He had arranged for Consuela to come to his room at eleven o'clock. It was announced that the morning would start off with a continental breakfast in the same room at eight, and it was suggested that everyone get a good night's sleep. The meeting broke up, and some of the attendees decided to go out to a strip bar on Jarvis Street. Jack declined, feigning jet lag, then hurried to his room to greet Consuela.

He ordered a chilled bottle of chardonnay, Consuela's favorite, and a nice assortment of imported cheeses, including his own favorite, Oka. He'd had just enough time to get everything set up, FM radio playing softly in the background, lights dimmed low, and he was extremely happy that they had assigned him a room with two queen sized beds, although only one would be required. There was a soft knock on the door, and Consuela fell into his outstretched arms. They kissed and fell onto the bed. The Righteous Brothers were singing "You've Lost That Lovin' Feeling." They enveloped each other and became one.

The morning came early, and the lovers parted. Consuela promised to return that evening. Jack got off the elevator and headed towards the skirted tables topped with croissants, jam, juice and coffee. He needed three cups just to wake up.

The day was spent role-playing, dealing with hard to please guests, disgruntled employees and all other possible scenarios that could occur in a major hotel. Lawyers have clients, doctors have patients, wholesale and retailers have customers, but hotels and restaurants have guests, and as long as that term is remembered, and you treat a guest like a guest in your own home, you will never have to worry about bad service and complaints. When someone asks for some eggs, you ask them, "How would you like them done?" then you prepare the eggs the way the guest requested. Service was driven home again and again, to everyone.

Jack found his mind wandering throughout the day, wondering how many people in the room had ever filled in a Form 15385B. He was sure that the facilitator of the meeting had never heard of such a thing or even considered some of the seamier things that go on in a hotel that the public never hears, such as keeping hookers off the floors and soliciting out of the lounges. Jack knew from experience that these women were brilliant in their guile. Some dressed in business attire with briefcases, others in long evening gowns, working the most fashionable dinners and fundraisers.

His mind also wandered to Colin, Clay and Clive. He must touch base with them while he was in Toronto. What was happening in Cape Breton? The day dragged, but eventually they wrapped it up and there was an hour break before a dinner, where everyone talked and laughed about some of the strange things that had happened over the years. Jack regaled them with stories about some of the questions tourists would ask, such as the weight of a certain mountain, or how long it took the bellmen to paint the lake in the spring in order for it to have such a beautiful pastel green color. The dinner ended as all went their separate ways. They looked forward to hearing a motivational speaker in the morning before everyone dispersed across the country to their respective properties and homes. Jack headed up to the room to make his phone calls then waited for the return of Consuela.

13

"Hi, Liam, It's Jack Souster. How are things in Glace Bay?" Jack checked his watch, remembering the one-hour time difference between Eastern and Atlantic zones. He kicked off his shoes as he lay back on the bed and loosened his tie.

"Jack, good to hear from you. Things are starting to come together. The *Cape Breton Post* did a fantastic editorial on Colin, his problems and our fundraising efforts. People are coming out of the woodwork to help. A local lobster fisherman has offered to supply all the lobsters we need. He hates the wholesaler Ocean Foam Fisheries, and when he heard that they were only going to give us a ten percent discount off the wholesale price, Dennis got together a bunch of his fisher friends, and they have pledged as many lobsters as we need. Natalie LeBlanc from Cheticamp has offered to do one of her famous hooked rugs of a picture of Colin in his Cornell uniform for auction, and there are tons of other auction items coming in every day. Tickets are almost sold out."

Jack knew of Cheticamp. It was a French-speaking community on the beautiful Cabot Trail. The women there were famous for their rug hooking. It was a tight-knit community. You were either a LeBlanc or a Chiasson, it seemed, if you lived in Cheticamp. Their main source of income was fishing and tourism. Jack remembered his parents taking him to the Keltic Lodge in Inverness as a special holiday as he was recovering from his heart surgery. They traveled around "The Trail" one day, and his mother had purchased a table runner that one of the ladies had hooked. His father, to this day, maintained that the finest seafood chowder he'd ever had in his life was in Cheticamp.

"Jack, can you contact Jerry Mosher in Digby? I don't know him, but he called me and he wants to put on a scallop dinner to help Colin. This thing seems to be gaining momentum. Boy, this is going to be some great! Dad's meeting with the manager of the Bank of Nova Scotia to set up a trust fund in Colin's name. So that will be the YN, the BMO, the Royal, the CIBC and Scotiabank all accepting donations across Canada. Have you talked to Colin lately?"

"Wow," said Jack. "No, I'll be calling him tomorrow. Have you set a date for the lobster dinner?"

"I'm thinking Saturday, October 9th, that'll be Thanksgiving weekend, and everybody will be ready to party and loosen up the old purse strings. Mom and Colin's mom are looking after the food, and my brother Sean is looking after the music. He's into that sort of thing. Any chance of you coming down?"

"I wouldn't miss it for all the tea in China."

They said their goodbyes, promising to keep in touch. Jack was invigorated by the news. His mind went to the letter he had sent to the prime minister. He wondered when, if ever, he would get a reply. He made a mental note to ask April to speak to her father when he got back to the Chateau. There was a gentle knock on the door, and Consuela fell into Jack's arms once more. They decided to go down and catch the last act of Tony Bennett in the Imperial Room if there was a spare table. If not they'd just have a drink in the lounge. He explained everything that was happening with the fundraiser in Cape Breton, and they talked about Consuela coming out to spend a week or two at Lake Louise. They were both giddy with the drinks and with the excitement of just being together. They held each other close as they went back up to the room.

Next day, the motivational speaker wasn't all that he was cracked up to be. The session wound up with each participant giving a brief synopsis of what they'd gotten out of the meeting. Everyone, without exception, gave a glowing report and said that it was most beneficial. However, the real reasons for their accolades were that it was great to get an all-expenses-paid company trip to Toronto and a break from their routine.

Jack went back to the room and quickly packed his bag, checked out and got a taxi to his parents' house. His mother had invited the neighbours and Consuela over for dinner, but Jack wanted to make a few phone calls. He opened the door from the garage to the kitchen, and Dylan, the dog, raised his head from his usual spot keeping an eye on the front door. At the sight of Jack, pure mayhem ensued as Dylan came running, bounced up onto his chest, then proceeded to go into his ritual of tearing in circles through every room of the ground floor. Jack just wished everybody could be that happy at the sight of him. It never failed to lift his spirits.

*   *   *

"Hi Clay, it's Jack. I'm just in Toronto for a couple of days and thought I'd check in. How're things?"

"Well they're moving pretty slowly, and we just had a bit of a setback. A couple of days ago the DA called me to tell me that they have an eyewitness. I don't know who. It looks like the trial date will still be October 19th."

Jack's stomach started to churn, and he began to feel a little lightheaded. *A witness! That's impossible!*

"Clay, something's wrong. I think he's being framed...I just can't believe what I'm hearing. I just wish I were down there to help. By the way, there's going to be a big fundraiser in Colin's hometown, so I fully expect there will be more than enough money raised to cover your fees...if you can wait 'til October."

"No problem, don't worry about it...oh, and thanks for the advance. That'll help cover some of Clive's expenses."

"How's Colin holding up?"

"Not too bad, all things considered. His agent just delivered a letter from the Leafs stating that his contract was null and void, since he missed training camp. But other than that he's doing fine. Ruth visits him every other day, and Clive and I are constantly in contact with him, but I'm sure that he'd like to hear from you."

"Yeah, yeah," replied Jack, "I just wanted to get the lay of the land from you. I'll keep in touch."

Almost afraid of calling his best friend, he decided to call Ruth instead to get her take on Colin's state of mind, although he knew his procrastination was just a way of avoiding talking to Colin about his problems. Ruth assured him that Colin was doing better than she would have ever thought anybody could, and that she called or visited him at least three or four times a week. Jack felt reassured.

"Hi guy, its Jack, how're you doing?"

"Hey, stranger, I'm doing great. What's new in the outside world?"

Jack told Colin everything that Liam and his parents, and aunts and uncles were doing, and went into every detail of the fundraiser. Colin mentioned that the conditions weren't all that bad in the jail as long as he kept positive and kept telling himself he would soon be out of there.

Jack told him not to worry about the Leafs. When this whole thing was over, any one of the other five NHL clubs would go after him.

"Anyways, there are rumors that there's going to be a major expansion within a couple of years."

Jack fought back tears as they said goodbye and promised to call more often, now that he was settled.

The dinner was fun, with a lot of laughs. Afterward, Jack drove Consuela home. "Jack, don't be late, your flight is early, and I'll need at least an hour to get you out to the airport," his mother said knowingly. Turning to Consuela, she said with a cool peck on the cheek, "Nice to see you again, dear. Don't keep him too long." Jack blushed, knowing exactly what she meant.

14

When the plane touched down in Calgary, there was a Brewster Taxi waiting to meet him. Jack was always in awe as he drove west from Calgary and saw the mountains rise above the rolling foothills of golden wheat like a jagged wall of rock. Within an hour he was looking out the side windows up at the snow-capped peaks. He could understand how those who lived by the sea would feel claustrophobic in the mountains. It was easy to see how these majestic monoliths could cause a feeling of confinement. "Majestic" was the term so many people used, and Jack thought that there was no better term, realizing these were remembrances of a time eons ago and the time of creation.

As the taxi left the Trans Canada Highway and started heading up the switchbacks to the lake and the Chateau, Jack once again felt the excitement he had experienced whenever he arrived at the hotel. He dumped his suitcase in his room and went directly to the front office to see Craig Simpson and get caught up on anything that might have happened while he was away.

"Same old crap, rah, rah, rah, but at least I got to see my folks and Consuela."

Craig smiled. "There's someone else here that seems a little sweet on you," said Craig. "Mandy Jenkins, the new Glacier Lounge waitress."

Jack proceeded downstairs to the lounge to say hello to Mandy, and since it was right next door to the Poppy Room coffee shop, he thought he'd also check in with April and see how she was doing.

Mandy welcomed Jack with a big smile and thanked him for putting in a good word for her, but she was too busy to talk. The Poppy Room, on the other hand, was fairly quiet, and April quickly came over to Jack to say how thankful she was to see him again.

"Jack, I know there's someone following me. I think there are two of them. I went riding yesterday morning, and I heard a couple of horses up the trail again. I caught a glimpse of them on their horses through the trees. They were riding pretty fast, but just then Chet came along with a trail ride of about fifteen people, and I asked him if I could join him. Then I heard them take off. Last night I was headed up to Hillside for a hootenanny and I heard a branch break just off the path. Jack, I'm not paranoid. I don't want to tell my dad, and if I need security I'll have to quit my job."

"By the way, I wrote your dad about Colin. I'm looking for some sort of government intervention, but I don't want to get you involved, so we'll just see what happens with my letter. In the meantime, let's go riding together, and if I'm not available, I want you to go out with someone else. Never on your own. Understand?"

April agreed. Jack decided he'd better report what April had been telling him to Geoff Entwhistle, the head hotel security cop. Geoff was on loan from the Vancouver rail yards and had been working the Chateau Lake Louise beat for the past seven years.

The next morning, Jack was up bright and early at six thirty and had breakfast in the Pipestone dining room, which was used strictly by the management and office staff. He came on duty at seven and found that one of the night auditors had left him a note saying that he should check into room 632 and have the guests pay down some of their account or at least establish some form of credit. They had only been in the hotel four days but had already rung up a bill of more than a thousand dollars. They continued to order Dom Perignon and the most expensive items on the menu. As well as their Brewster Limo, they also had rented horses. The last item made Jack take particular note, although he hated asking a guest to establish credit. It was embarrassing for both him and the guest, and he didn't know of a tactful way of dealing with the question. He often thought that it would be so easy if the hotels had a policy of taking an imprint of a guest's credit card as they checked in. There would be no need to single out any person in question to establish credit, nor would they have the problem of guests skipping out without paying. He figured that would happen at some point in the future.

He procrastinated about contacting the guests of 632, and at 4:45 in the afternoon the hotel received a telex from head office advising that there were two individuals who had been traveling across the country, ringing up large hotel bills, and then skipping out without paying their bills. It had started, the telex went on to say, at the Holiday Inn in Sudbury, and hit every CP Hotel, including the Saskatchewan in Regina, the Palliser in Calgary and the Banff Springs in Banff. They were described as both being over six feet, one blond and the other dark-haired with a pockmarked complexion. It was mentioned that they both had a slight New York accent. Aliases used were Sam Waters, Sean McKenzie, Scott Mandeville and Sonny Williams.

Jack went out to the Bell desk with the registration cards for room 632. Saul Weir and Seth Miller, both from Louisville, Kentucky.

"Gerry, do you or any of the guys recall checking in these two gentlemen?"

The bellhops gathered around, and Mike Trottier said, "I remember those guys, a couple of smart asses. They only had a couple of gym bags and said that they could carry them themselves. But you know hotel policy."

The bellman was talking about the policy where all guests must be shown to their room by a staff member. "They stiffed me," he said, "and then they started asking me if I knew April."

"Oh yeah, those guys," said Pete Rosen. "I just saw them down in the Glacier Lounge. They give me the creeps. I just had a coffee, and April's all excited because they've asked her to go riding after she got off duty."

"What?" exclaimed Jack "Thanks, guys." He went back to his office and called Geoff Entwhistle, who appeared within a couple of minutes.

"Geoff, close the door and have a seat." He motioned to the chair in front of his desk, pushing the account for room 632 and the Telex towards the hotel cop.

"These guys are down in the Glacier Lounge now and waiting for April Cadeau to get off duty so they can go riding with her. Remember my telling you about April being followed? I think we've got a problem."

They quickly decided that it would be best if they searched room 632.

"Is it legal?"

"Of course," answered Entwhistle. Jack got out his pass key as his phone rang.

"Jack? It's Mandy. I can't talk too loud, but do you remember I saw that guy from Cornell looking for a compartment on the train when I went to the washroom?"

"Yeah."

"Well, he's here in the lounge with another guy."

"Mandy, do not look around, do not do a thing, or even let on that you're talking to me. Just keep your eyes on them, and if they get up to leave, call me quietly and quickly in room 632. Tell Sissy, the switchboard operator, quietly so they won't hear their room number. It is really important not to let them know that you're watching them."

"Okay," she said and hung up. Jack went out to Sissy to explain that she might be getting a weird call from Mandy, and if she couldn't hear what the girl was saying, she was just to put her automatically through to room 632.

Jack and Geoff took an elevator to the sixth floor.

"Remember," Geoff said, "don't touch a thing. If you have to pick anything up, use a handkerchief or a tissue, or just lift it up with a pen or pencil." Jack was so nervous that he asked the elevator operator to open the doors quietly, and he put his right index finger to his mouth, fearing that the elevator would be heard all the way down in the basement and in the Lounge. He had never been in a situation like this, and was about as nervous as he ever wanted to be. The elevator operator looked at him as if he had gone a little mad.

"I'll explain later."

They arrived at room 632, where Entwhistle nodded and Jack knocked quietly on the door, as was hotel policy, before entering. There was no answer, so he slowly slipped the skeleton key into the lock and quietly turned it until he could hear the tumbles click. He turned the doorknob and gingerly opened the door. The room was a mess, although the chambermaid had done her job. The beds were made, garbage emptied and fresh towels, face cloths, bath mat and new complimentary toiletries were sitting in the white wicker basket on the shelf beside the sink. The gym bags were partially open and there was dirty clothing strewn around the room. Jack was amazed at how a maid could clean up around such a mess. It looked like she had tried to tidy up as best she could. Entwhistle signaled to Jack to look in one of the bags while he checked out the other. Jack, remembering what he had just been told, picked up a tissue and started to unzip his designated gym bag. He felt very uncomfortable.

He took his pen out of his inner breast pocket and with a tissue in his left hand started to lift up some of the bag's contents: shirts, underwear, socks and a large pack of Trojan condoms.

"I didn't know they came in such large packages, and it hasn't even been opened," Jack whispered. He then proceeded to the other corner of the bag and lifted up a Holiday Inn towel, from which he uncovered the cold stainless steel handle of a Smith & Wesson revolver. Jack started to shake and told Geoff that they had better leave before these guys came up from the lounge.

"Shit, that's a 9 millimetre," said Geoff as he carefully started to uncover it. As he lifted it by putting his pen in the trigger guard, they noticed a dried, blood-soaked rag wrapped around a knife under the gun. Jack looked more closely at the handle of the knife and soon recognized the very identifiable "JAS" initials, which he knew instantly were his, identifying the boning knife he had lost last spring at Cornell. The phone rang.

"Jack, it's Mandy. They've gone. They were here just a minute ago, and I turned around and they left. They haven't even paid their bill."

"Never mind, thanks." He hung up.

"Geoff, they're on their way up, let's get the hell out of here."

The cop attempted to put the items in the bags the way they were found as Jack opened the door. He could hear the elevator doors open, and the two sleuths quickly left room 632 and ducked into the stairwell of the nearby fire escape. They kept the fire escape door open no more than a quarter of an inch so they could see if it was the two occupants of room 632. They gradually came into view down the long hallway.

Jack froze. He felt his chest tighten and somehow made it down the stairs without knowing how he got there. He found himself squatting on the landing as Geoff Entwhistle crouched over him.

"What happened to you? See a ghost?"

"No, I know those guys," he whispered as he tried catching his breath. "The blonde guy is Sky Muncey, quarterback of the Cornell football team, and the dark haired guy is Sam Wainwright...his wide receiver. Shit, what do we do now?" They went down the fire escape.

"I'll call Bishop at the RCMP," said Geoff.

"Why him?"

"They've committed a federal crime."

"Really?"

"Yeah. It's illegal to carry a firearm in a National Park. That's enough to hold them until we get to the bottom of the bloody knife."

They eventually made it to Jack's office, where Geoff took over Jack's desk.

"Sarge? It's Entwhistle at the Chateau. We've got a situation here. We have a couple of guests with a 9 millimetre Smith & Wesson. We need you fast. They're presently in their room 632. You'd better call for back up from Banff....no sirens...there's also a bloody knife involved."

Jack was terrified. He didn't want to leave his office. "Could you and the RCMP handle it from here? I don't know what the hell is going on, with me knowing them and all."

"Sure," said Geoff. "It's better we let them look after it from here, but they'll want to get a statement from us, and they'll need a reason to go up to the room."

"Just tell them that there had been a sighting of two people who were skipping out on all their hotel bills across the country, and that they had been spotted as fitting the description. Treat it as a fraud case and get them to produce some I.D. to clear their names. That's pretty simple," said Jack.

Sergeant Bishop and Constable Morrow appeared at Jack's office door within minutes and were given the accounts

of Sky Muncey and Sam Wainwright, alias Seth Miller and
Saul Weir. Jack had never seen Bishop in his regular policing
uniform. He had always been in his famous Red Serge tunic,
complete with flat-brimmed Stetson and dark blue jodhpurs
with a thin yellow stripe that ran down the outside of the
pants until they tucked into the highly polished, calf-high
riding boots. The uniform was famous around the world
and represented everything that was good about Canada. But
today he was in his working uniform. They quickly discussed
how they were going to handle the situation, and Jack's idea
was put forward. "O.K., let's do it," said the Sergeant.

"If you don't mind, I'll just stay behind."

"Oh no you don't. You have to be there as a representative
of the hotel. We can't go up on our own. Don't worry, we'll
be right there with you. Let's go before they decide to leave."

Entwhistle, Morrow, Bishop and Jack emerged from the
office and proceeded towards the bank of elevators just past
the gift shop. A hush fell over the lobby. Jack was perspiring
heavily. He quickly glanced over at the bell desk, where
every bellman's eyes were on him. Gerry Graves gave him a
quizzical look, and Jack stuck out his left hand down by his
side reassuringly.

"Sixth floor," the sergeant said to Carole, and once they
were all in the elevator and the inner folding brass gate was
closed, he told her that he didn't want any of the six elevators
to pick up or drop off any guests or staff on the sixth floor until
he told her it was O.K. "Just tell people there's a malfunction
on the sixth which is being fixed, and that it won't be long.
And remember to tell the other elevator operators as soon as
you return to the lobby. "Do you understand?"

"Yes, sir." As usual there was the obligatory silence in the elevator, with Jack not knowing where to look. He noticed that Carole's white glove was not only dirty but had a hole in the thumb. He made a mental note to tell the chief engineer, to whom the elevator operators reported. As the elevator levelled off at the sixth floor and the doors opened, Miss Edith Cantwell, from San Diego, California, a wealthy spinster who had been coming to the Chateau for two weeks every year for the last twenty-five years, was waiting to get on. The four men stepped out of the elevator as Miss Cantwell marched in. The sergeant nodded his approval to Carole, as if to say, "This is the last, until I say so."

As the party proceeded down the long corridor towards room 632, Jack's stomach was in total knots, so much so that it was becoming painful. This was more than just simple butterflies. *What am I going to say to them, they'll obviously recognize me, they'll think that I've squealed on them. This carpet is getting threadbare, that exit sign is out, will the gun and knife still be there?* His mind was wandering frantically all over the place, and he was close to hyperventilating. Bishop noticed that Jack was walking slower than the rest and fell behind until Jack caught up.

"I want you to knock on the door, and as soon as it opens, step back and I'll take over from there."

"What am I supposed to say?"

"Tell them it's you, after all, you're the one who knows them."

"They're under false names. They don't know that I know they're here."

"Oh. Well, you'll think of something, and anyway, they might just open the door expecting the maid or someone."

The quartet reached the door and Sergeant Bishop

unsnapped the leather clasp on his holster, nodding to Jack to knock. All of a sudden Jack's butterflies left him, and he knocked on the door.

"Who is it?" came a voice from inside. It was Sky Muncey, there was no doubt in Jack's mind. He'd despised that voice ever since he'd met the jerk at the fraternity rushing party.

"Hotel plumber," blurted Jack. "There's a reported leak in your bathroom which is coming through the ceiling of the room below."

"Just a minute," came the reply as Jack heard the door unlock. He immediately stepped back and Sergeant Bishop moved into his place with his badge in his hand. Constable Morrow had his hand on his revolver handle and took a backup position. The door opened and Bishop stepped into the room.

"What the..."

"We've had a report that two young men were traveling across Canada and skipping out on their hotel bills, and the two of you seemed to fit the description. Now, if you can just give me some identification and settle up your bill to this date, we'll be on our way." Muncey and Wainwright started to look for something as Jack appeared in the doorway.

Sky looked at him and said, "You little weasel. I knew you could never be trusted."

"So Jack, I understand that you're familiar with these two gentlemen," said Bishop.

"That's Sky Muncey, quarterback of the Cornell University football team, and this is Sam Wainright, also from Cornell."

"You mean to tell me that they are not Seth Miller and

Saul Weir, as written on these registration cards? What have you got to say for yourselves, gentlemen?"

"Listen, here's my credit card. We were just having a little fun. This will clear up our account, and we'll be on our way."

"Not so fast, gentlemen. Let's just have a look around," the sergeant said as he headed towards the two gym bags.

"You don't have any right to search our bags without a warrant."

"I'm charging you both with fraud, and I can now seize and search anything of yours I want."

Sam Wainwright bolted for the door, only to be stopped by Morrow, who grabbed his arm, twisted him around, and slapped a set of handcuffs on him. Muncey was subsequently cuffed as well, and they were both told that they had the right to speak to a lawyer before being asked any questions. "Yeah, right, some Canadian dude, what the hell hope have we got of justice in this friggin' country?"

Sergeant Bishop put on a pair of leather gloves he had worn neatly folded on his belt and started to go through the first gym bag. He pulled out the large, unopened package of condoms. "These must have been bought on wishful thinking."

Entwhistle chuckled and Jack shuffled from one foot to the other, not wanting to make eye contact with the two Cornellians. He then heard some voices coming down the hall. He went to the door and saw four RCMP officers heading to the room.

"How did you know where we were?" Jack asked.

"Head bellman."

Jack felt much better now that he was with a total of six cops as well as Geoff Entwhistle. Bishop continued to root through the gym bag and gingerly pulled out the Smith & Wesson.

"Do you realize it's a criminal act to have a firearm in your possession in a National Park?"

"I have a licence..."

"You have squat!" asserted the sergeant. "And what's this?" He uncovered the bloodied towel and boning knife. Jack was going to say something about his knife but decided to keep quiet until later. The sergeant then searched the other bag and found a small black notebook with the names of hotels the pair had stayed at and the names they had used at each hotel, each crossed off. Chateau Lake Louise had the names of Seth Miller and Saul Weir.

"O.K., we're going to have to close this room as being out of bounds due to a police investigation. There is to be absolutely nobody, chambermaid, or anybody else permitted to enter this room until I clear it, and it could be a few days until that happens."

He continued, "Now you two are going to be taken to the city jail in Calgary until you've had a chance to speak to a lawyer and the charges are finalized and read in court. Now, Mr. Souster, I presume you don't want these two paraded through the lobby. How would you like us to take them out?" Jack suggested that they bring the cruisers up to the steward's loading dock and that they all go down the service elevators. Then Jack had a strange feeling that someone else had appeared at the door.

"Young man, What is going on here?"

"It's O.K, Miss Cantwell, everything is fine."

"Fine, how can you tell me that everything is fine when I see six policemen in the room directly opposite my suite? I had to take the elevator to the seventh floor and walk down those filthy uncarpeted fire stairs because there is no service to my floor. Do you realize how long I've been coming to this hotel, and now I'm treated to having a couple of thugs in a room almost adjoining mine. Look at them, just a couple of lowly thugs, I just feel filthy, this is outrageous! I want my suite changed...but not until after I have my tub!" Her tone was one of total indignation as she tried to peer around one of the officers to see who else was in room 632.

Jack knew that the hotel was overbooked and that there would be no way he could change the irate spinster's room; now room 632 was out of order, which would mean that they would be another room short. He mollified Miss. Cantwell by suggesting he treat her to dinner and that he would love to join her. This he knew would make her feel very special, since she loved to be treated as a conspicuously eminent guest.

"I'll have Giorgio reserve a window table for us."

"I'll wear my mink stole, I find it getting a little chilly in the evenings."

"I'm looking forward to it," lied Jack. "I just love to hear your stories, because they tell me so much of the history of the hotel and the old days." *She's really chuffed now,* he thought as she turned, went across the hall and entered her suite. "Until seven thirty."

Two of the constables had already left to retrieve the cruisers and drive them up to the loading dock. That left a party of seven, two in handcuffs, proceeding down the hall to the service area and down the large elevator, which held all of them. Sergeant Bishop had said that he'd be in touch with Jack in the morning.

As Sky and Sam were put in the back seat of their cruisers,

one car for each, Sky looked at Jack and said, "You watch your back, weasel, I've got your number."

Bishop said, "Shall we add threatening to your list of felonies and misdemeanours? Just keep it up, young man."

Jack requested that Bishop allow him to process Muncey's American Express card in order to cover his account. He called it in for authorization, and the quarterback had to be temporarily relieved of his handcuffs while he signed his receipt. As he put an illegible scribble on the piece of paper, he gave Jack a menacing look. At that, they all got into their respective cruisers and headed off to the Lake Louise detachment office to fill out some paperwork, and to the Calgary Jail for processing. It was the last time the two Cornellians would see each other until their court date.

Jack headed back to his office, passing the elevators and telling them that the sixth floor was now open. "O.K., Gerry told us a few minutes ago." Jack smiled. He continued to his office to meet with Geoff Entwhistle and Craig Simpson to rehash the day's events. Then he called Miss Krantz, the head housekeeper, to advise her that room 632 was not to be touched and that it was a police order.

"Believe me, Hilda, you will not lose your job if the room is not made up. Mr. MacIntyre has gone salmon fishing in B.C., and I'll explain everything to him when he returns."

He spent the next hour talking about everything that had taken place, and his mind was flooded with things to do and people to call. "Geoff, what about the knife? I'm sure that's mine, and I reported it stolen to the campus security office."

"You've got to tell Bishop as soon as possible. There's no question about that."

– 15 –

"Clay, sorry it's so late," Jack said, looking at his watch and remembering the two-hour time difference, "and I'm sorry to disturb you at home. It's Jack Souster, and something has just happened out here at Lake Louise that is really strange." He explained what had just happened with Sky Muncey and Sam Wainwright, the murder on the Canadian, and his boning knife found in one of their gym bags. "I'm just wondering if there might be some connection between these guys and Colin's situation."

"You might be on to something, what's the sergeant's telephone number?" Jack promised to send Clay everything he could find out. He then called Ruth and gave her the same information.

"There's no doubt in my mind that Colin's being framed," said Ruth.

"But these guys aren't smart enough to do this on their

own. There's something or someone much bigger than we know." They both decided to sleep on it, and Jack would try and glean as much information as he could from the sergeant, knowing that Geoff Entwhistle would have his ear.

April was closing up the Poppy Room. "Now tell me, what the hell were you trying to do this afternoon?" He startled her as she was sweeping under the counter.

"What?"

"You know what!" he scolded. "Going out riding with two total strangers. Especially after you complained to me that you were being followed and you promised me that you would only go riding with me or someone we mutually knew."

"But they were guests of the hotel, and they told me how much they loved horses and the freedom of riding in the mountains. You know that feeling, Jack."

"Well, let me tell you about what we found in your two friends' room. A 9 millimetre Smith & Wesson handgun and a very sharp chef's boning knife wrapped in a blood-soaked towel. They're now in the Calgary jail."

Tears welled up in April's eyes and she started to sob. Jack went around the counter to comfort her. She was now shaking, and Jack had to get a stool so that she could sit down. He called Mandy next door in the Glacier Lounge if she could get someone to be with April, as he had to have dinner with Miss Cantwell. Jack promised to see April back in Fairview after his dinner and that she was to promise to stay with someone until he returned. Mandy assured him that she was getting off duty in half an hour, so she would stay with April.

*   *   *

Jack felt that the staff residences were firetraps, having been built solely of wood, decades ago. His position allowed him to go onto the women's floors, but other male staff members were restricted. That was not to say that these rules were not broken from time to time. The Rotunda was the comfortable common area with numerous couches, coffee tables, a ping pong table over in one corner and a couple of dartboards. It was covered entirely in a dark wood paneling made up of thin pine slats, darkened by age. There was a magnificent stone fireplace that was lit whenever there was a staff party or the ever-popular hootenanny happening, or whenever someone had the initiative to simply warm up the room. Jack always felt that a fireplace was the emotional center of a room. There was a large bay window overlooking the lake, rivalling any view the guests would have. April was waiting for him, curled up on a couch watching a houseman laying a fire so that he and his girlfriend could spend some quiet moments together warmed by the flickering flames.

"Hi, how are you doing?" he said as he sat down beside her. She pulled her feet in closer to her to make some room for him.

"I'm scared, I don't know what to do."

"Personally, I have a funny feeling that your worries are over." He told her everything that had happened that day, including that he personally knew the two who were arrested. He continued to talk about Colin and his problems, and that he had actually written her dad, hoping that there was something that he might be able to do.

"Jack, I wish I could help, but I don't get involved in anything that my father does. In fact, I hate politics."

"I can appreciate that, and I didn't mention your name for that very reason."

They talked for a good hour and a half, until she fell asleep in Jack's arms. He just sat there looking at the fire. Twice a bus boy and a dishwasher entered the residence and seeing him, immediately turned around and left. He smiled to himself as he quietly stroked April's hair.

Harold McIntyre, the general manager, had returned from his fishing trip and was filled in on what had transpired since he had been away. He congratulated Jack on getting the payment for the account, because "That's all that really matters."

McIntyre was soon to be retired, and it was obvious he was just biding his time until the final day came. Jack admired him. He had started as a bellhop in 1929 when the Royal York Hotel was built and over the years had worked himself up to a senior management position, all with no education. Jack knew that times were changing for the hospitality industry, and with schools like Cornell, the University of Michigan, Ryerson in Toronto and many others in Europe, boards of directors were not going to entrust multimillion properties to someone without an education. Sergeant Bishop arrived just as the meeting was breaking up. Jack and Geoff Entwhistle took him up to room 632 so that he could glean any evidence possible before turning the room over to the hotel.

"I think we've got a couple of bad dudes here. Have you got an April Cadeau, the prime minister's daughter, working here?"

"Yes, why?"

"Her name was in the little black book we found along with some other names already scratched off." Jack's legs went limp. He sat down on the bed then told the sergeant about what he knew of Sky Muncey and Sam Wainwright, that he thought the boning life with the initials JAS was his, and how he had reported it stolen not only to the hotel school but also to the Cornell police. He coughed and started to shake a little. His mouth went dry and he asked Entwhistle to get him a glass of water from the bathroom. He had absolutely nothing to hide, but he was terrified that the boning knife would implicate him in the murders.

The sergeant, realizing Jack's fear, told him to take his time. They ordered some coffee from room service and Jack told everything that had happened to him from the last day at Cornell up to the present.

"There's no doubt that you'll have to testify, but that's not a big deal. I'll be in touch. I understand that Muncey has engaged the best and most expensive defence lawyer in Western Canada. He must have some bucks somewhere."

They ended the meeting and Jack called Hilda Krantz to let her know that the room could now be put back in order and cleaned. He also put a call in for Clive, who had already heard the basics from Clay and Colin.

"I'll look into a few things and see what I can find out," said Clive.

– 16 –

It was now mid August and just three weeks before Labour Day weekend, the end of the season for the hotel. The day was one of those dreary ones where the clouds came down and touched the mountains. You couldn't see any of the peaks. The hotel had been running very smoothly, and Harold McIntyre decided to take another week off.

"Do you want to go to Field tonight?" Gerry asked Jack.

"Why not? I'll see if Irene can lend me a car. Maybe Mandy and April would like to go as well."

After dinner the four climbed into the Brewster loaner and headed down the mountain, turning left at the ESSO station and west along the old #1 highway, across the Great Divide. The weather had closed right in, the road was slick and the windshield wipers were slapping time to their own beat. The conversation was lively. The four friends were all looking forward to an evening of relaxation and laughing at some of the things that happened over the summer. Suddenly Jack noticed a car approaching from the rear. Headlights splayed out on the back window, making the raindrops look like sparkling diamonds.

"Shit, this guy's really moving," said Jack. The car was soon on his back bumper. It hit the rear end and then backed off. "What the hell was that? I think he's trying to run us off the road."

"Slow down, Jack," yelled April.

"Hell no, I've got to shake this guy." The pursuing car came up and hit theirs again. Jack gunned it, and after a hundred feet or so, he slammed on the brakes, knowing that there was a sharp hairpin switchback directly in front them. The car started to fishtail to the right around the corner as it dropped with the steep grade of the sharp bend.

The right front wheel caught the soft shoulder, which caused the rear end to almost jackknife, but Jack was able to finally get control and bring the car back in line with the road. He caught a glimpse in his rear-view mirror as the pursuing vehicle went straight ahead, through the guard rail, and jumped into the steep grade of the mountain, clipping off the tops of some firs and pines in the way. He slowed down, went left around the next switchback, and found the offending car on its roof in front of them with its wheels still spinning and a thin whiff of exhaust threading skywards. Jack looked up the mountain. The path the car had taken was clearly visible through the trees and brush. He figured that it must have nosedived into a gigantic boulder at the side of the road, causing it to flip in the air and settle on its roof. Gerry and Jack got out and with only the headlights of their car to guide them through the cloud, walked through the drizzle to see if the driver was alright.

"He's gone."

"How do you know?" asked Jack.

"Look at his neck, it's almost done a 180, and look how the roof has caved in. That tree branch couldn't have been placed more perfectly through his chest had either of us tried it with a sabre." Every window had been shattered. The back window had actually popped out in one shattered piece and come to rest in the muddy ditch at the side of the road. They checked to see if there was anyone else in the car. There wasn't.

"What the hell are we going to do?" asked Jack. "We can't leave the scene of an accident. Let's wait here for a few minutes and see if anyone comes along." After fifteen minutes they decided to continue on to Field, since it was closer than heading back to the hotel or the Village of Lake Louise. No one was going to hang around the scene, especially since there had been a sighting of a female grizzly and her cubs on the road earlier that week. They could call the police from the Monarch and drive back to meet them at the accident scene. The girls were quietly sobbing and hugging each other for comfort.

Once again, Jack saw Constable Morrow as they both arrived at the scene of chaos within minutes of each other. The flashing red and white lights created an eerie, throbbing glow in the thick mist, which was becoming more impenetrable as the night wore on. An ambulance, a tow truck and two more cruisers were called from Banff, which seemed to take twice as long as the forty-five minutes it actually did. The distant sirens were haunting in the drizzle and heavy fog. The constable had tried to get a pulse from the victim by touching his neck, but he confirmed what the four already knew. He went to his trunk, pulled out a yellow tarp, and put it over the windshield and side window to prevent anyone from looking at the grisly scene. He offered the girls a warm blanket from his survival kit. They thanked him profusely and returned to the car to keep warm. Meanwhile he asked Gerry and Jack to get into his cruiser to take down their statements. He had made note of the wrecked car's licence plate and called it in on his police radio. It was an Ontario plate, and within a matter of minutes the radio crackled. "Go ahead," said the constable.

"That plate's registered to a Mario Curozzo, and there's an outstanding warrant for his arrest."

"Well, we've got him, but he won't be answering any questions."

"Pardon?" crackled the radio.

"He's deceased. I've called an ambulance to take him to the morgue in Calgary."

Jack told him how he'd felt that he was being run off the road and showed the dents in his rear bumper, which looked as if they matched the dents on the front bumper of Curozzo's car. April, Mandy and Gerry all confirmed Jack's story.

"I'm going to have to impound your car until we can clear this matter up,"

"It's a loaner from Brewsters," said Jack.

"Well, you'll have to tell them what happened. It won't be more than a couple of days. You're just lucky the four of you didn't end up the same as your friend here," he said, motioning to the overturned car, which was now spilling oil and gas all over the road.

"No smoking!" Morrow shouted as he noticed Gerry pulling out a pack of Rothmans. "Do you want us all to join Buddy here in the morgue?"

The help from Banff finally arrived, and the constable arranged to have one of the officers take the four friends back to the hotel. "Nothing more you can do here." He didn't want them to witness the unpleasant task of extracting Curozzo's twisted corpse from the car.

When they got back to the hotel, they immediately went to the kitchen, and the girls asked the night room service chef if they could get some hot chocolate and a couple of grilled danishes. Jack and Gerry raided the chef's daily allotment of beer and picked up a bowl of mixed nuts. They went into the darkened dining room, which was lit only by some red exit signs and a pathway light shining through one of the windows. They talked about the evening's events, and April and Jack opened up about some of the things that had been happening.

"I think this guy tonight was gunning for me, not you," Jack tried to reassure April. Finally, they all decided they needed a good sleep, and the men walked the girls back to Fairview before Gerry went his way to Gables, the bellman's residence, and Jack to the hotel.

*   *   *

There was nothing about the previous night's accident in either the *Globe and Mail* or the *Calgary Herald*. Jack's favorite meal of the day was breakfast, where he could skim through the morning paper and take his time over a cup or two of coffee. This morning was not unlike any other, as he rose an extra half hour early so that he could enjoy the morning and gather his thoughts before he went on duty. He was expecting that a report from the RCMP would be forthcoming shortly regarding last night's accident. He went down to his office and checked the day's reservations, making note of anything or anyone special that required his attention. Sheila Cook, the head mail clerk, eventually brought the morning mail, having sorted out that which was obviously meant for reservations, which went to Craig Simpson. The accounting mail went to Chuck Woodruff, head accountant.

Sheila was a high school teacher in Red Deer, about halfway between Edmonton and Calgary. She was one of the more mature staff members, having graduated with a Bachelor of Education more than ten years ago. Jack always wondered how she was able to start well into the season and leave two weeks early so that it would fit into her school year, until someone told him that she had an annual torrid affair with Chuck which permitted her to call the shots and name her hours. She was very outspoken about what she thought were the "meager wages" of teachers and needing the summer job to "make ends meet."

Chuck Woodruff Jack knew as assistant accountant at the Royal York, and like Jack he was transferred out to Chateau Lake Louise every summer. Jack and Chuck had always gotten along well, but really had limited contact except when discussing some guest's account or some form of supplier's credit.

Sheila was not the most attractive person, at first glance. When at work she always wore her hair up in a bun and had extremely frumpy, heavy-framed granny glasses. However,

Jack once saw her sunning herself at the pool. She was wearing a very skimpy bikini with her long honey-blonde hair flowing back over the pillow of the chaise lounge, and not wearing the glasses. Jack did a double take, not recognizing her at first. She merely returned his second glance with a warm smile.

"Here's your mail, Jack," Sheila said as she put down a bundle of various sized and colored envelopes bound by a thick elastic band. "I think the top one is meant for April, but it's got your name on it. Why the prime minister's office would ever want to write to you is beyond me."

If there was one fault that Sheila had, it was her habit of editorializing on just about every piece of mail that might be of interest. It was August 13th, her last day before heading home to prepare for the year ahead. She was also not ever short on opinions and never afraid to express them. Jack had just thought at breakfast this morning that it was funny how he had not heard from the prime minister since he had written and figured that he probably never would. He quickly opened the letter, tearing it with his right index finger rather than wasting time searching for the letter opener.

Office of the Prime Minister
August 6, 1965

Dear Mr. Souster,

Thank you very much for your letter explaining the problems your friend, Colin MacDonald, is having in the United States of America. I regret there is nothing the Government of Canada can do to help Mr. MacDonald's situation. All Canadians, when travelling abroad

*must live within the laws of that particular country,
and when it is a democratically elected government,
we recognize all of their laws. There is nothing in our
extradition treaty with the U.S.A. specifying the return
of persons who have committed a criminal offense who
are subject to the death penalty be returned to Canada.*

*Please keep in mind that the United States of America
is Canada's largest trading partner and I would not
want to do anything to jeopardize this relationship. I
thank you for your letter and I look forward to your
continued support.*

Yours very truly,

Pierre Cadeau

Prime Minister of Canada

Jack put the letter down and stared at it. He couldn't
believe what he had just read. He had never felt so let down
in all of his life. His own government couldn't give a damn
about Colin. He thought about going down to the Poppy
Room to see April but decided to leave her out of it. He still
had to phone Clive and see if he could find out anything
about Mario Curozzo, the deceased driver of the car, who
had tried to run Jack off the mountain.

"I've got a contact in Toronto. He may be able to help. You
do get yourself into the middle of things. Keep well Jack, and
I'll say hi to Colin for you when I go to see him this afternoon.
Just got a couple of things to clear up," said the private eye.

Jack with his mind still on the letter from the prime
minister's letter, asked Sissy to patch him into the Green Line
to Calgary. Then he dialled the number for the *Calgary Herald*.

– 17 –

Jamie Sutherland was a young columnist for the *Herald*. A graduate of Carlton University's esteemed School of Journalism, he had his own by-line and was well read. Jack had met him when he had come up from Calgary to cover the arrival of the Duke and Duchess of Kent.

"Jamie, it's Jack Souster of Chateau Lake Louise. I think I've got a story for you. It's got some political overtones to it and I'm not sure if that's the sort of thing you like to write about. If not, perhaps you could point me to someone who would like to hear it."

"Jack, I've been dying to get my hands on something political, this being an election year." The two decided to have dinner at the hotel the following night.

"My treat, and if you don't want to drive back home, I'll hold a room for you. It may not be the best, as we're sold out, but it'll at least be a bed."

Jack arranged for a quiet table on the Pipestone side of the dining room, so named because it supposedly looked over the Pipestone Range of mountains, but in reality the windows faced a hill of scrub brush leading up to a path linking the hotel and the staff residences. The waitresses who had been late for work, had not ironed their uniforms or had somehow otherwise gotten into the maitre'd's bad books, were assigned to the Pipestone tables because that is where the senior staff, tour escorts and guests who did not know the value of a decent tip were relegated. Jack was interested only in a quiet table where he could fill in the young writer on the problems of Colin MacDonald.

Sutherland arrived on time, and the two proceeded up to the Victoria Room, where they were ushered to their table. Giorgio was curious but didn't hang around, as he had a throng of paying guests at the door waiting to be seated. After they had ordered and started on their beers, Jack told the story of Colin and how he felt that he was being framed. Sutherland was well aware of the case, since it had been well-publicized nationally.

"How does this become political?" The question prompted Jack to bring out a copy of his letter to the prime minister and the reply he had received only yesterday.

"Wow, you mean Cadeau is more concerned about our trade relations with the U.S. than he is about the interests of our citizens?" exclaimed the young journalist.

"That's how I interpret it, and you're holding the evidence in your hands."

"Listen," Jamie said, "I'll make notes during dinner, and then if you can just give me a desk somewhere, I'll write the story. If I phone it in before eleven o'clock, I'll be able to make tomorrow's first edition. Then, again, thanks for the offer, but I think I'll drive home and meet with the editor."

Sutherland asked many questions and made quick notes. He wrote so fast that Jack thought that he must be using shorthand. After dinner, he declined coffee, so they went to Jack's office, where Jamie would have some peace and quiet to write his story. In the meantime, Jack got the key to the accounting office, since it housed the only photocopier in the hotel, and photocopies of the prime minister's letter were important to the story.

*   *   *

'TRADE MORE IMPORTANT THAN CITIZEN RIGHTS: PRIME MINISTER'

blasted the headline in the *Calgary Herald* the next day. Sutherland had gotten all of his facts straight. Jack nervously read every word with utmost attention. There was no doubt that the story was definitely slanted to Colin's side, giving all of his hockey records and achievements, the lost contract with the Maple Leafs, and it was worded in such a way that the prime minister couldn't refute it. There was a picture of Colin in his Cornell hockey uniform on skates with his stick firmly planted on the ice, the same picture that was hanging in Johnny's Big Red. Jack was quoted a number of times, and the letter from the prime minister was printed in its entirety. It mentioned that Jack was Assistant Manager of Chateau Lake Louise, which concerned Jack, who was sure that head office wouldn't want the hotel chain drawn into the debate. He was shocked back into reality as the phone ring. He thought that Sissy must have given it an extra long ring.

"Have you read the story yet?" It was Jamie Sutherland.

"Wow, it's fantastic," said Jack.

Sutherland continued, "Canadian Press has picked it up, so it will be national tomorrow, depending on which papers, radio and TV pick it up. So expect a few phone calls. If the Liberals thought that they had a chance of one seat west of Ontario, they've got another thing coming to them."

"I can't thank you enough."

"Not a problem...just have the beer on ice the next time I'm up there."

Jack picked up the phone and gave Sissy the number for the Elmira Correctional Facility. It seemed to take forever for the guard to get Colin to come to the phone.

"Hi, guy, how's it goin?"

"'Bout the same. What's up?"

"Well, I've got good news and bad news. What do you want first?"

"Well, I'm pretty used to bad news, so let me have it."

"The prime minister has refused to offer any help. I'm pretty pissed off, and I don't know where to go from here."

"What's the good news?"

"I met with a reporter from the *Calgary Herald* last night, and the story is headline news. It really makes the P.M. look like a total 'A' Hole. You never know, it's an election year, and maybe with enough pressure on him, he might do something."

"Don't hold your breath, but at least I've got you, Clay, and Clive in my corner."

"You've got a lot more than that, I can assure you. Just keep your head up, and you may be getting a few calls from the press...you never know."

"Thanks, pal, great talking to you...Jack, I mean it." Colin added, "I really appreciate everything you're doing for me."

"No problem, take care," Jack added as they hung up.

"CBC Radio is on line two," Sissy said as Jack punched the flashing button. They wanted to interview him for their national radio program "This Country in the Morning." Jack knew that it had a huge audience, and he was also aware that the CBC, Canada's national broadcaster, was particularly upset with the present government due to the fact that they had just been turned down for an increase in funding. They were going to use Colin's story to make the government look bad, which was just fine with Jack.

The interview went well, and life returned to normal at the hotel. Jack had a meeting with Chef Ernst Sommstrum to go over his latest food costs, which were very good. They also discussed the "Closing Menu," which was designed to create as small an inventory as possible once Labour Day arrived and the hotel would be closing down for the season. They had some latitude, since anything remaining would be transported to the sister resort the Banff Springs Hotel, which was slated to stay open for two more weeks than the Chateau. Chuck Woodruff would make the necessary debits and credits, which would be reversed when the hotel opened again in the spring of 1966.

"There's a television crew here to talk to you," Sissy said when she called the chef's office, interrupting a meeting that Jack had always enjoyed. Chef would usually have something specially prepared for them while they chatted; seared fois gras with melba toast was today's treat.

"I'll be right down. Just ask them to wait a minute. Thanks, Sissy."

It was the fledgling CTV network wanting to interview Jack about Colin MacDonald. Jack had never appeared on television before, but the questions were pretty direct and simple. The interviewer asked to see the letter from the prime minister, and Jack was only too happy to oblige. Within half an hour, a CBC television news truck showed up for yet another interview. They were a little annoyed to hear that CTV had already beaten them to the punch. By this time, word had gotten out among the staff of the hotel that Jack had turned into somewhat of a celebrity.

The story was carried on both national television newscasts later that evening. Jack had calls from his mother, Consuela and Heather that evening, all saying that they had seen the interviews and that he had come across well and credible.

"Jack, I'm so proud of you. I'm sure that Colin must be very thankful," said his mother.

The following morning at 6:15, he had a call from Liam in Cape Breton, who had forgotten the three-hour time difference.

"Jack, it's in the *Halifax Herald* and the *Cape Breton Post* this morning. Front page news. The phone hasn't stopped ringing. Everyone wants to know about the fundraiser and if there are still tickets left. I've given the two papers your number. I hope you don't mind, but you're better talking to them than I am."

"No, that's O.K. Are you going to be able to get enough lobsters?"

"Oh, yeah, you needn't worry about that, but I'm afraid Ocean Foam Fisheries is going to have to start looking elsewhere for their supplies for a few weeks, 'cause the boys are already talking about building their own pound to keep Colin's lobsters in. Looks good on them anyway. They're a bunch of bloodsuckers anyway. They've never paid the fishermen a fair price for their catch, and if the boys can help Colin and screw them, so much the better."

"O.K.," said Jack, not really wanting to create a war between the fishermen and the wholesalers, but as long as things were well in hand, that was all he cared about.

Jack had no sooner hung up than the *Cape Breton Post* called. He spent almost half an hour on the phone with reporter Alex McTaggart explaining everything about Colin, his family, his education, his prowess as a hockey player, his incarceration and the prime minister's lack of interest.

"He's not going to do that to one of our sons," the reporter said with great indignation. "This is an election year, and I'll do everything in my power to see that those bastards don't get into power again. At least not down here."

Jack was well aware that the Liberal Party held most of the federal seats in the Canadian Parliament, especially in Cape Breton. "The Island," as it was known locally, was continually financially strapped. There was talk of the closing of the coal mines, and the only people that made any money from the fisheries were the wholesalers. On top of that there was CapCo, a local diesel engine manufacturer that always seemed to be going to Ottawa with requests for financial bailouts. Locally it was known as "Cap In Hand Company."

Federal subsidies were just a way of life for Cape Breton, but blood is thicker than water, and Liam, Archie, Andrew,

Alex and thousands of others would give up every penny of federal subsidies if it meant helping one of their own. The rest of Canada didn't understand the resolve and the spirit of the Maritimers, especially the people of Cape Breton. The island had some of the most beautiful scenery in the world, only to be surpassed by the hearts of its sons and daughters.

The *Halifax Herald* called next. Jack was beginning to feel like a tape recorder. He was getting tired of telling the same story over and over again but knew that it had to be told in order to create public pressure on the government. It was Colin's only hope, or he'd face the possibility of the death penalty in New York State.

Due to the phone calls, Jack missed his much-relished breakfast and went straight to his office. He had checked the reservations for the day and was just about to go up to housekeeping to see Hilda Krantz, hoping to talk to her about the tardiness of rooms being made up, especially on the third floor. Miss Krantz was never very good at receiving criticism, especially when it concerned a complaint about "her girls." Just as Jack was leaving his office, April appeared in tears.

"What's the problem? Come in, sit down." He motioned her to a chair, and rather than sit behind his desk, he pulled up the second chair in the office and sat beside her and took her hand. "What's going on?'

"I just had a call from my dad and he wants me to quit and go home. He asked if I knew you, and I said yes, and then he told me to tell you to stop talking to the press and that his letter to you was 'in confidence' and was not for the public. He's pretty upset," she continued between sniffles and tears. "I told you that I didn't want to get involved."

"It's your father who's involving you, not me. I would

never do that to you. You know that. I don't understand why he wants you to quit."

"Because he thinks that I'll get involved in your friend's case and people will start asking me questions, and...you know how things are." April's next remark grabbed Jack by the stomach. "He said if you don't stop talking to the press, then he'll make sure that you'll never work again for any hotel in the country."

"He actually said that?" Jack said incredulously. *He's blackmailing me for my silence.* "Don't quit, let's just sit on this and think about it for awhile. Let's go for a ride after dinner tonight and get away from everyone and everything, maybe up to Lake Agnes or to the Plain of Six Glaciers. In the meantime, I'll just have Sissy screen my calls and take numbers from the press, and I can call them back later, depending on what I decide to do."

April dried her tears, and Jack gave her a little kiss on the side of her head. She left the room quietly. Jack sat down behind his desk and thought, *It's my job or Colin.*

"Yes, Sissy, who is it now?" Jack caught himself being a little short and apologized.

"It's Mr. Lawton from Head Office."

"O.K. Thanks, put him through."

"Hello, sir, it's Jack speaking,"

"I've just had a very disturbing call from the prime minister's office, and I want to see you in my office as soon as you can get a flight out. Call back and tell Heather when you'll be arriving, and I'll have someone meet you at the airport."

"Heather?" queried Jack.

"Yes, she quit. Couldn't handle the pressure at the bank,

and I couldn't handle the dipstick I hired to replace her. And Jack, if you know what's good for you, don't say another word to the press. That's an order. Do you understand?"

"Yes sir, I understand. I'll see you, hopefully, tomorrow." Jack hung up and put his head in his hands. He felt that he should have expected this, but had no idea that it would happen. He was now playing a game in the big leagues.

He arranged with April to get off early so that they could go for a long ride. He was able to get a seat on an early flight from Calgary that would get him into Toronto mid-afternoon, taking into consideration the time difference. He advised Harold McIntyre of what had transpired and that he would be off for a few days. The general manager was not pleased, because that meant that some of Jack's routine chores would have to be picked up by him. Craig Simpson chuckled when told that.

"I guess the old man isn't too pleased. That's going to mean that he's going to have to get up off his duff and do something for a change while he waits for that golden handshake." He continued, "Jack, you've got more balls than a brass monkey!" Craig had a knack for turning a hackneyed phrase around. "I'd no sooner take on the prime minister of Canada than try to swim the Atlantic. But if there's anyone that can do it, you can."

Jack and April met at the stables, and Ribbon had not been booked out. April was happy to take any horse that was available. She was an excellent rider and could get anything she wanted out of any horse. Jack was different. He had an affection for Ribbon that he didn't have for many other animals except Dylan, the family dog. They decided to ride up to the Lake Agnes Tea House, where they could sit and talk.

Lake Agnes was halfway up the Little Beehive and was cradled in one of the valleys as you headed for the summit. The lake was the epitome of pristine glacial waters and supplied all of the water for the Chateau, staff residences, Brewster stables and Deer Lodge. With saddles creaking, they headed out of the corral and down to the path that led between the Chateau and the lake. It was magnificent. The gardens were immaculate, and the poppies were in full bloom. Reflections of light from the swimming pool splashed upon the massive wind-guard windows surrounding the pool. Tears welled up in his eyes as Jack realized in his gut that this might be the last time he would be admiring with pride a building he had come to know and love. They passed a number of tourists who were either coming or going on their hike up to the Plain of Six Glaciers or Lake Agnes. They were quiet and just enjoyed the ride up the mountain, nodding to the odd hiker.

Once at the top, they took the horses over to the lake for a well deserved drink. Ribbon walked right in just up to her forelocks. They tied the horses up at the hitching post and loosened their cinches.

April and Jack started to climb the steps up past the solid stone foundation to the log teahouse and the large outdoor patio. Jack had to stop halfway up the steps to catch his breath. If Lake Louise was a mile above sea level, as advertised, then Jack felt Lake Agnes was a mile and a half above. The lack of oxygen and the climb up the steps had a definite effect on his heart and its ability to pump enough oxygen from his lungs to the rest of his body. He held on to the handrail and took a quick glance at his fingernails. There was a definite purple hue to them, and he stayed there a minute until he caught his breath, taking in the magnificent view of the valley floor below him. Lake Louise now looked no bigger than the bathroom sink, yet its incredible color made it look like a giant stone in the most magnificent ring that God had ever made. Jack soon joined April at a table by the railing so they could keep an eye on the horses and still enjoy the superb scenery.

"You all right?" asked April as Jack joined her.

"Yeah, why?"

"Your lips are all purple."

"Yeah, well, that's just me. You know all about that."

"Oh Jack, I didn't mean to…" she said as she grabbed his hand.

"Don't worry about it, Everything's fine," he reassured her.

"Hi, guys, what'd you care for?" asked Gunda when they arrived. Gunda Evanson had been running the Tea House for as long as Robert Rhind had been playing the piano. She was a fixture and featured in just about every tourist publication produced by the Province of Alberta. She was of Nordic and Germanic stock and loved every piece of "her mountain" and every drop of "her lake." Her long, honey-blonde hair was braided and rolled up and wrapped in a large ring around the crown of her head. Jack had gotten to know Gunda because she had all of her supplies delivered to the Chateau. If Jack was ever going to take a ride up to the Tea House, he would always check to see if there was any mail for her. He always threw in a current newspaper. Today it was a copy of yesterday's *Calgary Herald* and *Globe and Mail,* with Jack's story blasted all over both front pages.

"A couple of your tea biscuits with a little extra Devonshire cream," he requested.

"Oh, I'm always torn between your tea biscuits and...have you got any of your cranberry-lemon muffins?" asked April.

"Yes, m'am," replied Gunda in her thick Norwegian accent.

"Let's share a pitcher of ice cold lemonade with lots of ice."

Jack started his explanation. "Mr. Lawton had a call from your father's office, and I have to fly back tomorrow to meet with him. Your father's office called him and told him to make me stop talking to the press or something like that. I have a funny feeling that I've worked my last day at the Chateau."

April's tears started to flow again. She said, "I hate him, I hate him." Other hikers enjoying their respite stared at the couple as Jack moved his chair around to be beside April and put his left arm over her shoulder.

"It's O.K. It's not your fault, and it really isn't his fault either. It's all my fault, and I just have to figure out what to do. I'll know better when I meet Mr. Lawton." April gradually pulled herself together and they started to talk about some of the funny things that had happened over the summer.

"What if I did something that would embarrass him even more? Maybe I should run as a Conservative," laughed April, "then I could really torture him every day in question period."

Gunda refused to give the two of them a bill, and Jack asked her to sit down for a minute while he explained everything to her. "I have an old friend," she said with a glint in her eye. The distant look in her eyes suggested there might have been a relationship years ago. "Jurgen Nordstrum, he's Norway's ambassador to Canada."

"Wow, girl, this is getting too far out of hand. Let's leave him out of it."

"Listen, you are already up to your rear end in horse sheeet," she said, adding, "If you want to come out smelling like a rose, you're going to need all the help you can get."

"I don't know. Why don't you wait until we see how things unfold in the next couple of days."

They all got up and Jack gave Gunda a hug. They got the horses ready and started down the trail. Jack took in every breathtaking view and sucked in every cool clear pine scent that could fill his nostrils. They went back to the stables, unsaddled the horses, took off their bridles and put on their halters. April had to get back to the hotel for a meeting in the steward's office. Jack got a curry brush and started to curry Ribbon down, not something he often did, but this day was special. He put the brush down and went up to her head and she nuzzled her muzzle into his armpit. *How do animals know that something is up?* he thought. Her big brown eye was staring at him and there was a touch of goop oozing from the corner. He wiped it off with his thumb and then grabbed her gently under her jaw and kissed her on the cheek. He was now in tears. With one last pat on the side of her neck as he rubbed her ear, he slowly turned and started walking towards the gate of the corral, hoping that no one would see him. He felt that someone was following him, and as he reached the gate he felt a soft nudge in the middle of his back. It was Ribbon. He gave her another kiss on her velveteen muzzle.

"Goodbye girl, you keep well. Luv ya." Then he was off through the gate, heading down the laneway towards the hotel as she stood looking longingly over the top cedar rail of the fence.

The flight left Calgary at nine in the morning and arrived at 2:40 Toronto time.

Jack recognized Tom the doorman, who often filled in as a chauffeur whenever the hotel needed one. "Hi Jack, your meeting with Mr. Lawton is at ten tomorrow morning. He's booked you a room for the night." Jack wasn't sure how to interpret the phrase "the night." Would he be returning to Lake Louise right after their meeting, or would that be the end of his wonderful but short career with CP Hotels? He had left instructions with Craig Simpson to throw everything into his trunk, which he had left behind, and ship it to his parents' address should the meeting not go well. He checked into the hotel, greeting old friends who were on duty. He dropped his bag off in his room and immediately went down to the travel agency on the concourse level to see a very surprised Consuela.

She jumped out of her chair and came running over to him as he walked past the large glass wall and through the open door.

"Why didn't you tell me?"

"I didn't know until yesterday. I'll tell you all about it tonight...that's if you're free? I hope I'm not too presumptuous? We can order in a pizza or something, and we'll pick up a little vino on the way home."

"That's great, but I don't have anything for breakfast."

"I can't stay the night, I have a meeting with Mr. Lawton first thing."

"Perfect, we'll pick up some wine on the way back to your place. I haven't had pizza since I last saw you. I hope that you haven't had anything else that I give you," she said with a smile.

The reunited lovers went over all of the events while enjoying their meal, a double cheese pizza accompanied by some Chianti. Jack expressed his worry about the outcome of the next morning's meeting.

"Don't worry, things are so busy at the agency that I was thinking of hiring another agent. I'll teach you the business."

Consuela's warmth and compassion led to an early evening of tender lovemaking, after which Jack fell asleep. Consuela covered him up and kissed him goodnight.

The alarm went off at seven and Jack jumped up in a start. "What the..." They decided to grab a cab. Jack would shower and change when he got to the hotel then treat her to breakfast in the coffee shop.

Jack arrived early for his meeting with Gordon Lawton at the head office. Heather greeted him with a big smile then gritted her teeth. "This isn't going to be fun. I'll just warn you that he's not very happy."

"Coffee after?" Jack suggested.

"Sure, if you're still up to it."

That comment told Jack that the worst was going to happen. He braced himself for the final exit and gave himself a minute to decide how he would handle the situation and to make sure he'd be able to control his emotions.

"Send him in," instructed the CEO over the intercom. Jack entered the office and noticed that nothing had changed, except that he was not greeted with a handshake.

"Have a seat." There was a pause. "Now, what's this all about? You've got yourself involved defending a serial killer... and getting the prime minister involved. Do you realize what this has done to our business?" Lawton continued, barely taking a breath, "This is an election year, and the prime minister is making four scheduled stops in Toronto over the next three months. He was booked in here, on all four dates, and he has now cancelled and booked into the King Eddy."

The King Edward Hotel was the Royal York's biggest competitor. "Next year the Liberals are having their convention at Maple Leaf Gardens, and they've booked this as their headquarters hotel. The prime minister called me personally and suggested that if you continued to be employed by CP, he would pull all government business from all of our properties. I'm sorry, Jack, but I have no alternative but to let you go effective immediately. May I suggest that you grow up and forget about doing what you think is right. This is most disappointing, as I felt that you had a promising career ahead of you. I had some wonderful plans for you, but my hands are tied. I just hope that I can repair all the damage that you've done. Oh, and one more thing, after you check out, please do not set foot on any of our properties until this whole thing has blown over."

"I'm sorry, sir, to have disappointed you. Thank you very much for the opportunity. I've truly enjoyed working for you," Jack said as he got up and extended his hand.

Lawton looked at the hand and nodded, picked up a pen and started signing a pile of correspondence that had been sitting on the left side of his desk. Jack turned and walked out of the office, more disappointed in a man he had always admired than in losing his job. The swift dismissal only strengthened his resolve.

"It looks like Murray's for coffee," Heather said, referring to a family restaurant next to the hotel.

"You heard everything?" said Jack.

"Yep, he left the intercom on when he called you in. I'm so sorry, Jack. The prime minister didn't give him any choice. These guys play hardball, and if you think that's bad, you should see what I've just left. This is nothing to what I think is going on over there."

They agreed to meet at Murray's in half an hour, which would give him enough time to check out. He only had yesterday's clothes and his shaving kit to pack, and he decided to call Craig Simpson at the Chateau to let him know what had transpired. He figured he'd charge the call to his room as an act of defiance.

"Hi, Craig. Well, as I expected, the hammer has fallen. I'm no longer employed by CP Hotels. Would you mind packing and shipping my stuff to the address I gave you?"

"You've got to be kidding," the jovial front office manager said. "These guys couldn't manage their own sock drawer if their lives depended on it. Jack, I'm sorry, what more can I say, we'll all miss you. I'd patch you through to McIntyre, but he's off on another one of his mystery trips. Keep in touch."

"I will for sure. Thanks again for everything." They hung up, and Jack all of a sudden felt very much alone.

Heather ordered a bran muffin with her coffee, and Jack was so upset that he couldn't eat anything, so he stuck to his double-double. They talked about Colin, about the government's stance when it came to helping citizens outside the country, and they talked about the press coverage Jack had received that eventually led to his dismissal.

"What the hell am I supposed to do? Just lie down and do nothing and let my best friend face the death penalty?"

"By the way,' asked Heather, "do you know anything about a couple of kids that were arrested out west?"

"Yeah, why? It was all over the news. I was involved in it and probably will be called to testify. Why do you ask?"

"We never heard anything about it down here, but this banker jerk a couple of weeks ago flies out of a meeting and yelled something about, 'You tell your boys up in Ottawa to let those kids out or all hell's going to break loose.' At that point I'd had enough. The guy actually scared me, and that's when I phoned Mr. Lawton to see if I could have my job back."

They shared a parting hug and a quick kiss on the cheek, and Jack crawled into a cab to take him home. This would be a surprise for his parents. They had no idea that he was even in town. There was nobody home, and Jack remembered that Thursday was his mom's day to volunteer with the Hospital Auxiliary, and she would be working in the gift shop. The key, as usual, was under the front door mat and he made a mental note to have his parents change the location, because he was sure that every burglar in the city, if not in the entire country, always looked under the door mat for the spare key.

Once inside, he decided to call Ruth. She was excited to hear from him but saddened to learn of his predicament.

"Give me a couple of days at home with my folks, and I'll come down for a visit. Tell Colin that I'll be down and tell Clay and Clive as well."

"Jack, it will be so good to see you again. I'm sure that Colin will be excited to see you. He's been a little depressed lately."

"I haven't got much money, and I'm going to see if Mrs. Smithyes will put me up for a few nights." After hanging up he thought that he should check in with Liam to see how the fundraiser was going.

"Jack, the press we're getting is unbelievable. We have to put on a second night to meet the demand. We've decided to go for the Sunday."

"I didn't think you'd have the population to fill the arena twice," said Jack.

"They're coming from all over: Sydney Mines, Louisburg, New Waterford, Glace Bay, Mabou, Port Hawkesbury, St. Petes. The entire island, believe me, Jack, is coming out to support Colin. And guess what? The Liberals are taking a real hit in the polls down here. Also Gerry Mosher in Digby wants to talk to you." It was obvious that Liam was excited at the success he was having. He gave Jack Gerry Mosher's phone number, which Jack dialled as soon as he said goodbye to Liam.

"Gerry Mosher?" Jack asked.

"That's me, boy."

"Gerry, it's Jack Souster. Liam Macdonald said that you'd like to speak to me." The two men talked for over an hour about getting a fundraiser started for Colin down in the south western part of Nova Scotia, around Digby, the French shore, Weymouth and Yarmouth. As Digby was famous for scallops, he thought that it would be appropriate to have a scallop dinner. Gerry had already talked to O'Meara Fisheries Limited, and Tim O'Meara, grandson of the founder, who had heard what was happening to Ocean Foam Fisheries up in Cape Breton, told him that he'd call a meeting of the scallop draggers association and see what kind of a deal they could strike up. "Perhaps the boys will take less per pound than they're getting now, and we'll give them to you at cost." They talked about using the Digby Arena, entertainment, the best date, table and chair rentals, kitchen facilities and volunteers. "Oh, there's no shortage of those," he assured Jack. So it was decided that they would have the Digby scallop dinner on the same date as the lobster dinner in Cape Breton, October 9th, Thanksgiving weekend.

Jack decided to check out his car and give it a wash while he was waiting for his parents to come home. Dylan was tied up to his long clothesline. Jack remembered a saying about Siberian Huskies: "*They run in one direction, only... away.*" He couldn't count the number of times that Dylan had snuck out of the house between the legs of some unsuspecting visitor and go missing for days, until the SPCA would call the phone number stitched in his collar. It was futile chasing him, because he thought that it was just a big game.

His mother arrived home first and jumped out of her car.

"What are you doing home?"

"It's a long story, but the short version is that I've been

fired, and I'll tell you the long version of it over dinner when Dad gets home."

She asked him so many questions that she knew the full story well before they sat down for the pot roast, and he had to recount all of the events again for his father.

"Never liked the man from the day I met him," she said at least three times during the dinner.

"I've got enough money for at least three months if I can stay here, and I'll be happy to contribute to the food. Consuela's offered me a job whenever I want it, but right now I want to help Colin as much as I can."

"Jack, you're always welcome here. This is your home. We're behind you one hundred and ten percent. You know that."

"I know that, and thanks. I'm keeping track of all my phone calls, and there will be a lot, so we'll tally them up at the end of the month. I'll be here for a couple of days, and then I'm off to Ithaca and Elmira."

He thanked his parents again, helped clear the table and did the dishes with his mom. She washed and he dried and put away.

"Mrs. Smythyes? It's Jack, would you have a room for a few days? I have to come back to Ithaca, and I don't have too much money so I couldn't afford a motel." He heard the TV in the background and knew that she had a baseball game on, probably a Yankees/Red Sox game.

"Jack," she answered, "I'll have none of that. You can have your old room back, and I won't charge you. I have it rented for the upcoming year, but the new renter won't be moving in until after Labour Day, but it's all yours until then. It'll be nice to see you again." Jack was thankful for the generous offer.

"Just one thing," she reminded him, "the same rules apply: no visitors of the opposite gender."

"I fully understand. Wouldn't think of it," he said, smiling. "What's the score?"

"Yankees 7, Red Sox 5, bottom of the 7th , Mickey Mantle's up, so I think that'll clinch it." Jack smiled, knowing that he had her pegged.

"I'll see you in a couple of days."

Jack kept himself busy around the house, walking Dylan, and spent both nights at home with his folks.

*   *   *

Two days later, having caught up on his laundry, he hopped into his Mini and headed back along the highway system he knew better than the back of his hand.

"Hi Mrs. Smithyes."

"Jack, it's good to see you again. Here's your key. The phone's been disconnected down there. I don't know if it's worth signing up again, they have a minimum of one month plus a connection fee. There's always the pay phone across the street if you really need one, I suppose."

"I'll manage, thanks again for this." He held up the room key. "I really appreciate it."

As soon as he dropped off his suitcase, he drove over to Ruth's. She seemed extremely happy to see him. She talked for over an hour. They went out and got Jack some bare essentials at the supermarket then continued on to Johnny's Big Red for some beer and burgers.

"Does Colin know I'm coming?"

"Yeah, but I couldn't tell him when. He'll be very excited to see you. He's been getting a little depressed lately, and I think that he's starting to lose some weight."

"O.K. I'll go first thing in the morning. What time are visitors allowed to start?"

"Ten in the morning, that'll be a great surprise for him." They were both tired, so Jack drove Ruth back and promised her that he would see her after his visit with Colin. She gave him the key to her apartment so that he could use her phone, in case she was still in class when he got there.

At the correctional facility, Jack pulled up beside a gleaming new white Cadillac convertible with candy apple red leather seats. The top was down. As he climbed the impressive granite steps up to the heavy oaken doors that led into the jail, he noticed an attractive, well-dressed, middle-aged woman exiting a door which had a pebbled glass insert with the word "Warden" painted on it in gold with a thin black outline. Out of curiosity, he looked out a window before the guards buzzed him in and watched her go to her car, the Cadillac convertible. She looked at the little red Austin Mini, put her purse on her trunk, and proceeded to dig for a pen and notepad. It looked, from a distance, like she was writing down his licence plate number. Jack thought that very strange and made a mental note to find out who she was.

After the usual emptying of pockets and frisking, Jack was ushered into the visitor's room. Colin appeared with a huge smile. He seemed truly surprised and excited. He had lost considerable weight and was beginning to look gaunt and ashen. He listened to Jack's story with great intensity and concern and was shocked to hear about his own fraternity brothers being arrested.

"Listen, Liam's sold over twenty thousand dollars worth of tickets, so I've asked Clay to send us an invoice so I can pay him. It looks like there's going to be a lot more coming in."

"Phew, that takes a load of my mind. I've been worried sick about how we were going to pay for Clay and Clive."

Jack tried to cram as much information as possible in the hour. He mentioned the knife with his initials on it, they talked about the lobster dinner, and, of course they talked about Yvette. Their hour was up, and Jack told Colin that he would keep in touch on a daily basis. As they said goodbye, Jack could see a fresh step in Colin's walk as the guard took him back through the doors to the cells. Jack went back to Ruth's to set up an appointment to see Clay and Clive at Clay's office in Binghamton the following morning.

*   *   *

Clay's office was over an old hardware store and was reached via a steep set of stairs. *Why does every office I go to have to be up a steep set of stairs, particularly dentists' offices,* Jack thought. Clay had another appointment in an hour, so they didn't waste any time with chit-chat. The office was sparsely furnished but bright, with a large picture window overlooking the busy street below.

"You wanted to know about Mario Curozzo," said Clive. "My guy in Toronto tells me that he was a small-time hood who ran a protection scam in Little Italy along College Street, wherever that is, and was suspected to be a hit man for the Moretti family. In fact, he believes that Curozzo was a nephew of Giovanni Moretti. So it looks like that pine tree did everyone a big favor. The question is, who was he after, you or the prime minister's daughter…or both?"

Jack shivered at the thought that someone was actually out to get him.

"Speaking of the prime minister," Clay said, "since your correspondence with him, I asked the judge for an extradition hearing and was granted one. I argued that the treaty between the United States and Canada clearly states in Article 2 that persons charged with murder should be turned over to, I believe the term is 'delivered up to,' the perpetrator's home country, as long as his crime is punishable by more than one year…which clearly this is.

"The D.A.," he continued, "argued that under Article 9 of the treaty, the request for extradition should be made through diplomatic channels and not by the court. He produced a copy of the prime minister's letter to you to show that Canada is not interested in having Colin extradited. He then went on to tell the court that since there is a large debate in Canada as to whether the death penalty should ever be used again, Article 6 states quite clearly the state need not permit extradition unless the country requesting extradition could guarantee the same punishment as New York. The judge ruled in the D.A.'s favor without even thinking. He said it was out of his hands, regardless of the arguments."

Jack felt very dispirited but thought he really must get some more pressure on the government. He didn't have his job to worry about now. *What more could they do to me?*

"They also have an eyewitness," Clay said. "Brett Vaughan, he's on the heavy eights of the Cornell Crew and was a fraternity brother of Colin's. The D.A. just sent me his name, so I haven't had a chance to question him in discovery. Apparently he was jogging along the path around Beebe Lake and saw Colin throw Yvette's body into the lake."

"I know Brett," said a very surprised Jack. "He's a Hotelie, he's just going into his senior year. I think he's working for the summer somewhere in Ithaca. I'll see what I can find out."

He asked Clive if he could dig up something on Sky Muncey and Sam Wainwright, because of what had happened at Lake Louise. There was not much more to talk about. He just had to wait for October 19th. The jury selection was to begin the week before.

Jack left Binghamton and drove directly to the hotel school. Since summer school was in progress, parking restrictions were very much relaxed, and he found himself a spot just two spaces away from the main entrance. It was a warm summer day, and he felt the relief from the heat as he entered air-conditioned Statler Hall. He turned right at the end of the foyer and stood at the door of the office of Dean Myer's secretary, Mary Caldwell. She looked up.

"Jack, what are you doing here? What a nice surprise," she said. "You're supposed to be out at Lake Louise."

"It's a long story. Do you know where Brett Vaughan is working this summer?"

"Yes, he's a waiter at the Waterworks."

The Waterworks had only been open for a year and had become a favorite with the Townies. It was a replica of an old flour mill or a hydroelectric plant. Jack had always figured the designer missed on both accounts, but it did have considerable atmosphere. It was built out of solid granite blocks with large, wide plank wooden floors. It straddled the base of Falls Creek just below the gorge but was well above where the creek would empty into Lake Cayuga. Just off center in the main room was a giant paddle wheel which dipped down and touched the rushing stream under the floor, causing it to turn. The wheel was attached to an intricate pulley system that went up to the ceiling and turned about twenty ceiling fans, which circulated the air throughout the cavernous hall. With the water cascading off its paddles, the wheel also served as an interesting fountain. Keeping with university tradition, popcorn and peanut shells were strewn all over the floors, although today there was less mess because of the time of day and the fact that summer school was in session. There were much fewer students attending than in the fall and spring semesters.

Jack caught a glimpse of Brett at the far end of the room. Ignoring the "Please Wait To Be Seated" sign, he walked over to Brett's section and found a table. Brett was another Hotelie and Jack had had him in one of his HR seminars but nothing more than that.

"Hey guy, what brings you here?" said Brett as Jack rose up to shake his hand. Jack ordered a burger and an order of their homemade onion rings as well as a glass of Miller Lite.

"On tap?" Jack asked,

"You bet." The place was almost empty, so Jack asked Brett to sit down.

"Tell me, is it true that you saw Colin dump Yvette's body into the lake?"

"Jack, you know I can't talk about that. All I can tell you is I know what I saw. So that's why you're here?"

Brett gave him his check and left the table, but Jack couldn't help noticing the gleaming gold Rolex watch on Brett's wrist. Jack left his customary fifteen percent gratuity, paid the bill, and drove back across town to Ruth's. She got out of class early. They went out for a swim at Buttermilk Falls and just lay in the hot summer sun, cooling off every once in a while by jumping in to the refreshing waters. Over dinner they discussed their mutual feeling that there was something missing in the puzzle. There was something that they just couldn't see, but they agreed it felt that it was right in front of them. Jack had decided that there was nothing more he could do in Ithaca, so he would visit Colin in the morning then leave directly from Elmira for home.

He thanked Mrs. Smithyes as he gave her key back and headed to the correctional facility. The white Cadillac was not there, although there was a large black Lincoln limousine.

"Tell me, you know Brett Vaughan better than I do. Does he have a lot of money, or are his parents rich? Because I always thought that he looked as though he was on his last dime."

"No," responded Colin, "he never had a pot to piss in. He had to beg everyone for loans at the fraternity to see if he could pay his monthly dues. He even painted the front porch in order to pay off some arrears. Why?"

"Oh, nothing." Jack ended it there, thinking he'd better give Clive a call before he left town. There was a waiter whose bank account should be looked into.

Driving home, Jack thought that he should get a part-time job, because he wasn't going to start handing out resumes until after the trial was over. Because he had his own car, he was immediately hired by Panelli Pizza: *'789-9999 OUR PIZZA'S JUST FINE....PANELLI'S OUR NAME, PIZZA'S OUR GAME!'* So the jingle went across every radio station in Toronto and southern Ontario.

– 19 –

It was a beautiful mid-September day in Ottawa. The sky was a brilliant blue, and the sun was piercing through the cool morning air. Prime Minister Pierre Cadeau pulled on a light coat and picked up his briefcase. Without even a goodbye kiss for his wife Monique, he left 24 Sussex Drive, his official residence, to meet his waiting limousine. It was supposed to be a fairytale marriage, but shortly after they had given their vows in a huge public wedding, it had turned sour and was best described as "tempestuous." Monique always wondered how they ever had April, but her daughter was the only thing that kept her going.

He had a very busy agenda ahead of him. First a meeting with forestry officials looking for more subsidies for the softwood lumber industry, then a meeting with the Canada Council for the Arts, which was looking for funding for a new national gallery, then a private luncheon with visiting Prime

Minister Levi Eshkol from Israel, followed by attending a joint session of Parliament, where Prime Minister Eshkol would make a rare address to the MPs and the members of the Senate, Canada's "Upper Chamber." The message was to thank Canada for its support in its seemingly endless struggles against the Palestinians and its backing at what many considered a very anti-Semitic United Nations.

He then had a meeting with his cabinet, which would be attended by his chief of staff, his press secretary and the election strategy team so that they could discuss a worrying drop in the polls. Later that evening he was hosting a state dinner in honor of Prime Minister Eshkol. The Lebanese ambassador had declined. As the limousine glided up to the steps of the Langevin block, which housed the Prime Minister's Office, better known simply as the PMO, a few hundred yards away some peaceful protestors carried placards demanding fairer subsidies for wheat farmers and the abolishment of the wheat marketing board. These were being held at bay by removable fence sections and a few RCMP officers in working uniform. The scarlet tunics would appear at the main entrance to Parliament, half an hour before the Israeli party arrived.

Walking briskly past the numerous offices and suites which comprised the PMO, he nodded and said "Good morning" to everyone he passed. His personal assistant, Claudette Chapell, was busy at work, having already placed the day's correspondence on his desk. She was the one person he could trust beyond anyone else. She had been with him since the first time he won a seat in the Legislature for Ville St. Pierre, a riding on the west side of Montreal.

The office was rich in history, with heavy, carved wood

paneling, plush carpets, and sixteen-foot ceilings with leaded windows reaching as high as the ceiling would permit them. There was an ante-office with a full settee and television so that he could keep in touch with breaking news. This room led into his personal dressing room, which in turn opened into a full five-piece bathroom complete with shower and bidet. The desk in the main office was a gift of the Province of Québec and had been hand-carved. Three different sitting areas with sofas, coffee tables and armchairs were perfectly placed around the large office for private conversations.

On the coffee table to the right of the desk was a large box wrapped in brown paper.

"This just came by courier. I hate opening packages," Claudette said to her boss, who had placed his briefcase on the desk and thrown his jacket over a chair. He went over to the box and put his ear down to it.

"I don't hear a clock ticking," he mused with a smile. "I think it's O.K. Anyway, it's from Les Producteurs de Fromage du Québec. I'll bet it's just some samples of their cheese, 'cause they want me to put pressure on Health Canada to allow them to produce unpasteurized cheese. I keep telling them it's a provincial matter."

Claudette closed the door to let him open his parcel and attend to his correspondence. He took the brown paper off the parcel and cast it aside then took the top off the box. Inside he found a plain piece of lined paper, with the following letters in various fonts and sizes glued to the page:

*AllOw FoReiGn oWner*ship *in*
cAN*adian b*AnK*s*

At the bottom of the page was glued a Polaroid picture of a dead dove with its head severed from its body, and it appeared from the brown stain on the paper that someone had smeared the dove's blood across the picture and onto the lined paper.

Around the edges of the sheet were tightly-bound bundles of one hundred dollar bills. He gently lifted the page to expose the entire top layer of packets. He lifted one bundle and estimated that there were at least a hundred bills in it. There were ten bundles on each layer. He figured it out in his head then on the calculator on his desk that he had just been sent $500,000.00 in U.S. bills. He quickly put the lid on the box and placed it gently on the floor of his closet in his dressing room.

"Please ask Allan Gelsten to come to my office as soon as possible," he asked Claudette over the intercom.

Allan Gelsten was Cadeau's most trusted friend and advisor. They had met at McGill University in Montreal when they were both students and involved in the Liberal student organization. Cadeau had run for the student presidency, which he won handily with the help of his friend. Gelsten preferred to stay in the background and was often the broker of most back room deals. He was also the leading "bagman" for the Liberal Party. He twisted more arms across the country than most people would have thought possible.

"Alan, there's a box in the closet in my dressing room. Check it out."

His trusted friend opened the box and was shocked at what he saw. Bringing it back into the main office he said, "O.K. Now what?"

"Right after today's meeting, I want you to take the jet,

go to Grand Cayman and deposit it directly into our slush fund account. Be sure to take the government jet, because if you fly commercial, you will get stopped at customs with that much cash. Talk to Celia at the bank. She's very discreet and there won't be any questions. Keep a couple of bundles out to cover your expenses. I'll have Claudette make all of the arrangements. She'll have them bring the jet from Trenton to here so your limo can just whisk you out to the airport. Remember, do not let that box out of your sight and re-wrap it securely."

"What about the message allowing foreign ownership of our banks?"

Cadeau replied, "I don't know what the hell to do, these guys are playing hardball, but I'll figure something out. And that picture of that dead bird, what do you think that is?"

"Oh, that's not hard to figure out, that's well known to be the warning of the Morretti Family in New York. You and your family are marked if you don't do what this guy says. I'd strengthen your security detail and call in the commissioner of the RCMP. Tell him you just received this, and whatever you do, don't mention the cash at all." With that Alan Gelsten wrapped the box as best he could and tied it with the string. He left the note with the prime minister.

Cadeau sat behind his desk, definitely shaken. He put the threatening note in his top drawer and started to go through his correspondence, signing letters without even reading them. He trusted Claudette, and his mind was on his physical well-being. He was able to assuage the worries of the forestry representatives as well as those of the Arts Council by throwing money at them and assuring them that they had his full support. They hadn't realized that they'd reached him at a very vulnerable moment and that he would have given anything to anyone with the hope that everything else would go away. The luncheon with Prime Minister Eshkol also went well. Cadeau was aware of the large, influential Jewish community in Canada, particularly in Montreal and Toronto, and he needed every one of their votes.

Members of the cabinet and inner circle began gathering in the Cabinet Room just before two. Alan Gelsten nodded to the prime minister as he entered the room. This was an acknowledgement that all arrangements had been made for Alan's trip to the Caymans immediately following the meeting. Greg Sommers, head of Grant and Associates, the Liberals' private polling organization, had been asked to attend.

"Is it true what I've been reading in the papers and on the late night news about our plummeting in the polls?" asked Cadeau.

"I'm afraid so," responded the pollster. "It started with that article in the *Herald* about that hockey player in the States, and it's getting worse every day. We've never been very strong in the west, and as of yesterday's results, we are losing every seat in Nova Scotia and are starting to lose support in the other Maritime provinces."

"It's that Souster kid. Well, I've fixed his clock. He won't be working any more, I've seen to that, so I think we should just ignore it and it will go away. The electorate has a very short memory, and we still have over two months to go."

International Trade Minister Andrew Cameron was next on the agenda. He was probably the brightest member of the Cabinet, having attained both his Bachelor of Law and his Chartered Accountant's degree. He had made his name working as a forensic accountant and lawyer and had blown the whistle on the executives of Opal Trust Company, the salaries they were making, and the slipshod investment schemes they were creating. Pierre Cadeau had personally recruited Cameron knowing that with his high profile and a guaranteed position as Minister for International Trade, it would be a sure victory in his riding.

"I'd like to talk about the foreign investment regulations with our banks." said Cameron. "I'm getting incredible pressure from the States, in particular from their Chairman of the Federal Reserve. There's also some other pressure from our own York National Board of Directors and some odd behaviour from this man, Richardson, who is attempting the takeover."

Cadeau started to get restless at the mention of this, and his hands began to get clammy. Just then Claudette entered the room, quickly went over to her boss, and quietly whispered in his ear.

"Your wife is on the phone, she says it's urgent."

He asked the rest of the assembly to excuse him for a moment. He took the call in his office.

"Helen and Jack Pitman have invited me to the Met tomorrow night. Can you make arrangements for the jet to take me to JFK, say, sometime around four?" asked Monique Cadeau.

"It's already booked. It will be in the Caymans tomorrow. You'll have to fly commercial."

"Please," she said with great indignation. "You know how I hate flying commercial. It means that I have to go when the schedule is and not when I'm ready to go."

Monique Cadeau was the third daughter among seven

children. She was considered one of the most beautiful girls at her school, where she eventually became head girl. Her parents did very well for themselves and raised their family in the wealthy Montreal neighbourhood of Westmount. Monique became a debutante and was the star attraction at every coming out party. She met Pierre Cadeau in her third year at McGill University where she was studying Political Science and Economics. She was also on the senior women's basketball and volleyball teams. He recruited her to campaign for him for the presidency of the Student Liberal Organization. There was no doubt that her beauty and her popularity on campus would bring him a great many votes. He went on to get his Law Degree as she continued with her Master's degree. Their wedding in Notre Dame Cathedral took place to huge fanfare, with a who's who of Montreal and movers and shakers of the Liberal Party, both provincially and federally. Alan Gelsten was best man. After a two-week honeymoon in Barbados, the marriage seemed to take a turn for the worse. Pierre's law career and political ambitions seemed to take precedence over warm evenings by the fire. It was on one of these special nights in early spring when April was conceived, hence her name. Monique soon began to think that she was being used only for political purposes, since she was brought out to almost every public appearance to show her support for her husband. Pierre Cadeau began to feel considerably more jealous as his wife was drawing bigger crowds than he, and the television cameras were always on her. As soon as they got home he started throwing things around, slamming cupboards and doors for no reason. It eventually escalated into physical abuse when he slapped her across her face when she suggested that he spend a little time with April.

"She's all yours. You wanted her, now deal with her. I've got better things to do than look after a kid that I never wanted in the first place," he screamed with rage. One time, on the chef's day off, she cooked his favorite meal, a roast leg of lamb, and had the wine uncorked and ready to pour. Before dinner, while sipping on martinis, one with a twist and one with two olives, she cuddled up to him and quietly whispered in his ear, suggesting that they have some private time in bed after their nice dinner. He grabbed his wife's beautiful brunette hair at the back and held her head tight against the back of the sofa, shouting, "If I want to have sex with a fucking whore, I'll find one I like."

She dropped her martini glass and ran upstairs to April's room, dissolving in tears, and locked herself in with her darling daughter. The roast continued to cook until it had become a large lump of charcoal by the morning. Her tears had stopped, but her eyes had reddened, and she carefully unlocked the door and accompanied a frightened April down for breakfast.

From that night on she lived in terror of her husband but played any game he wanted, because she loved the lifestyle and loved her daughter. She often would receive a black eye from one of his outbursts, but she knew if she reported it to the police, no one would believe her. Furthermore, he had connections within every police force in Canada, and he hobnobbed with many judges. He knew every sitting judge on the Supreme Court by his first name. She knew that she could ruin his career, but loved the perks so much, she continued to publicly support him. His ascendancy to prime minister was fast and quick, as he had filled every cabinet position his leader had given him. All the senior cabinet positions he tackled he guided with great skill and aplomb, which was clearly publicized and appreciated by the Canadian populace. He could do no wrong. He won the election and became prime minister of Canada in 1954. His dutiful but saddened wife was always at his side, her radiant smile never betraying her inner misery.

*   *   *

Two years before in 1963, when April was seventeen, the Canadian Bankers Association was having its annual "Ice Ball." All of the members of Parliament, senators, and all of their spouses were invited. It was always considered one of the great social events of the year, traditionally held at the Chateau Laurier hotel in Ottawa. A giant ice castle had been fashioned at the entrance, lit up by various colored lights that changed every five seconds. Chefs had carved ice sculptures throughout the dining room, and the massive reception hall had large tables draped in starched white linen, each one holding iced carved statues holding trays overflowing with shrimp, lobster and crab. The Ice Ball was a play on words. At each table place setting was a pair of diamond earrings for the ladies and usually a pair of diamond cuff links for the gentlemen. These little tokens changed annually. The association figured it cost less to put on this dinner than to hire expensive lobbyists and meet the demands of each of the members whose favor they were trying to curry.

This particular evening Monique was seated at the head table with Pierre on her left. He was ignoring her, engrossed in a conversation with the wife of the president of the association to his left. Monique struck up a conversation with the new young International Trade Minister.

"How is it that some lucky young girl has not snagged you?" she asked as she took another sip of her white wine.

"Oh, I'm just not ready to settle down."

They had a wonderful evening. He seemed to admire her beauty, and she delighted in his warm brown eyes and a shock of blond hair. But more than anything, she hadn't had a man pay this much attention to her since the day of her marriage. Their hands touched as he passed her the butter, and she felt a definite tingle of excitement.

She also had the pleasure of meeting Helen and Jack Pittman. Jack was a banker from New York who was invited as a special guest to the dinner, since he did a great deal of trading with the various Canadian banks.

It was only a week later that Pierre was off to New York to address the United Nations. The phone rang and Monique picked it up. She had given all of the staff the night off. She was going to spend a nice evening curled up with the latest Leon Uris book. April was spending the night at a friend's house in Rockcliffe, the wealthiest part of Ottawa, where senior bureaucrats and foreign dignitaries lived.

"Hello, it's Andrew Cameron." There was a pause as Monique gathered her thoughts. "I was wondering if you needed any company this evening."

"Why, I'd love some company. The staff all has the day off, so I'm not sure what I can get you," she said.

"Nothing, I was just looking for some good conversation, and I recall the great time we had at the ball the other night. Knowing that Pierre is at the U.N., I just thought that you might be free."

"Well, it just so happens that I am. Give me half an hour to straighten up, and I'll let the guard at the gate know that I'm expecting you."

"Great, see you then."

They hung up and Monique started cleaning up the family room and looking in the large kitchen for something to feed him. She found some paté and a selection of Québec cheeses. She went down to the wine cellar and selected a bottle of Vosne Romanée, 1948, her most favorite burgundy. There was a knock at the door, and she welcomed the young minister into 24 Sussex Drive.

She ushered him into the family room, where he sat down on the sofa facing the warm fire. As he spread some paté onto a fresh piece of crusty bread, Monique passed him a snifter of cognac. Once again their fingers touched. They seemed to linger in midair as that electric feeling she had experienced at the Bankers' Ball returned. She sat down beside him and they began talking politics. She quickly changed the topic to her work with the Junior League and her initiative to improve education within Inuit communities in the north. Their hands touched again, which gave Andrew the opportunity to continue to hold Monique's hand, remarking how soft it was, gently rubbing the back of it with his thumb. She moved over a little closer.

"It's been so long since I've had a man around this house, if you know what I mean," she said. "Pierre has been so busy with running the country that he just doesn't seem to have much time. Oh, what am I saying, forgive me." Andrew leaned over and gave her a tender, lingering kiss on the lips.

"It's O.K. I understand."

She put her head on his welcoming shoulder and kissed the nape of his neck. She sipped her wine and suggested that he try it.

"It's like sipping velvet, I've never tasted anything like that before," he said. With more wine and cognac, their kissing became more intense, and finally they went up the stairs to the master bedroom. Monique had never felt so fulfilled in her entire life. "Nobody has loved me like that... ever. I've never felt so wanted and so special," she said as they lay side by side with only the moon casting a light blue ray over their spent bodies.

"Can we meet again?" she said, bending down and kissing his chest.

"I would hope so," he responded, "although perhaps it would be better either at my apartment or someplace neutral, but we can work that out later." The lovers got dressed and kissed goodbye. It was only ten thiry, too early for the guard to wonder.

*   *   *

It was now 1965, and her affair with Andrew Cameron was the subject of speculation among the wagging tongues of Ottawa. The plane settled down gently at JFK International Airport in New York. Jim and Nancy Pittman's driver was there waiting to take Monique to her hosts' beautiful upper west side condominium. The driver helped her with her bag as they went up the elevator, which stopped at their penthouse. She walked into the front hall of the most lavish living quarters she had ever seen.

Her old friend Helen Patterson welcomed her with open arms. "Mrs. Cadeau's bag will go to the Cranberry Room," the driver was instructed.

The two women sat in the floor-to-ceiling windowed living room looking out over Central Park and discussed the problems of flying commercial rather than by private jet or government jet, in Monique's case. The plan was to have dinner at the Stork Club and then off to the Metropolitan Opera to hear Beverly Sills perform works from Handel, Mozart and Puccini.

"I just love a good coloratura soprano," gushed Helen. It was not long before Jim arrived home and they parted to freshen up and change into their eveningwear.

The maitre'd guided them to the Pittmans' usual table. He had an arrangement with the club that the table was his every evening, and if he wasn't going to use it, he would call them. The menu had already been pre-selected in order to get them out in time for the opera: wild quail stuffed with wild rice accompanied by fresh asparagus with hollandaise. The meal was finished by a velvety smooth zabaglione. Monique enjoyed the attention as diners glanced at her as she entered the room. She had been there many times before with Nancy and Jim. Monique smiled and nodded to Tallulah Bankhead, who was dining with her friend Beatrice Lillie, better known to some as Lady Peel, at the next table.

After dinner, the driver dropped off his charges at the front entrance to the "Met." The door to the limousine was opened with great fanfare. He held a hand out to help steady each of them as they stepped onto the pavement. Cars were parked two deep, and yellow cabs were honking frantically so they could get to their next call or pick up one of the people waving them down within the block. The sidewalk was crowded with bejewelled theatre-goers as well as others just trying to wend their way through the crowd. Monique was jostled, momentarily, and in typical Canadian fashion, apologized to the person who may have bumped into her.

The opera was outstanding. Beverly Sills received a standing ovation and five curtain calls. Jim Pittman suggested that they return to the condominium for a nightcap before retiring for the evening. Nancy put on a pot of coffee, and assorted liqueurs were offered.

Jim had decided to be direct with Monique and his desire to get her to intervene on his bank's desire to acquire control of the YN bank. "Monique, There seems to be a bit of a problem of our bank acquiring fifty-one percent of the York National Bank. Our CEO, Chadwick Richardson, has had a number of meetings with the Board of the 'YN,' but he keeps running into government regulations which are preventing any success in the takeover. Do you think that you could talk to Pierre and see what he can do?"

"I'll try, but really I try to stay out of government business. I will mention it...that's the best I can do."

"Most appreciated," he replied and poured her another Drambuie.

The next morning after breakfast, Monique looked at her watch, thanked Nancy for a wonderful evening with a huge hug and left to catch her 12:25 p.m. flight back to Ottawa.

Once settled in her first class seat sipping a complimentary glass of chilled Champagne while economy passengers glared at her as they boarded last, she opened up the *Globe and Mail*. The headline said: "Liberals on Verge of Collapse: Polls."

According to the latest polls, Pierre Cadeau's Liberal Party was doomed for a definite defeat unless a miracle happened in the next two months. The mounting anger in the Atlantic provinces with regard to the way the government was handling the Colin MacDonald affair had spread to all four Maritime provinces. The Western provinces were basically a write-off, as usual, except for a couple of seats in Vancouver and Saskatchewan which were being seriously challenged by the New Democratic Party, Canada's third political party and the most left-wing. The Liberals' only hope for forming a possible minority government was to pick up a lot of seats in vote-rich Ontario and Québec, although support was slipping in the hockey-loving northern portions of these provinces.

Noted political scribe Curtis Kennedy started his column with: "The Death Bell Tolls for Cadeau." Monique had always told her husband that she would never move into Stornoway, the home of the leader of the Opposition. *I couldn't stand the shame, what a put down! Now's the time to get rid of him and move in with Andrew.* She was now gaining inner strength aware of how vulnerable he was, and she knew that he wouldn't dare hit her.

There was a small Canadian Press story buried on page five about two young Americans who had been arrested for firearms offences in Calgary being extradited back to the U.S. Her husband was quoted as saying, "The United States of America is Canada's largest trading partner, and I would not want to do anything to jeopardize this relationship."

Just prior to landing, she reached into her purse to retrieve her lipstick when she noticed a strange envelope. It was a standard #10 white, letter-sized envelope, with the words glued to the outside: "*PIERRE CADEAU*".

Monique turned the envelope around and checked out the back as well. She held it up to the sun-drenched window of the aircraft. She could see the outline of a piece of paper and a darker image in the center of it. Air Canada had left the seat beside her empty, so she felt comfortable that no one would see her opening the letter, even though she knew better than to open someone else's mail. Regardless of propriety, she decided to open it. She unfolded a torn blue lined piece of paper with a horrifying picture of a beheaded dove. Someone had taken what Monique presumed was the dove's blood and smeared it across the page and the picture. She was shocked and quickly folded it up and put it back in the envelope and her purse just as the stewardess came through the cabin to make sure everyone was ready for landing. Monique was shaken by the picture, wondering how the letter ever got into her purse.

Her driver met her at the Ottawa airport and took her bag as they proceeded to the limousine.

"You must have had a lot of rain last night," she remarked as she stepped over a large puddle to get into the car.

"It poured all day yesterday and didn't stop until early in the morning. It was a real drenching," replied the uniformed chauffeur.

He whisked her back to 24 Sussex Drive, where the butler took her bag and went ahead of her up the stairs to the master bedroom. She unpacked and slipped into some more comfortable clothes, but the thought of the gory picture of the dove remained in the front of her mind at all times.

As she went to put a tissue into the wastebasket, she thought of disposing of the letter. Looking down, she thought she saw the glint of a foil wrapper of a condom. She bent over and picked it up. She sat on the bed and started to weep. It was definitely over now. Somehow it was alright for her to love Andrew, but for the prime minister to cheat on her after all of the abuse she had received over all the years of her marriage was just too much to handle. She gathered herself and went downstairs and out to the guard house at the entrance. She asked the young RCMP officer if he could check the log and find out who had visited last evening.

"Mimi Belanger, Parliamentary Assistant to the Minister of International Trade."

That little slut, I'll fix her but good, she thought as she walked briskly back into the official residence. She contemplated calling Andrew to tell him what his parliamentary assistant was up to but thought better of it.

"How was New York?" asked the prime minister as he started taking his overcoat off and loosening his tie.

"It was wonderful. Let's have a drink. Martini?"

"Great."

She stirred the Beefeater with just a drop of Noilly Pratt over an abundance of ice cubes until the mixing glass was totally frosted. She poured the martinis over a couple of pre-chilled glasses, one with a twist, the other with two olives.

"You know better than that. I like mine on the rocks," he said in his demanding voice as he handed the drink back to her to fix.

"You'll need it straight up and as strong as you can handle it when you hear what I've got to say to you. Sit down!" she demanded. She was proud of herself.

"What's this?" She pulled out the condom wrapper from her jeans. "I know," she continued, "you've been having a little fling with that floozy Mimi Belanger. You think you're smart, but you're as dumb as they come." She couldn't believe that she was the one doing the yelling now. "And what's this mean?" she continued as she pulled out the picture of the blood-smeared dead dove on it.

"Where did you get that?" he demanded. He went to take it from her but she pulled it away from him. "Don't you fuck with me, woman. Give me that goddamned picture, before I slam that pretty face of yours into that table." He raised his hand to strike her.

"Not so fast, sit back down, and you listen to me," she said slowly and deliberately as she raised the empty condom wrapper and waved it ever so slowly in his face.

"You will never hit me again," she started. "You are going down the tubes, and if you want to have the remotest chance of winning this election, you will do exactly as I say. If I've told you once, I've told you a hundred times, that I will never move into Stornoway, so you'd better shape up and win this thing. Furthermore, if you touch me one more time, this little wrapper is going to be all over the front pages of every newspaper and magazine in this country, and that will be the end of your career, and the last you will ever see of me and April. Now...listen up...I have flown my last commercial flight as long as we are living here, so if you are using the government jet for the campaign, then you better have another one available for my personal use. Furthermore, if you want me to appear with you at any speaking events, you'd better make sure that we have a two-bedroom suite at all times, because I'm through with you, and it's very obvious that you've been through with me for a long time. Now, what's with the dead bird?"

Pierre was clearly shaken. His head was bowed and he was looking down at the broadloom. "There's an American bank that wants to take over control of the YN Bank, and we don't allow 51 percent foreign ownership of our banks. We think that they've hired the Mafia to do their dirty work."

"Who's we?"

"Alan Gelsten and I."

"What does he know about this?" she asked. "This isn't the first time they've sent a picture of a dead dove? And you didn't tell me, and now we know that they know my every move, because this found its way into my purse somewhere in New York or on Air Canada."

He looked at her square in the eye and said how sorry he was and how much he loved her.

"Too late for that. You should have thought of that twenty-four years ago." She remembered that Jim Pittman had asked her to speak on the Bastion Bank's behalf but decided that this wasn't the right time.

"Pull yourself together. I've moved into the guest room and, frankly, I don't care what the staff think or say." With that she rose and headed to the kitchen to see what the chef had prepared for dinner.

20

Jack woke up to the distant ringing of the phone. He had been delivering pizza until two a.m. and it was now eleven am. He jumped out of bed and heard the familiar voice of Craig Simpson, his friend from Chateau Lake Louise.

"A Jamie Sutherland of the *Herald* wants your phone number. Is it O.K. to give it to him?"

"Yeah, no problem. How's everything out there?" Jack asked.

"Starting to wind down. How're you doing?"

"Great," Jack said, trying to be positive in his foggy state. Within ten minutes, when he still had his toothbrush in his mouth, the phone rang again.

"Hi, Jack, It's Jamie Sutherland of the *Herald*. Have you read the *Globe* today?"

"No, why, what's in it?"

"They've extradited Muncey and Wainwright back to the

States. I got a great picture of the cops handing them over to the U.S. Marshals. I called the prime minister's office, and I got the press secretary, whom I've quoted in the article. 'Please keep in mind that the United States of America is Canada's largest trading partner, and we would not want to do anything to jeopardize this relationship.' Sound familiar? I was just doing a follow-up and was hoping to get a quote from you."

"It's quite bvious that this prime minister will do anything the United States asks him to do and couldn't give a damn about our own Canadian citizens, who are locked up in their jails and facing possible death sentences. And you can quote me. Furthermore, he uses blackmail to shut up those of us who speak out against him...and you can quote me on that too."

He told how the prime minister had forced Gordon Lawton to fire him or pull all the government business away from CP Hotels.

"Do you want me to tell that story too?"

"Sure, my life's toast now, anyway."

They hung up and Jack sat down, wondering if he had gone too far. But he thought if the prime minister was going to ruin his life, he was going to return the favor. He hoped April would understand and was thankful that she didn't have that much respect for her father. He got dressed and went out to get the paper. Dylan loved to go for a ride in the car.

Jack returned with the paper and found the story on page five, complete with a picture of the two Cornell football stars in handcuffs being handed over to the U.S. marshals as they were removing the handcuffs. He assumed that their fathers had paid off some federal authority so that their sons would receive preferential treatment. He read the story many times and became angrier each time. He made himself another piece of toast and poured a second cup of the coffee his mother had left for him. His mind was swirling with events from the first murder at the bottom of Cascadilla Gorge, and all of the others, especially Yvette. He couldn't stop thinking about the slaughter on the train that he almost witnessed, and the true sadness in his heart every time he visited his best friend in the Elmira Correctional Facility. He threw Dylan a crust, which he caught in midair when the phone rang.

"Jack, it's Ruth." She was crying. "Colin's in the prison infirmary. You've got to come down as soon as possible."

"Oh god, what happened?" Jack bleated.

"The warden released him into the general population of the prison, and apparently he was attacked in the showers. He's got a broken nose, two broken ribs, a punctured lung and a possible fractured skull. I just found out about it from Clay. I told him I'd call you."

"I'll be down there this evening. Please call Mrs. Smithyes for me. I'll be leaving here within the hour." He threw some things into a duffel bag, scribbled a quick note to his mother and headed out, first stopping at Panelli Pizza to let them know that he'd been called out of town on an emergency.

After the long drive, Jack checked in with his former landlady to pick up his key and drop off his bag and then drove immediately over to Ruth's apartment. She greeted him with a hug and tears. Since Colin was in the Elmira Hospital, he was allowed two visitors at a time, and visiting hours were far more relaxed than they had been in the Correctional Facility infirmary. They decided to go at ten the next morning. They were ushered to the elevators after asking at information for

Colin's room number. They were told 310 and were directed to the elevators. As they stepped off the elevator, it was obvious where Room 310 was. There was a guard with a rifle across his lap sitting outside the door of a room at the end of the hall to their right. They passed the nurses' station and asked if they had to sign in, which they did not. They nodded to the guard and just as they were about to enter the room, Clive came out. They talked quietly and briefly because of the guard sitting right in their midst.

"Call me," Clive said, and Colin's friends entered his room.

It was a private room, and he was in one corner in what only could be described as an adult crib with both sides up. His right wrist was handcuffed to a side bar, and his left ankle was shackled to another bar on the other side at the other end of the bed. His head was heavily bandaged, eyes black and swollen so that he could only see through a slit. His nose was puffed and pushed over to one side, and there was a big split in the right nostril. His upper lip had been cut and was bulging up towards his nostril. There were traces of blood around his wounds which the nurses had failed to clean up after he was brought in. His torso was tightly wrapped to hold his ribs still. He was covered by a sheet from the waist down. His left ankle shackle protruded from under the sheet. Ruth grabbed Jack's arm as they approached Colin, who forced a painful but thankful smile.

"Hi, guy," said Jack. "Who did this? Can you talk?"

"A little," mumbled Colin without moving his lips. "Two prisoners, in the shower. I've never seen them. Then a guard came in and took his boots to me when they got me down. Never seen him before either." He kept his words to a minimum as he turned his head slowly towards the night table. "Water, please!"

Ruth picked up the water jug and held it outside the crib then guided a long extended straw through his swollen lips. "Thanks." There was only one chair, which Jack offered to Ruth. The guard had taken the second one. They were able to get a additional one for Jack from a passing orderly.

"What did Clive say?" asked Jack.

"Something about bank records. I didn't understand."

"Don't worry, just get better. I'm going to be around for a while. You're going to get sick of me." Colin moved his right hand toward the edge of the crib and put two fingers through as if to wave goodbye. Jack shook them, and the Ruth bent over and kissed them.

"Thanks," mumbled Colin. They left the spread-eagled friend feeling almost as helpless as he was but determined to fight on. They returned to Ruth's apartment and Jack immediately called Clive.

"Hi, it's Jack. What's up?"

"I've got a friend at Ithaca Savings and Loan."

"I thought she was with Tompkins County Trust," interrupted Jack.

"Oh man, you are so far behind, I'll have to get you caught up, but anyway, my friend tells me that their so called eyewitness, Brett Vaughan, made a deposit of twenty-five thousand into his account two weeks to the day after Colin was arrested."

"Hmmm," mused Jack, "that's pretty cheap for proof. How do we link it up with whoever is framing Colin?"

"I'm working on it."

"Did you hear that Muncey and Wainwright have applied for and got extradition back to the U.S.?" said Jack.

"No, when?"

"Just a couple of days ago."

Jack was a little unnerved at the knowledge that there might be a possibility of Sky and Sam soon being set loose. He and Ruth talked about some of their options, and Jack didn't want to endanger Ruth by his association with her. She refused to opt out of being part of the team.

The following day, Jack drove to Binghamton to meet with Clay.

"I've got a special hearing this afternoon with a judge. I'm trying to get an order to have Colin put back in protective custody. I think that he'll agree after he sees these pictures." Clay laid out a number of 8 1/2 x 11 glossy photos, complete with handcuffs and shackles visible. "I've also written the governor to have an investigation to get to the bottom of this. He could have been killed."

"I think that was supposed to be the ultimate goal, and they failed," Jack surmised.

The hearing was held in the judge's chambers. Erik Wolfe, the district attorney, argued vehemently that the State could not protect every prisoner from the many grudge matches that arose every day in the prison population.

"Mr. MacDonald would not have these problems if he had not been a serial killer...next to child molesters, these people are the most despised in the criminal world."

Clay argued that Colin was still considered innocent in the eyes of the law and that there was evidence that a guard was one of the attackers. When he was asked about the evidence, he argued that only someone wearing hard-toed shoes or boots could inflict those kinds of wounds. It appeared that the judge was not really interested in any of Clay's arguments and had only his tee-off time in mind, as he kept looking at his watch.

"I'm afraid that your motion is dismissed to have your client be put into protective custody." He looked at the D.A. and said, "However, should this happen again, I'm afraid I will have no option but to rule in Mr. McBride's favor. Please advise the warden."

"Yes sir," nodded the pleased D.A., and the two left the judge's chambers.

Jack had been sitting on a bench in the foyer of the courthouse and rose to his feet as he saw Clay walking down the stairs.

"How did it go?"

"Not well, we'll just have to keep an eye on Colin ourselves, which is going to be an almost impossible job."

As they headed towards the large oaken doors, Jack glanced out a dusty window and saw the same older woman, in tweed, sliding into her white Cadillac convertible with the bright red leather seats. He had seen her just a few days earlier at the warden's office.

When Jack got back to his basement apartment in Collegetown, Mrs. Smythyes had left a note for him on his desk: *Your mother called and Mr. Lawton wants you to call him. She said that you'd know the number.* Jack checked his pocket for change and realized he didn't have enough for a long distance call. He thought he might try something.

"Canadian Pacific Hotels, Mr. Lawton's Office, Heather Stuart speaking." The operator broke in and said, "I have a collect call from Mr. Jack Souster, will you accept the charges?"

"Absolutely, Operator. Put him through. Hi Jack, how are you doing?"

After a few pleasantries, he said, "I understand that Mr. Lawton wants to talk to me."

"He sure does, and he's not very happy. Fortunately he's running a little late, so you won't have to endure his wrath for very long, I'll put you through."

"Gord Lawton speaking," came the CEO's voice just as a police car was speeding past Jack.

"Hi Mr. Lawton, it's Jack Souster," he yelled as a fire truck with sirens and horns blaring was approaching, following the police. "I'm in a phone booth in Ithaca, New York."

The CEO came back very firmly. "Listen, I've had just about enough of your nonsense. The prime minister's office has just cancelled all bookings in all of our properties across the country, and they've just sent me a draft copy of a memo that they will be sending out to all government offices in Canada and embassies around the world stating that no one is to use our hotels, and if they do they will not be reimbursed when they submit their expense account receipts. Now," he continued, "the conversation that you and I had was supposed to have been confidential, and I didn't expect to see it splashed all over the front pages. So just stop what you're doing. Am I making myself clear?"

"Sir," Jack answered as the ambulance wailed past. "With all due respect. If you recall, you fired me, and therefore I don't answer to you. If you want my advice, not that you do, but I'm going to give it to you anyway." He was shocked at his own insolence but continued. "Start telling the truth when you get a call from the press and get your sales teams out there and have them knocking on every Conservative and NDP voter's doors. Because," he added, "these are the people that you will be dealing with after November 8th. I guarantee you that Cadeau's going to be lucky if he becomes leader of the opposition. In fact, the way I'm reading the polls, he'll be lucky to get enough seats to retain his 'party' status. You've pretty well lost all of the government business anyway, so you might as well hedge your bet and start rebuilding it."

Finally he threw in a little philosophy his grandfather had once told him, "You know, telling the truth isn't all that bad. In fact, sometimes it just feels downright good." There was silence on the other end of the line, which probably was no more than four or five seconds, but to Jack it seemed like an eternity.

"Thanks for your opinion," Lawton said and the line went dead.

Jack walked up College Avenue to see if he could see any smoke, but instead he saw the flashing lights of the police car, the fire truck and the ambulance all at the bridge over Cascadilla Creek and Gorge. The officer had his cruiser parked sideways so that no one could cross the bridge. There were a few onlookers, but since it was a week away from orientation, when the thrilled crop of freshmen would arrive to have a week of excitement, the campus was still very quiet. As he got closer to the bridge, Jack noticed the firemen hauling up a cradle-like stretcher, with a body bag firmly strapped to it, swinging it over the stone bridge wall. His mind went back to his last day of school, and he found a window ledge outside of Collegetown Records on which to perch on. He knew that this was not a "gorge out," as school had not even started. He returned to his flat. He had made arrangements to bunk in at Ruth's, since Mrs. Smithyes was expecting her new tenant's arrival in a couple of days. He gathered his clothes and returned his key to his generous former landlady.

Ruth, having finished summer school a few days earlier, was at home and made sure that the extra long couch was cleared of magazines and other debris. "You're not going to believe what I've just seen," he said as he came in. He explained what he had just witnessed.

"Well, at least they can't nail this one on Colin. He's shackled to a hospital bed," Jack noted.

The following morning there was a picture of a lovely young woman with the caption, "Cathy Ward, Murdered." The sad story told of how she was a single mother of one child and that her husband, Todd Ward, had been killed in the Vietnam War, thereby orphaning her two year old daughter. The story went on to say that she was a teller at Ithaca Savings and Loan and then went on to quote a number of her fellow employees, all attesting to her being a wonderful person and a fabulous, caring mother. Child Services had taken Emma into their custody, and they were looking for any family who could take the sad little toddler into their care so they wouldn't have to put her into a foster home. Accompanying the story was a second picture of a crying Emma holding her soother in her flailing left hand while her right arm was wrapped around the neck of a caring social worker. Tears came to Jack's eyes as he looked at the desperate cry for help emanating from the picture of Emma's futilely pleading eyes. She had nothing, no one.

He left a message on Clive's answering machine. Then they went to visit Colin and both noticed that the swelling had gone down around his nose and eyes, and the black bruises had taken on a strange purple and green combination. They told him about what Jack had seen yesterday and explained to him that the victim was a bank teller named Cathy Ward. The trio was quiet as they reflected on the sad circumstances, but they all had a strange feeling of great relief that they were not involved in this murder.

Jack had to say a temporary farewell, as he had to get back to earning some money. He hoped that Panelli Pizza would rehire him.

21

The fall colors in Cape Breton were so bright, Jack had to wear sunglasses. He had never seen the brilliance of oranges, reds, pinks and yellows combined like this ever before in his life. It was now Monday, October 4th, a week before Canadian Thanksgiving, and only five days before the first sold-out lobster dinner at the Glace Bay Arena. Having just climbed Kelly's Mountain in his little Mini, Jack gave a sigh of relief as he and the car started their descent and pulled over on the St. Ann's Look Off to enjoy one of the most breathtaking views he had ever seen. The scenery seemed to go on forever over the Brador Lakes. It didn't have the grandeur of the view from Lake Agnes, simply because of the overwhelming size of the Canadian Rockies, but it sure had it beat in color. When he came to the outskirts of Sydney, he filled up with gas and took advantage of the washroom to shave and brush his teeth, since he had slept the night before, curled up in his car, at some truck stop near Perth Andover, New Brunswick. He asked the senior attendant if he knew Liam MacDonald, and if so, where did he live?

"Who doesn't know Liam, boy? You'll probably find him at his Uncle Andy's house, three roads up to the Glace Bay exit, turn left, two miles, turn right, and he's the third house on the left. He's putting on some big do this weekend. Ain't seen nothing like it in these parts."

"Maybe we'll see you there," replied a hopeful Jack.

"Me and the missus will both be there, as sure as the tide goes out."

Jack smiled and said, "Great. See you there."

He headed out to his final destination, the home of the MacDonalds. It was an older farmhouse. The family had a Border Collie, Jessie, and a Black Labrador Retriever, Glen, short for Glenmorangie, Andrew MacDonald's favorite single malt whisky. Jessie won the race.

Jack squatted down and patted them as they tried, with great success, to wash his face with their kisses. He recalled Colin's numerous stories of Glen and the times they went hunting together. He grabbed Glen and gave him a big hug. "That one's from Colin, boy." Liam appeared at the door and called the dogs off as Jack rose and introduced himself to Colin's cousin, and then they went inside.

The smell of freshly baked bread permeated the house, and everyone around the kitchen table got up to greet him, Colin's mother Moira; his father, Andrew; his Uncle Archie; Aunt Phyllis, and Liam's long-time girlfriend Gillian. There were to-do lists scattered all over the table with a huge Brown Betty teapot, a mixture of tea cups and mugs, a small pitcher of milk, a bowl of sugar and a plate of homemade oatmeal and raisin cookies cluttering the Formica table with chrome legs and matching chairs. Everyone welcomed Jack as if they'd known him all of their lives. Colin's mother gave Jack a hug that he thought would never end, and as she quickly brought up a chair, he noticed that she wiped a tear from her eye.

"Now, what can I get you?" she insisted.

"Nothing at all," Jack said, eying the cookies on the table.

"Nobody comes into our home and gets nothing." In the same breath, she said, "Drew? Please get Jack something."

"Rum? Whisky? Beer? Tea? Coffee?"

"Beer sounds good."

"All I've got is Keith's, if that's O.K."

Jack, not knowing his Maritime beers, said, "Sounds good to me."

Andrew nodded to Liam, who went to the fridge and produced an ice-cold Keith's Ale and handed it to Jack, saying the brewery slogan: "Those who like it, like it a lot!" They all settled down and asked Jack what seemed like hundreds of questions, and he asked almost as many regarding the fundraising dinners in return. The afternoon tea ran right into dinner as Moira, Phyllis and Gillian set the table, and put out a huge platter of sautéed fresh haddock.

"The fisherman was just here before you arrived, Jack," she said. A mountainous bowl of mashed potatoes, a large plate of butternut squash, fresh from Gillian's garden, and another large bowl brimming with Brussel sprouts were put on the table, accompanied by the warm bread Jack had smelled as he arrived. Hot apple pie was the dessert.

Jack tried to get up and help clear the table but Gillian said, "Sit, relax, you've done enough."

Liam's father Archie brought out his guitar, as did Colin's father, Andrew. They sang well past midnight, and Jack was fighting to keep his eyes open, but he didn't want the evening to end. Finally, Moira guided Jack to the small but very comfortable guest room. Jack thanked her for the wonderful dinner and evening, and she gently took hold of each of his cheeks and kissed him on the forehead.

"God bless you, Jack. Have a good sleep." He had never felt more welcomed anywhere by anyone in all his life. He went to sleep to the tune and words of "Farewell to Nova Scotia" swirling in his head.

The next day was down to business for Jack. Since he had a car, he was used as a go-fer to pick up all sorts of things from tickets for the 50-50 draws to thousands of Styrofoam cups which had been donated by the local K-Mart. The morning of Saturday October 9th arrived and Jack was helping as much as he could setting up tables and chairs on top of the plywood flooring which covered the ice in the arena. Old newspapers were spread over the tables to soak up any spillage from the lobsters. Knives and forks had been rolled up in paper napkins throughout the week, one of which was placed at every place setting. Audio technicians were setting up the sound and lighting system on the stage at one end of the arena. The stage had been erected earlier in the week.

There seemed to be a bit of excitement at the other end as someone yelled out "They're here." Jack wandered down and went past the boards of the ice rink where the Zamboni was parked. There he saw a number of men unloading huge gray plastic bins as a double chain line was formed and the heavy bins were passed from hands to hands into a large area beneath the stands where a temporary kitchen had been set up. The bins were open, and Jack was amazed as he looked at the slowly writhing, dark green crustaceans. He had never seen so many lobsters in his life.

"There'll be some good feed tonight, boy," said the man beside him.

"You got that right."

The ladies were starting to bring in their homemade apple pies. The refrigerated Keith's truck had already backed in and was running lines of draught to the bar. It was illegal for Keith's to donate beer, so they had sent Liam a ten thousand dollar cheque made out to the Colin Macdonald Defence Fund, and they were permitted to supply free plastic Keith's cups. The cheque was enlarged and put up on the glass behind the bar for everyone to see. Coca-Cola, not being restricted by any liquor laws, had donated tanks of fountain Coke, and other soft drinks. Their tanks were sitting in giant galvanized tubs filled to the brim with ice.

Both the CBC Radio and Television trucks arrived within minutes of each other. When Jack saw the national broadcasters arrive, he immediately thought, *Oh boy, am I ever going to get it now. I haven't got a prayer to get back into Mr. Lawton's good books. The prime minister is going to be really pissed off.*

Soon after, a van appeared with three different Cape Breton radio station logos covering every inch possible: MAX 98.3 FM, 94.9 FM "The Cape," and CJCB AM 1270 "Country Favorites." Patsy Cline was belting out "I Fall to Pieces" through the crackling roof-mounted loudspeaker.

People began to arrive around five p.m., even though the tickets had six printed on them. There was a great air of festivity surrounding the whole scene. A young boy, Ronnie

Rafuse, who was only ten years old, and recognized by most Islanders as a musical genius, was playing jigs and reels on the Hammond organ as people started filing in, handing over their tickets, and having their hand stamped. Their ticket stubs were returned for one of the many donated door prizes: one was a return ticket for two on the *Acadian Princess* ferry over to Newfoundland. Jack went back to the kitchen area to watch the cooking production and was surprised to see that they steamed the lobster rather than boiled them. "Doesn't waterlog them," was the statement from one of the cooks when he saw the quizzical look on Jack's face. He couldn't figure out why they were using water out of big buckets that had been carted in, and not water from the taps.

"Sea water, boy. The salt water sure makes them sweet." There was a whole crew of men splitting the lobsters and cracking their claws as soon as the rich red delicacies were taken out of the dozen steaming cauldrons. They were then placed in large Styrofoam-insulated bins and taken out to the "buffet table" where people would pick up their lobster, a small paper container of coleslaw, a bun, and some melted butter. The butter was kept in numerous slow cookers and everyone just ladled what they wanted into one of the nearby stacks of Dixie cups. Some people struggled with the plates and had to return for the roll or the coleslaw. The line was very efficient and moved quickly, although it seemed to go on forever. Jack caught a glimpse of Liam talking to a couple of men. Since most people had been served, Liam made his way over to Jack.

"O.K., it's time to get things rolling."

"All right," Jack said, "what can I help with?"

"Well, I was hoping you'd say a few words and open the

show, so to speak. I'll introduce you, and then there's a couple of politicians who want to say something and then we'll get into the music and the dancing."

"What, you want me to speak?" said a terrified Jack. "I've never spoken to this many people in all my life...and I don't even know any of them."

"You're a friend of Colin's and that's all that matters."

Jack turned in one of his tickets, grabbed a beer, and followed Liam on stage. The lights dimmed, and Liam had put together a film montage of Colin beginning when he was a young boy skating for the first time, throughout his hockey career, including pictures of him playing for Cornell and receiving the MVP trophy at the NCAA championships, a copy of his contract with the leafs and then the startling headline in the *Toronto Star*: "Leaf Hopeful Charged in Multiple Murders." This was met with a chorus of boos from the crowd.

Liam then quieted the crowd and introduced Jack. "Ladies and gentlemen, thank you all for coming out to support Colin in this most trying time."

"I love you, Liam," yelled a girl from the back of the arena.

"I love you too, Charlene." The crowd chuckled then Liam put his hand over the mic and quietly whispered to Jack with a smile, "Charlene loves every man in Cape Breton."

"You all know why we're here. To raise funds to pay for Colin's legal defence, and it is my privilege to introduce Jack Souster, a fellow student and dear friend of Colin's, who has been working tirelessly to prove Colin's innocence. After Jack speaks, there are a couple of other people who want to say a few words, then we're going to have a little entertainment and then the party will begin. Ladies and gentlemen, it is my privilege to introduce you to Colin's friend, Jack Souster."

There was a warm, welcoming round of applause, and Jack's mouth suddenly got incredibly dry and his knees shook. He took a large mouthful of beer and handed the cup to Liam. The crowd chuckled as he stepped up to the microphone. Liam had projected on the giant screen behind the stage pictures of Colin and Yvette as well as a multitude of photos of Colin's youth and even one of when he put on his first pair of skates. The silence was incredible for an arena holding over five hundred people. Jack could see many pulling out their handkerchiefs and wiping away the tears. It was not hard to feel the love these people had for Colin.

"WOW. Cape Breton, what an awesome place! WOW, what an amazing bunch of people!" The silence was broken, and the crowd cheered wildly. Jack had to wait for what seemed like an eternity for everyone to settle down.

"I was speaking with Colin just this morning. He sends everyone his love, and he thanks you all for coming out to support him." Again, the crowd stood on its feet and cheered, not settling down until someone started banging a large ladle on an empty beer keg. "I met Colin and Yvette on my very first day at Cornell. We became instant friends, and to tell you the truth, I have never seen any two people more in love than Colin and Yvette. They just lit up a room whenever they would enter it. I had the great pleasure of spending part of yesterday and last night with Colin's mom and dad, with all of their family, including Liam and Uncle Archie. I now know from where Colin gets his incredible character." There was a long period of applause that gave Jack the opportunity to take another gulp of beer. His nerves had now settled down.

"These days are probably the darkest days of Colin's

life, sitting in a jail cell, waiting for his trial on the 19th, and yet every time I have visited, his inner strength has shone outward, knowing that he will be found innocent. I know Colin, and I knew Yvette, and I know of their incredible love they had for each other, and I know in the bottom of my heart that he will be found innocent."

The crowd once again erupted with a chant of, "Co-lin, Co-lin, Co-lin...."

"We have been able to find the most incredible lawyer in Clay McBride and a private detective in Clive Scranton who took on Colin's case without charging a cent. Your being here tonight is going to help pay these two amazing individuals for all of their hard work, and for their belief in Colin's innocence, and for their faith that a great injustice has been done.

"You all know that we have a prime minister who would not nor will not raise a hand to help one of our own in a foreign country. Colin, as far as Prime Minister Cadeau is concerned, could rot in Hell."

"Shame, Shame, Shame...." shouted the crowd, and Jack noticed that the television cameras were panning the crowd.

"I want to close by thanking you on behalf of Colin. I want to thank Liam for all the hard work he has done putting this event on and for all of the generous donations that I understand have been made by the community: the lobsters, the pies, the music, the tables, the chairs, absolutely everything that has come together to make this evening such a great success. But this wouldn't be the success that it is if it wasn't for you, the people of Cape Breton. God bless you all. You are like no other people that I have ever met. Thank you."

The arena erupted into a frenzy. Again there were shouts

of Colin's name and eventually Jack's. While this was going on, Liam had projected a large picture of Colin, Yvette, Jack and Ruth in better times raising their beers. Jack handed the mic back to Liam and went back to his table on the floor, but the crowd kept yelling his name, so he went back up on stage and gave them a large wave.

Liam started to introduce Cape Breton's "Favorite Son," as the man liked to call himself. Alistair MacLean had been the sitting member of Parliament for over twenty years. He had a knack for pleading at the cabinet level to get more subsidies for Cape Breton. Almost everyone on the Island owed him something, their jobs or some spin-off monetary gain. He was a Liberal, and prime minister Cadeau's Maritime lieutenant. Every election was almost a coronation. There were two elections when he'd run unopposed, as the other political parties realized there was no use wasting their money when they knew he would obviously walk away with a victory once the polls were counted.

The portly, red-faced "Favorite Son" walked on stage as he was introduced, waving to the crowd, oblivious to their mood. He just assumed that they were being extra vocal and seemed to be relishing the attention. He got up to the microphone, still grinning, and then started to realize that they were all chanting "Shame, shame, shame." One shrill-voiced woman yelled out "Go back to Ottawa and get off the Island." The crowd was so loud that they wouldn't let him speak, and every time he tried to speak into the microphone, he was shouted down. He finally gave up, slunk off the stage and out a back door. Normally, he would have been glad-handing everyone in the arena and talking to everyone he could, looking for any baby to kiss, and at the same time on a constant lookout for a photo opportunity.

A CBC reporter had kept his eye on Jack and quickly grabbed him just as the music started. They went outside where it was quieter for the interview. Jack had finished the first interview with the television reporter when he noticed that there was a line-up of reporters waiting to talk to him. The *Cape Breton Post* and the *Halifax Herald* were also there, and Jack felt very comfortable discussing every aspect of the case with them. He was very relaxed after his speech had gone so well. With the interviews over, he went inside, and as he entered the arena, a gentleman at the first table, immediately in front of the stage, came and took him by the arm, insisting that he join their table. One of the ladies retrieved a two-and-a-half-pound lobster, which he started to devour. At this point the pupils of Heather MacAllister's School of Scottish Dance took center stage and gave a wonderful demonstration of the Highland fling, and then "The Gay Gordon" all to the strains of the Glace Bay Volunteer Fire Department Pipe Band.

However, the standing ovation didn't come until six-year-old twins Cailleach and Robbie MacInnes gave a superb demonstration of the Scottish Sword Dance, standing ever so erect with arms perched on each hip then flung over their heads as they kicked their legs out over the crossed swords placed on the floor and their toes jabbing the air, pointed as if they were stabbing some imaginary foe.

"Cute as buttons," said Vera Wright, who was the local apple pie baking champion, seated next to Jack as they joined the rest of the crowd standing and shouting for more. Shortly after they all sat down and the buzz and excitement of the dance performances settled down, Jack looked up and noticed a young man standing along the side of the arena, all by himself. He didn't look like he belonged and looked uncomfortable being there. He was dressed somewhat nattily and had his black hair slicked strait back with what must have been the contents of a half a tube of Brylcreem. His eyes made contact with Jack's, then he quickly looked away. Jack didn't know why, but the stranger's presence made him feel a little uncomfortable. When he looked back to the same area, the outsider had disappeared.

A group of men started to gather at the side of the stage. They were dressed in full miners' gear from head to toe, and as they mounted the platform, they turned on their helmet lamps. The overhead lights were gradually dimmed and as they rotated in unison to face the audience, the splash of their illuminated helmets completed a perfect outline of the group. They commenced to sing a Capella, a much loved song, "She's called Nova Scotia".

Jack felt a shiver go through him, and the hair on his arms and neck stood on end. "That's North America's only coal miner's choral group," said the lady sitting next to Jack as she put her hand on his arm. "They've been singing for years but have just formally given themselves a name, The Men of The Deeps.

Tears of joy started to well up in Jack's eyes. He didn't know whether it was the emotion of the evening, the lack of sleep, the wonderful people and the warmth he found surrounding him or the incredible support people were showing towards Colin. There were many 50-50 raffles going on, and buckets were being passed for people to make further donations. The bar receipts were the last to be tallied as it stayed open until one a.m. After every penny was counted and added to what was already in Colin's trust account there, was a total of $37,452.25…and still another day to go. Moira took Jack home for some rest, and as he climbed into her car, he was amazed that Liam had arranged for an army of men to clean up the huge mess and get it ready for Sunday's repeat dinner. Jack made a mental note to call the organizers of the other five dinners that were being held in conjunction with the one in Sydney: St. John's and Corner Brook, Newfoundland, Summerside, Prince Edward Island, Middleton in the heart of the Annapolis Valley and a scallop dinner in Yarmouth.

One of the luxuries Colin had in the hospital was a phone beside his bed, but when Jack got through, an orderly answered the phone and advised him that Colin had been returned to the correctional facility. He called Ruth, whom he had awakened, not remembering the one-hour time difference between Atlantic and Eastern Standard Times. He told her about the fabulous evening of support for Colin and about the amount of money raised. She was absolutely amazed and told Jack that she would be going to visit Colin in an hour or two. "They've got him in solitary again."

"Well, I suppose that's better than in the morgue," Jack said. Ruth said that the news of the lobster dinner would really buoy Colin's spirits.

Gerry Mosher, the organizer in Yarmouth, was brimming with pride as he announced to Jack that they had taken in $32,871.21.

"By the way," the scallop fisherman added, "the press was all over the place, CBC, CTV and tons of radio and newspaper reporters." Jack again started to chuckle as he imagined what this must be doing to the prime minister's polling numbers.

After calling all of the organizers of the other dinners, he then called Verna Martin in Corner Brook, Newfoundland who wanted to put on a dinner of "Fish 'n Brews' and then Sean O'Malley in St. John's who was planning a "Jigs dinner".

*   *   *

Summerside, Prince Edward Island, followed Sydney's lead and had a lobster dinner, although, since the area was known for its Malpaque oysters, they offered everyone a bowl of oyster stew to go with their lobsters for an additional fifteen dollars. Jack was amazed that the support from Canada's smallest province almost brought in the most money, more than thirty-six thousand. The event in Middleton, in the heart of the Annapolis Valley, also went well.

Jack totalled all of the receipts reported and came up with a grand total for the day of $158,971.03 He was shocked, and he still had the second dinner in Sydney tonight and a very large event in Halifax on Friday the 15th, only another five days away.

The second dinner in Sydney was much more subdued, since it was put on for those people who couldn't be accommodated the night before. Jack was able to meet a lot of the entertainers and told some of the Men of the Deeps about the voice of Clay McBride. The bar closed at eleven p.m. because it was Sunday, and yet they were still able to raise another $21,952.75. The greasy stranger was also in attendance for the second night. Again their eyes met, and again the man disappeared. Jack was perplexed and asked Liam if he knew who the stranger was when he was spotted coming out of the men's room. "Never seen him before in my life, must be from 'away.'"

Jack stayed over Monday to have Thanksgiving dinner with Colin's family. He felt a little embarrassed when they all held hands and Andrew, Colin's father said, "...and we thank you, oh Lord, for the friendship and the kindness Jack Souster has given this family and especially to our son Colin."

Moira, who was sitting to Jack's right, squeezed his hand as they all said "Amen," and Jack could feel Glen curled up at his feet. They watched the late night news and Jack was shocked to see that the fundraising events of the weekend were headline news, appearing before the stories of the first Cuban refugee boat arriving in the U.S. and the closing of the New York World's Fair in Flushing Meadow. For the first time, he saw himself on television during the interview he had given during the first lobster dinner. Apex Research Corporation was reporting that the Liberals had fallen in popular support from their lofty 38 percent down to a meagre 13.5 percent. The president of Apex linked the fall in popularity directly to the handling of the "Colin Macdonald Issue." They had been totally wiped off the electoral map in the Maritimes, never had much support in the west, and they were now suffering tremendous losses in Ontario and Québec.

Pierre Cadeau was being interviewed, and in his arrogant way, he said, "I'm not worried one bit. The U.S. is our largest trading partner, and I don't intend to do anything to jeopardize that relationship and, furthermore, the only polls that count are those on election day."

He started to walk away but one reporter shouted out, "Mr. Prime Minister, what about the two Americans you extradited at the request of the U.S. State Department, shouldn't the treatment be the same for Colin MacDonald?"

Cadeau glared at the reporter, turned and walked away, heading down the marble hallway to his suite of offices. "No further questions," interjected a press aide. However, the question was out there for all the country to hear, and the prime minister's arrogance was once again at center stage.

After a huge breakfast of orange juice, farm fresh eggs, lightly scrambled, along with Bounty Market's locally cured and smoked extra thick-cut bacon with the rind still on, toasted homemade bread and tea, it was time for Jack to leave his newfound family and head to Halifax for "The Big Do" on Friday.

As he climbed into his Mini Minor, everyone gathered around. He had shaken hands and hugged everyone, including the dogs Jessie and Glen, and promised to say hi to Colin as soon as he saw him. Both Moira and Gillian seemed to be crying as Jack headed down the long laneway. He checked his rear-view mirror, and they were still waving goodbye. He responded with a quick beep of the horn followed by a wave out the window.

They had all told him to take the St. Petersburg route, since it was closer to the Brador Lakes and would cut out at least half an hour off his time.

He was well on his way and just coming up a slight knoll in the road and a curve, just east of Big Pond, when suddenly a large black Lincoln appeared beside him. Jack hadn't seen the car approaching in his mirror. There was a steep embankment down to the lake on Jack's right, and no guardrail. The Lincoln, without warning swerved abruptly to the right, hitting Jack's left front fender and then continued to push sideways as it slowed down, scraping along Jack's door. The right wheels of the Mini were digging into the soft shoulder, and he was heading for the embankment, where he could see a scrawny pine tree coming up directly in front of him.

The Lincoln's driver seemingly assumed he had done his job and sped off as Jack struggled to get his car under control. Fortunately, it had front wheel drive, and Jack was used to driving in sleet, snow and gravel. The hills of the Finger Lakes region of New York in winter had prepared him well for the worst of conditions. He eventually got control of the car, and it jumped back onto the paved highway only feet before the drop-off. He caught a glimpse of the car that had tried to run him off the road climbing a hill in the far distance. The windows of the offending car had been tinted so Jack could not see the driver. The only part he could see of the Lincoln's licence plate was that it was from the state of New York.

The RCMP came out from Sydney to the Irving Oil station where Jack had pulled over to inspect the damage. The driver's door was damaged so that it couldn't be opened, so Jack had to crawl in and out of the passenger door. The police couldn't do anything except make a report so the insurance company would be satisfied that such an incident took place. After waiting for the police to arrive, going back to the scene, and holding the tape measure for the officer as he recorded all of the skid marks and ruts and took photos, Jack was a good two hours behind schedule.

*   *   *

This was Jack's first time in Halifax. He had to stop many times to get directions to the home of Robert Bennett, the city's most prominent developer. The developer had invited Jack to join him at the fundraising dinner he was planning on Colin's behalf. It was to be a black tie, business suit-optional affair, and Jack had been invited to sit at the head table and be a guest speaker. He was happy that he had still had his tux, dress shirt, bow tie and cuff links from his days at the Chateau, although he knew that they'd have to be cleaned or at least pressed, as they had been traveling all over Cape Breton with him. He had only talked to Mr. Bennett once on the phone and accepted his kind invitation to stay at their home "on the Arm." Jack had no idea what "on the Arm" meant until he started asking directions through the passenger's side window. The driver's side one was out of commission due to the accident.

One gas station attendant smiled as he gave Jack directions and said, "You drive this out 'on the arm,' and property values will take an instant nose dive." Jack eventually found "The Cedars," the estate of Robert and Susan Bennett, drove between the massive stone gate pillars, and continued on a large circular driveway which brought him directly in front of the granite steps leading up to a beautiful Georgian-style mansion. Two young children came running out of the house and an attractive woman in jeans, sneakers and red-and-white gingham shirt appeared as Jack emerged, having crawled over the gear shift and passenger's seat.

"Mrs. Bennett?" He extended his hand.

"Jack Souster. Please call me Susan...come in," she said as the large Irish Wolfhound tried to jump up on her guest.

"Bozo...get down. Please don't pay him any mind, he's such a clown. Bob will be down in a minute." Jack retrieved his suitcase and one of the kids took everything up to his room. He sat down and enjoyed a beer with his hostess as he started to tell her all the sordid details of his road trip adventure.

"Wait, wait, wait, here comes Bob, he'll want to hear everything, no sense repeating yourself."

"Jack? Bob Bennett, and it's Bob, let's get that out of the way."

The young developer was impeccably attired in a blue blazer and gray flannels, with a yellow paisley-patterned silk ascot and matching handkerchief puffed in the blazer's breast pocket. He was slightly portly, with a ruddy complexion and a handshake and smile that would warm the coldest of hearts. Jack was amazed at how young the developer was.

He had been told that Bob Bennett was perhaps the most philanthropic person in Halifax, if not all of Nova Scotia. He donated often to various charities, with a penchant for children's organizations. They started to talk, and before Jack knew it, an ordered-in party size pizza was finished, and the kids were sent up to do their teeth and get ready for bed. Bob was astonished at how much money had already been raised. He began telling Jack about what was going to happen the next night. Then Susan appeared with a large rolled up tapestry. As she unrolled it Jack saw an incredible picture of Colin in his Cornell hockey gear, looking up and leaning slightly forward, with his stick firmly planted on the ice. The artist had signed it, ever so small, in the lower right corner of the 3ft. x 4ft. wall hanging.

"She's even put in the small mole on the right of his mouth. I can't believe it. This thing is beautiful," exclaimed Jack. He was awestruck!

"Susan and I drove up to Cheticamp over Thanksgiving

and gave Natalie LeBlanc five grand for Colin's trust fund. I'm putting it in the silent auction. We'll see what it brings in." Bob continued, "We've sold out both the Regency and Imperial Ballrooms at the Lord Nelson, which fortunately are adjoining, and it's still going to be tight with eight hundred coming. Next to these rooms is the Georgian lounge where they are constructing a stage and dance floor for the Moxie Whitney Orchestra from the Royal York."

"Moxie Whitney? Really? I know him really well from my days at the hotel. It will be great to see him again."

"The tickets have gone for $250.00 each. All four provincial premiers and the lieutenant governor of Nova Scotia will all be attending, and a good business associate from Ontario is flying down for the event." Jack did a quick calculation and realized that the dinner receipts would be over $200,000.00, which would bring the total to well over $375,000.00.

* * *

Susan Bennett had shown Jack all the highlights of Halifax and made sure that his tux was sent out to the drycleaners. Friday, October 15th arrived sooner than Jack had thought possible. He had talked to Ruth on Tuesday and Thursday and to Colin on Wednesday and earlier in the afternoon before he started to dress for the party.

"Man, you have no idea what kind of support you've got up here in Nova Scotia. I'm freaking out about tonight's dinner. Black tie and all...the lieutenant governor's going to be there, and all the Maritime premiers. But it's going to be great."

"Jack, if I know you, you'll slay them...be sure to thank everyone for me."

"Absolutely, wish me luck, bud." Jack was nervous knowing that he had to speak to eight hundred of the most influential people in Atlantic Canada, with considerable clout in Ottawa.

"You'll do just fine. Jack, I know you know, but I want to say it again, I can't thank you enough for what you're doing for me."

"Not a problem, you'd do the same for me." As they hung up, Jack feeling very much alone, yet rejuvenated.

A large black stretch limousine pulled up to the front door, and they all climbed in. It wasn't long before they pulled up to the front door of the Lord Nelson Hotel, along with what seemed like an endless line of limos, some with government licence plates and one with the flag of the lieutenant governor on each of the front fenders. They proceeded up to the convention floor, where there were numerous people standing with drinks in hand, eyeing the canapés and hors d'oeuvres. Those with cigarettes in hand were trying desperately to figure out a way to hold a drink, a lit cigarette and delicious morsels.

Tables were filled with items for the silent auction, each one with a pad of paper, a pen and a place for names and amounts attached. There was a beautiful signed Jack Gray maritime print, and someone had driven down to Windsor, Nova Scotia, to pick up a couple of original Maude Lewis panels. Maude Lewis was considered to be the "Grandma Moses" of Canadian art circles, and being a little more primitive than her American counterpart, her works were quickly becoming collectors' items. There was an all-expenses-paid weekend at the Sword and Anchor Inn in the beautiful village of Chester, only an hour outside of Halifax on the South Shore.

Susan and Bob Bennett started introducing Jack to the numerous luminaries. Jack felt comfortable, having greeted members of the Royal Family, film stars and business icons during his brief career in the hotel business.

Out of the corner of his eye he saw the same young stranger that he had seen at both the lobster dinners in Sydney. His hair was still greased back, and he was the only male in the room not wearing a tie. Instead he had a loose-fitting white silk shirt opened halfway down his chest, exposing two gaudy gold chains. His pants were tapered to the point where they hugged his ankles, directing one's eyes to a pair of scruffy black shoes that were so pointed they could be considered dangerous. He was talking to an older man, balding, heavy-set, and smoking a very large cigar. Bob excused himself as he went to greet a friend, the same man who was talking to the stranger.

Bob returned shortly with the balding gentleman and introduced him as Enzo Costa. "Enzo is a major developer in Toronto. He's recognized the growing population of Italians arriving in Canada and settling in Toronto. Most of the surrounding subdivisions there are his. He's buying up as many farms as he can get his hands on for future developments. We call it 'land banking,'" Bob explained. "We've done some joint venture deals together."

Jack shook Enzo's hand then asked him who he had been talking to. "That's my cousin's boy, Guido, he's a good boy, not too bright, but does what he's told," said the developer.

"Who's your cousin?" asked Bob.

"Giovanni Moretti."

Bob went white. "Don't worry, Bobby, don't believe everything you read," said Enzo, and turning to Jack he added, "I'll talk to him, don't worry. He's a good boy." Jack and Bob looked at each other in distress, thinking of what had happened to Jack on the road just outside of Big Pond and the Mario Curozzo incident between Field and Lake Louise..

The head table guests were gathered in an anteroom, where Jack had the pleasure of meeting the lieutenant governor and the various dignitaries and their spouses. All four premiers assured him they had written letters of support for Colin to the prime minister, urging him to seek extradition from the U.S. They had also all written letters to the governor of New York asking for his intervention, at least in making sure that Colin was safe and kept out of harm's way.

Soon a piper led the head table through the ballroom, which Susan and her committee had decorated in red and white. On one wall behind the head table was a ten-foot high mural of Colin in his usual pose with his stick on the ice wearing his Cornell uniform. On the opposite wall was an equally high mural of Cornell's Big Red Bear appearing through the huge Cornell "C."

The television cameras, microphones and lights were all set up. "Would it be appropriate for me to slam the prime minister again in front of all of these people?" Jack asked Bob. "He's pretty powerful, and I would think that he's got the message by now, but you never know."

After a brief pause Bob said, "You never know, but Guido

could be his 'messenger.' He's been known to play hardball, so be careful ...it's your call."

There was a very festive atmosphere as members of the orchestra quietly played dinner music in one corner of the dining room. People were jumping up and down from their seats to go out to the lobby to place bids or to see if their bid was still winning.

Shortly after dessert was served, Bob rose, acknowledged the guests at the head table and thanked everyone for coming. He then introduced Jack, who was familiar to all of them via the media, and they eagerly awaited what he had to say. Jack had no notes, and when he approached the microphone and the lectern, he felt completely at ease. He started his speech by recognizing the head table.

"Your honor, Commander and Mrs. Scrivener, Premier and Mrs. MacKinnon, Premier and Mrs. Campbell, Premier and Mrs. Joudry, Premier and Mrs. Trimball, Mr. And Mrs. Bennett, ladies and gentlemen.

"I met Colin Macdonald on the first day I attended Cornell University. By mere happenstance, I sat down at a table in the student cafeteria next to two friends of Colin's, and shortly thereafter Colin and his then-girlfriend, the beautiful Yvette Bouchard, sat down to join their friends. As we introduced ourselves I found out that Colin was studying in the School of Industrial and Labour Relations. It was obvious he was studying in order to carry on the family tradition of his father and uncle to improve the lives and the lot of the coal miners and their families in his hometown of Glace Bay.

"His amazing athletic skills and his hockey prowess easily got him on the Cornell hockey team and his leadership abilities soon won him the honor of being named team captain. Last year, only months before his graduation, he lead the team to the NCAA championship and was voted the MVP. He scored a hat trick in each of the tournament games, a feat never before accomplished in the history of the tournament, and, I believe, it will be a long time before anyone accomplishes the same deed again. Colin was more than a hockey jock. He had a 3.9 grade average, and with his heavy school load as well as hockey practices and games, he still found time to help coach the local Ithaca High School hockey team, appear as a guest speaker at numerous charitable fundraising events, and often on a free afternoon you would find him visiting the children's ward at the Tompkins County Hospital, giving hope to all those youngsters whom life has dealt a bitter blow.

"Over the last few days I have had the great pleasure and honor to meet Colin's family and friends in Glace Bay. There is absolutely no doubt in my mind that he gets his amazing resolve and character from some of the finest people I have ever met. They say that it takes a village to raise a child. Well let me say this; the town of Glace Bay has raised one of the finest individuals that Canada has ever produced."

This was interrupted by a loud and long standing ovation.

"As you know, Colin is sitting in a jail cell awaiting his trial next Tuesday as a serial killer, and if he loses he faces execution by the electric chair. I probably know Colin better than anyone in this room, and I can honestly tell you that Colin DID NOT murder any one of those co-eds. Colin did not have it in him to hurt anyone. Having said that, I have seen him throw a pretty good body check or two."

Some in the crowd chuckled.

"I have never seen anything like the love between Colin

and Yvette. They were inseparable. They adored each other and they loved life. Wherever they were on campus they would bring huge smiles to everyone's faces. I will never forget that day, only a few short months ago, when Colin signed his first NHL contract with the Toronto Maple Leafs and he and Yvette announced their engagement. He had so much to live for and Yvette was the center of his world. There is no way that Colin could have committed these dastardly crimes."

Jack looked directly at the battery of television cameras. "Prime Minister Cadeau has repeatedly said that the Canadian government will not interfere with any legal matters of this nature, since the U.S. is our largest trading partner. Well, I ask the prime minister, 'What do you think a Canadian sitting in a jail cell, facing a trial which could eventually send him to his death, would think of your policy? What do you think the rest of Canada thinks of your policy, knowing that when travelling abroad they do not have the support of their government and could be incarcerated for any reason, depending on the quirky state of mind of the local authorities? One of Nova Scotia's finest sons, if not one of Canada's finest, I can tell you, doesn't think much of the government of the country of his birth...and neither do I. There is an election on the horizon, and we will see what the rest of Canada thinks of your policy."

Returning his gaze towards the audience, he said, "I firmly believe that next Tuesday, October 19th, Colin MacDonald will be found NOT GUILTY."

Looking down at the dignitaries at the head table, he concluded. "I wish to thank your honor, the premiers of the four Maritime Provinces for their attendance tonight, and especially to Mr. and Mrs. Bennett for their most generous support and for organizing this event. I also wish to thank each and every one of you for your support, and I know that Colin's spirits will be surely lifted when he hears about your presence here tonight and your backing. Thank you all, very much."

The crowd rose to its feet and applauded for what seemed like forever. Jack looked down the head table to see all were standing and applauding. The lieutenant governor, the representative of the Queen, was not permitted to take political sides and remained seated, stone-faced. Still, his honor, who happened to look up at Jack at the same time Jack glanced over at him, gave the young speaker a warm smile and a slight nod.

The Moxie Whitney Orchestra started up playing "Far Above Cayuga's Waters" as people sang along using the song sheets that had been passed out. It was announced that the dancing had begun, that the bar was now open, and that the silent auction would continue for one more hour. The sheets would be gathered and the winning bidders could bring their cheques to Susan Bennett and her committee at the auction table. She was overwhelmed when she saw that her husband's friend and occasional joint venture partner, Enzo Costa, had bid $25,000.00 for Natalie LeBlanc's hand-hooked wall hanging. Conservative Premier Gerry MacKinnon of Nova Scotia pleaded with Costa to allow him to hang the tapestry in the Nova Scotia Legislature until Colin was released. Jack wasn't sure if this was a sincere gesture or one to ensure his re-election. Enzo agreed and then headed over to talk to his nephew Guido. Something was said that required finger pointing while his large cigar was being clamped down in his vice-like jaw. Guido slowly slunk out of the room. Enzo found Jack and said, "Don't worry about Guido. You won't see him again, but all in all, he's a good boy."

People approached Jack throughout the evening, congratulating him on his speech and asking him to give Colin their best wishes. Many of them gave Jack cheques made out to the Colin Macdonald Trust Fund. These totalled another $3,765.00, and with the additional $43,650.00 from the silent auction, Jack made a mental rapid mental calculation and estimated that the trust fund had now reached over $425,000.00.

Bob, Susan and Jack were the last to leave at around one thirty in the morning. They had thanked everyone personally while the guests gathered their wraps and coats. The limousine swept through the gates of the Cedars and deposited the three tired but very satisfied partiers.

"One quick nightcap," Bob insisted, and they replayed all the events of the evening. Jack finally said that he had a long drive ahead of him. He hoped to get to Bangor, Maine, for the next evening, since Colin's trial started the following Tuesday the 19th.

"Oh, that Airline Route #9 through Maine is not the greatest. I don't envy you," Bob said as they all got to their feet and Susan gave Jack a kiss on the cheek. Bob had taken Jack's Mini to a local body shop, and it had been returned the previous day looking as if it had just come off the showroom floor. Every scrape and dent was gone, the window worked better than it ever had, and the car had been given a complete paint job, all a gift from the young developer.

"No sense driving up your insurance rates...whether it's your fault or somebody else's, they still find a way to raise your rates," Bob claimed. The children as well as Bozo the dog all came out to say goodbye. Susan gave Jack a farewell peck on the cheek. Bob who looked at the younger man and said, "Good luck, my friend. If there's anything we can do for you, you know our number. Safe trip."

Jack got into the Mini and checked his directions as he headed slowly through the gates of the magnificent estate.

– 22 –

Jack found his way out of Halifax without any problem and drove west on the #102 towards New Brunswick, where he would head south and cross the Canada/U.S. border at St. Stephen, New Brunswick and Calais, Maine. Then onto Highway # 9, which was extremely winding and hilly with many logging trucks bearing down on him. He was reminded of just how small the Mini was when one of the loggers would pass him and he'd find himself at eye level with one of the twenty-two-wheeler's axles. He was hoping to get past Bangor, where he would pick up Interstate 295 and head south to Portland, thereby having to stop only one night. The following day he would push on to Ithaca.

The Mini was small, and Jack's long legs sometimes cramped up. He finally pulled over at a small gas bar and diner just south of Bangor. He'd had enough driving for one day. The property had been carved out of a stand of tall lodge pole pines. Past the gravel parking lot was a forest floor of pine needles with the odd, low shrub fighting for some light, sharing the area with blueberry bushes. After filling up with gas, he asked the attractive attendant if she knew of a reasonable motel nearby.

"You're in luck today. I've got one room left out back. Twenty-five bucks cash up front," she said. He took it sight unseen and drove around to the back of the building. He hadn't been with Consuela for some time, and the very tight shorts and T-shirt on the attendant got him wondering what she was doing after work. There was a half-ton truck with some dogs in the back parked in front of his room # 2, so he pulled into the spot in front of room #3. He walked past the yelping dogs to room #2. The tarnished brass numeral was hanging upside down, swinging on one screw. He opened the door and was greeted by the heavy, thick stench of stale cigarettes and mould. He left the door ajar and opened the window to air out the room. Large pickup trucks were parked in front of the other five rooms. Two of them had gun racks in the back and another two had large cages with hounds howling, panting and looking for some sort of excitement.

Jack checked the room, and apart from the stench it was quite clean, although he wasn't thrilled at all the rust around the bathtub and shower fixtures. The towels were fresh and clean. He brought his bag in and decided to have some dinner before going to bed. As he rounded the corner of the building to go into the diner, he stopped and his heart jumped as he saw Guido Moretti filling up a black Lincoln with a scrape all down the side. Guido finished filling up his car and went inside to pay the attendant. Jack quickly went over to the car and crouched down low so that nobody would see him.

There were clear traces of red paint embedded in the scrapes. Jack ran back to the corner of the building, hoping that Guido would not see him and praying that he would not see Jack's car. His heart was racing. The mob boss's son came out and sped off. Jack was relieved but still nervous as he ate his burger and fries with a milkshake. He watched intently as the gas jockey/waitress scooped three servings of chocolate ice cream into the metal container and added just a splash of milk with some chocolate syrup. The old green Hamilton Beach mixer strained as it started and then within a minute produced a milkshake that none of the fast food restaurants which were popping up everywhere could duplicate.

The counter was in a double S shape, and every seat was soon filled. Many of the men were wearing their fluorescent orange hunting hats and red and black checkered quilted woolen jackets over their plaid Vyella shirts. "What's with the dogs?" Jack asked the gentleman beside him.

"Bear hunting season, dogs'll find 'em...the woods are busy this time of year, what with the moose season just starting and bear, got to watch yerself out there."

Jack struck up quite a conversation with a number of the hunters and explained that he was Canadian and just passing through. They were all Boston Bruins fans but promised that they wouldn't hold it against him that he rooted for The Maple Leafs.

Back in his room he tried, since it was a Saturday night, to get a hockey game on the small black and white television. When this proved impossible, he slipped between the sheets, but not before checking for bedbugs. Even though the curtains were drawn tight, they were thin enough to allow some of the powerful parking lot lights to filter through into his room. A couple of the hounds were howling outside, but he was tired enough to drift off into a deep sleep without any trouble.

Jack was woken by an incredibly loud blast coming from the room next to him, followed by another. They were coming from room #3, and Jack could hear someone through the wall yell, "Call the cops, hurry, someone call the cops." By the time Jack found the phone, retrieved his glasses, and started to look up the phone number for the police, he could hear the sirens coming down the highway. In less than a minute, two cruisers, with lights and sirens piercing the night air, pulled up behind his Mini in front of room #3.

By the time Jack pulled on his pants to go outside to see what was happening, a number of other voices had appeared on the scene. He carefully opened his door to see if it was all right to go out, and there, splayed backwards on the hood of the Mini, with his bloodied face looking skyward from the windshield, was Guido Moretti. The car was so small that the hood barely came up to the back of his knees. One shotgun blast had hit him in his chest and a second sprayed his neck and face. The force of the blasts had thrown the victim back onto the hood of the Mini. Thick blood was oozing from his open cavity and straining through his silk shirt. It was running down the hood of the Mini and forming pools on the gravelled parking space. The streams and pools of blood appeared black and were reflecting light from the glaring parking lot and service station light stanchions.

"I saw this guy's shadow through the curtain, and I saw that he had a gun. I grabbed mine in case he was coming into my room, and sure enough, he kicks the door in with his gun pointed right at the bed. I let him have it," the hunter was explaining to the police.

Jack immediately recognized Moretti's corpse, not so much for his unrecognizable face but by his bloody, matted greasy hair and his many gold chains, now knotted and covered in blood, flesh and sternum bone fragments. Jack's stomach churned even more as he realized that there was pink and white brain matter spattered all over his windshield. He didn't know what to say, whether to keep his mouth shut or tell the police what he suspected.

Without thinking, he said, "Excuse me, Officer, I think this man was trying to kill me." The assembled hunters and the police all looked at Jack, who continued, "He tried to run me off the road in Cape Breton, Nova Scotia...that's in Canada, and there is so much more to the story. He must have been gunning for me, mistakenly thinking I was residing in # 3," said Jack with nervous excitement as his adrenalin continued to pump.

"Would you mind coming with us to the detachment office and giving us a statement? I'll need you to come down too," the cop said to the shaken hunter, who was still pointing his gun at the ground.

The hunter was William Edwards, vice president of Traveler's Insurance in Hartford, Connecticut. He was on his annual hunting trip with a friend, also an insurance executive from Hartford.

Jack climbed into the back seat of one cruiser while Bill Edwards was handcuffed and put into the back of the second cruiser. They had to wait at the scene until numerous photographs were taken, and until the ambulance arrived and the body was put into a body bag, placed on a stretcher and taken to the morgue in Bangor. Yellow "POLICE LINE

DO NOT CROSS" tape was unrolled and went from the door of room #3, out into the parking lot and around Jack's car before returning down the other side and back to the motel.

Once in the station, Jack started telling the story of his friend, Colin MacDonald, and all the dangerous incidents that had occurred, many involving Moretti. One officer was looking through Guido's wallet for identification, and when he found it, he placed a call to someone in the New York City police department.

"There's a warrant out for this kid's arrest: attempted murder and threatening. Hmm, why didn't the border guards pick him up if he came in from Canada?" he asked the other officer.

"They're only interested in catching people with too many cigarettes or an extra bottle of booze," was the reply.

Having heard Jack's story, he turned to the insurance executive. "I'm afraid I'm going to have to charge you with murder, although it sounds to me that you have a pretty good defence. If you get yourself a good lawyer, he'll have you out on bail in quick order, and we won't object to that. But I'm telling you that you may be paying for this with your life. Nobody kills a Moretti without paying for it dearly. Get yourself some good protection when you're released."

After Jack recounted his story and signed an affidavit promising to let the police know of his exact whereabouts should he ever leave Ruth Golden's address in Ithaca, he was chauffeured back to his motel room, this time sitting in the front seat with the young officer, who wasn't much older than him.

Bill Edwards was concerned about his dogs in the back of the pickup. He asked Jack to tell his friend in room #4 what was happening, and asked him to call his wife and to look after the dogs. It was now six in the morning. Jack had had only four hours sleep and thought he'd try to get in two more hours until he arrived at the scene and saw the state of his car.

The young officer removed the police tape from around the Mini after taking a few more photographs, as Jack went around to the restaurant to get some water and some rags. The same young gas attendant/cook/waitress, and probably wife or girlfriend of the owner, went to get him a pail of hot soapy water, a sponge and a couple of rags. She was now wearing a Boston Bruins jersey with "Bucyk" and a huge #9 across her back. She asked him to dump the bloodied water on the lawn beside the parking lot, and if he needed some clean water, he should get it from the outside tap.

The clots and streams of blood had now congealed and turned black in the open air. It took considerable elbow grease with lots of soap and water to remove everything. He came close to vomiting when he found a small bit of flesh, or bone or the odd hair stuck in a clotted pool. The dogs, smelling the blood, started to howl like Jack had never heard before. One by one the other occupants of the small motel appeared at their doorways in various states of undress. Carl Swanson, Bill Edwards' friend, was most helpful and retrieved more hot water for Jack as he poured the bloodied waste down the bathtub drain.

"She's not going to like that," Jack said.

"She's not going to know," was the reply. With both of them working at it, they had the Mini cleaned up within half an hour. They kicked clean sand and gravel over the clots that had formed around the sides of the car, pooling close to the small tires. Jack took a shower, which took longer than usual.

He kept thinking that he hadn't completely washed all the blood off his hands. *Now I know how Lady Macbeth felt,* he thought.

He called Bob Bennett in Halifax and explained in great detail what had happened. There was silence at the other end of the line, then the Halifax developer said, "I'm sure that Enzo is legit. At least I hope so."

"I would like to think so, but how did Guido know my route back to Ithaca?"

"Hmmm, perhaps he just followed you the whole way."

That thought sent a chill through Jack's body. They decided not to tell Enzo until Jack arrived safely at Ruth's, for there was no telling what the Moretti family would do if they found Jack en route. At least in Ithaca there was some strength in numbers, and Clive might be able to suggest methods of getting some protection.

Jack threw his bag into the car, went around and checked out, grabbing a coffee to go, unable to face food for awhile. It was now his birthday, Sunday, the 17th of October, and the trial was to start on the 19th. He still hoped to make it back to Ithaca by Monday to allow a couple of hours to speak to Colin, Clay and Clive, and knowing how little sleep he'd had, he knew that it might not happen.

He had to drive past Portland to pick up the Massachusetts Turnpike west, which would eventually lead onto the New York Thruway, past Albany, down to Binghamton, and finally up to Ruth's in Ithaca. It was at least a ten- to eleven-hour drive, and with his lack of sleep, it would be doubtful if he could go the full distance without stopping. Having phoned his parents, Ruth and Clay, he was still somewhat shaken after repeating the night's events. Clive was with Clay, which saved him a fourth call. Clive was going to check in with some of his contacts and asked Jack to call him the next time he filled up.

"Perhaps around Lowell, and, hopefully, I'll find out if there really is a hit out on you. If so, you'd better get to the police as soon as possible...but I'll let you know. Watch your back," said the P.I. as he hung up. Those words didn't give Jack that much confidence, but he started the car and began backtracking to Interstate 295, then headed south to Boston.

The trip henceforth had been uneventful, and Jack's confidence was gradually returning to normal until he checked in with Clive from the gas bar in Lowell, where he had already located the Massachusetts's State Police office. "Where the hell've you've been?" asked the worried and angry P.I. after receiving Jack's call.

"Everything's O.K." said Jack. "Why?"

"Why, you ask. You've been named the mob's number one target. They're really pissed off. I don't know what to suggest. Maybe if you explained everything to the state troopers, they could drive you here...offer to pay them for their children's Christmas fund or whatever. Have them call me and I'll explain everything in police talk, maybe that'll help."

Jack explained his situation to the sergeant on the desk and asked him to call Clive as well as the police outside of Bangor. He produced Detective David Tattersall's card as well as Clive's phone number, which he had from memory.

The sergeant could see Jack's weariness and offered him a cup of coffee while he phoned Maine and New York to verify the story. Jack thanked the officer, sat down on a bench against the wall, and started to sip his coffee as the cop went into an inner office to make the calls. The last thing Jack heard was the crackling of the dispatch radio before he dozed off. He awoke to a gentle shake of his shoulder and quickly realized that there was a stream of drool coming out the right corner of his mouth. Embarrassed, he wiped his chin and mouth.

The sergeant said, "I think that you'd better spend the night here. You're too tired to drive, and I want to talk to my superiors about what we should do. There is no doubt that your story has been verified. The accommodation isn't great, but come with me and we'll give you a cot in a room that's normally kept for drunk drivers...the only difference between you and them is that we won't lock the door tonight." Jack was too tired to think, except he knew that he still had enough time to get to Binghamton before the trial on Tuesday.

*   *   *

It was now Monday morning, and no decision was made about what to do about Jack. After a full day of phone calls to headquarters, the Massachusetts State Troopers received permission to escort Jack to the state line and turn him over to the New York State Troopers. This was going to take considerable coordination and cooperation between the two Highway Patrol departments. Massachusetts was willing to go ahead with a plan of actually hooking Jack's Mini to a police-operated tow truck and have a cruiser take Jack and the Mini to the New York State line, at which point they would hand him over to the protective custody of the New York force. New York had not agreed to the plan, but due to the time constraints, Jack and the Massachusetts Police decided to leave, and hopefully when they got to the New York state line, things would be sorted out.

They crossed the state line and pulled into the New York State Troopers' Detachment Office at 8:25 p.m. The trial was starting the next morning at nine a.m. The Mini was lowered, released from its shackles and parked off to the side. The tow truck driver, the Massachusetts state trooper, and Jack all headed into the office, where Sergeant Muir had been expecting them. "I don't think that there's anything we can do to help you, but if you want to wait awhile, I'll try another avenue with my superiors...have a seat."

Jack felt most uncomfortable and unwelcome. Sergeant Muir was making a number of calls in a muffled voice so Jack couldn't hear exactly what was being said. Every now and again Muir would raise his head and look at Jack. Another inspector entered the office, introduced himself as Inspector Carlos Rossi and started talking quietly to the sergeant, also taking a furtive glance or two in Jack's direction. Jack decided to call Clive. He realized that he still had a three-hour drive to Binghamton and therefore would be driving through the night, which caused him some concern.

"What's the number of your pay phone, and I'll call you back as soon as possible, after I check with some of my friends," said Clive. "Just sit tight."

"There's nothing we can do tonight," said the sergeant, "but you can spend the night here and we'll figure something out in the morning."

"That's too late. I have to be in Binghamton by tomorrow morning." Jack went back to his chair and sat with his head in his hands, weighing the idea setting out on his own. He was very frightened of what the mob could do if they ever found him and was feeling more alone than at any time in his life. He decided it had best wait until the morning and asked Muir if there were a couple of more chairs he could put together so that he could lie down and sleep. All of a sudden the pay phone jangled, startling Jack as well as the sergeant. Jack picked up.

"Don't say a word other than 'yes' or 'no.'" It was Clive's voice. "Don't look anywhere," he continued, "just face the wall." Jack obeyed, his heart starting to pound. "Have you met a Detective Rossi yet?"

"Yes."

"Shit, again, don't look around or show any signs of emotion, but Rossi is what is called a 'dirty cop.' He's on Moretti's payroll. You've got to get the hell out of there without them seeing you go. Wait for the right time and quietly slip out. Maybe wait until the cop has to take a leak or something. You'll eventually want to get on to Route 88 just before Schenectady and take it south to Binghamton. You'll come to a town called Oneonta, and I want you to pull into the Mobil station at the edge of town. You'll see an Ithaca police car there. It's Bill Braxton, a friend of mine on the force, and he'll bring you into Ithaca. You'll have to leave your car at the Mobil station, and Bill will have made arrangements with the station to hide it around the back of the building. Don't worry if you can't slip out for a few hours. Bill will be waiting for you. Take care. Oh...and good luck."

Jack said "Thanks" into a dead receiver. He casually walked over to the water cooler, pulled down a paper cone and poured himself a drink of water, having not been offered even a coffee since he had arrived.

Rossi left shortly after, which eased Jack's mind. The following hours were extremely quiet and boring, as the only things to read were a couple of brochures in Plexiglas holders fastened to the wall. One was titled "What The Police Can Do For You." The other brochure was meant for children, with cartoon characters and was titled "Mr. Policeman's Your Friend."

Unless his name is Mr. Rossi, Jack thought. He spent most of the time turning around with his chin resting on his arms, which were folded on the window sill, watching the lights of the cars travelling on the Thruway. The eastbound traffic seemed heavier than the westbound. All of a sudden he heard a snort coming from Sergeant Muir, who was sitting at his desk, behind the counter. His head was tilted back and the snort turned into very heavy breathing and eventually serious snoring. Jack quietly stood up and slowly walked over to the glass door. He held the door gingerly as it closed so that there would be no sound. He quickly got into the Mini and pulled away from the State Trooper Detachment buildings, lights off until he started to ease onto the Thruway, joining the rest of the traffic. He kept checking his rear-view mirror to see if any cars were coming out from the detachment driveway. *So far so good.* Jack hoped that the sergeant had a good sleep and that the police radio didn't crackle too much so that it would wake him. The night was dark, the road was slick and there were pockets of fog.

Jack soon came to Route 88, which was going to take him directly to Oneonta. There were far more curves and hills on this road than on the Thruway. Jack had noticed in his rear-view mirror just as he finished paying the toll as he left the Thruway that a car was coming up behind him. It only had one headlight.

As he proceeded along Route #88, he noticed that the one-eyed vehicle seemed to be following him. He would lose it from time to time as he disappeared over the crest of a hill and into the low-lying fog patch, or turning around a sharp bend. There had been a comfortable amount of traffic about half an hour ago, but it seemed to Jack that it was now that just he and the single-lighted car were sharing the road. He was beginning to feel really uncomfortable. He knew how his car handled in wet conditions, with its front wheel drive, and was confident that his Mini had the power to outrun a lot of cars. It was a Cooper, and Jack had put it through its paces before. He sped up to see if he could put some distance between the two cars, but to no avail. He then decided to slow down and perhaps the stranger would pass, but again this plan did not work. The car seemed to keep a good ten lengths back. Just enough so that Jack couldn't tell what make or model it was, and since it was dark, he couldn't even see what color it was, let alone get the licence number. A sign announcing the town limits of Oneonta appeared, and Jack gave a great sigh of relief.

The haloed sign of Mobil appeared through the fog and drizzle. Jack geared down and was most thankful to see Bill Braxton sitting in his Ithaca police cruiser. They went inside to the all-night lunch counter and had a bite to eat. Jack hadn't anything to eat for at least ten hours. The Mini was hidden out back. Jack got into the front seat of the cruiser with Braxton, and they headed off towards Binghamton.

After chatting for about fifteen minutes, Braxton noted, "The guy behind us has only one headlight. If it was within my jurisdiction, I'd pull him over."

"That guy was following me," Jack said as he explained about his trip from Schenectady to Oneonta.

"Well, let's just see if we can get a license plate number." Braxton did a quick turn into the parking lot of a small plaza. It was so fast the following car had no chance to react and continued past them. Jack made a quick mental note of the plate number, which Bill Braxton radioed in to his station for verification. It wasn't more than a minute when the dispatcher called back with "Carlos Rossi."

"Mean anything to you?" asked Bill.

"No, but it means a lot to Clive. Apparently he's not the cleanest of cops, but you'd better get the whole story from Clive. I just know that I'm not thrilled to know that he's been following me."

The sun was coming up in the east, and it looked as if the fog was dissipating. It was only another hour from Binghamton, where Bill Braxton suggested they go to meet Clive at a diner just opposite the court house. "All the cops and court officials, as well as some of the lawyers, hang out there."

They entered the diner, where Clay was sitting at a booth in one corner going over some papers. He jumped up at the sight of Jack and gave him a relieved slap on the back. He and Braxton introduced themselves and sat down to order some breakfast. Clive was due any moment.

"We've got an hour and half to go over everything before we're due in court."

"Finally, the big day has come." After some small talk, Clive Scranton arrived and joined the trio. They were about to go over some of the details of the case when Clay glanced at Clive and then at Bill.

"It's O.K. Bill's on our side, we can trust him," said Clive.

"Listen, go ahead without me. I'm happier not knowing, but remember if there is anything I can do, just let me know." Bill rose and shook everybody's hand. Jack thanked him profusely.

"I'll bring your car back for you," Bill said with a smile.

Jack tossed him the keys. "Thanks."

23

Clay, Clive and Jack headed across the street and up the wide, curved, steep staircase to the granite hall. "Court of Justice" was carved in large bold letters into the stone above the door, and above that was a relief of the woman in a flowing dress, blindfolded, holding up a large set of scales. Jack always thought that this was his sign of good luck, since the scales were the symbol of Libra, his zodiac sign. There was a huge American flag softly fluttering atop a large flagpole just to the right at the top of the stairs. Jack had to stop for a minute, as he started to feel a little dizzy after climbing the stairs.

"You O.K.?" asked Clay.

"Yeah, thanks, just give me a minute," replied Jack, not wanting to get into a discussion about his heart condition. They soon walked through the gigantic twelve-foot oak doors.

The floors were highly polished terrazzo, and the clean

smell of a recent waxing permeated the air. It was a cavernous lobby rising four floors to a glass dome. The sun spilled onto the mahogany wall.

"Courtroom 4, up the stairs to your right, second door on your right once you're up there," said the disinterested information clerk, pointing to his left at another set of sweeping stairs.

Jack looked at the stairs. "Is there an elevator?" he asked.

"Nope, but there's talk of putting one in. Seems like we're getting more and more cripples in here every day, but right now the stairs are the only option." Jack bristled at the word 'cripples'. The others, sensing his dismay, told him to take his time and they'd meet him inside Courtroom #4.

When Jack opened the door, he saw that Clay had already taken his seat at the defence table at the front and to the left. There was a wooden railing separating him from the rest of the courtroom. People were beginning to arrive, and Jack was happy to see that Clive was sitting beside Ruth. He joined them and gave Ruth a warm hug and kiss.

As they sat down they continued to hold hands. They could do no more. They were at the mercy of the court, and they were frightened. Jack looked at the judge's desk and was surprised at the height of the dais. In large, raised gold letters on the mahogany wall were the words "In God We Trust." Jack closed his eyes and thought, *If there is a God, please help Colin.*

Far across on the right side of the room was the jury box, where there were six seats in the front row and six behind. As in the bail hearing courtroom, there was a large photograph of President Lyndon Johnson hanging on the wall directly behind the witness stand. There was a table directly in front of and below the judge's desk reserved for the clerk. The prosecutor's table was to the right of Clay's, and they were separated by a gate in the bar leading from the center aisle that divided the courtroom. The spectators were filing in with a great deal of excited banter and a peculiar morbid interest. *How often do they get to witness a judge sentencing a convict to the death penalty and therefore to the electric chair?* Jack read into the mood of the room. There was a great flurry of activity at the entrance as both doors swung open and District Attorney Erik Wolfe strutted in, followed by four of his staff members carrying boxes of documents. He seized the moment with his head held arrogantly high, almost begging the appreciative audience to applaud his entrance. As he opened the gate into the inner sanctum, he gave a disdainful nod to Clay, who returned it with a subdued smile.

There was restless anticipation in the crowd as the lawyers continued to shuffle their papers. Minutes later a door opened to the left of the defence table. The crowd all of a sudden became hushed as Colin walked in. He was pale, almost ashen, with an expression of pure fear on his face. He had clearly lost at least twenty pounds. One eye was still showing signs of distress from his beating, with some light green and purple bruising, and his nose was now slightly off center. Ruth had delivered a clean shirt, pressed pants, a tie and a sports jacket to the prison the day before so that Colin would have something decent to wear. His legs were shackled and his wrists handcuffed behind him. There was a guard on either side of him, each leading him by his elbows. As one guard removed his handcuffs, he looked at Jack and Ruth. He was clearly terrified, even though he tried to force a slight smile. One shackle was removed from his right ankle, which was then attached to a rung on the chair. He shook hands with Clay, and they said a few words before they both took their seats.

A few people on the far side of the courtroom were straining to catch a glimpse of the man now known to them as the "Hat Trick Murderer." A couple of flash bulbs went off, but the court clerk rose and said "No photographs! Guard, please seize those cameras."

The offending photographers gave no resistance and relinquished their cameras to avoid ejection. Jack noticed the woman in tweed, the same one he had seen coming out of the warden's office.

"Who's that?" Jack asked Ruth.

"I don't know, but she was at Colin's bail hearing."

Jack asked Clive the same question. "I don't know, but she looks familiar...come to think of it, she was hanging around the courthouse on the day of Colin's bail hearing."

"All rise!" shouted the court clerk as the door to the left of the judge's dais opened, and in walked an elderly, ruddy-faced, white-haired man dressed in black robes.

"You may be seated." Jack noticed a slight hint of kindness in the otherwise gruff voice.

Judge Harold Hyndmann had an excellent reputation for being just and seeing that defendants received an extremely fair trial, going out of his way to give the defence attorneys a little leeway, although once a verdict was given, the punishment could be severe if the accused was found guilty. There was very little room for leniency.

"He didn't get the nickname of 'Old Sparky' for nothing. If he thinks someone's guilty, he'd just as soon fry 'em," said

Clive.

"Please bring in the jury." At that order one of the court officers opened a door to the left of the jury box, and the jury entered in single file. Jack scrutinized each one carefully as they took their seat. There were eight women and four men. Five of the women were black, three white, and there was one black male, two white males and an Hispanic. All twelve appeared to be over the age of thirty-five. Jack wondered if this was truly a "Jury of Colin's peers." Three of the men and one woman looked directly at Colin as they took their seat. The others looked either at the judge or at the assembled gallery of observers.

"Will the defendant please rise," said the judge. "Will the clerk please read the charges against the accused?"

"In the case of New York State versus Colin MacDonald, the accused has been charged with first degree murder of Nicole Watson in the first count. The accused has been charged with first degree murder of Amy Schechter in the second count. The accused has been charged with first degree murder of Yvette Bouchard in the third count."

The judge looked down at Colin and said, "Does the defendant understand the charges against him?"

"Yes, I do, your honor." Colin's voice was clear and firm, although Jack could notice a slight nervous twitch in his right hand as he tried to steady himself on the table.

"How do you plead?"

"Not guilty, your honor."

"On all three counts?" asked the judge.

"Yes, sir," responded Colin.

"Are both parties ready to proceed?"

"We are, your honor," replied Clay in his beautifully resonant voice, which stilled the courtroom. Likewise, Erik Wolfe nodded towards the judge.

"We'll start with opening statements to the jury then," said the judge, nodding to Erik Wolfe. The smarmy district attorney stood and proceeded to walk towards the jury as if he was a preening peacock looking for a willing pea hen, but in this case he was looking for votes for his upcoming campaign. There wasn't a crease in his suit, except in his pants, which were as sharp as the knives that had slit the throats of the victims. A turquoise silk tie and matching puff accompanied a suit that was in between light and charcoal gray with brilliant, shiny black alligator shoes. Strutting back and forth in front of the jury, he said that he would prove without a reasonable doubt that the accused, Mr. Colin MacDonald, had committed all three of these heinous crimes.

"You will hear the testimony of a person who heard the accused and the victim have a violent fight the afternoon of the murder, and you will hear a witness who saw the accused callously dump the body of Yvette Bouchard into Beebe Lake."

There was a large map of the Cornell campus on an easel so that everyone on the jury could see the various sites where the bodies were found. All of a sudden one of the female jurors started to sneeze then gag as she held her throat. The judge called a fifteen-minute recess until the woman could get a drink of water. At this point she advised the judge that she was allergic to strong fragrances and she thought that the district attorney's strong cologne was the cause of her distress. He then called Clay and Erik Wolfe into his chambers.

The judge adjourned the case for a day and asked everyone to be considerate and not wear any heavy perfumes or strong deodorants. He instructed the jury not to discuss the case with anyone, and all were to be seated in the courtroom no later than nine a.m. the next day. Jack noticed that Ruth had not returned since the recess. He finally spotted her at the bottom of the winding staircase, talking to the lady in tweed, who quickly left as she saw Jack descending the stairs.

"Did you find out who she is?" asked Jack.

"No, I asked her if she was with the press, and all she said was that she was a friend of one of the victim's mothers, and she just wanted to make sure that Colin got what he deserved."

Clive joined the conversation and said that he didn't believe a word of that. "She's been skulking around too much to be a friend of the family. I'll find out exactly who she is. See you guys tomorrow, enjoy the afternoon off."

Jack and Ruth went to her apartment, where she had invited him to stay during the trial. The sofa was a hide-a-bed, and although they had slept one night together, they knew that it was more the beer speaking rather than any particular attraction. Jack had come to realize that Ruth was becoming fond of Colin, and he no longer wanted to be unfaithful to Consuela.

Ruth enjoyed the company and had great fun cooking with Jack, testing many of the recipes he had acquired from Quantity Cooking 301. They talked and talked for hours, weighing every aspect of the case, but believed that they were just too close to it to figure it out. The fact that Colin had admitted to having a heated argument with Yvette the day before she was found dead didn't help him, and yet everyone had lover's spats, Jack recalled as he thought of the one in which he had almost lost Consuela. Yet the lovemaking that followed was one of those sessions that he would remember for the rest of his life.

They coordinated the bathroom time, and Jack cooked a gourmet breakfast before they set out to meet Clay and Clive at the courthouse. They were there in plenty of time, and Clive announced that he had no further knowledge of the identity of the lady in tweed. Bill Braxton discovered that the mysterious woman's car was registered to a company in Rhode Island called Tri State Formal Rentals, "Tuxes and gowns for every occasion. If you look good…We look good!"

"We are doing a check on the principals of the company, and maybe we can come up with something." At that point the lady in question drove into the parking lot, and they changed the topic as they proceeded up the stairs to the lobby and then up the next set of stairs.

"Not built for 'cripples'!" Jack laughed as he started up the second set, resting halfway up with Ruth at his side. She understood, which comforted him. Everyone sat in exactly the same seat as they had on the previous day. Judge Hyndmann apologized to the juror and assured her that the problem had been remedied. Erik Wolfe tried to pick up where he had left off, but somehow the interruption had taken the wind out of his sails as he stumbled over his words, and his arrogance was quite obviously forced.

After Wolfe finished, Clay stood up and slowly walked over to the juror's box and in a very quiet, deliberate and resonant tone talked of Colin's background: coming from a hard working coal mining family in Cape Breton; his stature as one of the finest hockey players to have put on a Cornell jersey; his love and his plans for his future with Yvette; his Dean's List standing at Cornell's School of Industrial Relations; his signed contract with the Toronto Maple Leafs.

"This young man had the world by the tail. Why would he commit these crimes? The prosecution tells you that they have all sorts of evidence, including an eyewitness. I'll tell you right now that they have nothing that links my client to any one of these murders, nor do they have a shred of forensic evidence. A murder weapon has never been recovered from any of the three homicides, and there is actually no motive for my client to have committed these horrendous crimes. I will prove to you that their 'eyewitness' is a fraud. And I remind you, ladies and gentlemen of the jury, that the prosecution must prove 'without a reasonable doubt' that Colin MacDonald committed these murders for you to find him guilty."

There was not a breath of air in the courtroom. Not one person moved as every juror, every onlooker, and even those seated at the D.A.'s table and the judge sat spellbound by the presence and quietly assured tone of this lawyer from Pelham, Alabama.

Clay quietly went back to the defence table and slowly took his seat. There was dead silence in the courtroom, and had the proverbial pin dropped, it would have created a deafening echo. Judge Harold Hyndmann slowly looked up, and peering over his half moon glasses, he nodded to the D.A.

"You may call your first witness."

Erik Wolfe stood up and called Brett Vaughan to the stand. After he was sworn in, Wolfe began by confirming the various facts about the witness. He was a member of the Cornell Heavy Eight Crew, a junior at the school, a member of the Delta Chi Upsilon Fraternity, and that he knew the accused, Colin MacDonald, who was a fraternity brother. He then asked the witness to recall through the events of Thursday evening of June 10th.

"I like to keep in shape, and I was jogging around Beebe Lake when I saw someone throw a body into the lake at the west end...just by the bridge."

"Where were you at the time?" asked Wolfe.

"I was jogging on the north side of the lake, not far from the canoe storage shed."

"Can you point out for the court on the map exactly where you were and where the body was dumped?"

The witness reached into his inner jacket pocket, pulled out a pen, stood up and reached with his left arm over to the enlarged map on the easel, exposing his beautiful new Rolex watch. While everyone was looking at the Rolex "President Day-Timer," Jack sat in absolute shock as his eyes focused on the pen Vaughan was pointing with. It was identical to the Bastion Bank executive pen he had found on the bridge when he stopped to see what all the fuss was about, then saw Nicole Watson's lifeless eyes staring up.

"That's the pen I was telling you about," he whispered to Clive. The judge looked over at him with a frown.

"What did you do then?" continued the D.A.

"I ducked in behind the shed and some trees."

"Could you identify the person in the courtroom who threw the body over the bridge into Beebe Lake."

"Yes, he's sitting right there." He nodded towards Colin.

"Let the record show that the witness has identified the defendant, Colin MacDonald, as the person he saw disposing of Yvette Bouchard's body." Wolfe pointed to a very uncomfortable, red-faced Colin. "Your witness," he said to Clay disdainfully.

Clay slowly got up from his table, walked over to the witness stand with two pieces of paper in his hand, and quietly said, "Would you mind pointing out the exact location of the canoe shed where you were standing?" Again, Vaughan pulled out his Bastion Bank Executive pen and stuck out his left arm.

"Now, when did you report what you saw to the police?"

"A few days later."

"Wasn't it almost a week later, on Wednesday June 16th. Why the wait?"

"I didn't want to get involved, and I wasn't sure it was a body until I read that a co-ed was found floating in the lake."

"That's a nice watch you are wearing. When did you purchase it?" asked Clay.

"Objection, your honor, what has this got to do with anything."

"It has a lot to do with everything. I have proof that this witness was bribed for his testimony and that his entire story is a complete and utter fabrication," replied Clay, slowly and deliberately, totally unruffled by the D.A.'s objection.

"Objection overruled, but don't stray too far, Mr. McBride."

"Yes, sir."

"Now, please answer the question."

"A few weeks ago, I guess."

"You're wearing a five thousand dollar watch, and yet you are working as a waiter at the Waterworks in order to put yourself through college?"

"It was an inheritance from my grandfather, who died a few months ago, and I wanted something that I could remember him by," Brett Vaughan answered uncomfortably.

Clay passed Vaughan the piece of paper he had been holding throughout the interrogation. "What date do you see on this sales receipt from Tompkins County Jewellers?"

"Tuesday June 17th."

"And is your name on it?"

"Yes, sir."

"So it actually appears that you purchased your watch the day after you went to the police. Would that be a fair statement?"

"Yes, sir."

"Did you make a large deposit to your account at Ithaca Savings and Loan on the afternoon of the day you went to the Ithaca Police?" continued Clay.

During the questioning, Bill Braxton had come into the courtroom and made his way up to where Ruth, Jack and Clive were sitting. He gave Clive a document that looked like a police report. Clive read it with great interest then let out a long, muted whistle. He looked at Jack, and his eyes went up to the ceiling. Jack didn't know if that was a sign of good news or bad news. Clive caught Clay's eye, and the calm and collected lawyer slowly walked over and took the document.

"One moment, if you please, your honor," he asked.

While this was going on, Jack caught a glimpse of Carlos Rossi, in his state trooper uniform, enter the courtroom. He passed an envelope to Erik Wolfe, which the D.A. put aside. Jack couldn't help but notice Rossi's quick wink to the mysterious lady in tweed and his hasty exit from the courtroom.

"I caught that," Clive said to Jack.

"Something's going on there," Jack replied.

Clive knew exactly what was coming next with regard to Clay's line of questioning, and wanted to stay around for the excitement, but he thought that he'd better keep an eye on Rossi and the woman in tweed and sensible shoes. He quietly got up and left the courtroom.

Returning to the witness box, Clay asked quietly and deliberately, "Do you know a Jeremy Small?"

"No," was the agitated answer from Vaughan, who immediately blushed a flustered red.

Clay continued, "Before you answer any more questions, I want you to think carefully, and remember that you are under oath and what the consequences of perjury are." He paused to give Vaughan a moment to let the weight of his words sink in, and then said, "Where were you on the evening of June 10th, between six and ten p.m.?"

"The witness has already answered that question," exclaimed an irritated Erik Wolfe, jumping to his feet.

"Yes, he has, and now I'm going to give him this opportunity to answer it truthfully. Because I have in my hand a copy of an Ithaca police report stating that the witness and a Jeremy Small were arrested on June 10th for performing an indecent sexual act in a public place, namely in the stacks of Olin Library, and had been charged by the Ithaca Police Force for public nudity, buggery..."

"STOP, STOP, PLEASE DON'T, MY PARENTS DON'T KNOW, NOBODY KNOWS, PLEASE STOP, I'LL TELL YOU

EVERYTHING, PLEASE STOP!" Vaughan pleaded through his tears.

"Your honor, the defence is badgering the witness," shouted Wolfe.

Clay quietly handed Judge Hyndmann the document, and after scrutinizing it carefully, the judge turned to Brett Vaughan, who was sitting sobbing quietly, and said, "Is this true, young man?"

"Yes, sir."

"Well, you'd better start from the beginning."

Brett started in a soft voice between sobs, as if he was too embarrassed to speak and really didn't want anyone to hear him.

"On Monday, June 15th, the lady who was just sitting there and the state trooper who just came in to give Mr. Wolfe something came to the fraternity house and said that they were looking for me and asked if I'd like to make a lot of money. He was in jeans; I didn't know that he was a state trooper. We went down to the Purity Ice Cream Dairy Bar because they said they wanted privacy, and they said that all I had to do was tell the police that I had seen Colin throw a body into Beebe Lake, and they would give me twenty-five thousand in cash the day I went to the police. I'd get another seventy-five thousand after today's testimony. I was in trouble with the police because of what my friend Jeremy and I had done, and I was frantic. The man told me he knew about my problem with the police and that he could have it fixed so that it would go away. I didn't know what to do. I'm so...so...sorry." Looking at Colin, he repeated himself amidst a flood of tears.

"Is there anything else you want to tell the court?" asked

the judge as he looked over his glasses at the terrified witness.

"You mean about my meeting with Mr. Wolfe?"

"Well, yes, that might be interesting," smirked the judge. The district attorney started to squirm and one of his aides closed a couple of briefing books.

"Well, I met with him last week, and we went over my entire testimony. He told me to go up to Beebe Lake and walk around it so I would know exactly what I was talking about. Until then I never realized that there was a building there, where they stored the canoes. He also said that he had been in touch with Detective Roach of the Ithaca Police, and he was assured that the charges against Jeremy and me would disappear after today."

"And did you ever see anybody throw a body at any time into Beebe Lake?"

"No, sir."

The courtroom was hushed.

"Son," said Judge Hyndmann, "whatever you did with your friend, do it behind closed doors in the future, since it's nobody's business but yours. Under the circumstances, I'm going to have to dwell on what to do about your testimony, because it could have led to the execution of your fraternity brother. Perjury in this case could have been fatal. Do not leave Ithaca until I see you. Please leave your address and phone number with the court clerk, who will in turn give it to the Ithaca Police and the Cornell Campus Security Office. In fact, on second thought, I want you to check in with the Ithaca Police every day until I resolve this matter. Mr. Wolfe, have you got any evidence you would like to present to the court?"

"No, your honor."

"Mr. McBride, do you have a motion?"

"Yes, your honor, I'd like to motion that this case be dismissed."

"Granted! Case dismissed!" The judge slammed down his gavel. "The jury is excused. I thank them for their time. Mr. MacDonald, this court offers its sincerest apologies for everything you have been put through. This has truly been a miscarriage of justice. Guard, release Mr. MacDonald immediately, as he is free to go." He continued, "Mr. Wolfe, I'll see you in my chambers RIGHT NOW. Mr. McBride, it is not required, but you are welcome to join us."

Ruth and Jack were crying with joy as they hugged each other and jumped over the rail to embrace Colin as he was released from his shackles. It was obvious that Colin and Ruth had formed some form of relationship during Colin's incarceration. They continued to kiss. Jack was happy for them.

The courtroom was somewhat hushed, as if the spectators weren't sure what had just happened. Erik Wolfe and Clay had headed into the judge's chambers, and a number of people had come up to the bar to talk to the district attorney's bewildered minions. Jack saw the envelope that Carlos Rossi had handed to Erik Wolfe sitting off to the corner of the prosecutor's table. He quietly walked over, picked it up, and slipped it into his jacket's inner pocket while all of Wolfe's people were talking to the confused and disappointed crowd.

He caught a glimpse of Mrs. Smythyes at the back of the court and waved her down to the front. *Since the L.A. Dodgers beat the Twins in the seventh game of the World Series last week, I guess that she has nothing to do,* he thought. "I need a bed for a night or two, any room at the inn?" he asked.

"Jack, for you, there will always be room," she replied as she was introduced to everyone congratulating Colin.

They slowly started to exit the courtroom, and they decided that if Colin wanted to go to Johnny's Big Red for a burger and beer, then that's where they would go. They were fishing for coins so Colin could call his parents from the pay phone in the lobby.

"Hey, Mom, It's Colin. We won, we won. Yes, it's me. Yes, yes, yes. It's true, we won! I can't tell you how much I love you. Yes, Jack's here and we're going for a beer, that's all that matters right now. Yes, I promise. I will, I will. Where's Dad? Dad, we won, we won. I was framed. Heads are going to roll now! I'll be home in a couple of days. You'll probably read it in the newspapers. Dad, I love you, thanks for everything, be sure to give Liam and everyone all my thanks. Tell Mom I love her, but I think I told her already, but that's O.K. Tell her again. See you soon, hopefully in a few days, and then we'll have a real party. Bye,"

Colin hung up and went over to give Jack a huge hug. "Thanks, buddy. I couldn't have done it without you. You won it for me, Thank you, *fucking* thank you! Mom wanted me to give you a hug for her too, so here it is." He gave Jack an extra bear hug, and they looked at each other with tears of joy running down their faces.

They all walked together out of the courthouse onto the landing at the top of the grand granite staircase leading down to the sidewalk, where a number of television cameras were set up. As well, a throng of reporters was waiting to get a statement from Colin. Across the street and over to the left, in the courthouse parking lot, Jack saw a number of flashing lights from police cars. There were people milling around, and he thought he could pick out Clive's cherished Corvette as well as the mystery lady's white Cadillac convertible. Jack knew that Colin could handle himself well with the press, since he had been interviewed dozens of times over his four-year hockey career at Cornell. Jack left Colin and his supporters to deal with the press as he crossed the street to see what Clive was up to.

24

A lthough Jack noticed three police cruisers surrounding Clive's Corvette and the white Cadillac convertible, his mind was more on the exhilarating feeling of Colin having won his case and his freedom. He breathed in the fresh, sun-warmed autumn air, tripped slightly over some leaf-covered piece of uneven pavement, and approached Clive, who hadn't been in court to witness the dismissal, nor to feel the judge's anger.

"What happened?" the P.I. said.

"We won, wait until you hear. I can hardly wait to tell you about it. What's up here? Why's your car banged up?"

Clive took Jack aside. The police were interviewing the lady in the Cadillac. Carlos Rossi, who had no jurisdiction within the city limits of Binghamton, was assisting the woman with her answers.

"I had to find out who she is and what she's up to.

Between you and me, she started to pull out, so I pulled in behind her so that she would hit my car. That way I could get a copy of her driver's licence and insurance. Rossi's beside himself. Braxton's doing a check on her. The car is registered to Tri State Formal Rentals, which she says is her husband's sideline business. Rossi says that he knows the people at Tri State and that they're 'good people.'"

"Who the hell is her husband?" asked Jack.

"Chadwick Richardson, President and CEO of the Bastion Bank of America, but according to her driver's licence, she is Sylvia Muncey. I can't figure it out, but give me time."

"Holy shit. This is scary. I'm beginning to put some of the missing pieces to the puzzle together...but not here," said Jack as they went back to the accident scene.

Sylvia Muncey glared at Clive as they approached. Rossi came up to him and said, "You little shit, you're going to get yours," then left the scene.

"I don't know why you're so upset. All of the damage has been done to my car. Yours barely has a scratch on it. Here, I'll give you a couple of hundred bucks, and you get your hubby to get it fixed, and he won't have to claim it on his insurance." Clive knew that the president of a bank couldn't care less about two hundred bucks or an increase in his corporate insurance premiums, but just wanted to push her ego, which he did successfully.

"I don't need your filthy money, and if this had been my fault, I would have paid for a lot full of Corvettes to prop up your pompous playboy image. You people make me sick," she said condescendingly. She got into her car and went back and forth, and back and forth, and back and forth again, until she finally was able to manoeuvre carefully past Clive's vehicle. There was no way he was going to move it for her. He grinned, as did Jack and the officers on the scene.

*   *   *

The last of the reporters was just leaving and the television cameras and tripods were being folded up and stored away in the vans as Clay appeared at the top of the steps. There was a bit of a skip to his step as he came down the large staircase.

"Oh boy, heads are going to roll over this one. I've never seen anything like that in all of my life." A black Lincoln sped out of the parking lot, causing the tires to spin and stones to fly up. "That was 'former' District Attorney Erik Wolfe... probably going to try and salvage his campaign and career, if that is humanly possible," Clay informed them.

"Do you mean the judge fired him?" asked Jack.

"Well, not exactly. Old Sparky told him that he was never to appear in his courtroom again, and since lawyers are considered officers of the court, if they can't appear before a judge then they can't practice law. Actually, the judge will be making a formal complaint to the New York Bar Association, the Attorney General's Office, as well as to the Department of Justice in Washington, and possibly the FBI. There will obviously be a number of investigations, but I'd say his goose is cooked. They are going to be charging him with bribery and witness tampering."

"It looks good on him," said Jack. "We're off to Johnny's Big Red for a celebration, you'll join us?"

"Wouldn't miss it," said Clay.

The little party headed for their cars. Ruth and Colin, still holding hands, squeezed into Jack's Mini, and Clive, after giving his right front fender a tender little rub, headed off in his Corvette while Clay climbed into his old Valiant.

"Slant 6...best engine ever to come out of Detroit," he would always say whenever someone asked him why he drove such a pedestrian car. As they arrived at Johnny's Big Red, Cam, the affable bartender, came around from the bar to give Colin a big congratulatory hug.

"News travels fast around here," said Colin. Cam pointed up to the television hanging from the ceiling, on which Colin could see himself being interviewed outside the courthouse.

"They've shown that clip at least three times in the last half hour. What'll you all have? Drinks are on the house."

The bar was quiet, since it was early afternoon, and classes were on, so they had their choice of seats and chose a table over in the corner in the room. That way they could talk, celebrate and laugh without disturbing anyone. Two large pitchers were deposited on the table.

"It's Miller Time," announced Cam.

"Sorry, it's Colin Time!" They all laughed as Jack started pouring out the delicious draught. Fresh peanuts were provided with the menus.

"God, I never thought that I'd see this day, and I never figured I'd be having a beer with you guys," said Colin. "This is some special." He took a long, slow drink of his beer with great satisfaction.

"I can't seem to piece everything together, but I know that there's something there, and I'm not sure exactly what's missing," said Jack. Then he remembered the envelope he had stolen off the prosecutor's table and handed it to Clay.

"Why don't you open it up, maybe there's a clue in there."

"Better that you open it...leave me out of it. I've seen enough of Old Sparky for one day, thank you very much."

Jack tore the envelope open while everyone quietly watched. He pulled out the folded piece of plain paper, which read:

CREDIT SUISSE
0890 ZURICH SWITZERLAND
CLEARING NUMBER; 4753
ACCOUNT NUMBER: EW5890L651019
AMOUNT; $500,000.00 U.S.D.

At the bottom of the page someone had written the word, "DONE!"

Jack studied the paper then said, "It looks to me like someone has deposited half a mill into a numbered account for Erik Wolfe." He handed the note over to Clay and Clive.

"Yep, EW are his initials, and 651019 is today's date, not sure what the 5890L stands for, probably something internal. Considering the five- or six-hour time difference, it was probably deposited this morning," surmised Clive.

"So here's my take on it," said Jack. "Erik Wolfe was paid off to convict Colin, and with Vaughan's testimony they figured it was a 'slam dunk.' Mrs. Muncey, whom I presume is Sky Muncey's mother, has been around these parts a little too much for my liking, what with her visiting the warden and all. And we have a supposedly 'dirty cop' in Carlos Rossi, who delivers this note to Wolfe in the middle of a trial, and who happens to be very friendly with Sky's mother, and who was following me up in Maine. There's something staring us right in the face."

"Also," Colin added, "Sky, and Sam Wainright were arrested after a couple of murders were committed up in Canada, and they found your boning knife on them. And they've been extradited to the U.S. and are doing whatever they please. Fucking Liberals, I'll never vote for them again."

Ruth put a hand on his arm. "It's O.K., you're free now, you're with your best friends, and in a couple of days you'll be with your family, who all love you. Forget about Cadeau and let's just savour the moment." She kissed him on the cheek.

Cam came over to the table and said to Colin, "There's a Chuck Trimble from Toronto on the phone for you. Are you here?"

Colin exhaled loudly. "Ya, I'll take it." He got up and headed out to the bar.

"That's his hockey agent," Jack informed everyone.

"No, not a chance. You tell them that they voided my contract, and I'm going to have a bit of a holiday. In the meantime you can start talking to other clubs. I'll be at home in Cape Breton in a couple of weeks or so, where you can get me. Until then, please don't bother me."

Returning to the table, Colin said, "Can you believe that? The Leafs want me to dress for Saturday night's game at the Gardens. Piss on them! We're going to have some fun. Let's plan this. First we'll go to Jack's house and then fly to Sydney and spend a few days with my folks. Clay, you're going to love them, and Ruthy, they're going to love you. Then Clive, we're heading over to that little island off of Scotland. What's it called? The one with the good Scotch?"

"Islay. The Isle of Islay," affirmed the private investigator.

"Listen, I've got another case I've got to prepare for, and then I have to clear my calendar," said Clay. "Why don't you guys do the Toronto thing and then Clive and I'll join you in Sydney, after that we'll all go off to Islay. Jack, I'd love to meet your folks, and I'm sure that will happen sometime, but I just have to get things organized with this new case."

"I understand," replied Jack. "I'll get Consuela to make all of the necessary flight arrangements."

"The trip's on me," said Colin. "Is there still enough left in the trust fund? If I have to pay it back, I will, once I get a signed contract."

"There's tons, so don't worry about that." Two more pitchers of Miller arrived with the burgers. Just as they were all biting down on their long awaited burgers and fries, Jimmy "Hoss" Cartwright appeared.

"Hey, congratulations, Colin," he said as he slapped Colin on the shoulder. "I never felt that you did it."

"You mean you weren't holding Nicole's murder against me?"

"Not for one minute, so get that thought out of your head. I mean, I'm going to miss her for the rest of my life, but I really feel that her killer is still out there.

"Mind you," the big center continued, "Muncey and Wainright have had you convicted from day one, and they've convinced everyone in the house that you did it. I don't know what their problem is...maybe they just hate Canadians. Funny how all three girls' fathers were in the financial industry or were financial bigwigs in their governments."

"What?" exclaimed Jack.

"Yeah, I've been racking my brain trying to figure out if

there's any connection. I was wondering if their mothers were members of the DAR, or if they all went to the same school or if they had any brothers or sisters that were somehow connected. But two of them were Canadian, except for Nicole, so I was at a dead end until I woke up one morning and thought I'd see what their fathers did for a living. Amy's father is the chair of Canada's Senate Banking Committee, Nicole's father is the chair of the U.S. Federal Reserve Bank, and Yvette's dad is Canada's finance minister."

"WOW!" said Jack. "The guy murdered in the Royal York was the deputy finance minister of Canada, and Allison Svendson, who was murdered on the train, was the executive assistant to the governor of the Bank of Canada. So, apart from everyone in the world, who hates banks so much that they'd want to kill some of the top U.S. and Canadian bankers' children and executives?"

"Well, we know that everyone on Wall Street hated Carl Watson, Nicole's dad, because he was trying to get the president and Congress to impose more regulations on the financial industry," said "Hoss."

"I guess I was too close to the situation to figure all this out. What do they say? Too close to the forest to see the trees," said Jack

"And then there's poor Cathy Ward, the single mom teller at Ithaca Savings and Loan. What's she got to do with international finance?" added Ruth.

Clive, knowing the answer to this question, elected to keep this information to himself for the time being. They all decided that they should get a good rest, pack and head off tomorrow for Toronto. Ruth and Colin would continue to celebrate in their own way back at her place. Clay and Clive would find their own way to Sydney by October 27th.

"What's the new case that you're working on, Clay?" asked Jack.

"Alvaro Correa, the kid who's been charged with Father Murphy's murder, has asked me to represent him...after I cleared Billy Eckler. He's been through a couple of lawyers who he's not very happy with, so I'll see what I can do."

The celebrants left the bar. It had been an exhilarating rollercoaster of a day.

*   *   *

The days in the life of a finance minister can be extremely hectic. This one was perhaps worse than most for Pierre Bouchard. It had started off with the weekly Liberal Party caucus. Every member of the party was extremely nervous about the polls and the party slipping in popularity with the Canadian public. Members from Atlantic Canada openly challenged Prime Minister Cadeau on his handling of the Colin MacDonald extradition case, refusing to request this from the U.S. secretary of state and yet releasing the two Americans without giving it a second thought.

"Canadians are furious, and it's proof that we are just puppets to Johnson," said one.

Another: "We'll be lucky if any one of us is re-elected."

It was October 19th and Pierre Bouchard's mind was on the MacDonald trial and how the kid soon would be found guilty. He secretly wished that the death penalty would be given, because he could hardly stand the anguish of not having his adorable, loving Yvette around anymore. After the daily question period in the House he had to fly to New York, where he was one of two speakers at the *Wall Street Journal*'s annual Our Continent's Finances dinner. The other guest speaker was going to be Dr. Carl Watson, Chairman of the U.S. Federal Reserve Bank.

While he was having lunch with the prime minister, an aide came to the table and quietly informed Pierre Bouchard of the events in the courtroom in Binghamton. The words, "The case has been dismissed and thrown out" caused the finance minister to choke on his mouthful of Atlantic smoked salmon. As he coughed and gasped for air, the prime minister tried to hold his minister's hands above his head and the aide went to get some water.

Finally he got his breathing back and sat down to ponder what went wrong with the case. This meant the killer was still out there or that lawyer was smarter than everyone thought. Being a Francophone in a mainly Anglophone country, Pierre Bouchard never thought of himself as a racist or an anti-Semite, because he knew what it was like to be a minority. However, he recalled laughing when he heard that Colin MacDonald's lawyer was black. "This kid hasn't got a hope in hell," he remembered telling his wife. Pierre Cadeau excused Bouchard from question period, seeing the agony on his minister's face.

*   *   *

In the office of the chairman of the Federal Reserve Bank, Carl Watson was having a working lunch with Irving Shapiro, the senior Republican senator from New York. The senator had ties with the financial community in New York. In fact, his major financial backers were the banks, the trading houses and the insurance companies. More goverent control was the last thing they needed, and the senior executives could all see that this would be a direct hit on their annual bonuses. Bank regulation was the least of the chairman's concerns, as he was preoccupied with what might be happening in an upstate New York courtroom. The waiter had been asked to leave the office so that they might have some privacy. Just as they were about to have coffee, the chairman's executive assistant, Timothy Wentz, knocked and entered.

"Excuse me, sir, I'm sorry to interrupt, but I thought that you'd like to know what has happened in Binghamton."

"Go ahead."

"Well, the judge dismissed the case. It appears that the witness was bribed for his testimony. The judge is pretty upset with the D.A."

"Jesus Christ," exclaimed the chairman. "Senator, I don't give a damn about banking regulations at the moment. We'll have to continue this conversation at another time." He asked his executive assistant to clear his calendar for the rest of the afternoon so he could spend it with his wife, but he would still take the short flight from Washington to New York for the Wall Street dinner.

Both government jets landed within half an hour of each other at La Guardia airport, and the respective limousines were lined up on the private portion of the tarmac to take each of their parties to their suites at the New York Hilton. The head table was to assemble for cocktails at seven p.m. and then would be piped onto the dais at seven thirty. Grace would be said by The Right Reverend Archbishop Sloan, the

Episcopalian archbishop of New York. Both the chairman and the finance minister had been requested to keep their remarks to less than forty-five minutes each. The Grand Ballroom was set up for its maximum number people of 2,800 and it was sold out at a hundred dollars per plate. Microphones and television cameras had been set up well in advance. It was a black tie affair.

The minister and the chairman had not met each other in person, although they had spoken a number of times on the phone, more recently with the regards to their daughters' murders. The chairman was already in the reception room when Finance Minister Bouchard arrived, and they instantly stopped, went to each other and gave each other a very warm handshake. It was not long before all the guests were seated at their numbered tables. They all rose for the head table as it made its entrance.

After the archbishop said grace and all were seated, a phalanx of waiters swarmed through the kitchen doors with massive oval trays, shoulder high, heading to their stations. The bisque had barely been served when Chadwick Richardson, CEO of the Bastion Bank of America, mounted the dais behind the long line of head table guests. He stopped, bent over between the finance minister and the chairman of the Federal Reserve, and said, "Gentlemen, I cannot tell you how deeply sorry I was to have heard of your losses. It must have been a terrible time for yourselves and your families."

He continued, "It must be even more devastating to you to hear of today's events, where the killer has virtually walked free. Obviously, nobody talked to the judge and told him how important this case was to the cooperation between our two countries, especially in the financial sector. There's someone out there trying to make a point. As you both know, I am a proponent of free trade and that American and Canadian banks be allowed to be jointly owned. I'm afraid that until this is allowed and regulations on both sides of the border be loosened, then tensions such as we have just witnessed will probably continue. Again, gentlemen, you have my sincerest sympathy." He left before either one of them had a chance to talk to him. They both sensed a veiled threat.

"What did he mean by tensions?" asked the chairman, and Pierre Bouchard shrugged. If there was to be any life and enthusiasm in either of their speeches, Chadwick Richardson had put a complete damper on their spirit. They spent the rest of the meal confiding in each other about what their daughters had meant to them, and when it was their turn to speak they gave almost identical speeches in simple deadpan, monotone styles. The only difference in their talks was the dreary statistics they parroted from their notes: GDP, unemployment rates, consumer confidence and other economic indicators. At the end they were each applauded politely by those in attendance and thanked profusely by the managing editor of the *Wall Street Journal*. If anything beneficial came out of the dinner, it was that the two senior financial officers were bound together by each other's grief. They parted the next morning on their respective jets, still pondering what the Bastion Bank CEO had meant by 'tensions.'

25

Jack said a final farewell to Mrs. Smithyes and picked up Colin and Ruth before the trio headed up the west side of Cayuga Lake. It was new territory for the two passengers, and in spite of their hangovers, their spirits were buoyant, if not giddy. The radio was on, and they started to sing along with the Byrds' version of Bob Dylan's "Mr. Tambourine Man." Jack, being a purist, had never liked the Byrds version of the song and thought that the Colin, Ruth and Jack trio did a far better job.

Before they knew it they were pulling into Jack's driveway in Scarborough. They piled out of the Mini and stretched.

"We're here, Mom," Jack yelled as Dylan jumped up and ran into the foyer to welcome him. Jack's mother came down the stairs to greet her guests. "Colin, I presume. You poor dear, what you have been through is beyond belief," she said. "And you must be Ruth; it's so nice to see you and put a face on you. Jack has told me so much about you. I have Colin and you in the guest room just to the left, and Jack, Consuela and you will be in your own room.'

"What? Consuela is coming over and she's going to stay the night and…?"

"Absolutely, I've invited her and she will be here by six. I told her to take a taxi and I'd pay for it.

"But..."

"Never mind the 'buts.' I'm a grown woman and I'm not having her steal you for the two or three nights that you're here. Anyway, we love Consuela, so just don't try and pull the wool over my eyes. You're in the same room, whether you like it or not." She kissed Jack and winked at Colin and Ruth.

Jack felt as if he had finally been liberated. It was almost better than when his dad had given him his first beer, even though he had been drinking beer in his friends' basements for a couple of years before.

The trio picked up their bags and headed up the stairs.

Back downstairs again, Jack gave Colin a Molson Canadian and his mother asked Ruth what she would like.

"Just a cup of tea, if it's not too much trouble."

"No trouble at all. How would you like it? Clear? Milk? Lemon? Orange juice? You know that Jack drinks his tea with a little orange juice?"

"Oh, yes, I think all of Cornell knows that Jack drinks his tea with orange juice...I'm surprised that they allowed him to graduate from the hotel school."

They all laughed then headed out to the back deck to take advantage of the late warm rays of sun while Jack excused himself to make one phone call which had been on his mind.

"Gord Lawton's office."

"Heather, it's Jack, how are you"?

"Fine, congratulations."

"Thanks," said Jack.

"I'm so happy you called," continued his old friend. "Corrine Clancy has been after me. She said that if I ever hear from you, that I'm to have you call her. She wants to host a press conference for you so that you can explain everything and somehow clear the name of the hotel."

"You know my thoughts about Corrine," replied Jack. "Personally I'd like you to tell her to stuff it, but to be political about it, why don't you tell her that I'm busy and I'm taking a vacation."

"O.K., not a problem."

"Listen," continued Jack, "I know that you signed some sort of confidentiality agreement with the York National, but I was wondering if you could answer a couple of questions just by saying 'yes' or 'no.'"

"Well, I guess I could do that, I'm not sure what you're fishing for," she said.

"I'm just trying to put the pieces of a puzzle together, and no one will know how I found out, O.K.?"

"O.K."

"Was the Bank of America trying to get control of York National?"

"No."

"Was Citi Bank trying to get control of York National?"

"No."

Jack, hoping he knew the following answer, said, "Was the Bastion Bank of America trying to get control of York

National?"

"Yes."

"And the final question: Was the CEO of the Bastion Bank, Chadwick Richardson, the man who was doing all of the negotiations, and was he the same man that you told me was extremely rude and even threatening?"

"Jack," Heather said nervously, "you didn't hear any of that from me, O.K.? But the answer is yes."

"Not a word, I promise. I'll give you a shout when I get back from Cape Breton, or Scotland, if we go there. Thanks again. Bye."

Jack grabbed another beer and re-joined his friends and his mother on the back deck. "I think I've got it figured out, but let's wait until Consuela and my dad get here.

Soon after the doorbell rang. "Well we won't have to wait long," said Colin. It was Consuela. After introductions, the two girls started to help Jack's mother prepare the salads for the barbeque. Jack and Colin opened another beer, and Jack decided to bounce his idea off his friend.

"Listen, everything points to the Bastion Bank," he started. "I found one of their executive pens at the scene of Nicole Watson's murder on the bridge over the Cascadilla Gorge. The president of the Bastion Bank is Chadwick Richardson, who's been trying to get control of the York National, and Canadian laws won't permit majority foreign ownership of our banks. He's supposed to be a real prick and has been threatening all sorts of people, bank officials as well as government people, and everyone has just accepted his volatile personality as a cost of doing business with the man. We know," he continued, "that Sky Muncey is his stepson and that Muncey was found in Lake Louise with my bloodied boning knife, and my friend Mandy saw him on the train the night that Allison Svendson was murdered.

"We also know that Richardson is linked to the Moretti family with his partnership in Tri State Formal Rentals." Jack went on to tell how he had been tracked by Guido Moretti, who had mistakenly tried to kill a hunter instead of him. "I think the D.A. is dirty too. That bank transfer to a Swiss bank account, I bet, if it could be traced, would have come from Richardson, who probably promised the D.A. big bucks if he put you away. He transferred the money a few hours too early. He figured with Vaughan's testimony it was an open and shut case. He must be just fuming now. Did you see that Vaughan had a Bastion Bank Executive pen as well?"

"No, I was too scared to take much in."

"Well, he did, and if it wasn't for Clive and Braxton digging up Vaughan's little rendezvous in the stacks, then you could be sitting on death row."

"Let's not go there, I can't bear to think of it," said Colin.

"Furthermore," added Jack, "the timing was just perfect, as Clive left the courtroom just in time to find out that that woman was Sky Muncey's mother. She was probably sent there by Richardson to keep an eye on the proceedings and report back to him. It looks like the only person that Richardson didn't get to was Old Sparky."

Jack's father arrived home, and they had a barbeque. They discussed Jack's theory, and they all agreed that he should call Clay to bounce it off him. It was a wonderful evening, and Jack's parents could not have been happier for him.

"Clay?" Jack asked the brilliant lawyer who had become a good friend, and who was still answering his own phone. "It's Jack. Listen, I have been trying to fit some pieces to this puzzle together."

The young lawyer listened with great intensity. When Jack was finally finished, he said, "If what you're telling me is true, I think I should apprise Judge Hyndmann of this, but before I do that, I'd like Clive to call you, and you tell him exactly what you told me. I think that this may be a case for the FBI and the RCMP because of the international nature."

Within the hour, Clive called and Jack repeated his theory.

"Very interesting," said Clive. "I'll see Clay tomorrow, so leave it with us. We'll see you in Sydney in a few days."

Jack was satisfied that he had done everything he could do. The conversation turned to the flight and the visit to Sydney and Glace Bay to meet Colin's folks. Consuela gave Jack his own ticket as well as one from Halifax to Glasgow. One night there then a quick thirty-five minute flight from Glasgow to Port Ellen, the main town of Islay. With fond hugs Jack's father drove everyone to the airport, from which they would start their journey of joy and thanks.

26

As they stepped out of the plane and onto the tarmac of the small Sydney airport, they could see a large banner that said "WELCOME HOME COLIN." There was a huge crowd of cheering well-wishers. Two girls wore his Cornell jersey with the "C" designation near the left front shoulder, his number 34 and "MACDONALD'" across their back. Jack looked at Colin, who was clearly embarrassed, and said, "You didn't win the Stanley Cup, did you?" Colin gave Jack a playful shove, and they laughed. When they got into the terminal, there was a mad rush of supporters, and Colin finally saw his parents and Liam. There were hugs all around when over the loudspeaker declared "Colin MacDonald, will you please join Mayor MacTavish on the luggage belt."

He made his way onto the belt, which served as a makeshift stage in a small airport, hoping that someone would not press the "start" button. The mayor talked of the trials that

Colin had faced and how he had gotten through the hardest of times like a true "Caper," the endearing term by which the people of Cape Breton often referred to themselves. Colin was presented with the ceremonial key to the city.

Just before he was to speak, Liam came up to him, and said, "Tell them they're all invited to the thank-you party at the Glace Bay Arena on Friday night."

"What?"

"Never mind, just tell them." Colin thanked everyone in Cape Breton for their support and their prayers and invited them to the party, as Liam had told him to do. Ruth and Consuela were introduced to Colin's family, and then they all headed back to Colin's home.

The whole MacDonald family was there, and it was an evening of joyful tears, laughs and sharing of experiences as Andrew and Archie took the two girls, Ruth and Consuela, under their wings and started answering all their questions about Nova Scotia, Cape Breton, coal mining, lobster and cod fishing and any other topic that entered their minds.

"Well, it's been a busy day, but we better get some sleep, because we have to be up early and pick up Clay and Clive and their girls, and then it's off on tour around the Cabot Trail," Colin said.

The following morning, Moira, Colin's mother, woke up the entire household with the permeating aromas of homemade, fresh out of the oven cinnamon buns. They had to hurry, since they didn't want to be late meeting Clay and Julia and Clive and Ellen, his date of the month. Ellen was a research assistant at the Cornell Agricultural School.

Liam had been able to coerce a twelve-seat shuttle bus from a friend who ran the Sydney-to-Halifax shuttle service.

They piled into the minibus and Liam took the wheel as the designated tour guide. They headed down the highway and eventually took the small Englishtown Ferry which would put them on "The Trail." Ellen and Ruth were very much into photography and wanted to stop at every bend overlooking some of Canada's finest scenery.

"We can't stop everywhere, or we'll never get home. Mom has something special on for us tonight...I have no idea what it is, but we have to be home by six," Colin insisted.

They eventually arrived at Cheticamp, where Liam had arranged a meeting with Natalie LeBlanc, the famous weaver who had done the gorgeous hooked rug of Colin that had been auctioned off by developer Bob Bennett. This was one meeting where Colin felt a little choked up, and tears welled up in his eyes as he thanked this elderly woman. He was just amazed that someone would do something so beautiful and raise so much money for someone she had never met.

Consuela was particularly interested in learning about the technique of hooking, and the shutterbugs went crazy as they took pictures of all the different pieces Natalie had around her modest living room.

Afterward, the little band proceeded down the road to the Chowder House, where they had what Clive said was the finest chowder he'd had ever tasted.

"Perhaps if we get home in time, a nap would be in order," said Clay after the huge lunch.

"Yeah, no problem, Mom's got you staying at the Isle Royale, as there isn't enough room at the house, and then we can pick you up around six."

– 27 –

Operation "Dead IV" was a complicated plan, with many logistics for the FBI to orchestrate. After receiving a formal complaint from Judge Hyndmann, they went into action, gathering all of the evidence and put into effect a strategy where four raids would all be conducted on the same day and at exactly the same hour. The following are the scenarios of each of the four FBI operations which made up "Dead IV." It was twelve thirty p.m. on Wednesday, October 27, 1965.

* * *

OPERATION "DEAD IV"

GREENWOOD ESTATES — ESSEX CONNECTICUT

WEDNESDAY, OCTOBER 27TH, 1965, 12:30 pm

A magnificent horse was being led down the gangplank of a huge horse van, which had been driven into the luxurious paddock at Greenwood, the palatial 412-acre country estate of Chadwick Richardson and his wife Sylvia Muncey. There was a crowd of onlookers as the steed was led down the gangplank, walked over, and presented to Cicely Muncey, Skylar Muncey's sister. Firewind had been purchased from internationally-known German Olympic equestrian, Hans Mueller. Mueller's Olympic medals were countless, but he used his equestrian prowess to promote his business, which was to breed the finest jumpers in the world. The horse was a Dutch Warm Blood, and there wasn't a finer breed to be found for jumping. Firewind cost Richardson roughly $375,000, which was almost half of his annual bonus.

"So I hope that she appreciates it. He's a gelding, so there's no stud fee here, which pisses me off, so he'd better win her a gold medal," he had grumbled to Sylvia a few days earlier. The horse was skittish as two grooms gently cut the thick wrapped plastic sponge blankets from around its body and legs.

The head of the American Olympic Committee, as well as a number of the American Olympic equestrian team members, reporters and photographers from many equestrian and sporting magazines such as *Sports Illustrated* were on hand to witness the much-heralded arrival of Firewind. Local newspapers were also well represented. Cicely's long time friends and teachers from the Old Lyme Pony Club, where she had learned to ride, had come to see what an incredible horse Cicely's step-father had bought their friend. This was Sylvia's big day, one where she could show her friends exactly who she was. Firewind was one of the finest pieces of horseflesh that money could buy, and she certainly intended to let society know it.

In the distance, two, black, highly polished station wagons slowly started driving onto the field and headed towards the assembled group. There appeared to be a crest on both of their two front doors, and as they approached, one could read in a small font: "The Federal Bureau of Investigation." Everyone was silent as four officers emerged from the vehicles. They were all armed and wore bullet-proof vests with "FBI" splayed in large print on the front and the back of the vests.

The head officer walked up to Sylvia and said, "Sylvia Muncey, you are under arrest for the conspiracy to murder Nicole Watson," and continued with each count. "You are also under arrest for the conspiracy to murder Amy Schecter. You are also under arrest for conspiracy to murder Yvette Bouchard." He went on to name Aaron Hodges, Allison Svendson and Cathy Ward. "Furthermore, you are under arrest for bribery and witness tampering," the officer added.

Everyone was staring with utter disbelief. The photographers couldn't believe their luck and flashes seemed to be endless. Firewind was getting more skittish, and the two grooms started to lead him around in circles to keep him distracted. One groom could not contain himself and started smirking. One of the two female officers walked up to Sylvia Muncey and asked her to put her hands behind her back, telling her that she had the right to counsel and anything that she said may be held against her.

"I know my rights, and I have a right to call my husband. You people make me sick," she said with venomous disdain.

"Yes, ma'am, you will be able to talk to your husband

eventually, but right now, as we speak, he is on his way to Rikers," said the officer.

*   *   *

OPERATION "DEAD IV"
60 WALL STREET, NEW YORK, NEW YORK
WEDNESDAY, OCTOBER 27, 1965, 12:30 pm

On the 49th floor of the Bastion Bank of America Building, the board of directors of the bank was meeting. Apart from the regular items on the agenda, it was now approaching the end of the year and it was time to determine the annual bonus packages for the bank's executives. Lunch was catered by Chadwick Richardson's personal chef. Under his direction, the kitchen team created the meal in a large kitchen adjoining the boardroom, separated only by a serving pantry. Plates of the finest beluga caviar in iced crystal bowls placed in the center of platters, along with, crust less toast points chopped egg yolks and whites in separate piles, and finely chopped red onion along with two small sterling silver serving spoons.

The four brushed brass elevator doors opened almost in unison as they deposited their cargo of eight FBI agents into the luxurious reception area, where they were greeted by a stunned and shocked receptionist. Behind the reception desk the large logo of the Bastion Bank of America, the famous "B" spiralling down in ever decreasing concentric circles, shouted "wealth" as its polished brass finish complemented the rich, dark mahogany wall. The receptionist was a most attractive and efficient gatekeeper and was rumored to regularly do "personal favors" for the CEO. She had been with the bank for thirteen years and also received a generous bonus each year as well as a substantial personal gift from her reported lover.

"We're looking for Chadwick Richardson," said one of the officers.

"I'm sorry, he's busy at the moment. May I tell his executive assistant what this is all about?"

"No, you needn't bother her. If you can't tell us where he is I'm sure that we'll find him ourselves."

"He's in a board meeting and cannot be disturbed," replied the receptionist irritably.

"Where's the boardroom?" whispered the officer, leaning over her large mahogany reception desk. "Do I make myself clear?" he added.

"First door to your left, down the hall, second door on the right," she answered as she picked up the phone to alert security.

The double doors to the boardroom swung open without notice and the eight FBI agents walked in. The treasurer started to choke on a piece of toast heaped with caviar, and another board member spat out the gulp of Italian sparkling water that he had just taken.

"Mr. Chadwick Richardson. You are under arrest for the murder of Aaron Hodges, Deputy Finance Minister of Canada. You are under arrest for the conspiracies to commit the murders of Nicole Watson, Amy Schechter, Yvette Bouchard, Allison Svendson and Cathy Ward. You are also under arrest for racketeering and money laundering, committing bribery and conspiracy to tampering with a witness. You have the right to remain silent, and you have the right to obtain an attorney. If you cannot afford an attorney, the State will appoint one for you, and please remember that anything you say from here on may be held against you."

At this point six servers appeared from the servery each carrying two plates holding a half an avocado filled with a generous portion of baby bay shrimp on a bed of lettuce, as it was now time for lunch, and these were the appetizers. Upon seeing the FBI, almost as one they turned around and quickly retreated back into the kitchen. Two of the servers were convinced that the FBI was after them for immigration offences.

Chadwick Richardson had been caught. His ego, however, would not let go, and through his embarrassment he maintained that there was an incredible act of injustice being perpetrated against him. Being arrested in front of the icons of American business whom he considered his peers was almost too much to take. As he rose and put his hands behind his back to be cuffed, he turned to his assembled board members and said, "There's obviously been a huge mistake here. Will someone please get in touch with Hoover in Washington and tell him what has happened. He'll straighten this whole thing out."

Turning to the eight FBI agents, he said with incredible arrogance, "Gentlemen, enjoy the moment, this will be your last day on the job."

*   *   *

```
OPERATION "DEAD IV"
101 SOUTH SWAN, ALBANY, NEW YORK
WEDNESDAY, OCTOBER 27, 1965, 12:30 P.M.
```

On the north corner of South Swan and Washington Avenues in Albany, New York, directly opposite the State Capitol Building, was an innocuous twelve-storey glass, steel and concrete office building, with less architectural design than a shoebox. It was named the Hudson Building. Erik Wolfe, being "the" district attorney, had a large corner suite on the twelfth floor overlooking the Capitol Building. The reception area on the twelfth floor could only be described as opulent. The floors were marble and the walls were painted light pea green, with a New York state seal hanging on the wall just to the left of the bullet-proof one-inch glass behind which a very efficient bespectacled receptionist would speak through a microphoned speaker hole. An armed security guard stood off to the side.

Erik Wolfe was having a private all-day meeting with his chief campaign adviser and bagman, Bernie Clawson, his wife of thirteen years, beautiful Candice Wolfe, a former runner-up in the 1951 Miss America Pageant, and his lawyer Mr. Bill Cranston of Fuller, Cranston, Whelan and Smith LLP, reputedly the finest criminal defence lawyer in America. Candice Wolfe was not only beautiful, but the she was the brains behind her D.A. husband and knew that he had the ego to eventually bring her to the governor's mansion. She had her Masters degree in criminology and had gone on to get her doctoral degree in Law. The four were scrambling with numerous scenarios about to how to handle the complaints that Judge Hyndmann was going to be making to the FBI.

The Hudson Building had a large underground parking garage where four black FBI limousines parked and the eight agents, all wearing bulletproof vests, emerged and proceeded to the bank of elevators. The first four agents reached the top floor and advised the guard and the receptionist that they were to let them into the offices and direct them to the district attorney's office without any further questions. The second group of agents arrived just as the buzzer went and their partners were entering the office. Phones were ringing, but no one was answering them as all eyes followed the agents. They wove through the myriad of desks and the labyrinth of offices to the D.A.'s office. The office door opened and everyone looked up in shock at this invasion of their privacy.

"Mr. Erik Wolfe, you have been charged with bribery, witness tampering, and the conspiracy to commit murder of Mrs. Cathy Ward." The officer continued to read the D.A. his rights as another officer went behind the desk and handcuffed him.

"A little bit of overkill, wouldn't you say?" exclaimed campaign manager Bernie Clawson. Erik Wolfe looked to Bill Cranston for some guidance.

"Listen Erik, I'm going to have to recuse myself from this case, as Clay McBride was a junior at Cranston Fuller. In fact, if anything I was his mentor, and my presence may be construed as a conflict of interest." The lawyer then looked at Candice and said, "I'll try and think of someone who might be able to help. Gentlemen," he added, nodding to the FBI agents as he left the office, grabbing on his way out a couple of crustless egg salad sandwiches.

One agent couldn't help but smile as he noticed the lawyer sneaking out.

As the group was leaving, Wolfe looked at his executive assistant and optimistically said, "Clear my calendar for the rest of the week." As he walked through the large general office, the phones seemed to be ringing even louder, and the staff didn't know exactly where to look.

*   *   *

OPERATION "DEAD IV"

SCHOELLKOPF FIELD, CORNELL UNIVERSITY

ITHACA, NEW YORK

WEDNESDAY OCTOBER 27TH, 12:30 P.M.

It was a golden Wednesday autumn afternoon when Cornell's Big Red football team was preparing for its annual battle with the Princeton Tigers in Cornell's ancient crescent, Schoellkopf Field. It had been home to Cornell's football team since 1915. The offensive and defensive lines were sparring while wide receivers were running their intricate routes with second and third string quarterbacks. Sky Muncey and San Wainwright were working closely with the offensive coach on a few new plays that were going to be introduced into tomorrow's game. Eight FBI agents, two brandishing rifles, walked onto the field and headed to the bench, where head coach Bud Aldridge was reaming out the first string center, "Hoss" Cartwright, for not putting his heart into the game.

"Gentlemen," he said to the bulletproof vest-clad officers in surprise. "What's the reason for your visit?"

"We are looking for one Skylar Muncey and one Samuel

Wainwright," said the lead officer. The coach put two fingers between his lips and sent out a piercing shrill that stopped everyone on the field. He motioned to Muncey and Wainwright to come to the bench. The two slowly started towards the sidelines, when all of a sudden Sam Wainwright started to run towards one of the exits. There was no point in pursuing him, as he could do the hundred-yard dash in almost world record time. In fact, he was on the Cornell track team and anchored the four-man relay. As he approached the exit, two more agents appeared with rifles pointed at the speedy receiver.

"Stop or we'll shoot!" they ordered. He stopped so quickly, he slid on the grass and fell down. After he got up he was ushered over to the bench, and all eyes focused on the officer reading the charges to the handcuffed Sky and Sam for the murders of Nicole, Amy, Yvette, Allison and Cathy. A group of Christian players formed a circle off to the side and holding hands, knelt down, bowed heads, and started to pray. Without incident, the two football players were led out of the coliseum and into the phalanx of waiting black vans with tinted windows.

*   *   *

Before dropping Clay, Julia, Clive and Ellen off at the Isle Royale, the weary but happy band of sightseers stopped in at Colin's house to introduce everyone to the family. As they got out of the minibus, Colin's parents emerged from their modest home. Andrew immediately went up to Clive and said, "You must be Clay. Thank you so much. Colin and Jack have told me so much about you, thank you so much. Welcome to our home." He gave Clive the warmest of handshakes.

"Actually, I'm Clive, this is Clay." Clive introduced the brilliant lawyer from Alabama. Andrew immediately blushed, which showed through his soot-cratered face. He had obviously never heard of a black lawyer.

"Oh, I'm so sorry, nobody told me that...."

Clay cut him off and said, "That's O.K., I understand, and I'm just happy that I could help. It's a real treat to meet you and see your beautiful home. I'm now beginning to realize why Colin is the fine young man that he is." The handshake turned into a warm hug as tears welled up in Andrew's eyes, partly because of the shame of his ignorance but mostly for the newfound love of a man who had saved his son's life.

After everyone had a quick nap at Colin's parents' house and freshened up, Liam got all of his charges into the minibus and they headed into Glace Bay for an evening of Cape Breton entertainment at the Savoy Theatre, which had been the cultural center for the performing arts in Cape Breton since 1927. For some unknown reason, like many old auditoriums, the Savoy had probably the best acoustics of any auditorium in Atlantic Canada.

Liam pulled up to the front door and everyone went to their seats, front row center. A number of people came up to Colin and congratulated him. Most of them remembered Jack from the fundraisers. Shortly, the house lights dimmed and everyone took to their seats as a hush fell over the audience. The theatre was in total darkness when suddenly from the back, the voices of the Men of the Deeps could be heard as they came single file down the aisles, dressed in their traditional black miners' work clothes, faces smudged with black charcoal and their path lit only by the mining lights beaming from the front of their hardhats. As they climbed up to the stage and walked behind the heavy velvet curtain, the audience could still hear them singing, although somewhat muffled, but suddenly the massive curtain swept aside and the assembled choir was facing the audience, hardhat lights glaring at the audience as they began to sing "Out on the Mira," and a soft amber light slowly lit up the miners as they continued to sing.

At the end of the song, Clay stood up, initiating a standing ovation from the audience. It was an evening of pure Cape Breton music, and at the end Colin was asked to go up on the stage, where he was presented with an honorary Men of the Deeps hat complete with a working lamp. He thanked them profusely for their support then turned to the audience inviting them all to the party the next night at the arena.

The following night at the Glace Bay Arena, fishermen, breweries and local merchants again had come forward with offers to supply everything. Liam and Colin firmly refused and insisted in paying for everything, since there was still almost three hundred thousand dollars left in the trust fund. Liam had hired a local DJ because he wanted the entertainers who had so generously donated their time and talent before to enjoy this one. Colin took to the stage to a thunderous round of applause. It seemed like forever but they eventually quieted as he began to speak.

"Ladies and gentlemen, friends, fellow Capers. Thank you, thank you so much for all the support you have given me over the past six months. There really are no words that can express my gratitude."

"I love you, Colin!"

"Oh, Charlene, you have no idea how much it means to me to be able to stand up here and say 'I love you too.'" The crowd went wild, and again it took minutes to quiet down.

"I'd like to introduce you to some very special people who have made my freedom, and tonight possible. First of all I'll ask Cousin Liam, whom you all know, to come up here with me."

"Next I'd like to ask Ruth Gordon to come up. Ruth is a fellow student and a good friend of Yvette's and mine, and she stood by me all the time through thick and thin and visited me in prison every day that they would allow her." Ruth was embarrassed and blushed but went up on the stage to give Colin a kiss on the cheek.

"Next I'd like you to meet the slickest and most professional private eye you'll ever meet in your life. Clive Scranton didn't leave a stone unturned, and he is a huge reason for my victory. Clive, C'mon up." Clive, in his natty light blue button-down shirt, tan chinos and brown penny loafers, joined the others on stage and waved to the crowd.

"The next man is the most incredible lawyer anybody could ever want. He took my case, believing in my innocence, after only one brief meeting and knowing that I had no money to pay him...or Clive, for that matter. In court he was absolutely brilliant as he kept everyone spellbound with his reasoning and his incredible voice. Ladies and gentlemen, the man I am in constant awe of, my lawyer, Mr. Clayton McBride."

Again there was a thunderous applause as Clay walked up the stairs to the stage, and yet there were a few hushed comments from people who hadn't known that he was black. Clay waved and then gave Colin a big hug.

"Now, last but not least." The crowd hushed. "I don't believe that there could ever be a truer friend to anybody than this man. You've all met him before at the fundraising dinner, but I have to say publicly that without his persistence, his perseverance and his undying friendship, I would probably be sitting on death row right now. Ladies and gentlemen, the greatest friend in the world, Jack Souster."

The arena went crazy as Jack walked up on the stage and gave Colin the biggest and longest bear hug possible.

"I love you, Jack," shouted Charlene as the crowd roared with laughter.

"I think I'd love you too, Charlene, but Colin's your number one love tonight!" Again the crowd roared its approval.

Colin asked Gerry Stephens, his former Peewee hockey coach and president of the Glace Bay Minor Hockey Association, to come onto the stage and presented him with a cheque for twenty-five thousand dollars then invited Bill MacPherson, a local councillor and chair of the Arena Renewal Fund, to the stage. The posters, which were plastered all over Glace Bay, Sydney and New Waterford, had a cartoon character of a Nova Scotian Duck Tolling retriever on skates in a 'Capers hockey sweater barking "ARF...ARF," the acronym for Arena Renewal Fund. Colin handed the councillor a cheque for a hundred thousand dollars to go to repairing the old arena.

"If my hockey career ever gets off the ground, it will probably take me all over Canada and the U.S., but I want everyone to know that I will never forget Cape Breton, and I will think of all of you wherever I go. I will always be a Caper."

Jack had never witnessed such adoration for a single

individual as the crowd chanted, "Co-lin, Co-lin, Co-lin, Co-lin..."

Colin finished his speech by saying, "Thank you again, I love you all, and now, let's party!"

The following morning had to be an early start as Jack, Colin and the rest of the little band of celebrants had to get to Halifax in order to catch their flight back to Toronto, where they would pick up a direct flight to Glasgow.

The British Airways flight touched down at Glasgow's International Airport. Jack, Consuela, Colin, Ruth, Clay, Julia, Clive, Ellen, Liam and Gillian disembarked and made their way to the hotel where they would spend the night before catching the thirty-five-minute air shuttle to Islay.

As they walked out of the airport, looking to get a taxi, they heard the stirring tunes of the bagpipes. A young Scot in full regalia, kilt and all, was tapping his foot next to his bagpipe case, and looking straight ahead as he pumped out "Westering Home," one of Jack's favorite Scottish tunes. Jack dropped a pound note into the young Scot's case.

After they all got settled in their rooms, they met in the bar, where Clive had ordered a round of Bruichladdich single malt Scotch. "This is something I've been waiting for, for years," he said as the other nine sipped it with mixed enthusiasm.

Ellen, being Clive's partner of the moment, seemed to force her appreciation, but Jack, Colin and Clive really enjoyed it. Consuela pushed her glass towards Jack. She asked the waiter, "Have you any tequila, *por favor*?" He brought the lovely Guatemalan a shot of tequila, some salt and a plate of freshly cut wedges of lime.

Jack woke the next morning to see his lovely Consuela only half covered by the sheets. He resisted his urgings and decided to let her sleep. He quietly showered, gave his lover a gentle peck on the cheek, and went down to the dining room for breakfast. After fixing his customary tea with a couple of drops of orange juice, he started to scan the paper for the international news. Buried on page five was a story from the *New York Times:* "Bastion Bank CEO Chadwick Richardson Charged in Murder of Deputy Finance Minister of Canada."

The article went on to talk about Sylvia Muncey being charged with conspiracy to commit murder. Sky Muncey and Sam Wainwright were charged with all of the other murders, and Jack was extremely confused how the CEO killed the deputy finance minister. It also mentioned that District Attorney Erik Wolfe had been charged with conspiracy to commit murder of Mrs. Cathy Ward as well as bribery and witness tampering. Jack had figured that it was Sky who'd done all of the killing. On the next page he saw another headline which caught his interest: "FBI Shootout in Rhode Island Kills Three."

Jack sat dumfounded as he read how the FBI had raided the Tri State Formal Rental business in Providence, Rhode Island, and when they presented their search warrant, they were met with gunfire, killing one officer and two armed employees, one being Carlos Rossi. The reporter wasn't sure why Rossi was there, as he was a New York state trooper, but concluded that the investigation continued and that there would be an internal investigation of Mr. Rossi's killing. The others soon joined Jack for breakfast.

"Clay, read these," suggested Jack.

"Well, we know about Rossi, so that's not a surprise, but I'm not sure about how they figured out how Richardson committed the actual murder of Hodges," Clay said. "Judge Hyndmann gave me the name of the lead FBI detective on the case. I may get a call from him just to verify some facts." Pulling out his wallet, he found the name and phone number of Detective David Fowler. Looking at his watch he said, "Considering the time difference between here and New York, I think I'll wait until we get to Islay this afternoon and phone him from there." Everyone else had arrived by now, and the newspaper was passed from new arrival to new arrival. Colin and Ruth were the last to emerge and it was obvious that they had partied later than everyone else,

"Looking a little rough there boy," Jack said. "There's some good blood pudding on the menu....that'll give you the old shot of iron you need."

They arrived with time to spare at the airport and took a short flight to Islay, where they picked up the two rental cars. It was a short drive to the Machrie Hotel and its championship golf course, windswept and overlooking beautiful Laggan Bay. The road was narrow and none of them had driven on the left side of the road or driven a car with the driver in the right seat and the gearshift to the left of the driver's seat.

They meandered through a number of sheep pastures and witnessed men cutting peat out in the fields. The men were anxious to play some golf, and Clive was in charge of the distillery tour.

They settled into their rooms, then met in the bar to determine their plans for the next few days. When everyone but Clay had arrived, they decided to visit one distillery today then just drive around and get a feel of the island. The men would golf tomorrow, weather permitting, and the ladies would visit the famous Islay Woollen Mill, noted for its intricate tartans.

The affable, ruddy-faced bartender greeted them all and produced a map of Islay as well as a number of brochures about the distilleries and other points of interest. Having determined that Colin and Liam were both MacDonalds, he told them that it was a must for them to visit Finlaggan, the home of the MacDonalds, who were the Lairds of the Isles. Clay had been absent for over an hour, when he suddenly appeared.

"Well, here's the long and short of it," he began. "Sky Muncey and Sam Wainwright have been charged with all of the murders except for Aaron Hodges, and that was committed by Richardson himself."

"But how did they figure that out?" asked Jack.

"Well," Clay continued, "there apparently was a secretary who had complained to the investigators that Richardson was very rude to her and even threatened her. She mentioned that she was particularly incensed one time when he interrupted a meeting and sent her out for a jar of olives, and she came back with the wrong kind. He apparently didn't like them stuffed with pimentos and sent her back to get a jar with pits in them. They found two martini glasses in Hodges' suite."

"Yeah, I remember that, I found those two glasses in the adjoining room," interrupted Jack.

"Well, they put two and two together and showed a number of photos to the room service waiter, and he pointed out Richardson's picture. He also remembered that he was stiffed that night, because as you know, these guys depend on tips for their livelihood. They checked the glass with the four olive pits, which fortunately had been kept as evidence by the Toronto Police, for fingerprints, and sure enough they matched Richardson's. Sky and Sam were in the hotel that night and caught the same train as you were on. It's amazing that you didn't bump into them, but then they may have seen you first and kept inside their own compartment."

"But Mandy saw Sky and has already identified him to the RCMP, and yet they're still free."

"Not so fast," said Clay. "Sky and Sam were picked up at football practice two days ago and are presently residing in your old haunts, Colin."

"I hope they enjoy it. Wouldn't it be ironic if one of them is occupying my cell?"

Clay continued, "The warden has also been relieved of his duties and has been charged with receiving a bribe from Mrs. Muncey. That is why he put you into the general population, where you were attacked. It is presently being investigated whether he actually orchestrated your beating."

Tears welled up in Colin's eyes. "God, I don't know how I can ever thank all of you. You just have no idea what I went through, and if it wasn't for you, I never would have made it."

"Colin, you don't have to say thanks to true friends. We all understand and we know that you would do the same for each one of us," said Jack.

"One last thing," Clay said. "Tri-State Formal Rentals was well known to be a mob business and was quietly being investigated, but when the connections of Carlos Rossi, the Moretti family and Chadwick Richardson were thrown into the mix, all of a sudden some bells went off, and it appears that Richardson was the final piece to that puzzle. This boy can forget about flying in his private jet to his villa in Cannes or in West Palm Beach for many, many years, and if I can add my two cents worth here, the way I figure it, is that Richardson knew his stepson Muncey was a psychopath and just kept feeding him victim's names. The kid loved what he was doing and got paid well for doing it. Poor old dummy Wainright just went along for the ride."

"But the D.A.'s being charged with conspiracy to commit the murder of Cathy Ward. How does that fit in?" asked Jack.

"Oh, that's easy. He knew exactly what went on, since Richardson had paid him a friggin' fortune to convict Colin, and he knew that Cathy Ward was the direct link to Vaughan's money. He didn't want her to be called to testify about Vaughan's deposit or bank balance. Vaughan had probably told him who at the bank knew of his deposit."

"And so this was all about Richardson wanting to get control of the York National, and he was going to keep threatening and killing until he got his way?" surmised Jack.

"Right on," confirmed Clive.

"Bizarre and creepy."

"Can anybody explain to me where the term hat trick comes from?" asked Ruth.

"Yeah," said Jack. "I asked the same question just a few months ago."

Jack had asked the diminutive but strong bellman, Iggy Metzger, how the term came about. Iggy was a walking encyclopaedia when it came to hockey. He knew the statistics of every team and almost every player in the National Hockey League. He was also the person to see if you needed tickets to the constantly sold out Maple Leafs games, as he was a professional scalper and had a steady clientele who were regular guests at the hotel. Iggy told Jack that the term originated in the late 1800s in England in the game of cricket. When a bowler would knock off three consecutive wickets the team, would buy him a bowler hat. Later, in the 1940s, a haberdasher in Toronto would give any hockey player who scored three goals in one game at Maple Leaf Gardens a brand new fedora. Therefore, a hat trick is when one hockey player scores three goals in a game. A "perfect hat trick" is when a player scores his three goals in succession without another player scoring a goal between the three."

They decided to forgo golf for the day, as there was probably only time to visit one, maybe two distilleries. The closest of Islay's nine distilleries were Lagavulin and Laphroaig. They decided that they would have enough Scotch by the end of the day, and then the men would golf in the morning while the ladies would visit the Woollen Mill. The afternoon would be reserved for Colin and Liam to visit their ancestors' home at Finlaggan. The day after that would be a visit to the distillery of Clive's most cherished single malt: Bruichladdich.

Jack had golfed a few times before in his life but found the walking a little stressful and only played the first nine holes before renting a cart. They all found the course really challenging, and they started to keep count of who lost the most balls. After lunch they piled into their two rental cars and followed the map out to Finlaggan. Jack noticed a lovely white stuccoed farm house up on a hill.

"Look at that," Jack said to Consuela. "That would be my dream retirement home. I'd turn it into a five star B&B and call it the Killmeny House." The name he got from the mailbox at the end of the driveway.

Finlaggan was a very emotional experience for Colin and Liam as they looked over the granite-walled ruins of the center of the Laird of the Isles. They learned that their ancestors had ruled the isles by boat. They almost bent over in unison to pick up a rock and placed it on one of the crumbling walls, as if to say to their ancestors, "We are here and we are with you."

The next day was all Clive's. They traveled on a one-lane road and had to pull over into the pasture in order to let another vehicle pass. The entire distilling process was explained to everyone, as they'd heard at Laphroaig and Lagavulin, but what was most interesting was that Bruichladdich had its own spring from which it got the purest of pure water, which bubbled up through the peat and gave their whisky a softer, mossier flavor. Clive came out of the gift shop loaded with different vintages of his favorite nectar.

They all headed back to the Machrie and decided to have a drink in the lounge. It was their last night. Jack picked up the newspaper as they all sat down.

"Well, look at this," he said. "'Wife of Canadian Prime Minister Files for Divorce Ten Days before National Election,'" he read. "Well, I guess she sees the writing on the wall. There's no way she wants to become second fiddle. Serves him right."

The conversation was lively as they talked about this wonderful little island and thanked Clive for loving his Scotch so much that it would bring them all together here. Not a word was said about the ordeal that Colin had been through.

The phone at the bar rang. The bartender placed the receiver down on the bar, walked over to Ruth and said, "Ruth, there's a Suzanne Kramer from New York on the phone for you."

"Hi, Suze, It's Ruth, what's up?"

"Oh no... Really? Where? When? Wow. Oh, God, that's terrible. We're leaving tomorrow. I'll call you when I get home. Thanks." Ruth handed the phone back and quietly headed to the table, noticeably shaken. Once sitting, she looked up and said, "Brett Vaughan gorged out yesterday. They just found his body on the rocks under the Suspension Bridge over Falls Creek."

There was deadly silence. Ruth slowly twirled one of her rings, Ellen and Gillian just stared blankly at the table. Colin fidgeted with his coaster while Liam picked up a Coke cap and quietly juggled it between his fingers. Clay's eyes closed and then his chin seemed to rest on his chest and he opened his eyes, quietly staring at the rich brown stout while rubbing one index finger up and down the side of the bottle. Clive threw back the remaining Bruichladdich and stared blankly into his empty glass. Jack didn't know where to look and could only think of the absolute agony, the despair, the humiliation, the shame, the scorn that Brett must have felt to cause him to take his own life. His pleading, the look in his eyes, the fright on his face and his plaintive, despondent, and mournful cry at the trial came back and flooded Jack's mind: *"STOP, STOP, PLEASE DON'T, MY PARENTS DON'T KNOW, NOBODY KNOWS, PLEASE STOP, I'LL TELL YOU EVERYTHING, PLEASE STOP."*

There was a slight whir from the ceiling fan, and a barely noticeable flutter of the tartan curtains as a breeze swept in from the ocean, over the first tee, through the slightly open window. Other than that there wasn't another noise to be heard in the room.

Was it a call he had received from Judge Hyndmann? Had his parents found out? Was the shame too much to handle? Jack looked vacantly down at his pint of McEwans, the fingers on his left hand gently caressing the top of the wooden table as if they were searching for an answer in braille in the grain. He picked up a lonely crumb on the table, rolled it around between his thumb and fingers and mindlessly flicked it in the air. "That sucks!"

*   *   *

The following morning, everyone flew to Glasgow, where Clay and Clive and their girlfriends would catch a flight to New York, while Jack, Colin, Liam, Consuela, Ruth, and Gillian would head back directly to Toronto and spend a couple of days at Jack's house before disbanding.

"Hi, everyone," Jack's mother said as the gang came into the house. "Colin, there's a Mr. Trimble trying to get hold of you. He said that you would know his number. And Jack, Heather Stuart wants you to call her as soon as you get in."

Colin went to the phone first while others were starting to unpack.

"Hi, Chuck, it's Colin MacDonald. I'm in Toronto now, you called?"

"Yeah...yeah...really? Yeah, well let's talk to both of them. I'm free anytime, so you set up the time and place and I'll meet you there. Let me know, I'll be at Jack's for a couple of days, or so... great...bye."

"What was that all about?" asked Ruth.

"Both the Boston Bruins and the Chicago Black Hawks want to talk to me, so I told him to set up the meetings, and we'll go and see what happens."

Jack next phoned Heather at Gord Lawton's office.

"Hi there, it's Jack."

"Hi, welcome home. Listen, Mr. Lawton wants to have lunch with you. I think he's pretty embarrassed about the whole situation. Between you and me, he wants you back... but don't let on that I told you that."

"O.K. but I'm not sure when I'll be free, 'cause I just got in. Would it be O.K. if I called you tomorrow?"

"Sure. Talk to you then."

Jack hung up and turned to Colin. "Do you want company on your trips to Boston and Chicago? I'm thinking I might want to pass out a few resumes while I'm down there. Both cities have some great hotels."

Acknowledgements

To me, family is everything; there is no more joyous time than when we are all together. The laughter they bring to me is nothing short of "falling on the floor" hilarity. I dedicate this book to all of them. Their combined support throughout my life has been nothing but overwhelming in whatever venture I have undertaken, and therefore I wish to thank Barbara and our incredible children Lisa, Jenny, Drew and Jeff.

I would also like to thank my many "first readers" of The Hat Trick Murders. Their comments were invaluable as I pulled the story together. In particular I wish to thank Gloria Stoppenbrink, Bill Ross, Mary Jane Pheeney, Judy Mosher, Carol Brennan, Alice Morrison, John Paull, Tom Ross and son, Drew, for his design direction and creative input.

My editor, Allister Thompson, was extremely patient and understanding and soon learned that there are a thousand stories in the hospitality industry happening every day, not all of which could be used in this work. His knowledge of the writer's craft kept me in focus and his guidance was immeasurable.

It is with sincere appreciation that the lyrics of "Four Strong Winds" are reprinted with the permission of legendary folk music icon Ian Tyson and Slick Fork Music.

Made in the USA
Charleston, SC
05 July 2012